CRAZY LADIES

CRAZY LADIES

Michael Lee West

HarperPerennial
A Division of HarperCollins*Publishers*

To the memory of my grandmother,
Edyce "Mimi" Hughes Little

Shine on, Mississippi moon

The old age law of an eye for an eye leaves
everyone blind. . . . It leaves society in monologue
rather than dialogue. Violence ends by defeating itself.

—The Reverend Martin Luther King, Jr.

Part One

Miss Gussie

1932

*M*y baby had the spring colic, and I remember just as plain as day, there was nothing I could do to calm her. All morning I walked up and down the length of the porch, jiggling her in my arms, watching Charlie plow the garden. The air around him seemed dust-charged, fine particles wafting in the March sun.

"Look at your papa," I'd say, but Dorothy just wailed. Charlie wasn't a farmer. He was a teller at Citizens' Bank, and he was proud to bring home fourteen dollars every week. Before the Depression, he'd had hopes of advancing to cashier. I always expected the bank to close. In spite of his good job, I was of a mind to stuff our money into a mattress. Stick it in a jar and bury it next to the climbing roses. Charlie just shook his head when I talked like that. But I knew what I knew. Mr. Wentworth, who owned the bank, gave Charlie and the other tellers thick stacks of one-dollar bills; then he'd cover the stacks with fifties and hundreds. People would come to the bank, see all the money, and go home satisfied.

I'd been hankering to start me a garden early. I thought it would ease my mind from worrying about the baby, worrying about the awful things going on. There is so much good in a garden, if you don't count what happened to Adam and Eve. When I was a girl, my favorite hymn was "In the Garden." I would sing at the top of my lungs, _I come to the garden alone, while the dew is still on the roses._ I pictured me a mess of butter beans and squash, not roses. I pictured squatting between the long green rows, me working in the sun, Dorothy sleeping in a wicker basket.

We lived on the edge of town, but we had no close neighbors. Before Dorothy was born, I'd watch Charlie shoot cracked milk bottles in the backyard. I was a better shot than him, on account of my brothers learning me, but I didn't have the heart to tell him. I let him think he showed me everything I knew. You have to coddle menfolks on account of their pride.

The Depression had made us all prouder. A man on the radio said too much prosperity ruined the fiber of the people. I wondered why he'd say a thing like that. When I looked around town, all I saw was poverty and slow living, Tennessee ways. I didn't know about the big cities, but there were tarpaper shacks beside the railroad in Crystal Falls. Most of the men held signs, WILL WORK FOR FOOD. They were skinny as chickens. Hoovervilles, the papers called those shacks. Charlie said he didn't see how President Hoover would be re-elected in November. I didn't know what to think.

I had plenty on my mind. My nerves were laid wide open from Dorothy's high-pitched cries, which I could not soothe and could not help but take personal. She was my first baby. I was eighteen years old, a bride of one year, the youngest child from a family of seven. So I just didn't know what to do. There had never been babies for me to help Mama raise. To make things worse, I could not seem to turn away from the terrible news on the radio. It was the middle of March, and the body of the Lindbergh baby had just been found. The Philco radio was paid for, and it had a glass dial like a single eye. From the porch, I listened to the radio and watched Charlie turn the soil. I held my Dorothy and offered her my breast, which only made her cry harder. I moved the rocker into a patch of sunlight and rocked her back and forth.

I couldn't get the handsome Lindberghs out of my mind.

That was also the year a series of murders shocked Crystal Falls. The victims, four total, were all young women. They had been stabbed, but I'd heard that the newspaper hadn't reported everything. I didn't want to know. It was such a large crime, in such a small town, that people were cowed by the news. Women whispered among themselves, but mostly they didn't like to think about it. It didn't seem real. Instead we hovered around our radios for news of the Lindberghs. It was a relief when music came on, playing over the static. I always liked "Star Dust"—*Sometimes I wonder why I spend the lonely nights/ Dreaming of a song?* Saturday evenings me and Charlie sat in the dark and watched the glowing dial while we listened to the Grand Ole Opry on WSM.

It was late afternoon when Dorothy, all red-faced, fell asleep chewing her fingers. I set her in the bassinet, rolled it into the kitchen, and looked out the window. Charlie was moving his plow into the barn. The garden was long and narrow. It was almost in the center of the backyard. Most every place else was full of limestone—the rocks jutted out like broken bones. One end of the garden, the east side, was shaded by a huge oak tree. Charlie said that tree had been there forever. Beyond the tree was the old graveyard, past the barn and the barbwire fence. I didn't cotton to living next to it, but I held my tongue. It was Charlie's land. The old homeplace, which I didn't have a memory of, had burned in 1902. Over the years, some of the markers had sunk into the ground or been knocked over by cows. Others stood tall and gray, carved with dates, names, and epitaphs:

Mary Beatrice Hamilton
Her children arise up and call her blessed
Nov 18, 1843–April 14, 1887.

Charlie stomped his feet on the back porch and lumbered into the kitchen. He poured a glass of buttermilk and drained it in three swallows, his Adam's apple jerking up and down. Because of the sleeping baby, I did not fuss at him for tracking up my clean floor with mud. I just gave him a harsh glance from under my eyebrows. He was too tired to notice. He gave me a kiss on the cheek and went upstairs to bathe.

I sat down at the kitchen table and laid out packets of seeds as if they were a deck of cards. Watermelon, cantaloupe, radishes, lettuce, cucumbers. And we already had starter trays in the window, cabbages and onion sets, bought from a farmer on the town square. The old man had given me a sack of white corn seed. He said, "Don't plant your corn on a full moon or it'll shoot up sky high. You'll get nothing but little bitty ears. And plant your cabbages when the moon's on the wax. Onions on the wane."

Well, I already knew that, growing up on a farm like I had, with Papa and all those brothers of mine. But I thanked the man. Mama had taught me how to can when I was a little thing. It seemed as if we spent whole summers putting up tomatoes because they'd never come ripe at the same time.

The screen door was open, and a cold breeze pushed into the room. I glanced up, thinking I ought to close the door before Dorothy got chilled, and that was when I saw the man. He was outlined against the screen mesh.

Lordy Jesus, I thought to myself. How long had he been

standing there, watching me study my seed packets? My next thought was, this is the man who kidnapped the Lindbergh baby. And I knew he had come for my Dorothy. I pushed away from the table and stood up. I was determined to fight. I had me a gun in the pantry, too. I would not let this man see my fear, even though my knees twitched and shook under my cotton dress. Growing up with mean-natured older brothers had taught me aplenty.

"What do you want?" I asked real icy, staring back at him.

The man opened the door and stepped into my kitchen. A great stench filled the room. Corn whiskey. He was a young man, barely out of his teens. His hair was blond, combed over to one side. His eyes were deep-set, dark and empty, hardly no lashes at all. His cheekbones were high, like two slanted rocks, and dropped off into dark hollows. Something nagged at me, but I couldn't place his face. I looked down at his feet. His shoes were crusted and muddy. Why, he had been walking through my garden. Maybe he'd been standing there for Heaven knew how long!

"I didn't ask you to come into my house, now did I?" I hollered.

He answered by reaching into my dish drainer, yanking out my best butcher knife, and pointing it at me. Then he slogged forward. His eyes burned, hard and black, and I knew then he had not come for my baby girl. He had come for me.

He waved the knife. "Take your clothes off and get on the floor," he said. There were red moles on his cheek. Red moles and pimples. He looked too young to be telling me what to do.

"I most certainly will not!" I said, sticking out my chin.

He grabbed my arm, making me cry out, and pressed the tip of the knife against my throat. Something slid down my neck and dripped onto my dress. Blood. I closed my eyes and waited for him to plunge the knife into my windpipe. He grabbed my collar and ripped my dress to the waist. My breasts popped out of my slip. He put the knife to my chest and scraped the blade across my skin. I didn't feel it. Above my head, I heard water running through the pipes and splashing into the tub. I knew Charlie couldn't hear me. But the murderer didn't know it.

Three seconds passed.

Then I screamed.

The man jumped back, startled.

"You get out of my house!" I yelled. "My husband's going to blow your head off! He's right upstairs! Listen!"

The man looked toward the ceiling. Then he turned his burning eyes on me again. I saw then that he would kill Charlie, too. Dorothy awakened. Her cries filled the room. The man cocked his head, puzzled, then turned to the baby. He seemed to have forgotten all about getting his head blown off. He walked across the room, lowered the knife to the pink blanket, and flipped it back with the blade. Dorothy screamed.

I could not breathe. Blood dripped down my neck as I watched him lean toward the baby. He seemed spellbound by her hysterical cries, the rise and fall of her chest. Upstairs, the water continued to gush into the tub. Would it never stop?

I stepped backward, reached blindly for the pantry. I flung open the door, grabbed Charlie's shotgun. It was loaded. It had been loaded since the newspaper first carried the news of the murders. I was no country fool. I planned to raise me a big family, and nothing but God would stop me.

The man stared at Dorothy, the knife flashing in his hands. His back was to me. I lifted the gun and took aim down the length of the barrel. Then I paused. I was terrified the buckshot would hit Dorothy.

"You old hog you," I yelled. "Get out of my house!"

He turned, and his eyes went completely black. He lunged toward me. Dorothy was screaming. How could my Charlie not hear?

Lordy Jesus, I prayed, let me shoot him in the heart. I squeezed the trigger. The blast knocked me backward against the stove. I blinked and saw the jagged hole in his stomach. The Lord had made me miss his vitals, but dark blood, mingled with torn fabric from his shirt, poured out of his belly. He looked down at his stomach, touched his fingers to the blood, and I took aim again. Before I pulled the trigger, he slumped to the floor, still clutching the butcher knife. All at once Dorothy's screams snapped off.

Charlie came running down the steps, dripping water, holding a towel around his waist. His eyes bugged as he looked at the man, now gasping for air. "Oh, mercy!" he said. "Oh, merciful heavens!"

I lowered the gun and looked at my kitchen. Blood was splattered across my pine cabinets, across the counters, across Dorothy's bassinet. *Dorothy.* I ran to her. She looked up at me, her face puckered, and she let out a long wail. Her legs thrashed. I saw a red flash on her gown. I jerked up the fabric. A long, ugly scratch ran up the length of her side. In the bassinet itself was a piece of buckshot, which had only grazed her. I gathered her into my arms. Charlie was feeling the man's neck, feeling for a pulse.

"He's still alive," he said. "He's just fainted. What in tarnation happened?"

"He tried to rape me," I said, holding the baby against my shoulder. "And he was going to kill Dorothy."

The truth was I didn't know if he would have killed her. But I had no doubt he would have killed me. I looked down at the man. His chest heaved just the slightest bit. Blood poured from the hole in his belly. I had never seen so much blood.

"We've got to get a doctor," Charlie said.

"Wait!" I shouted, and Dorothy screamed into my ear. "Just wait a minute!"

"Honey, do you know who this boy is?" Charlie stared.

"No. And I don't care. Let's just get the sheriff."

"This is Claude Wentworth's son," he said. "His youngest boy, Sawyer. You remember him, don't you?"

I felt the breath leave my body. Claude Edmund Wentworth was the president of the bank where Charlie worked. Claude Edmund Wentworth owned half the town. Claude Edmund Wentworth had once met Charles A. Lindbergh in Washington, D.C. There were photographs on Mr. Wentworth's desk, pictures of his wife, Willadean, and their two boys. The youngest, Sawyer, had a reputation. He was the one who'd slammed old Mrs. Beatty's cat into a stone wall. The oldest, Claude Jr., had a son who was a few months older than Dorothy. His name was Claude III. I stared at my husband. "Tell me what to do," I said.

"Why didn't you just lock the door?"

"I've never locked a door in my life," I said coldly. "Look at my dress, Charlie. Look what he did to me. He told me to take off my clothes and get on the floor. That's what he said."

"Let me think a minute. Just let me think." He blinked at the Wentworth boy. The boy's eyes flickered open, and he moaned.

"Oh, Gussie." Charlie's broad forehead wrinkled. "This is so serious. I'm afraid of what Mr. Wentworth will do."

"He can't do anything." I stared. "Can he?"

"He could foreclose on our house."

"His boy would've murdered me," I said, almost to myself. "Like he did to those other women."

"The thing is, Gussie, we'll never prove it was self-defense. I can hear the Wentworths now. They'll say you thought he was a prowler, that your nerves got the better of you. That you shot an innocent boy."

"He wasn't innocent."

"What if Mr. Wentworth fires me, Gussie?"

"He won't. Not when he hears the truth."

"Maybe he already knows it." He paused and looked down at the boy. "Blood is thicker than water. And Wentworth blood is thickest of all. They'll die before dragging their name through mud. They'll run me out of town first."

I patted Dorothy's back, but she rooted for my breast. I touched my finger to the dried blood on my chest. I imagined us taking in boarders or selling apples for a nickel, eating up the profits to keep from starving. Or I could hire myself out as a maid. The Crash had reduced most of us to paupers. Jobs were hard to find, harder to hold. When I looked up, Charlie was staring at me.

"Let's bury him now," I said, not believing my ears. Surely I hadn't said such a thing. The boy's eyelids flickered again.

"Gussie, *no!*" Charlie pushed his fingers through his hair. "He's not even dead," he said. "Can't you see that for yourself?"

"I don't care." I looked at Charlie, but he refused to catch my eyes. "Then I'll do it myself. Look, he's already fainted again."

"No." Charlie's face darkened. "We won't do this."

"Oh, yes we will," I said. "You're the one who's afraid of the Wentworths. Not me. I wanted to call the sheriff. You can't have it two ways, Charlie. Unless you know something I don't."

He looked up at the ceiling and blinked hard. His eyes watered.

"Unless you have a better idea, we'll do it," I said. "We'll bury him at the east end of the garden. There's not much limestone there. The ground is soft. Then we'll never talk about it again. Ever. Not to another living soul."

He didn't answer. He stared at the boy. Finally he looked at me.

"We'll burn in hell," he said and walked out of the room, leaving me with that bleeding man and my screaming baby.

I wrapped the boy in an old sheet. A time or two, he weakly struggled, batting the linen, like something in a cocoon. He moaned, called for his mama. *"Mother?"* he'd cry. I felt no pity. I remembered the knife at my throat. I remembered the faces of the dead women in the newspaper.

While the afternoon stretched into night, I passed time scouring my kitchen, wiping down the cupboards. Each time I squeezed out my dishrag in the pail, the water turned to blood. That night there was a full moon. Charlie came downstairs and we carried the boy's body to the edge of the garden. Above us, branches on the oak tree moved back and forth. We dug in silence, grunting softly when our shovels struck rock.

We seemed to work forever, digging throughout the night. I remembered when I was a little girl, how I'd make mud pies in the yard, and Mama would tell me I was digging all the way to China. Now I pretended I was fashioning a complicated tunnel, that when we dropped the boy in it, he would fall soundlessly through the earth, passing through layers of rock and ore, until he reached the other side. Chinamen would gather and stare.

We rolled the boy's body into the hole. It fell with a hard thump. The sheet looked too clean beneath the moonlight. I heard a muffled moan, *"Mother?"* I picked up the shovel. From the house, I heard Dorothy's wails start up again. I was grateful for not having neighbors. I let her scream. It was me who wanted to howl at the moon, but I shoveled harder, getting into a rhythm. For a time, the earth seemed to swallow the dirt. I could still see the sheet through clods of soil. There was no way I could plant vegetables over this. Just the idea of cabbage or corn growing over this dead boy took my appetite clean away.

I could plant zinnias there. I could plant marigolds and sunflowers. I dropped to my knees and pushed dirt into the grave with my hands.

"Stop it, Gussie!" Charlie said, trying to pull me away.

"Just leave me be!" I snarled and shrugged off his hands. I scraped the dirt with my fingers. All I could think about was what that old farmer had said. It was a good thing we weren't planting corn. It would grow to the sky, all stalk, the green ears packed with nothing but yellow silk. I pictured the boy, his mouth full of dirt, clawing his way toward the moon.

"Gussie, stop it! For the love of God, stop it!" Tears poured down Charlie's face, but I felt no mercy.

"I told you not to talk about this!" I cried. Then I looked up at him. The moon skated over his head.

He wiped his face on his shirt, and I went back to filling up the grave.

*T*hat summer, my garden produced enormous cucumbers and cabbages. The corn was so sweet and soft you could cut it from the cob with a spoon. My tomatoes were full of red juice. Charlie wouldn't go near the east end of the garden, even though it was the coolest place to work on account of that oak tree. He said he wouldn't eat anything that grew in that section. I planted me a flower garden, but I didn't bring any blossoms into the house. Instead I picked wildflowers—honeysuckle, Queen Anne's lace, black-eyed Susans.

The Wentworths ran a full-page ad in the newspaper, showing their crazy son's solemn face. They offered fifty dollars for news of his whereabouts. They, too, had been affected by the Lindbergh kidnapping. I heard down at church that Mrs. Wentworth had fully expected to receive a ransom note.

Finally, they decided he must have strayed to the railroad and crawled into an empty boxcar like an ordinary wanderer. They believed he was living in some city, standing in breadlines or shining shoes for a nickel. They believed that he had simply forgotten the way back home.

Queenie

1938

I come to work for Miss Gussie in 1938, before her second baby is born. It is late summer, August, and she is sitting on the front porch, stringing beans, wearing a huge pink-flowered top. Her yard smells like wild mint and fresh-cut grass. She looks close to my age, twenty-four, only she be big pregnant. And it look like she spaced her children out too far. The Lord didn't see to bless me and Talley with babies, so I treat Talley like he's a big old baby. He helps Mr. Dempsey break mules. You won't see Talley without his church clothes ironed. And I know how to feed a man right, I sure do, no matter what Talley's mother say.

Miss Gussie's little girl is sitting in the wooden swing, fussing at her dolls. She has light brown hair, all pulled back with wide yellow ribbons. She stop talking to her dolls when I climb up the porch steps. Then she stares at me with these milky blue eyes.

"How old is you?" I ask her real friendly-like, but she don't answer. She just keep staring. Those eyes remind me of something, but I can't think of what.

"Dorothy, where's your manners?" says Miss Gussie. "Tell Queenie how old you are, honey."

Dorothy, she look at me from under her eyebrows. "I'm six," she says.

"Six going on thirty-six," says Miss Gussie, smiling. She eases herself from her chair. Her belly huge. She's got the same blue eyes, only her hair is blond, wrapped on top of her head in two braids. "I'm sure glad you came," she tells me. "Aren't we glad, Dorothy?"

Dorothy looks at me and scowls.

"Dorothy?" says Miss Gussie again.

"Yes," the child say like the word hurt her throat. Then she goes back to dressing her doll.

"When's your baby due?" I ask Miss Gussie, shifting my eyes from the little white girl and her china-faced dolls.

"Not till the middle of September," she say. She pauses in the doorway and rubs her back. "Come on inside, Queenie," she tells me. "I'll show you where things are."

I set up the ironing board in the kitchen and stare out the window. Miss Gussie's outside, paying no attention to that girl of hers, who's busy dragging a mama cat across the yard. Miss Gussie walks into the garden. It is big and green. I see her pink-flowered top and big belly move through the corn. The corn taller than she is. She comes out the other side, her hands empty, her belly poked out to here. Her forehead is wrinkled, and her mouth turned down at the corners, like maybe she saw something that disturb her in there. I know that look, I've seen it on womens all my life, and it don't have nothing to do with bugs in her garden. She do not look like a woman happy because she having a baby, she sure don't.

Then, as if my own thoughts be nothing but lies, she turns her face up to the sun and shuts her eyes like she be praying.

What a white lady like that be praying for? I have worked for
stranger folk. I have worked for rich peoples, too, and Miss
Gussie sure ain't rich, but the rich be strangest of all. They sure
are. I worked ten years for the Wentworths and quit the year
before Mr. Sawyer, they crazy son, ran away. It was the year of
all those bad murders. After he run off, there never was another
murder, not a single one. Not even a shooting at the bootleg
joints. So don't you tell me he wasn't the one that killed those
womens. He is probably living in some big city, driving the
polices crazy. From the time he was young, he never looked
right to me. They kept him in the house, wouldn't let him go
outside. Not after what he done to his little brother's dog. No,
they just kept him upstairs, and I wouldn't go near him. Once,
I found a human finger under his bed. That's right, a human
finger. I sure found it. I showed it to the cook, and she told me
to put it back and shut my mouth if I knew what was good for
me. I knew. I put it back. But later he stared at me like he seen
what I'd done. I was glad when he run off.

Now Miss Gussie stands in a patch of sunlight and rubs her
hands over her belly like it aches. The whole time, Dorothy just
tormenting that poor mama cat. She drags it to the edge of the
garden, right in the middle of her mama's flowers.

"Get out of there, Dorothy!" cries Miss Gussie.

Dorothy ignores her mama and reaches for the cat's tail.
The cat hisses and scratches Dorothy across the cheek. She
throws down the cat and runs screaming across the grass. She
slams right into her mama's belly and they both fall down. Miss
Gussie look surprise and says "Oof!" like she catch a baseball.
The color drain from her face. She winces a little and holds her
belly.

"Mother Dear!" said Dorothy. "I'm hurt! Look at my
cheek, Mother Dear."

Miss Gussie's mouth open, but she don't say nothing. She start rubbing her stomach.

"Mother Dear!"

"Well, I told you not to play in the flowers," Miss Gussie says finally. She takes a deep breath and stops rubbing her belly. She gets up. Dorothy, wailing louder and louder, scrambles to her feet. She hold her hand against her face, hopping on one foot. Her cheek bleeding a little.

"Well, let's go wash your face, Dorothy," she says, sighing hard. They walk in the screen door. Dorothy's face be streaked with dirty tears, not much blood. Her mama rinse out a cloth and dab it against the scratch.

"Ouch!" screams Dorothy. "That hurts, Mother Dear!"

"You teach her to call you Mother Dear?" I ask without thinking. Sometimes it's hard to know what to ask and what not to. But all this time I been thinking about asking this.

Miss Gussie says, "No, she thought it up herself. She's always been one to think things up."

"Oh," I say and nod my head. But it do make sense. A child like that, with those old eyes hooked on her mama's belly, like she scared something bad going to come out of there. I myself hope it ain't another one like what she already got. Maybe that's why she waited so long to have this baby.

Miss Gussie turns to rinse the rag in the sink. All of a sudden like, she moans and grips the counter. "Oh, my," she says and sinks to her knees.

Dorothy says, "Mother Dear? Get up, Mother Dear."

I set the iron down on the stove and go to Miss Gussie. She grips my arm, breathing hard, but she don't say nothing. I run my hands over her stomach. It feel tight as a drum.

Dorothy shouts, "Get your nigger hands off of my Mother Dear, you nigger, you!"

Miss Gussie licks her lips and rolls her eyes over at Dorothy. "Shut your mouth, Dorothy," she says. "Shut it now. Or I'll wash it out with soap."

Dorothy's eyes fill with tears, her face screws up and turns red. She slides off the stool and fixes me with those blue eyes. *"Nigger, nigger!"* she hollers and runs out of the room. She runs so fast, she slips on the rug and I hear her bones knock against the floor. She gets up, whimpering, then she flies around the corner, and her shoes pound hard up the stairs.

I prop Miss Gussie's head in my lap. "I think the baby's coming," she says.

"You want me to run down to the bank and get Mr. Charlie?" I ask. "Or you want me to fetch the doctor?"

"There's no time. Just call the doctor. The phone's in the hall. On the table. Tell the operator to call Dr. Butler."

"Yessum."

"Oh, Queenie. It feels like the baby's head's about to drop out of me this second," she says. "It hurts so bad."

Then she squeezes her eyes shut and grits her teeth. She starts moaning. I push the heel of my hand against the floor and stand up. My hand feels wet. I'd mopped the floor earlier, so I just think it's water. Only it be blood. I look down at her skirt. Underneath be more blood. My mama brought many a baby, and I heard her say that some bleeding was natural and some wasn't. The difference be how fast it comes, and hers coming fast. I run and get a thick towel and push it between her legs. She is breathing funny, strained like. Her belly still be hard, like it's drawn up in one big knot.

"Now you stay here, Miss Gussie," I tell her. "I'll be right back. Right back, you hear?"

"Why am I bleeding so much?" she says weakly. "I don't remember doing this with Dorothy."

"You sit tight. I've got to call the doctor. You just busted a vessel is all, just a vessel."

"No." She shakes her head and grabs my sleeve. "It's God. He's punishing me. An eye for an eye. Queenie. A life for a death."

"Now you know the Bible don't say no life for no death," I tell her. I pat her hand and she closes her eyes.

"But you don't understand," she says.

"Oh, yes I do. Queenie understands," I say, but I think maybe I don't understand. I think maybe she is going to die. I think about yelling for that bad Dorothy to come downstairs to see for herself what she done done, but she holed up in her room pouting, and I don't have no time for sweet talk.

"It all started with the Lindbergh baby," she says. "It was on the radio. Don't you remember? And then that woman chopped up bodies and stuffed them into a trunk? Oh, I can't remember her name. Do you remember? Her last name was Judd, I think."

I shake my head and try to shush her.

"It was, let's see, 1932. No, 1933. Do you remember that song? 'Love for Sale.' Libby Holman sang it. She killed that tobacco man. Married him and killed him. I told Charlie, I said, 'It's an unsafe world.' I told him and I told him. He didn't believe me. He should have. I'd never hurt anyone on purpose, Queenie. I never would. He said I should've locked the door—"

"You're talking out of your head, Miss Gussie."

"No." She closes her eyes. Her chest rises and falls. I get up and walk backward into the hall. I pick up the telephone and right away I hear two old women gossiping on the party line.

"Who picked up this line?" one of the women says sharply.

"I did," I tell them.

"And who are you?" the woman wants to know.

"I'm Queenie LaFevor, and I need to make a phone call, please."

"Why, I don't know no nigger who has a phone," the other woman says.

"This is an emergency," I say, breathing hard. "I have to call the doctor for Miss Gussie. She's bleeding bad."

Silence. I hear breathing. After a moment, one of the women say, "Why, Gussie don't have her a nigger maid. And her baby's not due till next month. So you just hang up this phone right now, gal, or I'm calling the police."

"Miss Gussie's bleeding!" I holler. "I need this phone to call!"

"Get off the phone, nigger," the other lady says.

From the kitchen, Miss Gussie groans. I throw down the phone and run out the front door. I run down the sidewalk, and I don't stop running until I reach Dr. Butler's office six blocks away. I'm sweating heavy when I open the door. All these sick white folks just stare at me like I've lost my mind. When colored peoples are sick, they have to stand in the street and wait until they names called. The nurse, who is sitting behind a glass window, rises to her feet.

"Get Dr. Butler now," I say, panting hard as Miss Gussie was earlier. I tell her Miss Gussie Hamilton's girl punched her in the stomach and it's brought her baby, and now she's bleeding awful bad. That she fall to the kitchen floor.

The nurse runs to get the doctor.

Then here he comes running, holding his doctor's bag. All the sick white peoples just stare. Dr. Butler buckles his bag shut. Now I know him from way back. He's old and knows my mama. He knows I am not one to stretch the truth. "Did you say Gussie Hamilton's bleeding?" he asks me.

"Yessir."

"Is she bleeding real heavy, girl?"

"Yessir."

"Well, let's go."

He and his nurse rush out of the office and climb into his car. They slam the doors and drive off and don't see me running behind them, waving my arms. I'm so full of fear for Miss Gussie I take off after them. Let her and that baby live, Jesus, I think. I get a hitch in my side, but I just ball up my fist and poke it hard and keep running.

*M*r. Charlie sits in the kitchen, his elbows propped on the white enamel table. Dorothy sits on the floor, fussing at her dolls. She won't look at me. If she was mine, I'd wear her out but good. But she ain't mine. And I'm too busy to think. I go in and out of Miss Gussie's room, bringing towels, pans of steaming water. My feet move like they've never moved before. Dr. Butler takes out long curved blades, shiny metal, what I've never seen before. Then he fits them inside of Miss Gussie, fits them around the baby's head, although I don't see how he knows a head from a bone, there's so much blood.

He pulls, he hollers at Miss Gussie to push. He props his feet on the bed. He grunts and sweats. Finally the baby's head pops out. Miss Gussie pushes again, her face all purple, and the rest of the baby slides out, slick as a trout. It be another little girl, and she lets out a big scream. She so skinny you can see her ribs under her skin. Her bottom lip just quivers like it got a motor. Her hands and feet are a deep plum color. Her little legs pump the air like she riding a bicycle. She has blond hair, a pinkish scalp, but one side of her face red and scratched from where the blades mashed her. But she's alive and screaming for her mama. Dr. Butler's nurse gives her to me, and I wrap a blanket around her. She don't have no fingernails or toenails, and I hear Dr. Butler say it because she come so early.

"You going to be just fine, baby," I tell her, and she opens her two big blue eyes and looks around.

The door cracks open and Mr. Charlie's asking if everything's all right.

"It's a girl," hollers Dr. Butler.

"Well, I'll be. Another girl. How's my Gussie?" Mr. Charlie says.

"She's going to be just fine," Dr. Butler says, his head stuck between Miss Gussie's legs. "Just fine and dandy."

"It's a girl," Mr. Charlie tells Dorothy, who looks at me and don't say nothing, nothing at all. Before Mr. Charlie can close the door, I see her face, the dark, slanted eyebrows.

"Thank you, Queenie," whisper Miss Gussie. "You saved the day."

"She sure did," says Dr. Butler.

I look down at the baby, what Dorothy almost killed. She roots for my breast. I'll protect you, little gal, I think to myself, I'll protect you, and when she opens her eyes, I know she knows.

Dorothy

1945

First, we dropped a bomb on Hiroshima, then three days later, we dropped another on Nagasaki. I stood in the yard and looked into the blue sky, the scratch of blackbirds. I pictured the whistling bombs, the horror of it, the screaming, the twisted faces, the seared skin. Sister said she felt sorry for the Japs.

"They almost killed Papa," I reminded her. And it was true, even though he hadn't been wounded. He didn't even have a Purple Heart.

"But when they dropped the bombs little babies were killed," Sister said. She was six years old, almost seven. A stupid little child.

"Who cares about Jap babies?" I cried, thinking of the way Papa had been when he'd first come home from Guam. All he did was sit in his maroon stuffed chair, smoking cigarettes, his eyes pale and glassy.

"Those babies didn't hurt my papa," Sister said.

I wanted to slap her. Instead I clenched my fists and thought: *my* papa.

Mother Dear's eyes filled with water as she listened to Sister carry on about the Japs. "Clancy Jane is the most tender-hearted thing," she said.

"She sure is," said Queenie. "Tender-hearted as can be."

"And what am I?" I asked Queenie.

She fixed me with her brown eyes, the color of mud pies, but she did not answer. She had hated me since I was a little girl. Her husband, Talley, was killed by the Japs. He was carrying supplies to troops—hand grenades—and he was killed by mortar. It must have been some bad war, let me tell you, because Papa refused to talk about it. What I knew I had learned by eavesdropping. After Pearl Harbor, he got all patriotic and signed up. That was in 1942. Sister was only four. Men all over America were going off to war. Papa was afraid they wouldn't take him because he was thirty years old. He said the Marines wanted them young, so they could mold them. But they took him, made him a private, and shipped him to Guam, where something awful happened.

When he was discharged, Mother Dear had rushed off to the VA Hospital in Nashville, leaving me and Sister with Queenie. I thought he'd been shot in the stomach. I imagined his scars, great puckers of flesh, and my whole body shuddered and drew up in pain. When he came home he was thinner, but mostly he looked the same.

Mother Dear whispered things to Queenie. She said Papa had cracked up. I was shocked all the way to my drawers. The Marines, Mother Dear told Queenie, called it a severe case of combat fatigue. Mother Dear never volunteered this information to *me,* no indeed. I hid behind doors and listened to her and Queenie talking. Their voices moved back and forth like minnows in a pail. When Papa was on Guam, his first sergeant had gotten hit by a Jap artillery shell. It had landed right on top of him. The man shattered. A huge piece of bloody flesh slapped against Papa's face. When he realized what was oozing all over him, he went stone raving mad. He shook all over. They had to tie him to a stretcher. That was what I'd overheard Mother Dear say. She hadn't been there, so I didn't believe her. My papa hadn't cracked up. Why, he acted as normal as anyone. A little quieter, maybe. And he didn't seem ever so interested in us anymore. Sometimes he'd abruptly leave the room, but that was all. I swear to God it was all in Mother Dear's imagination. She was just embarrassed because he didn't have a Purple Heart to hang on the wall.

I didn't mind the way he'd sit in that chair of his and smoke one cigarette after the other. He was clean. He kept himself shaved, kept his hair combed. But there was something about his eyes. They'd turned all blue and gauzy, and he'd stare right through you. It was scary. You'd tell him to do something, and he'd do it. Taking orders in the Marines must have rubbed off on him; he didn't want to think up chores for himself. He'd let us do anything to him. Mother Dear and the others caught on fast. They ordered him around. I just knew they'd wear him out. One day he'd just keel over in the garden while planting Mother Dear's bitter lettuce. Cleaning out the chicken coop. Raking leaves. They'd made him do all the dirty work, just like he was a nigger. I thought we'd hired Queenie for all that. They didn't care about him the way I did. He had blackheads and would let me pick them for hours on end, until his face was blotched with red marks. Mother Dear thought it was disgusting, but I could tell that she wanted to pick the bumps, too. To watch them pop open, like milkweed pods. I'd lean over him so she couldn't watch, and then I'd go to work.

Finally Mr. Wentworth sent for Papa and turned him back into a teller. I kept waiting for the whole of him to return to his old self. Papa seemed scared of Mr. Wentworth, and there was something real sad about the way he shuffled between the bank and our house. I liked to think he was working his fingers to the bone so Mother Dear could afford Queenie, even though I knew everybody in Crystal Falls had colored help. They'd work for practically nothing. Queenie worshiped the ground Sister walked on. Mother Dear did, too. Sister was their favorite, no matter how hard they both denied it. I was not blind nor deaf. Their love for her was a fact of my life. The thing about Sister was she always came out smelling like a rose. She could drop a full bottle of milk on the back porch and all Mother Dear said was, "Watch out for the broken glass, Clancy Jane." Then Sister would go and prick her finger on purpose. I knew she did it on purpose because I had seen her do it many a time. I had done worse, but that was my special secret.

Our troubles went way back, to when Sister nearly died. She was born prematurely because I hit into Mother Dear's stomach. This I did not remember, but I should. If I had heard it once, I had heard it a thousand times. I could almost see Mother Dear falling, my hands firm on her stomach. After Sister was born, my mother seemed flooded with love. She lay on her bed as if floating on the white sheets, the baby in her arms. I ached to cry, but I did not allow it. I stood in the doorway and tried to remember the last time Mother Dear had held me.

All I remembered was her mouth, slightly turned down at the corners as she worked in her garden, a lean, tired woman who had little good to say to me. *Stop it, Dorothy. Get out of the flowers, Dorothy. Hush your whining, Dorothy. Stop bothering me, Dorothy.*

The first time I called her Mother Dear, she picked me up and kissed me. I loved feeling her arms around me. I wanted nothing so much as I wanted her love, and when Sister was born, I knew I had lost any chance of ever winning it. From the time she could walk, Sister would sneak into my room and rearrange all my dolls, and no one said a word, not one blessed word. They didn't even notice. But if I went into her room and touched the least thing, you'd think I'd robbed a bank. When I complained, Mother Dear would say, "She's just copying you, Dorothy."

Most of my life, I have been sad and blue. I have suffered personal slights. Favoritism at the hands of Mother Dear. She broke my spirit at an early age, like you break a horse, and taught me how to mind and not talk back. I have a clear memory of that day. It was spring, and Mother Dear was kneeling at the far side of her garden, sprinkling zinnia seeds. I knelt beside her. I couldn't have been more than four years old. It was before Sister was born. I reached for the packet of seeds, but Mother Dear shook her head. "You'd best not play here," she said.

"Let me plant just a few flowers," I begged.

"No." She stared down at the soil. "You'll get dirty. Just run on, Dorothy."

"But I want to help you plant flowers," I said.

"No, Dorothy." She set down her spade and lifted one gloved hand to her forehead. Colorful seed packets were scattered beside her knees.

I reached for a packet and looked her square in the eye.

"Put it down, Dorothy."

"No." I held the packet to my chest. She reached down, snatched the seed packet, and spanked my legs. I screamed as loud as I could, and she stopped hitting me. My legs were red and stinging, but as soon as she turned her back, I reached for another packet. This one had pictures of red and pink flowers. I looked her square in the eye and ripped it open. That did it. She whirled around and smacked my face so hard the seeds flew out of the envelope. My eyes were swimming, but I picked up another packet and ripped it open. I started flinging seeds everywhere.

"What's the matter with you!" she cried. She grabbed my arm and spanked me again. I was still determined to plant those flowers, but she was *more* determined to keep me out of her garden. When I tried to bite her arm, she carried me into the house. I gave up. I couldn't fight her. I grew up pretending not to want the flowers of life. I turned my nose up and said, "No, thank you."

So you can see why I grew into a "Yes, ma'am, girl." I learned from Papa to appear to go along with things and not rock the boat. I learned from my own self to have nice manners and put on a front. Nice manners could get you far. Behind everyone's back, if I thought I could get away with it, I did what I pleased. I pleased Dorothy and gave Dorothy what she needed. I had to love me because no one else did. It was a real sad and terrible way to live. Everyone thought I was so sweet and shy, but they just didn't know how much anger I had in me. I was tired of being a good girl, but I didn't know how to change. Then I stopped wanting to.

To make things worse, I was not the least bit pretty until I turned thirteen. It was terrible. I developed early and took to hunching my shoulders to hide my breasts. They were huge, like two pink apples. I looked deformed. "Oh, for goodness sakes" was all Mother Dear said. But she did not understand how the boys stared and how the girls hated me. All Mother Dear had on her mind was Papa, Sister, and Yalta. She was half in love with President Roosevelt. Anyway, it was a real long time before my face grew into my body, and until that time Mother Dear knew something was just the least bit off about me. If she hadn't doted so much on Sister, she would have seen, clearly, that I was misshapen. Listen, you grow up as your mother's least favorite child and see how much you like it. There is no other hurt like it. Believe me.

The first time I tried to hurt myself was after the girls at school laughed and called my breasts jugs. They called me Dottie the Cow. I came home crying. Queenie was in the kitchen making chicken and dumplings. Mother Dear was in the backyard planting marigolds around the edge of the garden. Sister was playing dolls under the oak tree. Mother Dear loved Sister best, then Queenie, then her garden, then Papa, then me. I hated gardening. It took so much of her time. As I watched Queenie cut out dumplings with a knife, I prayed for root rot. I prayed for locusts. I prayed for drought. She kept humming a song that no white person knew the words to, and when I couldn't stand it any longer, I wandered upstairs. From the guest room, I heard this strange sound, like someone was strangling. I tiptoed down the hall. I held my breath and peered into the room. The curtains were drawn, making everything gloomy. Papa was sitting on the bed, rocking back and forth as tears leaked out of his eyes. The whole front of his shirt was wet. It was real clear that he'd left the best part of himself in the Pacific. The Japs had killed my real papa and had sent back an impostor.

I swallowed hard, leaning against the wall spread-eagle, staring straight ahead. The bathroom was across the hall. I crossed the floor in three steps and locked the door behind me. I picked up Papa's straight-edge razor and held it over my wrist. The blade reflected the light pouring in from the window. I could let the blood drip down the sink, real neat-like, or I could draw up a hot bath and open my veins there. I had read about a lady doing that in Paris, France, when the Germans took over. I nicked the blade on the side of my wrist, just to see how much it hurt. The scratch filled with blood. I cut another spot, then another, but I was too scared to cut any deeper. Pretty soon my arms looked like I had fallen into a briar patch. I stuck toilet tissue to the scratches and walked into my bedroom and put on a long-sleeved blouse. I did not want anyone to see my wounds. They were mine, the ones Papa had denied us, and looking at them gave me a rush of dark pleasure.

Mother Dear knew something was wrong with me. She didn't know my secret, so she must have thought I was another bored teenager. She signed me up for art lessons since I liked to doodle on the back cover of the telephone book. Every Tuesday night I walked to my class, which was held for free in the basement of our church. The teacher was a strange lady who had once lived in New York. Miss Dial was her name. She wore black dresses, just black. And she brushed her long dark hair into a strict and shining bun at the nape of her neck. Her eyelashes were thick and dark, like sable brushes. I thought maybe she was a World War II widow, like so many others, but she never wore a wedding band. I didn't have the nerve to ask. Her black dresses were cloaklike, real mysterious, and they thrilled me. I loved the long sleeves and wondered what was under them, what she was hiding. For my next birthday, which was not for another whole year, I wanted a black dress with crisp white cuffs.

I took to painting at once, and for a while I stopped hurting myself. I still had to wear long sleeves, though, because of the scars. They had not yet faded. Miss Dial showed me how to mix colors and clean my brushes. Still lifes were my favorites. I would arrange colorful glass jugs on the kitchen table and paint all day. I painted pears, daylilies, squash. I painted tulips, iris, and jonquils. I painted the dogwoods in our front yard and won first prize in the 4-H exhibit at school. I was so proud of that blue ribbon. That was when Sister decided to paint, too. She was almost seven. She had a leggy, lean look to her, no baby fat to speak of. She didn't look like Mother Dear's darling little infant girl but more like a child going through a growth spurt, like what the doctor said had happened to me. You shoot up overnight and see if you don't suddenly look old. It happens, believe me.

It was summer, and Sister walked into the kitchen, holding a blank canvas, which Mother Dear let her steal from me, and she didn't say a single word as I set up a still life on the table. It was real pretty but stark, as Miss Dial would say, Concord grapes and a pitcher of water. Sister watched everything I did. I set up a canvas on my easel, then uncapped my paints. I poured turpentine into a dish. She did not have an easel, so she propped her canvas on a chair.

"What do you think you are doing?" I asked her.

"The same thing you're doing," she answered. "Painting a picture."

"Well, be my guest!" I said loudly, hoping Mother Dear or Queenie heard, but if they did, they paid no attention. As usual. Now if the shoe were on the other foot, if Sister had been the one yelling, they would have rushed in with their knitting needles raised like knives. I know this to be a fact and a half.

Sister just helped herself to my paints. She used up all of my burnt umber. And her picture was terrible, just terrible. The grapes were not shaped correctly, tiny as buckshot, and the water glass was oversized, a rectangle of lavender water. I made no comment. Mother Dear and Queenie moved behind us in the kitchen, like fish gliding in clear water. I didn't see a lick of talent on Sister's canvas, which relieved me. At last I had shown her up at something. She turned her face up to me, and I saw a splotch of purple paint on the tip of her nose. I wanted to hate her, but she did look cute. Younger somehow. "Well? What do you think?" she asked, cocking her head, staring at her painting.

I didn't know what to say! I could tell the truth and hurt her feelings, or I could lie. I decided to kill two birds with one stone. It was on the tip of my tongue to say her painting looked like the work of a blind monkey, but I just happened to look up and see Mother Dear standing in the doorway. Behind her was Queenie's broad face, her gleaming forehead.

"I know the grapes are a little small and off-center," Sister said eagerly. She could not see Mother Dear. "But it's not too bad, is it?"

I paused in front of the canvas, looking at Mother Dear from the corner of my eye. "Sister, I think you are extremely talented."

From the doorway, Mother Dear smiled and nodded at Queenie.

"You really do?" A huge grin spilled across Sister's face. She was not beautiful then, but it was clear she would be.

"I really think you ought to take lessons from Miss Dial," I added for no good reason. But once you start lying, you can't stop. There's a momentum to it.

"Really and truly?" Sister peered again at her pitiful little grapes.

"Would you like to take lessons?" Mother Dear asked.

Sister turned, smiling. "Oh, I'd love it! May I?"

"Yes, darling, you may," said Mother Dear.

I stared at my oils, dreading the thought of sharing them. I should not have lied, but I did. Later, those lies came back to haunt me, bread cast on the water, tenfold.

On the fifteenth of August, Sister's seventh birthday, V-J Day, Mother Dear gave her a whole set of paints. It was not a real good set, not as expensive as mine, I noticed. We worked in the kitchen, painting everything from peaches in a wooden bucket to daisies in a glass vase. I taught her how to hold the brush different ways, and she started tagging along to my art lessons on Tuesday nights. We painted vegetables and flowers from Mother Dear's garden, and we entered our best pictures in the county fair, in different age groups. We won red ribbons, second place. She was so excited, let me tell you. And her picture was good—a slice of cantaloupe and a paring knife with the palest sliver of melon on the blade. She called it *Still Life with Cantaloupe,* after my own prize-winning *Still Life with Gladioli.* That was the summer Mother Dear won a blue ribbon for her pepper jelly.

Toward the end of August, right after the fair ended, the Crystal Falls Home Demonstration Club had a big meeting and invited Mother Dear, who was not a member, to demonstrate her method of making pepper jelly. I will never forget it. It was on a Saturday morning, and the heat rose up in sheets while the club secretary read the minutes from the last meeting. The windows were open, and bees knocked against the screens, drawn to a huge pitcher of lemonade on the counter. Old wooden ceiling fans batted the hot air back and forth over our heads. I was perspiring all over, even between my legs. But when I looked around, the other ladies, who were mostly old, were cool and collected. Not a trickle dripped down their powdered throats. Sister had a little mustache of perspiration on her upper lip, which told me she was hot, too. I kept looking at the sweating pitcher of lemonade, imagining how cool and sweet it would taste.

After the treasurer read her report, the president of the club, Mrs. Willadean Wentworth, stood up to introduce Mother Dear. Miss Willadean was rich. Her father-in-law was Papa's boss down at the bank. The Wentworths liked Papa, Mother Dear always said. She hoped he would get promoted to cashier. They knew he was good with numbers, that he had a mathematical brain. I didn't. I was an artist. The Wentworths had a son my age. His name was Claude Edmund Wentworth III, and he was as ugly as they come. I would not be caught dead dating him, rich or not. Queenie said Claude's uncle, Sawyer Wentworth, ran off to become a hobo. With all of his family's money, he had to be stupid to do something like that.

"I'm real happy to introduce our special guest, Gussie Hamilton," said Miss Willadean, "even though most of you already know her. She's going to demonstrate the preparation of her prize-winning pepper jelly." Miss Willadean twisted her neck and stared toward me and Sister. She smiled so broadly, her moles appeared to crawl on her face like bugs. "And say, if I'm not mistaken, Gussie has brought her sweet daughter with her today, who is a prize-winning artist, and she's only seven. Clancy Jane? Why don't you please stand up, honey?"

Sister stood. The women clapped. Sister hunched her shoulders and stared down at her scuffed shoes. I waited for Miss Willadean to call out my name, to introduce Mother Dear's other sweet, prize-winning daughter, but she just turned to my mother and said, "We're ready when you are, Gussie."

She wasn't going to introduce me! My heart stopped beating for a moment, and when it started again, everything had changed for me. All my life I had been kind to old ladies. I had been polite and held my tongue and hid my true feelings. No more, my beating heart said. *No more, no more, no more.*

I thought I would start small.

After Mother Dear finished making the jelly and was holding up the green jars to the light, I watched Miss Willadean pass a tray of lemonade. She handed one to Sister, who said thanks and slid off her chair. She walked over to Mother Dear. I took a cup from Miss Willadean's tray and thanked her. She made a sharp little sound in her throat, un-hmm. As soon as she turned away, I took a sip. I had never tasted such watery lemonade. I really expected better from a home demonstration club. I stared down at the waxed tile floor. I set my cup on Sister's empty chair. Then I bumped it hard with my knee. The cup knocked over, rolled slightly, and spilled its contents onto the tile. Lemonade, pale gray and sticky, dripped from the chair, spreading into a puddle on the polished tile. I hoped it dried into a hard, filmy layer and Miss Willadean Wentworth had to scrub it off with her bare hands. But I knew she would not. She would make a nigger do it for her.

I got up and walked over to the counter. I had to squeeze between two fat ladies who smelled of dime-store perfume, My Sin. As I stared at the green jars of Mother Dear's jelly, I told myself it wasn't Sister's fault. No one had twisted Miss Willadean's arm and made her slight me. She probably didn't even know I was an artist. The women were eating jelly on crackers, spread with cheese. They were going *mmmmmm!* Little pieces of saltine gathered in the corners of their wrinkled mouths. I worked my way over to Miss Willadean. I was already forming the words in the back of my mind. She swallowed her cracker and reached for another. "My, this is delicious," she said to the woman next to her, pushing her tongue over her lips, just as I hoped she would later push a mop over this floor. I tapped her arm.

"My, this is excellent jelly," she said, staring me full in the face.

I felt my cheeks turn warm, but I gathered my nerve and said, "I'm a painter, too. Or did you not know." It wasn't a question.

"Really?" Miss Willadean stared at a fleck of pepper on her cracker. "Was that *your* painting at the fair? The gladiolus?"

"Gladioli," I corrected her. It was the first time in my life I had ever corrected anyone, much less an adult. It did not feel good. My cheeks flamed, but my brain was pure ice.

"Oh, I thought it was your sister's." She gave me a chilly smile. Then she reached down to spread jelly on a hunk of cheese. I was left staring at her back, the floral cotton dress with the lace collar, the fine wisps of gray-blond hair that had escaped her loosely gathered bun. The hairs were weathered and cottony, and I knew she wasn't aging well. That was unfortunate because I decided right then I was going to be Somebody if it killed me. I was going to make something out of myself. And gray-haired Willadean would not be there to see my glory. I hoped with all my might and with all the new blood passing through my heart that she would live a long and healthy life. That she would come to me when I was a famous artist and invite me to speak at the Home Demonstration Club. I would say, "No, thank you. My calendar is full. It is full until the end of your life."

She turned abruptly, a cracker in each hand, and almost knocked me down with her elbow. "Oops" was all she said and smiled this powdery smile that made me want to reach for her throat. Just you wait, I thought. Bread cast upon the water, Miss Willadean, bread cast upon the water.

I went home and took a box of matches from the top of the stove. I walked straight toward Mother Dear's flower garden. I crouched under the sunflowers and lifted my skirt. I struck a match, touched the flame to my pale stomach. I held my breath as a blister popped up below my navel. I prayed for the sky to fall, for lightning to strike. The pain was nothing compared to my wish to die. I just did not know how to do it. Instead I killed off one piece of myself at a time.

*T*hat November, I was still alive, but I saw a chance when the town flooded. A wintry rain had fallen for two days, grating hard against our house. Sister and I stared through the windows, the glass slightly blurred by moisture, watching driftwood backstroke down the lawn's yellow roll. Water beat against tall husks of corn in the garden, battering the soggy ground.

Then flash floods began, and the man on the radio cautioned people to move to high ground, to stay away from the square, which the town fathers had foolishly built over an underground creek. The town had been settled in 1780, next to a salt lick and a creek, which dipped into a cave and emerged some distance farther into a small, if breathtaking, waterfall. In those days, Crystal Falls must have looked like paradise, with its abundance of deer, ducks, and wild turkey. No one thought about its being in a valley, so near a creek, with so much limestone beneath the topsoil. The pioneers, Papa said, had Indians and bears to worry about, not the town's location.

We sat around the radio, listening for news, worried sick about Papa. I myself was worried that he might crack up right there in front of God and Mr. Wentworth. Businessmen were trapped, the man on the radio warned. Phone lines were down. I had an image of Papa falling through layers of dirty water, falling through the earth, and emerging in Guam. Outside the rain continued to fall, chilled, hard, and gray. It was the flash floods that made Town Creek spill over its banks and gush toward the business district. I imagined the courthouse filling with muddy water. I imagined men wearing yellow raincoats, stacking sandbags in front of the doors and windows.

Our house stood on a hill, which meant it was safe from the advancing waters. Mother Dear snapped off the radio and called out to me and Sister. "We're going to save Papa," she said, and a thrill shot through me. We put on raincoats, grabbed our umbrellas, and ran into the barn, skipping over mud puddles. Mother Dear and I lifted Papa's silver canoe and carried it down the hill, where the flood waters began. Once I had let the bathtub overflow, and water had dripped through the ceiling. The creek was like that, seeping through the grass, a relentless push of cloudy water.

I looked back at my house. It seemed huge and white, suspended above the surging brown water. I believed with all my heart that nothing bad could happen there. And Mother Dear was not about to let our papa drown at the bank. I imagined dollar bills rising, floating like scum on the creek. Coins would sink like flat rocks. Mr. Wentworth would wring his hands and sigh. "Dive!" he would yell at Papa. "Dive for my money!" And my papa would peel off his jacket, walk to the building's edge, and make a perfect swan dive into the muddy water.

We paddled toward town. When we reached the corner of Broad and Main, Mother Dear said, "Lordy Jesus." The water had spilled over the porches, right up to the windowsills, and people were hauling out their furniture, trying to salvage what they could. It would break your heart. We paddled toward the square just in time to see emergency crews stacking sandbags in front of the doors and windows. Water had risen above the basement windows.

"Oh, my Lord," said Mother Dear, lifting one hand from her paddle and pointing toward the north end of Broad Street. Miss Willadean Wentworth's long black car crested the top of the hill. I could not imagine where she thought she was going. The bottom of the road was cupped with water. I looked again. Her car crept forward, the tires parted water, just like she personally owned the road. As soon as she reached the bottom of the hill, her car was swallowed by brown water. She pushed open her door and began screaming. She was wearing a plastic rain hat, the cheap kind, which surprised me just the least, her being old money, as they say. But Mother Dear had once said the rich were always stingy.

A young policeman waded into the water, waving his arms. He yelled. "STAY RIGHT THERE, MA'AM! DON'T MOVE!"

Of course Miss Willadean moved.

The policeman shook his head and pushed forward into the water. He did not know Miss Willadean like I did. She probably thought she owned the water. From the canoe, I held my breath and squeezed my paddle, waiting to see what she would do next. She stepped forward into the water, sinking hip-deep. Then she waded forward, her mouth open, as if she were both astonished by and furious at the flood. I thought she looked like a goldfish, but of course it would not have been ladylike for me to say this out loud.

By this time a huge crowd had gathered on the roof of Citizens' Bank. My heart slammed against my ribs when I saw my papa standing next to Mr. Wentworth and his son. They waved their arms and shouted something nobody could hear. The water now reached Miss Willadean's starched white collar. The policeman screamed at her to turn back, but she slogged forward, her thin neck leaning into the wind and rain. Her legs buckled, but she steadied herself and trudged toward the policeman, who stood chest-deep in the water, holding out his arms, wiggling his fingers.

"Stop!" he cried. "Stop!"

Miss Willadean was two feet away from the man, but she did not seem to understand. Perhaps, in her terror, she thought he was yelling, "Hop! Hop!" She must have thought he meant to catch her in his arms. I could almost read her mind, that she had always been taken care of by menfolk and weren't policemen there to protect and serve her? She took a deep breath and jumped. The policeman reached forward to snatch her shoulders, but his fingers closed on her plastic rain hat.

We waited and waited, but Miss Willadean did not surface.

Someone shouted that she had fallen into an open manhole cover, that she had been snatched up by the current. I pictured her being sucked into a pitch-black underground creek. I knew about the creek because before the war, Papa had once drawn me a picture of it. I remembered the curved pencil lines on the Big Chief tablet, Papa sketching the creek's path beneath the square. It navigated beneath the courthouse and coursed blindly under the hardware store, under Citizens' Bank and the Ben Franklin Five-and-Dime. There, beneath the dime store, the creek made a sudden turn and washed upward into the waterfall, which now gushed one hundred yards from the corner Esso station.

The following morning, the rain had ended, and sunlight washed down, pale and fluid. It fell through the leafless woods, and birds called out in faint, shaking voices. Around the square, the water level slowly receded. It was ankle-deep, still not safe, but late that afternoon, Mother Dear let me walk to town with Papa.

We arrived just as Miss Willadean's body appeared in front of the Esso station, hitched against a stop sign. Her palm was frozen at a right angle to her wrist, in the stern, unforgiving posture of an officer directing traffic. As I watched the volunteers remove her body, I squeezed Papa's hand and wished it had been me that had drowned. Way up in the dusky sky, a small plane wafted above the square. As I stared at its silver wings and hammered metal, I pictured an aerial view, the drenched look of everything, and me, a tiny speck, a target among the minions. I turned my face upward and wished the plane would fall. I imagined gears grinding, the motor snagging. Then a rush of silence, like dead air in a windpipe, followed by the whistling drone of descent. I could hear everything—the water draining, the soft darkness rising from the ground, the white stars pulsing above me. The earth moved, pulling constellations through the air. I heard the silver sheath of bombs falling, the moment of impact, the sharp wild cries flung upward into the November dusk. I let go of Papa's hand and spread my arms wide into a V for victory, praying with all my might for the sky to fall.

Miss Gussie

1953

Every spring, until my Charlie's death, he plowed our garden. After that, the colored preacher turned the soil, and I always expected the blades of his plow to strike a bone. A skull. I would do it myself if I could. I knew country women who plowed whole fields walking behind a mule. But I was no country woman. Living in town had changed me. The women from my childhood had been strong as men from toting buckets of water. They had died without knowing the miracle of electricity.

Preacher came this morning, and I watched him plow the brown dirt. Nothing turned up. I suppose Charlie and I planted that boy fairly deep. Lung cancer took my Charlie, a definite smite by the Lord. Charlie never killed a living soul, not even a Japanese. He started coughing up blood, and Mr. Wentworth, fearing it was TB, made him stop working at the bank. Charlie had worked his way up to head cashier, in spite of his nervous prostration. He wasted away in our bedroom, skin just a-hanging from his bones. The room took on an odor, like Jergen's lotion spread on dirty feet, a yellowed, dead-skin smell. He never quit smoking until the end, either.

But he did not die at home. He died at the Crystal Falls

Hospital, on Dorothy's sixteenth birthday in 1948, and she had a party all planned. Of course, we had to call up everyone and postpone. Only we never got around to having another. And I didn't know, I guess she never forgave me for it, even though she never threw it up to me, not the first time. Even Queenie was amazed.

When Dorothy turned twenty-one, she had two babies of her own, a girl and a boy. They stayed sick all the time. Clancy was almost fifteen. Her birthday was coming up in August, but I'd made no plans. No need to. I didn't need a fortune-teller to predict that my girl's life would be ruined, that she wouldn't be needing a party. It liked to have killed me. When I thought about what she'd gone and done, my throat turned to rust. My heart dropped low in my belly. I had known heartbreak, and I had known death. I had buried my husband while I was still fairly young and not withered. I had buried someone who was young and not quite dead.

Still, I always thought I would have my Clancy Jane.

I had Dorothy and her family. They lived right next door. Who would have ever thought it? Now that she was grown and married, she talked down to me as if my mind was gone. Suddenly she was an expert on everything. Queenie said it was a shame, a doggone shame. Everything went too fast with Dorothy. All of a sudden she'd grown up, and I couldn't remember how she'd looked as a baby. I had to sift through her albums.

But with Clancy Jane it was different. She was a child for a long time. I paid attention to small things, and sometimes my memory would be larger than the thing itself. One day she was in the front yard helping her daddy rake leaves. It was before the war. She wasn't as big as a toot, couldn't have been more than three. She was wearing a bright red coat with brass buttons. Her little coat stood out in the front, making her tilt backward. She had on white stockings, and her legs looked so sturdy. Her blond head bobbed up and down as she gathered leaves. As I gazed out the window, my whole body fairly pulsed with love. As my breath fogged and shrank against the glass panes, it came to me that it was a sin to love someone too much. And I loved Clancy Jane too much. I saw it plain as day. Dorothy had accused me of it all the time, and I thought she was crazy with jealousy. I didn't pet Clancy Jane, I didn't love her more, the Lord knew I didn't. Well, maybe just a little. Maybe because she was my last child. Maybe I had always known it.

I tried to raise my girls into little ladies. I don't know about little boys, but girls will wear you out. There is a sneakiness about girls that they keep hid under sweetness and pouting and crying. Their giggles can sound like water falling from a fountain, but it can turn on you and fill your lungs with grief.

You had to watch girls. I only had the two, and Queenie always said it was one too many. She just never took to Dorothy. Lots of people didn't, and I thought it must go back to when she was a baby. She had that finicky temperament. She howled from daylight to dark. When she got older, she was always so sad and blue. She'd let out these long sighs like she was breathing her last. Or else she'd snap your head off. I couldn't help but wonder if that evening in the kitchen, so long ago, had marked her. When I remembered Dorothy's childhood, my mind turned dark with her squalling.

It was a long time before I worked up my nerve to have another. Charlie was a gentleman. He never complained, especially after that night in the garden. Sometimes I'd look up quickly and catch him staring at me. His eyes were so blue I could see all the way to the backs of them. He knew how far I'd gone that night. It was as if we had buried little pieces of ourselves, and we couldn't get them back.

I'm not sure what got us started again. There was six years' difference between my babies, six long years. I tried not to think about it. Sometimes I'd see a pregnant woman, and I'd pooch out my own flat stomach. I'd hear a baby's gurgle in church, and it would start me thinking that a little boy would be nice. A boy for Charlie to take to the baseball games. Then it turned into a hankering. Oh, I wanted me a baby! It was the strongest hankering I'd ever had. Strong enough to make me work up my nerve and go upstairs and open the door to the guest room. I stared down at Charlie. I was skittish as a bride.

"Is anything the matter, Gussie?" he asked. I answered him by untying my robe, letting it drop to the floor. His eyes got big. Then he pulled the covers aside, got up from the bed, and drew me into his arms. It was a night of surprises, and I went to him every single night thereafter. I couldn't stop myself. In the dark it was hard to feel shy or ashamed. We made up for lost time. A time or two, when Clancy Jane was just a little thing, I thought I'd gotten in the family way again. I was so proud. Charlie would kiss my stomach and talk to my navel. We'd laugh and laugh, and sometimes we'd wake Dorothy. She'd holler from her room until I just knew she'd wake Clancy Jane. Charlie wouldn't let me out of the bed. He'd pull on his trousers and go tend to Dorothy. Then he would come back to me. I wanted lots of babies, but his seed never took root inside me again. When he came back from the war, that whole other part of him had gone. Pretty soon it left me, too.

When Dorothy accused me of playing favorites, I'd get so mad. I'd think to myself, why does she do this? Why was she so jealous of her sister? Especially when she played favorites with her own two. She thought Mack, her boy, hung the moon. And he was a handsome little fellow, just as dark-headed as his mama was when she was little.

Bitsy, her youngest, had just learned to crawl. Her whole name was Lillian Beatrice, and Queenie started calling her Little Bit, then Little Bitsy. Now we all called her Bitsy and left it at that. That child was a general busybody, into everything. She got into my sewing and tangled all the spools of thread. Young as she was, she'd laugh and laugh when Dorothy fussed at her. It drove Dorothy fairly crazy. She was all the time bursting into my kitchen, holding Bitsy like she was a sack of apples and complaining about how she wasn't getting any sleep. How Bitsy cried all the time. How she got into Mack's toys and made him cry. She couldn't have her Mack crying over anything. I just nodded my head, but I didn't say anything. I remembered how Dorothy used to squawk. How her face would turn purple, and I'd think, well this is it, she's breathed her last, her lungs will burst, and I'll have to pick out a tombstone with a little lamb.

"I just had these babies so close together," Dorothy said and wiped her eyes like she was crying, but I could tell she wasn't. You'd think she'd pet her only girl, but it was the opposite. Bitsy put me in mind of Clancy Jane. Pretty honey-blonds, both of them, with crystal-blue eyes. It fairly irked Dorothy, who always had dark hair until Bitsy's grew in blond. Then she colored hers though she swore she hadn't. Her eyes were gray-blue like mine. She looked better as a blond if you asked me.

When the girls were little, I knitted them matching mittens and hats. Clancy Jane was always losing just one mitten, but I'd just whip up another one. Dorothy hated it. She would get this pinched look on her face as she watched me work. She never lost her mittens.

"She can't keep up with them, can she, Mother Dear?" Dorothy said, resentful like. From the beginning she called me Mother Dear, and when she was little, it came out *"Duh-dear."* It was the cutest thing when she was little. I don't know where Dorothy learned how to call me that. The older she got, though, the more she'd twist her voice. She'd say "Mother Dear" like she'd say "stupid idiot." Clancy Jane never picked it up. She always called me Mother.

"Why do you keep making her extra pairs of mittens?" Dorothy asked.

"Because her hands will get cold, that's why," I said. Dorothy rolled her eyes like I had lost my mind, but I kept on knitting.

I was real strict. I had to be on account of me being a widow lady. You had to watch girls when you didn't have a man in the house. I would not hear of the girls dating until their sixteenth birthdays. And those weren't real dates. I gave them a sharp curfew, ten o'clock. I had to meet the boys, too. I insisted they come right up to our front porch, which was all screened, and meet me.

"Where're you all going?" I'd ask. And the boy would say, "To the movies, Mrs. Hamilton." Or, "To a church picnic, Mrs. Hamilton."

Clancy Jane was too young to have a real date—none that I knew of, to be exact—but Dorothy had plenty. After the boys brought her home, I searched real quiet like for danger signs. Smeared lipstick. Hair all messed up. Or else combed too neatly. Wrinkles in her skirts and dresses.

Dorothy had every single solitary sign.

"Look at your dress," I'd say. "And why's your face so red?

What's that purple mark on your neck? Why weren't you home an hour ago?"

On and on and on.

"It's nothing, Mother Dear," she'd say. That was Dorothy for you. "Don't you worry your sweet head about it, Mother Dear."

I always thought she would get a reputation. Or get pregnant by some boy she did not love. I always expected the worst with Dorothy. Which only goes to show you that people can surprise you. The next thing I knew she was planning a big church wedding. She was in love with Albert McDougal, whose daddy owned the Ben Franklin Dime Store. She thought he hung the moon. He was a quiet sort, but I thought that was just what she needed. A rock to lean on. There is nothing harder than being your own rock.

At her wedding, she burst into tears and cried and said I was fussing too much with the bows in Clancy Jane's hair. Clancy Jane was a bridesmaid, of course. The truth was, she'd caught a necklace in her hair, and I was just trying to untangle it. But just try and tell that to Dorothy, who went off on her honeymoon without even kissing me good-bye.

Ten months later, she gave birth to Mack. She had a terrible case of the baby blues. Cried every single afternoon, then she'd blow her nose and go cook supper. When she got pregnant with Bitsy, I gave them some land next door and they built a great big brick house. The whole time the house was going up, I had these little spells of misgivings. I just didn't know how it would work, me living next to Dorothy. Sometimes I had the feeling she loved me better than life itself, and other times I'd think she fairly hated me.

After Bitsy was born, she started talking about having another baby, even though she complained all the time about the two she had. Plus, she had a tipped womb. Albert just rolled those pale blue eyes of his and let her do what she wanted. He could afford children, I guess, but she never got pregnant. I couldn't help but wonder what would have happened if she had given birth to another son, if she would have loved Mack any less.

She always had a way of filling up her life and yours. To this day I seem to spend all of my energy and attention trying to keep that girl in line, trying to cheer her up, helping raise her babies, and I just failed to notice what Clancy Jane was up to.

Clancy Jane, at fifteen, was not interested in her sister. I am not bragging to say she was real pretty, a cheerleader, the leader of this and that. Girls always coming out to the house to drink Coca-Colas and listen to records. Straight A's in math. And she was so religious. She could name all the books of the Bible in order. She was the first one dressed of a Sunday morning. She had the best manners you'd ever want to see, too. Both my girls did. Everyone said so.

Anyway, I would be baby-sitting little Mack and Bitsy, and Clancy Jane would breeze in and pick up one of the babies and say, "Mother, I'm going on a church hayride Friday night," and I'd say, "Fine." On Saturday afternoons, she would say, "I'm going to the movies," and I'd say, "Have fun." There were hayrides, pajama parties, football games, sock hops, dances. All this time, I thought she was my good girl and that Dorothy was the bad one.

*H*art Jones was a football player, and Clancy Jane cheered at all the games. So I should've put two and two together. That boy would meet girl and who knows what all. I just did not figure on her falling for a greaser. Last year Hart's parents had moved to Chicago, and they left him with his Aunt Estelle. Before I put my finger on what was what, Clancy Jane was crying her pretty blue eyes out and telling me she was in trouble. Going to have a baby. I felt my heart rush up into my neck, then it split both ways and shot out my ears. That was when I'd thought she hadn't dated, not the first time.

"How can you be . . ." I broke off and shut my eyes. I breathed hard. "How can you be in the family way when you haven't dated a boy?" I finally said.

Her eyes got real watery. "I sneaked out with him."

"Lordy Jesus," I said. "You're not even sixteen years old!"

I thought to myself how such a thing could happen. We weren't trash, although I knew people would talk. Every now and then a girl would get pregnant and have to marry. When her baby was born, the family would call it "premature." Premature, my foot, was what people said in private. But they all went along with it on the surface.

How can my darling be pregnant, I thought. Like a fool. How she got pregnant wasn't the mystery. I knew *how,* I just did not think she *would.* "Mother, I'm in real trouble," she kept saying. She was ashamed to tell me who the daddy was. When she finally did, my heart gathered itself and turned cold. I couldn't even feel it beating. I fairly like to have died. And me, a widow lady. I was scared of Hart Jones. He had dark eyes, no color at all, really. And his legs were bowed, which gave him this spraddled, nasty look. Clancy Jane was fragile-boned. Narrow hips and a tiny waist. I hated to think of him touching her there.

Dorothy said that Hart had probably seen our house and thought we were rich. Now our house wasn't anything special unless you were a Jones. It struck me that Dorothy might have a point. A Jones might think Clancy Jane was a rich girl. The house was white with green shutters, and the colored preacher kept it painted. The front yard was a mass of color from spring to fall—plums, redbuds, dogwoods, tulips, iris, magnolia, holly, gladioli, daisies. It was real colorful. People drove slow just to stare at the flowers. And that didn't even count the ones in my vegetable garden, which couldn't be seen from the street.

Now. Even though my Charlie had been head cashier at the bank, we were not anywhere near rich. But, over the years, bankers made deals under the table, and Charlie was no exception. Even in his weakened state, he had a talent for turning one dollar into two. That was why Mr. Wentworth liked him. Charlie made land deals and bought real estate on Broad Street, two shops downtown. As his widow, I collected a nice sum of rent money every month. So you could see where a Jones would have gotten the wrong idea. And I knew about meanness. All I had to do was look at my garden and remember.

When Dorothy found out about Clancy Jane, she said, "This is the most awful thing! How am I supposed to hold my head up now?"

"Your head?" I said. "You're married to a man with a dime store. What do you have to do with this?"

"Because I just do, Mother Dear. You know this is a disgrace. Sister's gone and ruined her life."

I couldn't deny it. The idea of Clancy Jane being an unwed mother was bad enough, but Hart Jones for her husband was worse. All I could study about was his Aunt Estelle, the way she'd sit in front of her trailer with her legs hiked up, picking her nose and snapping beans at the same time. She took in ironing for people, too, but I never used her. I was inclined to send Clancy Jane to a home for unwed mothers in New Orleans.

Dorothy agreed. "Sister's made her bed, now let her lie in it," she said. "She's disgraced us all. And with trash. And that poor little unborn baby will be half-trash. Don't look like that, Mother Dear. You know it's the truth. She'll just have to give that baby up for adoption."

Well, Lord help me, Clancy Jane sneaked out of her upstairs bedroom window, climbed down the trellis, and ran away with Hart Jones. They were underage, and I wondered how they'd find a justice of the peace to marry them. Old Estelle rounded up some fool with a Bible, some distantly related Jones who was an alcoholic.

They got married. It was legal and everything. Clancy Jane brought that boy to meet me. Lord, I can shut my eyes and see them just as clear as day. Clancy Jane on the screen porch, holding his hand. He had a great big blackhead beside his nose. Dark hair all slicked back. A chipped front tooth and all the rest crooked. Even standing still, his legs looked spraddled, and his pants were too tight. Clancy Jane was wearing a dark blue skirt with a white poodle appliqué. I'd made it. There was just the hint of a swell to her stomach. Her breasts stretched the fabric of her blouse, pulling the buttons tight.

"If we can just stay here until the baby comes," Clancy Jane was saying.

Tears sprung into my eyes so fast my glasses fogged. I couldn't speak for a full minute. They had the most pitiful looks on their faces. So full of hope when none was to be had. Before I opened my mouth, I knew I would spend the rest of my days regretting what came next. But I couldn't hold back. In the back of my mind was Dorothy's voice, and when I spoke, I used her words.

"No, you may not stay here," I said. Tears kept dripping onto my blouse. "You made your bed. Now lie in it."

Clancy Jane

1954

*P*USH!" the doctor said. "Push now, sugar!" I could see nothing except his eyes, slate gray, and a bush of silver eyebrows, above his white mask. Behind him was a wall of green tile. My hands were strapped in brown leather, hooked to a hard metal table. There was this curved handle, which I was supposed to squeeze. The nurses told me to. I thought of all the women before me who had touched it. I couldn't believe they strapped you down to have a baby. Or maybe they did things differently in New Orleans.

"Push!"

I squeezed my eyes shut and pretended to push. I imagined my face turning red, then purple, with blue, wavy blood vessels popping out on my temples.

"Push harder, sugar! There, there! You're doin' good, sugar. That's a girl. That's a good girl."

I wondered if the doctor would be nicer if I barked and licked his hand. *That's a good girl, good dog.* Push, sugar lump. Push those puppies out.

My baby was a girl, which disappointed Hart a little. I could see it in his eyes. He could have hidden it better. The nurse saw it, too, and said, "Well, Mr. Jones, at least you won't have to pay for a circumcision."

"I wish to God I did," said Hart.

I could've just cried. Later, I did.

I stayed at Charity Hospital almost two weeks because when the baby was born, her head cracked my tailbone. And I had fifty-nine stitches. The nurses counted them. I asked them to. The windows on the ward were long, with striped screens. Through them I saw a patch of blue. Below, on the sidewalk, colored ladies waited for the bus. They climbed up the steps and walked all the way to the back. I missed Queenie so much I thought I'd bust a stitch. And Mother. I needed her, but Hart said she'd hurt his feelings real bad, and he didn't think he'd get over it. Part of me wanted to cry and call her collect, and another part of me was boiling mad. I cried for two hours, but I didn't call. I upset the nurses so much they made the doctor give me a shot.

"It's your hormones, sugar," he told me. "You've got those baby blues."

Well, I sure knew about the blues. My sister had had them her whole life. Her room was across the hall from mine. She had a big cherry canopy bed. When she married Albert, she took all of her furniture, and Mother had to buy more. There was no telling what she had taken from my old room since I'd been gone. Just no telling.

Hart said it didn't matter, to forget my old room, that I had him now.

"Just let it alone," he said. "They'll calm down, and then you can visit them and show them the baby and everything'll be fine. And we've got my family. They may be in Chicago, but we Joneses stick together." He stuck his fingers together and held up his hands. "Just like this."

I didn't say anything. I hadn't been impressed by his people. His aunt Estelle, who'd raised him after his parents moved to Chicago, was a nasty woman. He always called her Ain't Estelle, like her name was sawed in half, Es telle. Then there was his mother, Mrs. Jones, who never saw fit to tell me her first name, even when we spent two weeks with them in Chicago. Hart thought he might want to work in one of the big factories. Mamaw and his daddy lived in a red and white trailer, the size of two cars jammed together. When I asked Hart what his mother's name was, he said, "It's Goldie, but everybody calls her Mamaw."

And she sure looked like a mamaw. No front teeth, the rest rotted off into black hunks. A snarl of gray hair. Faded brown eyes. I told Hart he could live up North if he wanted, but I could not. Chicago turned out to be too cold for him, so we drove south until our car went dead. We were in Slidell, Louisiana. I was wearing some old maternity clothes I'd bought at a thrift store in Oak Lawn. We hitched a ride with a Methodist preacher who treated us to a hot lunch. Then we drove across Lake Pontchartrain. One of the preacher's deacons was big in the oil business. He gave Hart a card and told him to call.

*H*art loved working on the oil rigs. We rented a little silver trailer in Myrtle Grove, south of New Orleans, in bayou country. We bought a car for fifty dollars, and the man let us pay five dollars a week. Our trailer stood in a patch of live oaks, with gray moss hanging down. When the sun was shining, you could see it for miles. It looked like a star. Hart said it reminded him of a piece of scrap metal in shallow water.

The bayou country was rough and swampy. It was full of mosquitoes and unshaved men. At night sounds would rise up, strange moans that Hart said was owls. Queenie always said when you heard an owl to quickly tie a knot or else someone would die. I told myself an owl couldn't make a noise so hooked and wild and long-throated. Still, I tied knots every time.

By the middle of March, I was ready to have my baby. We lived a fair distance from New Orleans, and I was afraid of the clinic in Myrtle Grove. It just didn't look clean, even though the Cajun doctor was nice. It was hard for me to understand half of what he said. All that French talk, mixed up with English. I was always asking him to repeat what he said. He just stared at me like I was rude.

There I was, almost sixteen years old and no mother to tell me it would be all right. Sixteen years old and didn't have the first idea how to diaper a baby. I stabbed me and Violet while I learned. The women in town, who were all kin somehow, scared me with their talk of polio.

"Bake her toys in the oven," my neighbor-lady advised. Her name was Irene, and she was part Irish, part Cajun. She lived up the road in a white house that didn't look big enough for her six children, who seemed so healthy I couldn't help but wonder if they had springs for bones. So I guess she knew. But I had this oven that ran on alcohol, and I was half afraid of it. Hart said it was safe, but I hated the fumes. The mosquitoes swarmed around the hot trailer like it was a silver moon. They buzzed and crawled through holes in the screens. I had to buy a mosquito net to drape over Violet's crib.

Hart was off doing this and that. He ran with a wild crew of men who had rotten teeth and stank and went with trashy women. He was never home, and I didn't have a car. My shoes

quickly wore out, and I hated to spend money on new ones.
We needed so many other things. I found some black electrical
tape in a drawer and mended the holes. The neighbor-lady kept
Violet while I walked to the market. It was an open-air grocery,
and it smelled bad. Flies hummed all around the bins of ice,
which were full of crabs, crawfish, shrimp, and other dead fish.
I didn't have the first idea how to cook them. I could barely
sterilize Violet's bottles on that alcohol stove. There were rows
of vegetables and fruit, which felt warm from sitting in the sun,
but I bought potatoes and peas, tomatoes and okra. I bought a
hen. I bought familiar things that reminded me of my mother's
garden back home.

When I thought about my family, how small it was, my heart
seemed to drop in my chest. Like gravity was pulling it down
and I would give birth again, this time to a large, permanent
grief. And trouble was in the air. It wafted like a sharp odor. I
didn't understand it. Violet was a good baby, which was lucky
for both of us, but I was lonesome. I ached for home. For the
cool spring nights that carried the scent of honeysuckle, for my
mother's deep feather mattress. But she had turned me out,
and even though I suspected Dorothy was somehow behind it,
I longed for them. They didn't even know about Violet. That
I'd had a baby girl.

Once I went as far as to buy a postcard at the dime store.
It showed a bayou that was much prettier than they are in person. I bought a pen, too, and I sat down on the curb to write.

Dear Mother,
        We're living down here. I had a baby girl, and I named
    her Violet Jane. Hart's real proud. He has a real good job on
    an oil rig. We live in a silver trailer, and it's real cute.

I couldn't think of what to write next. I just ripped up the
card. I hated to lie. And I knew she would write back. If she

wrote me, I didn't think I could stay in Louisiana. I'd leave Hart for sure even though I loved him.

Then he stopped coming home.

Two whole weeks went by. I thought he was dead. Then one Saturday afternoon he drove up in a new car. At least I thought it was his car. It was bright red, with a white rabbit's foot hanging from the rearview mirror. I walked out of the trailer, the baby in my arms, and stood on the metal steps. I was angry but relieved to see him. Then I saw that he wasn't alone. Sitting next to him, so close they looked attached at the hip, was this skinny woman. When she saw me, she quickly scooted over to her side of the car. Hart parked under a live oak. But I wasn't interested in him. I stared at her. Her black hair was piled on top of her head, a hornet's nest, and there were two spit curls, hard as bent nails, on each cheek. Her eyelids were blue, rimmed in so much black I thought for a minute she didn't have eyeballs, just two black holes. She lifted one bony hand and took a drag from a cigarette. She looked French to me. The Cajun kind with black hair growing out of her armpits, the kind that did not bathe. The kind who smelled like she had been keeping company with sweaty men.

Hart said something to the woman. Then he got out of the car.

"Where've you been all this time?" I asked.

He looked down at the yellow grass spearing through the sand and scuffed his new shoes back and forth.

"Just been working double shifts is all," he said. He shrugged and walked toward me. Then he pulled a thick white envelope from his pocket and held it out. "Here's some money for food and things. For you and the baby."

I just stared at it.

"Go on." He waved it. "Take it."

I ignored the envelope. "Who's that woman in the car?"

"Oh. Well." He cleared his throat. "That's just Laverne Pichard? I used to work with her husband? I'm having my car worked on, and she's just loaning me hers."

"She was sitting right on top of you, Hart. I saw it." I felt tears start behind my eyes, but I held them back. My face felt hot.

"We're just friends is all," said Hart.

"Well, you can take your friend and stick her up your ass, Hart Jones!" I yelled. My throat muscles ached. Violet started crying. I walked back into the hot trailer and slammed the door. I heard his new car start up. Then he and the French woman drove away. I yanked back the curtain in time to see red tail-lights moving through a cloud of gravel dust. Later, I found the envelope of money on the steps, seventy-five dollars, which smelled faintly of perfume. If I hadn't needed it so much, I would have burned it.

Two days later, I found Hart's old car in our driveway. No note, no money, nothing but the car with the keys dangling from the ignition. It was full of gas. The next week, I went to get in the car and found an envelope on the front seat. It was addressed to me in Hart's handwriting. I set Violet down in her basket and ripped the letter open.

> *Dear Clancy Jane,*
>
> *I have fell in love with Laverne. I will send you money so you and the baby can go on back to your momma in Crystal Falls. Or you can stay here. It don't matter. Whatever you think is best is OK with me. I'm sorry to spring this on you.*
>
> *Love,*
> *Hart*

I drove straight into town and bought rouge and lipstick and eyeshadow at the dime store. I didn't think it out or anything. It was just like I knew what to do. That night, I painted my face and put on my best dress. I took Violet down to Irene, the neighbor-lady. I told her all about Hart. She said, sure, she'd baby-sit. She already knew about my troubles from the grapevine. Her husband worked on the rigs, too. She even called the name of Hart's girlfriend, Laverne Pichard. Said she was the foreman's twenty-five-year-old widow. Well-off but trashy. A man-chaser, but a young-man-chaser, if I knew what she meant. I knew. Frenchy liked her men fresh, while they were still hot to trot. And Hart wasn't the first. Irene told me I could find them at the Blue Marlin Bar and Grill. They went there every night to eat oysters and dance. Irene even drew me a map so I could find it.

And I did. The Blue Marlin was a squatty cement building, painted turquoise, with a big plastic sailfish in the window. There were fishnet curtains. It was dark inside, full of wafting smoke, but I spotted Hart right away. He was sitting at a round table with Laverne. Between them was a platter of oysters on the half shell, a bottle of Tabasco, two Jax beers.

Hart's eyes about bugged out of his skull when he saw me. "Why, Clancy Jane!" he said. "What're you doing here?"

Laverne just glared with two ice-blue eyes, the color of Dorothy's. She tapped one red fingernail against the Jax bottle. Then she lit a cigarette.

"I just thought I'd get me some beer and oysters," I said sweetly.

Hart swallowed. His eyes switched back and forth, from me to Laverne. "Where's your baby?"

"The same place your baby is," I said.

"Did you leave her with Irene?" he asked.

When I didn't answer, he flushed.

"You left her with Irene, I know you did."

Frenchy narrowed her black eyes and glared at me through a veil of smoke.

"How'd you know where to find me?" he asked, and his eyes went a shade darker.

"What makes you think I was looking? Anyway, rumor has it that your Frenchy here has got hot pants for young men. That she loves to rob the cradle."

Laverne stood up, making the table shake. "I'm not gonna take that shit from you," she said real fast and foreign like.

I ignored her. Facing Hart, I gave him my sweetest smile. "Looks like she's got a trash mouth, too. Are you coming with me or not?"

His eyes swam back and forth.

"Hart?" Laverne said, but it came out like "Hot." She gave me a long icy stare.

"You need to be home with the baby," he said.

"No, he's not coming home with you," said Laverne. "Are you, Hot?"

"Just leave, Clancy Jane," he said. He wouldn't look at me.

"My pleasure," I said. "And I sure hope you don't catch some nasty disease from your Frenchy."

I was so mad, if I'd had a pistol, I would've shot him. Then I would've shot her. I turned and walked straight out of the bar. A bunch of men whistled, but I acted like I didn't hear. I got into the old car and drove down the sandy highway. I didn't even know where I was going, I was so mad.

Queenie used to say that some men chased women their whole lives. "It's like a passion with them," she said. "They never stop. Even after your heart be broke."

My heart felt good and broken. I sniffed and wiped my eyes. I had left home and my mother for this no-good man. They all told me he was a no-good, but I was blind with love.

And he wasn't even a real man. He was just a boy, not even a high-school graduate. And now he had left me for a fast-talking French woman. The child between us meant nothing to him. He was pure Jones. Trash. Dorothy had been right the whole time.

I thought of all the things I could have done. I could have stayed in Crystal Falls and married someone like Dorothy's Albert. I could have had a sweet-sixteen party. Right this second I could be sitting on Mother's screened porch, waiting for a date.

I drove past an old brown grocery, past a sign that said NOTARY—SHRIMP FOR SALE, past a stucco Catholic church. A fog hung over the road like sheets on a clothesline. The lights of my car picked out the steel supports of a bridge. It stretched across Bayou Lafourche, as if floating on top of the fog, delicate as a spider's web, all metal and spindles. I had driven over it in the daytime. The water reminded me of weak coffee.

The full moon was caught between two water oaks. Pale light filtered through the fog and shone on the bridge. I knew then what I was going to do. I parked my car, which was now clinking loudly, on the side of the road. I opened the door, climbed out, and stared at the rising fog. Owls called out back and forth. The night air was warm, heavy with the smell of brackish water. The cicadas sawed. Bullfrogs croaked from the weeds.

"Jump!" they said. "Jump!"

I walked down the worn pavement, toward the center of the bridge. I climbed over the side and pulled off my shoes. I wished with all my strength that no car would drive across the bridge and save me. I looked down. There, moving in and out of the fog, was a patch of black water, dark as the air itself, swirling a good twenty feet below. It could have been farther. I wasn't sure. I heard the water lap against the weeds. It all seemed hopeless. I could not raise a baby by myself. I couldn't even get a job. And I had nowhere to go. Maybe I could have been a waitress.

I thought of everyone I'd ever loved—Violet, Mother, Papa, Queenie, Hart, Dorothy. It seemed to me that I should have called Mother. Told her where we were living. I could have saved my money and caught a bus to Tennessee. A sob broke loose from my throat, like a chunk of something solid, as I pictured the long summer evenings in Crystal Falls, the lightning bugs sparking in Mother's corn, the wind shaking petals from her roses, dropping to the grass, colors wheeling in the breeze: Perfecta, Seashell, American Beauty, Tropicana.

I gazed down at the water, imagining how sorry Hart would be. How he'd cry at my funeral. He'd bring roses to my grave, and he would realize, too late, that he loved me. He would spend the rest of his life making it up to Violet. I climbed down and grasped a metal beam. It felt so cold, I pulled back my hand, thinking it was wet. I expected to see my flesh beaded with water. But my palm was dry. I took hold of the beam again, closed my eyes, and swung forward. I held on to the steel pole, and my body swayed back and forth, long and heavy.

I thought I'd just hang there awhile and think about what I wanted to do next. If I wanted to jump or climb back up. The frogs croaked, *"Jump! Jump!"* But I wasn't sure. I didn't know. The water seemed so far away. What if I just broke my legs? And what was in those weeds, alligators? I hated snakes. And how would Hart work and take care of Violet? If he decided to raise her, that was. I could see him leaving the baby with Irene and her six children. She would grow up talking Cajun and eating crawdaddies and running barefoot. She'd get ringworm, like all of Irene's kids. I could not imagine him marrying Frenchy Laverne, but men married women all the time just so someone would take care of them. And I would just die if he let Frenchy raise my baby.

My forearms ached, the blood was draining out of my hands, and I was losing sensation in my fingers. I strained hard to move my body. I tried to kick my legs toward the closest beam. I pumped hard, trying to hike my leg over it, but I lacked the strength. I squinted my eyes and tried again, rooting for leverage.

I knew then I did not want to die.

I didn't want to die for anything or anyone. I just wanted to get back in my car and drive to Irene's house and get Violet. I just wanted to go to sleep. Then I'd figure out what to do. I could write my mother. I could get a job at the Blue Marlin. I could move to New Orleans and be a whore. I felt like a huge tomato hanging from a vine. It was just a matter of time, I knew, before I dropped.

I prayed for a car to drive by and see my hanging body. I couldn't see the road, but I knew it was long and dark and empty. In the distance, light blinked through the trees like fishing boats in the Gulf.

"Jump!" the frogs said.

I hung on. I sang "Old Rugged Cross." I prayed. I lost all feeling in my hands. Moonlight shone down hard and hooded. I felt my hands slipping.

"Goddamn French whore!" I yelled, and the crickets fell silent.

Then I let go.

I fell screaming, feetfirst, tilted just the least backward. I heard the gush of water, the slap of it, as if it were solid. I shot down, heard the buzz of bubbles. Everything was black. My head nearly burst with pain. My ears popped. I never touched bottom. I moved one arm, then the other. No pain. I moved my arms in great hoops, pushing down water. I thought my lungs would burst, that I was drowning. I didn't know if I was swimming up or down or deeper, toward the muddy bottom. At last, I surfaced. There was a moment of utter silence. Then the crickets shrilled. *"She lives! She lives!"*

I ached all over, as if I'd been slammed against the pavement. I swam with the current, moved with the fog, passed under the bridge. I kicked toward a pier. It was crusted with barnacles, and crab traps were moored around it. I held on to the side and shut my eyes. My head felt full of water, full of silt and mud. I didn't have the strength to pull myself up. I clutched the rotten piling, feeling something nibble my toes. I felt the hard pinch of a crab, and I screamed.

That was when the fishermen came running to the pier and pulled me out of the foggy water. I looked at them and said four words. "Charity Hospital. New Orleans."

I felt myself sag in their arms, and then everything went gray, then black.

When I woke up, I was in a long ward. It smelled like a hospital. There was chicken wire on the windows, and I thought to myself *Now you've done it. They've gone and locked you up in the loony bin.*

And they had.

"Why did you jump?" asked the doctor. He wore round glasses and wrote down everything I said in a big notebook.

"I didn't really jump," I told him. "I let go. My hands gave out. There's a difference, you know."

"But I don't understand," said the doctor. "What made you do this?"

"Well, it's a long story." I looked out the chicken-wire window. "My husband left me for this French lady?"

"Yes?" The doctor nodded. He seemed bored. "Go on."

"And I don't know. I just thought I could jump and get it over with. That Hart would be sorry."

"I see." The doctor wrote something down. Then he looked up. "You were going to jump, but you changed your mind?"

I nodded.

"And when did you change your mind?" he asked.

"When I was hanging there."

"Oh." The doctor scribbled something else down.

"And I'm not crazy," I said. I had already had my eyes opened by the other women on this ward. There was one lady who came out of the bathroom wearing a stocking hat. At least I thought it was a stocking hat until I got up close. The smell almost knocked me down. I looked at her head and saw that she had shaped her own bowel movements into a ribbed and layered hat. It had dried on her hair. Later the nurses pulled her off to the shower. The woman screamed and hollered.

"But it coats my brain!" she yelled. "My brain'll leak out if you warsh it off!"

This other woman stared. She was perched on a red vinyl chair with her legs balanced on the armrests. She twisted her head from side to side.

"Chirp!" she said. "Chirp! Chirp!"

"We'll have to keep you here for observation," said the doctor.

"What kind of observation?"

"Well, just to make sure you haven't damaged your insides. That you're not bleeding internally."

I knew I looked bad. They didn't have mirrors here, but I could see my reflection in the metal bed. One whole side of my face was red and mashed looking. I looked like I'd been slapped, hard. And I could see for myself that my chest and arms and neck were bruised up. The nurses told me that the water did it to me. I heard them say that two people had died from jumping off that very same bridge. They said God must have spared me for a reason.

"I'm not staying here with these crazy people," I told the doctor.

He smiled weakly, but that evening the nurses moved me to a regular ward. The windows were full of normal glass. Clear. When I woke up the next morning, Hart was right by the bed, sitting in a chair. He picked up my hand. I jerked it back.

"Where's Violet?" I asked coldly.

"She's out in the hall. One of the nurses has her. She's fine. Just misses her mommy is all."

"Where's Frenchy?" I stared at him, hoping he'd get a good look at my banged-up face.

"Don't you worry about her," he said. "That's all over now. It's all over. We're going to move right here. To New Orleans."

"I don't know," I said, narrowing my eyes. I didn't trust him.

"Oh, Clancy Jane." Tears filled his dark eyes. "You could've killed yourself, girl. You know I love you. You shouldn't have done it."

He pushed a newspaper clipping in my hand, from the *Times-Picayune*. I looked at it.

WOMAN SAFE AFTER BRIDGE JUMP

MYRTLE GROVE—A Myrtle Grove woman is in stable condition at Charity Hospital after she jumped from a bridge over Bayou Lafourche. Clancy Jane Jones, 16, jumped from the Grande Bridge at 9 p.m. The woman swam to a pier, where she was pulled from the bayou by two fishermen. Jones told the men she had jumped because she was despondent over treatment by her estranged husband.

I looked up. Sunlight dropped through the window, and suddenly Hart looked old. I wondered if it was me or Frenchy who had aged him.

"Just give me one more chance, honey," he said. Then he put both hands on my face. The gesture was tender, as if he'd invented it just for me. I felt his youth and his eagerness to be shed of it. I felt his love and confusion. I drew all of that from his touch, but I said nothing.

His hands dropped to his knees, and his eyes filled like dark bayous.

"Oh, Hart," I said at last. I turned to prop the clipping against my water pitcher. When he reached for my hand, I didn't move it.

Part Two

Violet

1966

The checkout ladies at the market stared and asked where my mama was. "Sick," I said. But I hated the way they raised their eyebrows. It made me want to drop a whole carton of eggs right where they had to walk. I would've dropped those eggs in a heartbeat if I hadn't thought I'd have to pay full price for them.

"Well, tell Clancy we hope she feels better," they called out.

"Sure thing," I said, real natural like. Then I walked home and set the eggs on the counter. Mama took them out of the carton and wiped each brown oval with a dishrag, like they might have chicken germs. I asked her about it. "Well, they can't be clean," she said, this real wild look in her eyes. "Not the way they're squeezed out of hens."

"But we don't eat the shells," I said, and she gave me another wild look, like maybe I was the crazy one. She grew up in a small town, so I didn't know. She probably knew everything about chickens.

I had not seen hide nor hair of Mama's people since I was a little bitty girl. I had a small memory of Miss Gussie, my grandmother. Mama has a sister, too, Dorothy, who has two mean kids.

Mama hadn't always been this way, lounging around the apartment crying and listening to records. She kept the curtains drawn all day, hot as it was, and us dripping sweat. Wouldn't let me crack open the windows, said she'd smack me good if I tried. But she wasn't being mean. She was just scared.

The trouble started in June, after we got the news about Daddy. I'd just turned twelve. He got himself blown up in Qui Nhon, what I can't pronounce. I never thought it would happen, but Mama did. She said he'd never come back a second time from Vietnam, and he didn't. Won't. The news shook her up so bad, she couldn't remember my name, Violet.

Now it was 1966, the middle of July, ninety-eight degrees in the shade, and the Mississippi River steamed like a brown cauldron over New Orleans. Our cotton blouses stuck to our shoulders, and the apartment smelled like something dead, worse than boiled cabbage. There were days when she almost snapped out of it. She would climb out of bed and put on a clean dress. Only it wouldn't be zipped up all the way. She brushed on mascara but forgot to wipe off the smudges when she blinked. Or she forgot her underwear. Things like that.

The idea of leaving the house made her vomit. Her hands would shake so hard she had to clasp them, and sweat dripped down her back. She would go into her bedroom and pull on her stockings and come downstairs wearing a neat A-line dress, what she herself made at the factory. She would be shaking. "Look at my hands," she'd say. "I can't do it, baby. You'll have to go by yourself." Then she'd run into the bathroom and vomit.

The doorbell rang, and Mama was so shocked she squeezed a raw egg in half. "Did you hear anything?" she asked. Nobody

ever knocked at our door, unless it was that boy who fetched
Mama's beer for a quarter. The doorbell rang again. She stared
at her hands. Yolk slid through her fingers like yellow blood.
She jerked her head to the side, meaning for me to go to the
door. It was the Orkin men. The landlord sent them every
month to spray for bugs. I'd been hoping they'd come. I swung
open the front door, but Mama ran toward me, this stretched,
white look in her eyes.

"Did I say let them in?" she hissed, rubbing yolk off from
her fingers with a tea towel. She knocked me aside with her
elbow and kicked the door shut.

"I don't mean to be rude, but I'm contagious," she hollered
through the door. "I've got spinal meningitis. Come back in six
weeks." She coughed once or twice, beating on her chest to
bring up the phlegm. "You won't catch it then!"

The men didn't say anything. After a moment, they climbed
into their truck, which had a great big bug on the roof, and
drove off.

You didn't have to tell me it was getting worse.

*L*ate that afternoon it started raining, and the trees dripped
dark water. No thunder, just one of those long, green summer
drenchings. It was cooler now. I sat next to my bedroom window, listening to the rain, because she was downstairs carrying
on like you wouldn't believe. Playing one record after the other.
The Temptations were singing "My Girl." Before Daddy joined
the Army, he worked as a mechanic at the Esso on Poydras
Street. His tour of duty was twelve months. He went into the
1st Air Cavalry at An Khe, and he wrote a lot about a place
called Bong Son. It was on the coast. After ten months they
told him he could come home if he'd sign up for an extension.

He said he'd cut a real good deal. He even got promoted to
Specialist 4th Class. The catch was he had to go back to Viet-
nam. Mama said no, he said yes. So he came back to New
Orleans and shipped out in thirty days for a second tour.

Outside, the air was dark and slippery, almost black. The
rain washed down hard, and wind pulled itself through the
trees. Somewhere a dog barked. Our apartment was in an old
house on Camp Street. The house was pretty once, Mama said
almost a mansion, but now it was ugly—peeling white paint and
a long front porch with broken gingerbread trim. The paint
made us sad, but there was nothing we could do. The landlord
was cheap, out for a profit, Mama said. Anyway, it passed time
when I picked off long curls of paint. It was like that greenish
stuff on trees, lichen. I learned me that in school.

My bedroom windows were open, to cool things off, and
rain sweated against the screens. I couldn't help but wonder if
the other tenants were listening to Mama. Maybe they turned
up their radios or TVs. Maybe, because of the rain, they didn't
even hear. Except for Mrs. Massey, who is an old, old woman
with yellow eyes, most of our neighbors were students at Tulane
or Loyola. There was a nursing student upstairs, who couldn't
stand dorm life, and a bunch of fraternity boys across the way.

Downstairs, Mama talked up a storm, like my daddy was
here. "You bastard," she said. "You no good, pig-in-a-poke,
shit-for-brains bastard!"

She moaned like someone was killing her dead. "What am
I going to do now?" she cried. *"What am I going to do, what am
I going to do?"*

I made believe that I didn't live here. That someone else's
mama was crying her own self sick. I thought about me having
a dog named Jiffy and brothers who caught jars of grasshoppers
and me setting the table with real china and watching this

pretty, smiling mother, who was not drunk or crazy, walk around the kitchen. She asked if I wanted more macaroni, honey, and the pretend daddy said grace and didn't have grease under his nails and was a doctor, maybe a brain surgeon.

We didn't even have a tombstone for the real one.

Mama used to work days at the dress factory, and she wore this blue smock. She matched seams. Every night she'd roll up her hair in pink curlers, her mouth full of bobby pins. In the morning she'd comb it into a flip, her bangs teased a little. When Daddy came home from the Esso, they'd sit on the porch watching traffic and listen to the radio. Patsy Cline was singing "Crazy." He wore a blue uniform of his own, stitched with his own name on the pocket: Hart. Inside his pocket was chewing gum, Juicy Fruit, all wrapped in yellow paper. When I was a little bitty thing, I'd beg for gum. "Dum!" I'd yell, sticking my fat hands into his pockets. He got a real kick out of it.

The Tulane students would come onto the porch and slap Daddy on the shoulder and talk about Vietnam. Daddy had already signed up with the Army without telling Mama and me. When the truth came out, the students said they sure as hell weren't ready to die. And if the French couldn't win the war, why did we think we could?

"Because we can," Daddy said and blew smoke rings. "We beat the Japs, didn't we?" He laughed. They talked about a trail called the Ho Chi Minh, named after this skinny man with a tuft of white hair poking out of his chin, where he got his name, I reckon. It wasn't one big footpath like I'd pictured, but a whole bunch of paths. It was full of tunnels, too. As soon as the Americans bombed one section, the enemy would rush out and fix it. Daddy said the Vietcong were like a well-organized colony of ants. "Red ants," he said and laughed. But I didn't know. I imagined him mashing fire ants with his boots. Stamp, stamp, stamp.

*A*fter the rain stopped, the sun skittered out from the clouds. The apartment was completely silent. No records were playing, and the windows were closed. I thought about pressing my ear to the wall to see if I could hear one of the fraternity boys snoring. The cicadas started shrilling from the trees. It was hard to tell if they were angry or relieved by the dampness. There was a photograph on my dresser, happier days, Mama and Daddy at Audubon Park feeding peanuts to the monkeys. I couldn't remember where I was. School, maybe. I stared at the picture. My mother had pretty teeth, but my daddy had bad ones. He grew up in Mama's hometown, Crystal Falls, Tennessee, but his people moved to Chicago so his daddy could work in a big factory. They moved into a trailer park on South Cicero, in Oak Lawn, where gangsters used to machine-gun people on the streets. I remember the summer we drove north to visit Daddy's mama. I was six. "Call me Mamaw," she said. Her front teeth were false, and she would spit them out to make me laugh. A dentist was a luxury, and when they got cavities, they plugged up the holes with cotton and chewed aspirin. After a month or two, the pain would stop. My mother didn't much like Mamaw Jones, called her white trashy and said my crooked teeth and dark hair came from Daddy's people. I had blue eyes like Mama, only she was pretty, and I was just this side of ugly. Daddy's eyes were dark like blueberries. Mamaw's were like that, too.

"You should tell Mamaw about Daddy," I'd told her, even though she hadn't told her own family. Both of us had dead daddies now. She wasn't being secretive, keeping the news from her people. She was too upset about Daddy getting killed, and she couldn't keep her mind hooked on anything. I wondered if all our kinfolk thought my daddy was still changing oil filters on Poydras Street. Maybe they didn't know we still lived in New Orleans.

But she wrote Mamaw. Her hand trembled so hard she couldn't hardly make the pen write. I licked the stamp and walked down to the corner and mailed the letter. We never heard from Mamaw, and my mother said, "Well, she *could* have written. The Joneses are just that way."

When it started raining again, I got out of bed and opened the window. I pressed my hand against the screen, feeling the rain drip against my skin, and tried to remember Mama's people. Her family hadn't thought much of my daddy. Mama ran off with him in 1953, the year before I was born. He was living in Crystal Falls with his aunt Estelle, his daddy's sister, so he could keep playing football at the high school. He was a star and made bunches of touchdowns. His family didn't make him move to Chicago, and he was glad. He told me he hated the North. He said the houses were built so close together neighbors could reach out and shake hands. But they never did. People weren't friendly in Oak Lawn. Back home, Aunt Estelle's neighbors brought squash and tomatoes from their gardens. People helped each other in the South, he told us. And the air in Crystal Falls smelled sweet, and the mountains were so blue. Oh, he hated the trailer park on South Cicero. Police sirens screamed up and down the highway all night long, and traffic smells blocked his sinuses. People made fun of the way he talked. Then they'd turn around and say "yous guys" to each other, like they were talking good English.

Mama dropped out of school to run off with him. They couldn't get a judge to marry them, on account of her being underage. Daddy himself was only seventeen. His aunt Estelle finally found a justice of the peace over in the next county.

And then I was born.

Now it was late in the afternoon. The rain had stopped, and the wind blew a stench from the river. I wished I had a book to read, but all I had was an old white Bible. Mama's maiden name was written in little gold letters: Clancy Jane Hamilton. When there was nothing else to do, I read the Bible. I'd read anything. Cereal boxes, record albums, baseball cards for five cents a pack. I shut my window and went downstairs. Mama set her beer on the floor, then she fanned herself with her hands. Dark strands of hair were stuck to her neck. A record dropped, and the Castaways started singing "Liar, Liar."

"Lord, it's hot," Mama said. "Go tell Hart we're running low on beer."

When she got like this, I didn't know what to do. Mostly I walked away and pretended I'd gone to fetch Daddy. Then she would sit back and wait for him to come home from Vietnam. She'd wait all day for his whole self to fill up the apartment with smells of gasoline and perspiration.

"It's just so hot," she said again. "Do you think it gets this hot in Vietnam? I do. I think it probably gets hotter." She sighed and picked up the Pabst can. She pressed it to her forehead, then fit it in the crook of her arm. Pretty soon she fell asleep.

Another record started playing, "Turn! Turn! Turn!" I pushed open the living room window. Mama said she'd beat me with a switch the next time she caught me with the windows open, but I knew she didn't have the nerve to go outside and break off her own branch. And she'd quit making me break off my own switches. I just snapped off the no-count, skinny ones.

I decided to play movie stars. It was one of my oldest

games. All you needed was a movie magazine, and you picked out your parents and sisters and aunts, things like that. I made a little pencil mark next to Paul Newman for the daddy. I couldn't decide if I wanted Julie Andrews or Elizabeth Taylor for the mother. I remembered *Mary Poppins* and that decided it for me. Then I looked under the sofa for our Monkey Ward catalogue. I drew *X*'s next to dishes, vacuum cleaners, air conditioners, bedspreads, toasters, lamps. I circled two bald babies and even a curly-haired granny. I thought up a pretty house with a swimming pool and a big yard and a swing set and a redwood picnic table. Movie stars made a lot of money, so I circled whatever I pleased. I got Paul Newman an apron printed with blue checks that matched his eyes. He stood in front of a barbecue grill turning T-bone steaks, long red hot dogs, hamburger patties. He whistled "What's New Pussycat?" The scent of charcoal rose into the trees. Julie Andrews's head moved back and forth in the kitchen window like anyone else's mama.

Only we didn't have a window in our real kitchen; we didn't even have an air conditioner. I put down the catalogue and looked out the window. Steam lifted from the pavement. The room smelled sour and felt hot. Another record dropped, and "Oh, Pretty Woman" started playing. From the sofa, Mama stirred. I pulled down the window and latched it. I guess she was afraid somebody would break in and get us. Two females alone in New Orleans weren't safe, she'd said after Daddy shipped out. And that was when she thought he would come back. She was never a real brave person, but after he died, she seemed to get more and more scared. Going around checking the locks, sucking in air when a floorboard creaked. I didn't feel safe, either.

It was a good thing I'd shut the window because she

uncurled from the sofa and looked around. She got up and walked over to the record player and sifted through a pile of black disks. Behind her, our kitchen was dark. Thinking about my movie-star family and the sizzling meat on the grill had made my stomach growl. I pictured these little bombs going off in my belly. Mama's face was stretched tight and she was still drinking beer. I was not about to ask her about supper. When she got herself all worked up and drunk, she just sang and danced barefoot. But it was better than listening to her cry. She put on a new record and started dancing barefoot while the Beatles sang "Help." She glanced over at me, sort of guilty like, like she was just now seeing me, and said, "Hi, honey. What you doing, honey?"

I did not answer because what was I supposed to say? That I'm watching you dance like you're some fool ballerina? You crazy thing, you. But she had already started twirling again, singing with her eyes closed. When I couldn't stand it any longer, I went into the kitchen and opened the refrigerator. I swung on the door, hunting me something to eat. Cold air blew all over my hot self. There were a dozen cans of beer stacked on the bottom shelf. Two lemons, a green plastic bottle of lime juice, a half-empty carton of milk. I slammed the door, rummaged in the cupboard, and fetched a bag of marshmallows. Kraft miniatures were my favorites, and these were just the least bit stale, nice and crisp on the edges, which meant they'd take longer to melt down with spit.

I took the whole bag outside and sat on the porch steps. Mama was so wrapped up in her song she didn't even notice. Right before Daddy went to basic training, Mama almost got her own self killed. If she had died, it would have been murder. It was the fall of 1964, almost eight o'clock, a night so warm it felt like summer. The Esso station closed at five o'clock, and we began to worry that something bad had happened. Maybe a jack had collapsed? Oh please, god no, I thought and pictured him trapped under a car. It kept getting later and later, and I went into the kitchen. I was eating marshmallows that night, too, and I sat on the counter eating, watching Mama get herself all worked up. She put on a stack of records and opened a beer. The Animals started singing "House of the Rising Sun." Then she paced the room, talking to herself, which would have been sort of funny if I hadn't been so worried about my daddy.

"Here he is," she said over the music, "going off to Vietnam, and where is he now? Hmmm? With his family? *No.* Off drinking beer with a bunch of rednecks. Or else playing poker. Or else—" She broke off and glanced at me.

"Or else what?" I said.

"Nothing. Will you fetch me another beer, honey?"

By the time Daddy's old Monza chugged into the driveway, Mama was half-drunk. I listened to his shoes go click/thock on the sidewalk. There was a six-pack of Pabst under his right arm and two bags from McDonald's in the other. He walked up the porch steps sort of drunk-like and said hello to old Mrs. Massey. She fixed him with her hooded yellow eyes like he might hit her. She said something I couldn't hear, and he threw his head back and laughed. She pressed her powdered lips together, pushed out of her rocking chair, and scuttled sideways across the porch. She darted inside her apartment. When she locked her door, I heard the bolts click. She even slid on the chain lock.

Our screen door ticked open, and right off the bat Mama got up from the sofa and started yelling. "Where have you been, Hart? You'd better tell me right this instant."

"Calm down, Clancy Jane, honey," he said, rolling his eyes.

"Don't you look at me like that! I *am* calm! Where've you been?"

"Been?" His eyes were glassy, which meant he had been drinking plenty.

"Hart!"

"Oh, darlin'. I just lost track of time is all."

"You've probably found yourself another Frenchy."

"I haven't, I swear it."

"Well, you'd better not. Anyway, you're leaving soon." Mama frowned. "I don't know when I'll see you again. *If* I want to be with you, honey."

From the stereo, another record dropped. The Beatles started singing "A Hard Day's Night."

"Baby, you're with me now, ain't you?" He grinned. Then he held up one of the McDonald's sacks and smiled at me. "Violet, here's a snack for you. And I brung you some gum, too."

"Thanks, Daddy."

I took the Juicy Fruit and the sack and walked outside to the porch and sat down in old Mrs. Massey's rocker. I tried to figure out what a frenchy was. The McDonald's sack warmed my lap. Daddy had brought me fries and a cheeseburger. Last night's rain had sweetened the air. Lightning bugs sparked in the bushes. I thought about finding me a jar under the sink and punching holes in the lid and maybe catching me some bugs. Even though I was twelve, I still loved catching fireflies. I'd set them in the window and watch the strange yellow lights. You couldn't guess when they would blink. When I was little, I'd never let them go, but I would now. No sense in letting something that pretty and sweet die in an old mayonnaise jar.

I licked grease from my fingers. From inside our living room, I heard Mama shout. A beer bottle shattered, and Daddy cursed. I drew up my knees and rocked faster and faster, hitting my head against the cane back. The music kept playing, and I knew if it stopped we would all die.

"You were *gambling?*" Mama yelled. She sucked in her breath like she might scream. "A stupid *card* game!"

"Will you listen? I didn't lose no money," he said. I stopped rocking. I got up and knelt beside the screen door. The stereo clicked and another record dropped on the stack.

"I *won* me five dollars," Daddy said. "Listen, baby. Let's don't fight. We ain't got much time left."

"The only reason you're going to Vietnam is because you want to play soldier," she said. "Oh, Hart. This isn't playing. This is real." She gave him this long look and her eyes got watery. He kissed her neck, then her mouth. After a minute, she turned up the stairs, not taking her eyes off from him, running her fingers along the banister. Daddy just stared and watched her climb the steps. Then he followed her. She had long, beautifully shaped legs. I don't. My knees are too far down, like all the Joneses'. And they're full of scars. When I first started roller-skating, I fell down a lot. Now I can chase the pigeons on Jackson Square like an expert.

I was glad they'd stopped fighting. The record player was still on. I knew most of the songs by heart. Elvis was singing "Return to Sender." I went in and got a jar and headed down the sidewalk. I walked all the way to Tulane. When the jar was full of fireflies, I let them go and started over. Houselights turned off along the street, which meant it was real late, so I headed back home. I had at least twenty lightning bugs, and they made me a pretty lantern. Before I reached the porch, I could hear them screaming at each other. I couldn't remember them fighting before Daddy enlisted. After that, the fights flared suddenly, like struck matches. She didn't want him to go, and somehow the fights made it easier. Maybe she thought she would grieve less if she had bad memories, if she could hold on to those fights.

Across the porch, a curtain moved and Mrs. Massey peeked out of her window. I opened the screen door and stood inside the house, hoping they'd see me and shut up. The phonograph had stopped playing, and the needle scraped at the end of the record. I squeezed the glass jar until my heartbeat filled the room. Why didn't they hear it?

Mama stood at the top of the stairs. She wasn't wearing anything but a white slip that had been washed so much the lace was fuzzy. Her face was red, mascara streamed down her cheeks. "You'll get your idiot self shot."

"Stop it, Clancy Jane! Don't say things like that. You'll make them come true."

"No, I won't! *You'll* make them come true! And you didn't even tell me you'd signed up. You didn't ask my opinion. Maybe you didn't want it. Maybe you don't love me and Violet."

"I do so!" Daddy blinked hard, and his lips moved like he was struggling to think of something else to say.

"Then why are you leaving us?"

"Because it's the right thing to do," he said. "It's about freedom, Clancy Jane. Just listen to yourself, how you're acting. *This* is why I didn't tell you."

"I don't care about freedom in some backward country. Let them fight their own war. And you didn't have to enlist! I'll never forgive you, I swear it!" She slapped wildly, using both hands to strike his head and arms. "Are you trying to make me jump off another bridge?"

He threw out his hands to ward off the blows and knocked her sideways with his elbow. She teetered on the edge of the step, her arms whipped through the air, then she fell backward. I heard her head strike the steps, over and over, oh lord, please make it stop, please.

At the bottom she rolled over and blood streamed out of her mouth. I dropped the jar. It crashed to the floor. Daddy looked up, startled. "Violet?" he said in this whisper-voice, which didn't sound like my own daddy but some fiend from hell who'd knocked my mama down the stairs. He blinked hard at the broken glass. I ran to Mama and pulled her head in my lap.

"Mama?" I held my dress against her lip to mop up the bleeding. I glared at my daddy. "You killed her!"

"She ain't dead. Oh, God. *God.* I'd better call us an ambulance." He walked backward out of the apartment. The screen door flapped hard behind him.

"Mama? Mama, wake up!" I kept saying, but her eyes stayed closed. The fireflies lifted from the floor, toward the closed window, and blinked yellow light all over the room.

When the ambulance arrived, people cracked open their doors and stepped onto the porch. The nursing student, the girl who lived upstairs, asked my daddy what was wrong.

"My wife fell down the stairs," he said, running his fingers through his hair. He looked at the girl. "Is it okay if my little girl stays with you while I'm at the hospital? I don't have nobody to leave her with."

"Well. Sure," she said, blinking real fast. What else could she have said? I wondered if Daddy had caught her off guard. Maybe she was scared. Me and Daddy looked dangerous, all covered in blood. The student nurse reached out to take my hand. I looked back at my daddy. He seemed ashamed, and I didn't know how to make it right between us.

"What's your name?" the student asked me. She smiled this brave smile.

"Violet."

"Oh, that's a pretty name. I wish I had a pretty name like that. I'm Merrily, but everybody calls me Merry. I sure wish they wouldn't, but they do."

We walked upstairs to her apartment. I looked around the room. There was an overstuffed brown sofa, and the windows were full of plants. Textbooks were laid open on her kitchen table. She fixed me a Coca-Cola and found me a clean T-shirt that fell like a tent from my shoulders. It smelled good, though. Later she made me a bed on the sofa. The windows were open, and a breeze stirred the curtains.

The next morning, my daddy knocked on Merry's door. I pulled the sheet over my head, pretending to be asleep. I heard him say that Mama was at Charity. I knew where that hospital was. It took poor people and didn't make them pay. He said Mama had a concussion of the brain, but she would be just fine. The doctors had to put a stitch in her lip; when she fell, she bit clean through it. They were only keeping her overnight, which meant it wasn't real serious. She would be coming home later this afternoon.

Merry told me to make myself at home. Then she left for morning classes at the college. As she walked to her car, she reminded me of a big pear rolling down the sidewalk. I froze me a Coca-Cola and washed a bowl of green grapes and turned on the TV. When Merry came home for lunch, she fixed us melted ham and cheese sandwiches, and we drank iced tea, real sugary, with lemon rounds floating in the glasses. She asked if Mama and Daddy fought a lot. I told her no, that he was leaving for Vietnam.

"Your mother might need some help. Do you have a grand-mother?" she asked. "Somebody I could call?"

I shook my head. The Bible said not to lie, but I couldn't help it. My stomach muscles tensed as I pictured living in Chicago with Mamaw, moving into the cramped bedroom in her trailer. Watching her pop out her false teeth. Her other teeth hanging down long like a vampire's. I thought of Mama's people but didn't even know their last names. McSomething. I had me two cousins, a girl and a boy, near my own age. In a little town I couldn't remember, somewhere east of Nashville, Tennessee. Crystal Falls. A long, long way from here. I couldn't let Merry call them. We couldn't go there. I thought about telling her I was really Julie Andrews's daughter, to call Hollywood if she didn't believe me.

"All our relatives are dead," I said.

"I'm so sorry." Merry patted my shoulder.

"Don't you worry about me and Mama. We'll be all right. I know how to vacuum and dust. And Mama lets me iron. I know how."

"Oh, honey." Merry put her arms around me and hugged me tight.

When I finished the marshmallows, I went back inside. Mama was asleep again on the sofa. The arm of the record player bumped against the record. Her arm dangled in the air like a skinny branch. Her fingernails were all chewed off. I switched off the player. My stomach was still making noises, so I walked into the kitchen and ran water into a saucepan. What I really wanted me was a fried egg and bacon sandwich, but we didn't have bacon, and besides, boiled eggs wouldn't make a mess. Not if you peeled them outside. Then they wouldn't stink.

I peeled the eggs on the porch, dropping the shells into a paper sack. Outside, the rain started up again, falling out of a sky so dark and grainy you could almost touch it. Night was coming fast, like a dark blue fog. Along the road, houses lit up one by one. Women all over New Orleans were turning on lamps, cooking supper, standing on their porches and yelling for their children to come home. Daddies were coming home and stretching out on the sofas to rest their eyes. Or else they went into the backyard and started up the charcoal. I pretended Julie Andrews was calling my name.

"Violet? *VI*-LET! Supper's ready! Time to wash up!"

I pictured Paul and Julie's house in Hollywood, the long picnic table with the blue-checked cloth. Grilled hamburgers, corn-on-the-cob, baked beans. A platter of lettuce, garden tomatoes, red onions, pickles. Jars of mayonnaise, mustard, ketchup. And Paul Newman was over there in the hammock, just a-swinging. Mama Julie did not listen to songs like "Woolly Bully" but sang her own music. She sang me and the bald babies to sleep. Daddy Paul smoked a pipe and sipped iced tea and read the newspaper like any other daddy.

It hurt to think about the real one. Mostly I didn't. She did, and it had turned her mind, the way a farmer turned the soil. And the soil of Mama's mind was a dark place. We got the news about Daddy from a telegram, followed by a bunch of official-looking letters. Jones, Hartley P., Sp/4, Bravo Company, 2nd Battalion, 1st Air Cavalry Division, An Khe, KIA, 15 June 1966. Somebody mailed us a Purple Heart and a letter signed by President Johnson. Daddy's platoon sergeant wrote us a letter. They were in a "hard core" village, and this little bitty girl came up to my daddy, begging for candy. He handed her a stick of Juicy Fruit. The Vietnamese girl reached out to hug my daddy, and when he picked her up, she exploded in his arms.

*   *   *

*B*ehind me, our apartment was so dark, it might as well have been empty. It was sinful to want my movie-star family. I wasn't special, I wasn't anything. I was just here. I pretended I was part-heat, part-grass, part-rain. But the real me was biding my time, trying to stay alive, trying to keep her alive. Waiting for summer to end, waiting for school to start. Waiting for something to happen.

The first part of August, our electricity got shut off because we forgot to pay the bill. Daddy had left us money. We weren't paupers. Mama had explained all about the Army insurance policy.

"What's a benny fishy airy?" I'd asked.

"Beneficiary." She spelled it. "It means we'll get a little money."

The apartment swelled with heat, but Mama couldn't get to the bank. She said she'd vomit if she had to drive, and it was too far for me to walk. After the third day of no lights and no music, she told me to run up and get Merry.

Merry opened her door and the air conditioner blew into my face. It felt so good, my mind went blank. I just stood there, feeling the cold air.

"What's wrong, Violet?" Merry asked. "You look sort of peaked."

"They cut off our lights," I said. "And Mama told me to fetch you."

She squeezed my shoulders, and we walked downstairs.

"You've got to help us, Merry," said Mama as soon as we walked in the door. "I'm at the end of my rope. I think I've lost my mind. And that's the least of it." Then she glanced at me and said, "Go outside, Violet honey."

The least of it? Do tell, Mama. It was just like her to make me leave when it was getting interesting, wouldn't you know it. But I went outside and left the screen door cracked open. I sat on the steps and listened hard, but they were whispering too low. Then Mama started crying hard, boo-hooing like a big old baby. I couldn't believe it. In a little while Merry came out of the apartment and put her arms around me.

"It's going to be all right," she told me, and I thought sure, sure, that's what you think.

But I was wrong. The next thing I knew the lights were back on, and Merry was hauling in two sacks of groceries and started fixing us a spaghetti-and-meatball supper. Right in our own kitchen. I watched her chop bell peppers, onions, and celery. Then she dumped everything in a skillet and started frying it. Saw-TAY she called it. It was French. They did things the French way down here. And it smelled so good, my stomach set itself on fire. Merry found some tea bags way up in a cabinet, and we made us a jug of tea. She sent me up to her apartment to fetch a tray of ice cubes. Pretty soon we were ready to eat.

Merry talked while Mama twisted her fork in the spaghetti. Mama nodded her head and kept winding her fork and stared at the noodles like they were white worms all mixed up in red sauce. She never ate anything these days. "When I was a little girl," Mama said, "I'd beg my mother to cook spaghetti. I'll bet she still cooks it every Tuesday night."

"Your mother?" Merry looked up. "But I thought she was dead."

"Dead?" Mama's eyebrows drew together, and a shiver went up my backbone.

"That's what Violet told me. A long time ago, when you were in the hospital. She said all your relatives were dead. I remember."

"Did you say that, Violet?" Mama fixed her eyes on me. I was too scared to answer. She looked at Merry. "My mother lives in Tennessee. And as far as I know, she's still living. I don't know why Violet would tell such a lie."

Merry gave me a look and helped herself to another serving of noodles, more sauce. She wound spaghetti with her fork and fit the whole thing in her mouth.

"I'm not on the best of terms with my mother." Mama looked down at her plate. "It just about killed her when I ran off with Hart."

"Didn't she like him?" Merry reached for her glass and took a long swallow of tea, keeping her eyes on Mama.

"No. She was always partial to me. Which made my sister jealous. Dorothy's my older sister. But I met Hart, and we ran off and got married. I was sixteen. Well, almost." Mama looked over at me. "There was a little trouble, if you get my drift? Then my mother disowned me."

"Oh. Well. I do see what you mean." Merry lifted her eyebrows like she understood Mama's drift. "When's the last time you saw her?"

"A long time ago. Years." Mama's fork twirled and twirled. "Hart was working two jobs, and I took Violet for a visit. She was a real little girl, maybe four or five. We stayed two days. I couldn't take any more. My sister has this tendency to just take over. You do things her way or else. But Mother was pretty bad, too. She thought Hart had ruined me, that he was a greaser. Redneck, she called him."

"But you're not giving your sister or your mother a chance," Merry said. "They might have changed."

"Yes. I know." Twirl, twirl, twirl. She stared down at her plate. Big tears fell in the spaghetti.

"I'm sure they love you, Clancy."

Ha. That's what you think, I wanted to say. They cast out my mama when she married my daddy. In the Bible people got cast out of places all the time. It was the thing to do. And once they cast you out, they didn't let you back in. Look at Adam and Eve. Look at Cain.

I thought Mama's family probably hated us. I wondered what they would say. Go away, you trashy things. Just look at how you're dressed and smelling up our pretty porch. And no luggage, just paper sacks. White trash does that. Lord have mercy. What have I always told you, Clancy? If you sleep with trash long enough, you'll draw flies, sure thing. Just go. And take your flies with you while you're at it.

But I didn't say anything. I was too busy eating. I'd never eaten food this good. I couldn't get full. I mopped up the sauce with a piece of French bread. I drank two glasses of tea.

"I'm not sure my mother will help me," Mama said.

"At least give her a chance to say yes or no." Merry pushed her plate away. "I shouldn't try to talk you into something you're against. Look, I'm not going to say another word. If you change your mind, you can always call your mother."

"*If* I change my mind," Mama said.

I wasn't worried. I couldn't hardly believe she would call them. Not when they hated my daddy the way they hated him. They were hating a dead man, and the fools didn't even know it.

Miss Gussie

1966

*T*he phone rang, and I said, "Lordy Jesus." Which made me think I'd had a premonition.

I was shelling butter beans into a newspaper, sitting on the screened porch. Minding my own business. So it took me a long time to answer the phone. I had to set down the newspaper and the pot of beans. Then I had to walk all the way into the kitchen. And me with hardly no spine. I've got arthritis, the worst in the world.

You could have knocked me over with a feather when I heard Clancy Jane's voice on the phone. It sounded like a meow, *"Mother? Mother?"*

She told me about Hart. That he was dead. Killed in the very place Walter Cronkite showed pictures of on the news. Vietnam. I told her to get ahold of herself, that I would drive to New Orleans to get her and Violet. I didn't hardly know that child, but I couldn't think about it just yet.

Well, I set down the phone. My eyes were watering some. I thought about calling Dorothy, but I decided against it. Then I went back to the screen porch and started shelling beans again. Long ago, years ago, I had forgiven Clancy Jane for fornicating in the flesh with Hart. For getting pregnant and having to marry trash. For running off to New Orleans and not coming back home except once. And she only stayed a day or two, on account of Dorothy.

I remembered the day she drove up in this old car, which sounded like it was gargling a motor full of mouthwash. I hadn't seen her since the day she was wearing that cute poodle skirt and ran off with Hart. I'd gone over it and over it, and I just didn't know what made me turn them away. Pride, I supposed. And hurt, I was real hurt. But there she was, climbing out of that rusty old car, and this little dark-headed girl peeped from behind Clancy's skirt. She looked to be four or five years old. Cute as a button. Then Dorothy had to get in on the act, comparing her girl Bitsy to Violet. Can she tell time? Dorothy wanted to know. Can she do this, can she do that? I knew Clancy was holding in her temper. She always did with her sister. If you tried to argue with Dorothy, she'd shout you into the ground. She'd curl back her lip and get right nasty. That was Dorothy for you, always hitting below the belt, dragging up everything you ever did wrong in your whole life. She always did have a good memory.

Of course the kids fought, and my girls fought and pretty soon names were flying back and forth.

Dorothy started it by calling Violet out-of-wedlock.

"Prude," Clancy Jane said back.

"Mother Dear's favorite."

"Ball breaker."

"Trash."

"Bitch."

On and on and on.

Dorothy's voice got louder and louder. Pretty soon she was bellowing, like she always did. You'd never guess she was big in the Mary Martha Circle down at church, which hadn't done her a bit of good. She was mean as a snake. I just shut my eyes and prayed to the Lord that the shouting would stop. Next thing I knew, Clancy Jane and the little girl were driving off, going back to New Orleans and her dark-eyed man.

Now Dorothy's children were teenagers. Mack was sixteen, and Bitsy was thirteen. Pretty children, but spoiled as all get-out. She tried to give them airs. She taught Bitsy to call her Mummie, but Mack out-and-out called her Mama. Albert had that dime store, and those kids just took what they wanted. I got a discount, which was nice since I was on a fixed income. It just seemed as if I'd spent my whole life raising two families. She'd take advantage if you let her. Give her an inch and she'd take a mile every single time.

Especially when it came to her bridge clubs. She would claw and kill to get to play bridge with her friends. They played at night, and I suspected they drank wine, ate little finger sandwiches, and gossiped about everything going on in Crystal Falls. Who'd just had surgery. Whose daughter was running wild. Whose son was going to Vietnam. Who was fornicating in the flesh. Dorothy's friends were all wives of merchants, like herself.

Now Albert was a good man. Gentle like my Charlie was. But he let Dorothy run all over him. Wouldn't say a single blessed word. Just nodded his head and went about his business. When Dorothy got her temper up, she was liable to say anything that popped into her head, but Albert just let her blow steam, and it didn't get to him the way it got to me.

"She's just high spirited is all," he once told me.

"You mean she's fine as long as she gets her way," I said back.

Then when you tried to tell Dorothy she wore the pants in

her family, she puffed up like a fat toad and turned red in the face and called you a liar.

When I finished shelling the beans, I just sat there on the porch, the pot in my lap, looking out at my front yard. I'd let things go a bit on account of my arthritis. My rosebushes needed pruning. Last week, Mack had begged to cut them for me, but Dorothy said she was afraid he'd get hurt on the clippers. And him half grown. Lordy Jesus. She coddled him too much. Now if Bitsy had asked to prune those roses, Dorothy would have put the shears in her arms and said go to it. It was favoritism, pure and simple, but if you tried to point it out, Dorothy would say that I was a fine one to talk.

All I could do was shut my mouth, because a part of me knew she was right. I didn't understand it. She wasn't a bad person. Still, I'd never pick her to be my best friend. She had this way of turning, with her eyes narrowed, which always made my blood run cold. She didn't get that from my side of the family.

I didn't understand how you could love a person and dislike them at the same time. How could this be? It made me kindly ashamed to feel this way about my own flesh and blood, and every night I prayed to the Lord that I'd change. Or that she would.

I settled down and thought about what I needed to do before I drove down to New Orleans, where I had never been. I didn't even drive to Nashville alone these days. It was Queenie's day off, so I made a mental note to call and tell her I was leaving to get Clancy Jane. Then I made a note to change the sheets in the upstairs bedrooms. I had to clean out my refrigerator. I could give my perishables to Dorothy. And it wouldn't hurt for

Mack to water my garden while I was gone, even though I knew Bitsy would end up doing it.

I stared out past the garden to where the old graveyard started. In my younger days, before Dorothy was born, I liked to slip under the barbwire fence and walk through the field. Sometimes I'd take the Hamilton family Bible out there and try to make sense of it all. In summer, the Queen Anne's lace was as tall as some of the markers. The inscriptions were worn off in places. I'd kneel down and rub my hands over the carved letters and try to imagine myself back in the olden times. The long dresses and hoop skirts. Making lye soap and rocking sick babies.

Some of the inscriptions stood out plain as day. Like the one that said *John Gray (colored), 37 years old.* In the family Bible, someone had written, "Bought slave—freed." Then there was my favorite, *Here rests Addy Hamilton. She was Amiable in Person. Born May 15, 1782, in North Carolina—Died Dec 1, 1849.*

The children were the saddest of all. Little rock markers, *Lillian Dorothea Hamilton, April 26, 1802–July 1, 1802.* In the Bible, Lillian Dorothea's mother, Addy, had written: *Good-bye, Little Darling. You are just asleep, a sweet unbroken sleep, till resurrection's dawn.*

My Dorothy, little Lillian Dorothea's namesake, angled her car into her driveway. The car stopped. Bitsy jumped out and ran toward my house. She came onto my porch, bringing the smell of her mother's perfume, and flopped into one of the wicker armchairs. "You need some help snapping those beans?" she asked.

"No, child." I kept my eyes on Dorothy. She tucked a package under each arm and wiggled up the driveway. She'd just had her hair done. Teased out to here.

"You, Dorothy!" I hollered from my screen porch.

Dorothy crossed the yard, mashing the bags to her chest. She was wearing nylons, hot as it was, and her legs swished back and forth. I'd been after her to lose weight, but every time I hinted at it, she puffed up and got insulted. You couldn't be truthful with Dorothy. She climbed the porch steps, just a puffing, and yanked open the screen door. It banged shut behind her.

"I've been shopping," she said. "All the sales started today. I can't believe you're sitting home when there's sales going on."

"I can't be worried about sales today," I said.

"Are you all right, Mother Dear?"

"Not especially."

"Why not?" She rubbed her neck and stared down at the beans. She set down her packages. "Did you save me a mess of beans? You know how I love them."

"You can have them." I held out the bowl.

"Oh, I couldn't take all of your beans," she said. But she picked up the bowl. "My, these are fat and pretty. Are you sure you don't want them?"

"Yes. I won't be in town to eat them."

"You won't what?" She looked up, smiling that smile of hers that said I-don't-believe-what-you-just-said.

"I'm going to New Orleans," I said.

"New Orleans?" She narrowed her eyes. "Why?"

"I just am." I shifted my dentures and thought to myself why in the dickens did I have to open my mouth and call Dorothy over here.

"What's brought this on? You don't need to be going there."

"Well, I'm going, and that's that."

"The niggers down there will kill you dead. Why, they'll slit your throat for a quarter."

"I can't help it if they do."

"You'd better help it!" She narrowed her eyes. "Does this have anything to do with Sister?"

"It most certainly does," I said.

"I knew it, I just knew it. Don't you try to be cute, just tell me what she's done now."

"She hasn't done anything."

"Then I don't understand."

"Something bad has happened." I was silent a moment. "Hart's dead."

"Hart?" said Bitsy. "Who is Hart?"

"Just hush, Bitsy," Dorothy said. Then she sat down hard in one of the wicker rockers. It gave off a loud creak. "Did he get murdered or what?" Dorothy asked.

I shook my head. "Vietnam."

"Vietnam?" Dorothy looked confused, as if she were trying to puzzle out the word. Her eyebrows pushed together. "What in the world was he doing over there?"

"I don't know. Fighting, I guess."

"The stupid thing." She squeezed the bowl to her chest and gave me a funny stare. "You're going to fetch Sister, aren't you?"

I nodded.

"Why can't she just drive up here? She's got a car, doesn't she?"

I was silent.

Dorothy sighed. "I don't know why I'm surprised. You always did baby her. But if you ask my opinion, I think you're crazy to go to New Orleans. It's no place for a woman your age."

"A woman my age, my foot." I gave her a strong look. She was starting to rile me.

"Why're you going to New Orleans?" Bitsy said.

"She has to go to New Orleans because my sister's between a rock and a hard place," said Dorothy.

"Where's that?" said Bitsy.

"Nowhere. Will you please stop interrupting?" Dorothy glared at Bitsy. Then she looked at me. "Honestly, you ought to just send Sister money for a bus."

"I will not."

"What makes you so stubborn?"

"Dorothy, her husband is dead."

"You never liked him. Don't try and say that you did. And I know for a fact and a half that New Orleans isn't safe."

"If it's such a terrible place, then why don't you drive me down?"

Dorothy's jaw sagged. "Me drive you down? Why, what would I do with my children?"

"Albert could watch them." I glanced over at Bitsy. Her eyes were huge.

"Albert has a business to run," she said. "He's a busy man. He'd never let me drive you down there."

"Then I guess I'll go alone."

"Well, be my guest! There's bayous everywhere. If somebody took a notion to throw you into one, the alligators would eat you alive." She leaned back in the chair. Her forehead wrinkled. "If you had any sense you'd be scared to death."

"I'm not scared in the least."

Dorothy sighed. "I just can't get over it. Sister's coming home. With that strange little girl of hers, no doubt? What's her name? I never can remember. It's something floral."

"Violet," I reminded her.

Bitsy sat up straight in her chair, but she didn't say anything.

"Yes, of course. Violet." Dorothy gave a little laugh. "Well, if that doesn't beat all. I wonder what'll happen now."

Now that was a good question. I didn't have the least premonition. They said that Jeanne Dixon tried to warn President Kennedy not to go to Dallas. She called the White House, even. That was what you call an actual premonition.

I looked at my pretty granddaughter and said, "Come here child and give your Miss Gussie a kiss."

Violet

1966

*T*hree days later, I was sitting on the porch and the grand-mother, Miss Gussie, drove up in a long green Buick. Mama had said to expect her. We had even cleaned the apartment. I knew it was the grandmother although I didn't remember what she looked like. She rolled down the window and hollered at me. Even from here, I could see that she had the car doors locked. We didn't live in a real good neighborhood.

"Oh, little girl?" she called out. "Can you help me, honey?" She glanced down at a piece of paper. When Mama had phoned, Merry had given the grandmother directions to our apartment. Only I hadn't thought she would come all the way to New Orleans. I really hadn't. Mama had been too upset to talk, so Merry had taken over. "Your daughter needs you," Merry had said into the phone. "Her husband just got killed in Vietnam, and she's nearly lost her mind with grief. I'm afraid she can't take care of her little girl."

I didn't get to hear what the grandmother said. I didn't care. The next thing I knew, Merry was telling her how to drive through New Orleans, how to find our apartment on Camp Street.

"Little girl?" said the grandmother again. At least I thought she was the grandmother. "I'm looking for Clancy Jones's apartment?"

"You're at it," I hollered back.

"At it?" The grandmother looked confused. She blinked hard.

"You're at it," I said again. "This is our house. Clancy's my mama."

"Well, I'll be." She sat back against her seat and stared up at our apartment house. I noticed something strange on her dashboard. It looked like a ceramic frog perched there, and I wondered if it slid around when she turned down a road. I wondered how long it had taken her to reach New Orleans. She unlocked her car door, got out, locked it again, and walked toward me.

"Violet? You're half grown. You just can't be my little Violet."

"I'm her." I nodded. "I'm Hart's girl."

She blinked again. I noticed she blinked a lot, and her eyes were full of water like she was going to burst into tears any second. She had short silver hair, all wound up like a Brillo pad.

"Well, goodness gracious, child," she said. "I'll bet you don't remember me. But I'm your granny. Everybody calls me Miss Gussie. But you can call me what you want."

I didn't know what to say. I wondered why she wanted me to call her Miss. I thought about starting in about what a fine man my daddy was and how I knew she hated him, but I didn't. Instead, I got up from the porch and walked toward our apartment. From the corner of my eye, I saw her glance at the peeling paint and rotting lumber on the steps. She sighed. I pulled open the screen door. It was dark inside.

"Mama? Your mama's here," I hollered out, swinging back the door, holding it open for the grandmother to go inside.

Music was playing, of course. Little Peggy Marsh was singing "I Will Follow Him."

The grandmother took one look at Mama and burst into tears. "Oh, my little Clancy Jane," she said. "You look like you're half dead!"

"Mother?" My mama got up from the couch. Her eyes filled with tears. "I knew you'd come, I just knew it."

"Shhhhhh, little one," said the grandmother, pulling my mama against her chest. "I know it, I know it. Your mother's here. It's all water under the bridge, now. Don't cry, baby. Hush-hush-*hush.*"

We put clean sheets on Mama's bed, then put her in it and closed the curtains so she could rest. Then we got in the grandmother's car, just me and her, and we drove to the market on the corner. I tried to tell her about the French Market, but she said it wasn't safe.

We came home and cooked us a big supper. We cooked us meat loaf, a lettuce salad, mashed potatoes, and frozen peas because the grandmother hadn't found any fresh at the market. She let me mash the potatoes, and said aren't you the biggest helper she's ever seen. Lord. And me twelve years old. Did she think I was a baby and that a little sweet talk would make me mash those potatoes harder?

That night, she slept in Mama's room. I listened to them talk. Their voices ran back and forth like two birds smoothing each other's feathers.

"You should have called me the minute he died, Clancy Jane. There wasn't any need for you to carry this burden all by yourself."

There was a long pause. "I know."

"You just ran off with that boy like there was no tomorrow and had yourself a baby when you were still a child. We weren't angry with you. We were just upset. And I'm not going to bring up all those years you didn't call or come to see us. We'll just let bygones be bygones."

I wondered who she meant by "we." I thought she must mean Mama's sister. She couldn't mean my mama's daddy because he'd died when she was a little girl. She was nine or ten. He had this disease that rots your lungs. Charlie was his name. Mama once said if I had been a boy she would have named me Charlie. I was glad I wasn't a boy. Daddy said the enemy in Vietnam was nicknamed Charlie. Wouldn't that have been something? Me, a boy named Charlie, and my daddy killed by one. It would've marked me for life.

Now Mama said, "But even if we moved back home, we've got all this stuff. Furniture and things. It would cost a fortune to move it to Crystal Falls. And you don't have room, do you?"

"Honey, I didn't mean move all your things," the grandmother said. "Why not have a moving sale? It's done all the time. We'll put an ad in the paper, and people will come out in droves."

I sat up in bed and strained to hear.

"Oh, I don't know," Mama said in this little-girl voice. She sounded younger than me, even. "I hate to just sell everything."

"Well, I didn't say everything, now did I?"

"No. And the furniture *is* sort of old and junkie. And I haven't gone through Hart's things. I don't know if I can."

"It's the best thing, honey. I'll help you."

"Wait a minute," I hollered real, real loud. "What things? Mama? You hear me? You can't sell my daddy's things!"

Silence. From the other side of the wall, I heard Mama

start to cry. The grandmother called out, "We'll talk about this tomorrow, Violet. Let's all get our beauty sleep, hear?"

But I couldn't sleep. I had no beauty to get, and I'd never wanted any to begin with. She couldn't just come here and throw away our whole lives. I was so mad at my mama for letting this happen, I could've burst wide open.

The next morning I waited until the grandmother went downstairs to cook breakfast. I waited until I smelled bacon frying. Then I slipped down the hall and crawled into Mama's bed and shook her until her eyes opened.

"Hmmmm?" she said. Her eyelids fluttered and closed, like bird wings.

"Are we really moving to Tennessee?"

"Mmmmmhum," she said.

"Where're we going to live?"

"In Crystal Falls," she said slow like. "With Mother."

"Are we really?" I screwed up my face on purpose.

"Mmmmmhum. We really are."

"And we're going to sell all our things?"

"Not all." She was still talking with her eyes closed. "But a lot."

Then I thought about something that made me want to cry. "What're you going to do with my daddy's things?"

"I don't know just yet. We'll just cross that bridge when we come to it."

"No. Let's cross it now."

Mama's eyes blinked open, and they were so blue, the rest of her face looked pale and washed out. "Mother lives all by herself, Violet. In a right big house. Don't you remember?"

"No. And if she has a whole house, then why're we having to sell our things?"

"Because she already has a full house. Sofas and chairs and

pictures on the wall. Much nicer things than we have." She glanced at the old dresser. Daddy had bought it at some junk shop when we moved to New Orleans. But it was all ours.

"I guess it's been lonely for Mother to be all alone," she said. "My sister lives right next door. Listen, it'll be good for you. You have a family you don't even know. Cousins."

"Does she make those cousins call her Miss Gussie?"

"She doesn't *make* them. Lots of people call her that."

"Like a nickname?"

"Sort of. Her real name is Gussie, short for Augusta."

I thought about that a minute. "I don't care what her name is. I don't want to sell our things." I ached to cry, but I made myself breathe hard.

"Violet, honey. Listen. We have to. I wouldn't do it otherwise."

Her voice sounded funny, like thread pulled too tight, so I just stared at cracks in the ceiling. I didn't say anything else, because it was real clear that her mind was set on selling our things and on going home. I didn't have a memory of Crystal Falls or the grandmother or the people who lived around her. I had me some cousins. And Mama's sister. And her husband who owned a dime store. But I didn't know them. When I tried to remember, there were little flashes, like little sparks from a match, and then nothing.

*T*he day of the rummage sale, the fraternity boys moved our furniture to the front lawn. Me and the grandmother walked around the grass, tagging chairs, beds, lamps. She told me how much to price things. She called me sweetie pie. She was beginning to seem more like a Miss Gussie than a brand-new grandmother. Mama arranged herself in a lawn chair. There was a

Tampa Nugget cigar box in her lap, full of money, so she could make change. She was wearing green shorts and a white sleeveless blouse. Her arms were thin and freckled. Pale. There were circles under her eyes, purple smudges. I noticed that her legs were still good, even if she was a little thick in the middle from drinking beer. I wondered if she'd try to slim down and get her another man.

People parked on the street and climbed out of their cars. I had never seen so many people on this street. Almost everything we owned was either arranged on card tables or stuffed into boxes. There were dishes, slotted spoons, aluminum saucepans, sheets, records, towels, curtains. Clothes I'd outgrown. Glass figurines just yea-big. My daddy's flannel shirts, a stack of trousers, three fishing poles, and a green tackle box. It was hard to watch people poke inside the boxes, holding up our things. They haggled over prices.

"This ain't worth five whole dollars," a fat lady said. She was wearing a huge polka-dot dress with perspiration stains under her armpits. She pointed to our record player. "I'll give you one dollar for it, and not a red cent more."

"No," Mama said. "It's worth more than five dollars."

The fat lady bought it anyway, frowning as she counted out the dollar bills. You got yourself a bargain, I wanted to say, but I didn't. The fat lady looked mean. Still, I'd known that record player my whole life.

*T*hat evening, the apartment was full of echoes. Everything was gone. We had whittled our lives down to nothing, just empty space and swatches of dust in the corners. All gone. The Monza, our beds, the old sofa where Mama had slept so much, the Mason jars under the sink. We had us a roll of money in the Tampa Nugget box. At dusk, we packed our things into Miss Gussie's green Buick. We didn't have much. Three green suitcases Miss Gussie had bought us at Maison Blanche. Four cardboard boxes, a dozen paper sacks. Mama said she felt bad about those sacks, but we had to put our clothes in something. She didn't act nervous when Miss Gussie drove us to a motel. The ceramic frog zoomed across her dashboard when she turned the car, but it never fell off and broke.

We stopped at a Travel Lodge. There was a sign out front with a teddy bear toting a pillow. He wore the cutest little hat. I had never stayed in a nice motel before. That time we went to Chicago, we stayed at a place in Indiana that charged two dollars a night and we got bedbugs. You wouldn't get bedbugs at the Travel Lodge. There were two beds, and a long dresser with a TV on one end. In the drawer, there was stationery with more pictures of the little bear. And postcards that said Travel Lodge, New Orleans, Louisiana. These I kept. Along with the cute little soaps. In the bathroom, there were stacks of white towels. There were four glasses, all wrapped up so that you knew they were clean. The toilet was wrapped in strips of paper to let you know nobody had sat on it. Me and Mama got in one bed, and Miss Gussie got a whole one to herself. Nobody talked much. We let the TV play, and it filled up the room. I fell asleep watching *Dragnet*.

The next morning, we drove to the old apartment house to say good-bye to Merry and to make sure we hadn't forgotten anything. We hadn't. Merry gave us coffee and doughnuts. She wrote down our new address in Crystal Falls, Miss Gussie's house, but I thought maybe we would write letters back and forth for a year, maybe two, then we'd just exchange Christmas cards, and finally one day she'd move away and forget to send us her new address. Or maybe we'd be the ones who'd forget.

Years would go by. Now and then we would think of her and how she had called Miss Gussie. But we'd never see her again. I knew in my heart that I was looking at Merry for the last time.

We climbed into the car. Merry dropped a paper sack into my lap. "Just some little snacks, in case you get hungry," she said. I started to say thank you, but a big knot swelled up in my throat and I couldn't breathe.

"Now what do you say, Violet?" Miss Gussie said, looking over her shoulder at me.

"Thanks," I said, but I couldn't look at Merry. Mama glanced at the old apartment house and waved to Merry. Miss Gussie started the engine.

"Y'all be careful, now," Merry called out, lifting her hand, waving good-bye. The car pulled away from the curb. I looked back at Merry. She was waving, a big pear with arms, all backlit by the sun. Behind her the windows of our apartment were bare, waiting for new tenants. Bye, Merry, I thought. My grandmother angled her Buick away from Camp Street, the ceramic frog scooted across the dash, towards Mama, and Merry shrank to a pinpoint. My eyes watered up. We turned down another street, and I wiped my eyes. When I looked back, Merry and the old apartment had dropped out of sight.

The whole time we drove, I couldn't get over how the land changed. Louisiana was real flat. Miss Gussie kept her car pointed north. We spent the night in Memphis, and I got to see the Mississippi River again. This time we stayed in a Holiday Inn. Mama turned on the television. The announcer said, "In our next segment, we'll have an update of total U.S. casualties in Vietnam since January." Mama's hand was quick. She switched channels until she found a cartoon. Me and Miss Gussie went outside to look at the swimming pool. "Why don't you take a little dip?" she asked. I shook my head. I didn't have me a swimsuit. Plus, I didn't know how to swim. She must have read my mind because she told me I could wade in my shorts. I took off running and jumped into the shallow end.

That evening we ate in the restaurant. It wasn't like McDonald's. The walls were made up of windows which overlooked the blue pool and metal lounge chairs. The waitress led us past an arrangement full of plastic flowers, past a dessert tray showing cakes with whipped cream and cherries, past a man and woman who were holding hands. The waitress stopped in front of a corner booth which, to my disappointment, didn't have a view. After we slid across the length of red plastic, the waitress handed out thin books.

"You get anything you want," Miss Gussie said to me.

I opened my book and stared down at the fancy script: chicken à la king on a bed of rice; sirloin steak, grilled to perfection; broiled red snapper, fresh from the sea. I thought, what sea? I wanted one of those desserts I'd seen. Inches of whipped cream, long-stemmed cherries, shaved nuts and coconut.

"You ladies ready to order?"

I looked up and saw our waitress. She was holding a pencil over a green pad. I told her what I wanted. She glanced over at Mama and Miss Gussie.

"Don't she want some nice fried chicken instead?" the woman asked them.

"She'll have the ground beef platter," Mama said. She looked at me. "You can have the dessert later. If you clean your plate."

I glared at her from under my eyebrows. She wouldn't know a clean plate if it hit her in the face. Who was she trying to fool, the waitress or Miss Gussie?"

"Mashed, fried, or baked potatoes?" asked the waitress, still looking at Mama.

"Fried," I hollered. Miss Gussie raised her eyebrows, but she didn't say anything. I could have told her a thing or two. I could have told her about our old refrigerator. What was in it before she came. The moldy limes and cans of beer. Cupboards full of stale marshmallows, Hostess Twinkies, and Ring-Ding Jr.'s. My eyes met Mama's. I was one heartbeat away from telling Miss Gussie everything I knew and then some.

Mama glanced up at the waitress. "Well, let's see," she said briskly. "I think I'll have the breaded veal."

Miss Gussie ordered the daily special, liver and onions. The waitress gathered our books and left. I looked at everything on the table. A red netted candle. Little packets of sugar. Squares of butter stuck to white paper. A place mat showing the Tennessee state flower, bird, and flag. I'd never seen such finery, and I wanted to remember everything.

The next morning, we traveled east. We passed through a bunch of swamps. Then something called a wildlife refuge. Mostly the highway was empty. I'd never seen so much empty land. There were old gray barns alongside the road, miles of empty pasture. We crossed a bunch more rivers: Hatchie, Tennessee, Duck. I stretched out next to the paper sacks and smelled our things and tried to sleep. It felt as if we'd been driving forever. I wondered why driving made you so tired.

When we reached Nashville, First Avenue, we drove next to another river, the Cumberland. It was not as big as the Mississippi. But I noticed a range of mountains toward the east. "That's where Crystal Falls is," said Miss Gussie, like she owned the place. It didn't matter. It looked like a cool blue place to me.

We reached Crystal Falls at dark. It was nothing like I'd imagined, everything was so different from New Orleans. Mountains were all around us, and the trees were huge. Many of the buildings were built out of limestone. The air smelled different, like minerals. I didn't see a single banana tree or hibiscus. But, then, it was dark, so I didn't know. Anything could have been out there.

On the outskirts of town, there were little trailer parks, which put me in mind of Mamaw. Inside Crystal Falls, the scenery got prettier. Mama pointed out the names of places. There was a big creek that ran through the center of town, Town Creek. Miss Gussie said it dipped right under the courthouse. She said a woman drowned there a long time ago when the creek flooded. There were trees and benches all around the courthouse. She called it the square. And it made sense because the road was shaped in a big cube, with all of these stores lined up around it.

She drove around the square and pointed to her son-in-law's Ben Franklin, a five-and-dime. Next was a Western Auto, a drugstore, and a beauty salon. On one corner was a bank and on the other was a movie theatre. She said the creek ran under those stores, too. She stopped the Buick at a red light, and I looked up and down the street. It was called Broad Street, but I didn't think it was very wide. All of a sudden, I didn't much like this town, not the trees or the mountains or the cool evening air. It was a firm dislike, like something solid in my throat.

Miss Gussie turned down a shady street. There was a sign at the corner, Dixie Avenue. It was a straight street, and we drove for a long time. The houses were pretty, like St. Charles back in New Orleans, only not as big. She angled the car into a driveway, and looked up at the house. I didn't have a memory of it. It was a white house with green shutters, a screened front porch. Rosebushes had shed pink petals onto the grass. The yard was full of trees with fat trunks.

"Well, we're home," said Miss Gussie. Her hands still clutched the steering wheel.

Now what? I thought.

Next door, a woman got up from a rocking chair on her front porch and peered down at us. Her blond hair was teased in a Jackie Kennedy bouffant. She looked like an older, spread-out version of my mother. Wide hips and fat arms. I guessed she was my aunt.

"Mother Dear? Is that you, Mother Dear?" the aunt woman called out.

"Is that your sister?" I asked.

"That's right. My sister, Dorothy," said Mama. "Your aunt. Don't you remember her?"

I shook my head. It was strange to see my mother's features all mixed up on someone else's face.

"It's almost a shame," said Miss Gussie, looking back at me. "Her growing up like she has."

A pinched look swept across Mama's face, but it only stayed there a minute. I looked up at the aunt woman's house. It was a larger, prettier house than Miss Gussie's. Red brick with white shutters. The porch light was burning. I stared at the aunt woman again. The fact was, I did have a small memory of her. I think it was near Easter, a long time ago. Me and Mama drove by ourselves to Crystal Falls. Daddy stayed in New Orleans. What I remembered about the aunt woman was a lady with purple Bermuda shorts that matched the veins in her legs. What I remembered was a blond little girl who threw sand in my eyes when we went to an Easter egg hunt. I didn't recall her name. I cried, and Mama washed my face. Right after that, we got into our car and left Crystal Falls. Mama kept saying, "Never again. Never, never."

Now the aunt woman stared right back at us, like who were

we to be sitting in her mother's car. I wondered what Miss
Gussie had told her about us. I wondered if she knew how sick
Mama had been. Then the aunt woman's face sort of changed.
Her jaw dropped open. She got up from her chair, poked her
head into the house, and called out, "They're here!" She
walked down the steps, the screen door banging hard against
the wooden frame. She folded her arms, like maybe she was
cold. Miss Gussie and Mama got out of the Buick, but I just
sat there, watching the screen door open close open close as a
girl and a teenage boy came outside and crossed the yard to
stare at us.

"Get out of the car, Violet honey," Mama said. She
watched until I opened the door and stood up. Then she looked
up at her sister.

"I was getting so worried about y'all," the aunt woman said,
smiling, walking over to us. "Mother Dear doesn't drive as
good as she used to. She can't see worth a hoot. And she's got
that bad arthritis."

"Why, I can drive as good as you, I'll have you know." Miss
Gussie's eyebrows slanted down. "I made it to New Orleans
and back, didn't I?"

"I was sick the whole time, worrying about you. Now come
here, Sister, and give me a hug." The aunt woman held out her
hands. "It's about time you came for a little visit."

They embraced, stiff like, and over Mama's shoulder, I saw
the aunt woman blinking at me. I didn't know what she was
thinking. Maybe she was thinking a little visit, my foot. I wondered if she could see all those boxes and paper sacks in the
back of the car.

This girl with blue eyes and long blond hair stared. The
teenage boy with most of his hair shaved off stared, too. I
noticed his pinkish-looking scalp. His bangs stuck straight up,

like a chunk of brown grass. They were all staring at me and Mama. But no one stepped forward to slap or hug us.

My cousins, my family, the McSomethings.

"And you must be Violet," the aunt woman said, letting go of my mama.

"Yes, ma'am." All of a sudden, I felt shy.

"Well. Aren't you all grown up? I'm sure you're just as sweet as you can be."

Sweet. She didn't know the half of it. I could see right off the bat that she was disappointed in the way I looked. I didn't have the sort of face that made people say oh, isn't she the cutest thing or oh, isn't she pretty. Not with that blond girl cousin over there, who had dainty bones and a beautiful face. Even the boy with the peeled scalp was handsome.

"She favors her daddy and his people." The aunt woman looked at me.

"I don't think so," said Miss Gussie. "I think she looks like our side of the family."

She opened the trunk and called out to the teenage boy to fetch our suitcases. She called him Mack. Mack McSomething, I thought to myself. What a name.

"How long are you planning to stay?" the aunt woman asked Mama.

"Let's don't talk about leaving just yet," said Miss Gussie, putting her arm around my mama, hugging her real close. The aunt woman smiled, but a line appeared on her forehead.

"Oh, it's just so good to be home." Mama smiled, too, but I knew that smile. It was sort of wavy, the way water got when you threw something in it. That smile could change into tears in a heartbeat. "Where's Albert? At the dime store?"

"Oh, no," said the aunt woman. "We close at five o'clock. He's at a Jaycees meeting."

"What about Queenie?" Mama said. "I'm just dying to see her."

"She'll be here in the morning," Miss Gussie said.

A small silence sprang up. I wondered about this Queenie person. I could hear the crickets singing from the trees. It was getting darker and darker, and I wondered if we'd just stay out here or what. The cousins were staring holes through me, the girl especially.

"Y'all hungry?" asked the aunt woman.

"Oh, we don't want to be any trouble," Mama said.

"It's no trouble," the aunt woman said. "We've already had supper, but it won't take a minute to heat things up. Y'all come on over right now."

We sat down at a long kitchen table, Mama and Miss Gussie and myself, while the aunt woman heated up the leftovers.

"Now don't go to any trouble," Mama said again.

"I wouldn't do it if I didn't want to, and you know it."

"Can I help you do anything?" asked Mama.

The aunt woman shook her head. I looked around the kitchen. There was a big window which curved out, and this was where the table fit. The table itself had a bowl of shiny fruit in the center. Behind me, the cabinets were made of knotty wood, polished a warm honey color. Each cupboard door had a curved black handle. The counters had recently been wiped down, and on the surface stood a track of beaded water. There was a toaster, a mixer with a plastic cover dropped over it, a shiny metal coffeepot. A calendar showing a basket full of daisies hung on the farthest wall. August. There was an air conditioner up near the ceiling. Somebody had to cut a hole in the wall to make it fit. It chugged out cold air. All around me, smells rose up. Fried meat, the floury smell of heated biscuits.

The aunt woman told the blond girl to set the table, honey. The girl frowned and opened a drawer. She took out the silver. Miss Gussie fetched a jar of blackberry jelly, a butter dish, a bowl of sugar. The blond girl smacked down a white china plate in front of me. A fork, two spoons, one with a real long neck on it. A knife. A tall blue glass. A paper napkin. I wanted to say something to her, since she was my cousin and all, but she gave me this cool, drop-dead look. Her eyes were pale blue, like some of the color had leaked out. She set a plate in front of Mama, but she didn't smack it against the table.

"I don't suppose you remember me?" Mama asked the girl. "Do you, Bitsy?"

So. That was her name. Bitsy. Bitsy and Mack. Like two parakeets.

"Yes, ma'am. I remember you. Would you like iced tea or milk with your meal?" She sounded like the waitress from the Holiday Inn.

"Buttermilk, please." Mama's smile dimmed a little. "If you have it."

"We have it." Bitsy looked at me. "Do you want buttermilk, too?"

"Iced tea," I said.

The aunt woman set steaming bowls on the table. I didn't know leftovers could smell so good. Fried pork chops. Stewed apples, cornbread, biscuits, snap beans. Mashed potatoes, fried yellow squash patties. Blackberry cobbler with one whole section missing.

"Anything else, Mummie?" said Bitsy.

"No, dear," said the aunt woman.

Bitsy left the room, giving me one last look.

"Oh, my aching back," Miss Gussie said to no one really.

My mouth watered as I stared at the food. I felt half-starved. I remembered the spaghetti Merry had cooked for us.

Oh, Merry. Don't think about her. You're long gone, Violet. And you've got yourself a new granny and a bunch of other kin to boot.

I picked up my fork and stabbed a hunk of porkmeat. I dipped it in the creamed potatoes, then took a bite. From under the table, Mama kicked my shin. She lifted her eyebrows and cleared her throat.

"What?" I asked around the food.

Mama pointed to my napkin. "In your lap, please," she said, like I really had good manners but had just forgotten and was acting like a brat.

"And you know better than to talk with your mouth full," she said.

"No I don't," I said, and Mama kicked the fire out of me again.

"Ow!" I hollered and leaned over to rub my shin.

Miss Gussie acted like she hadn't heard. She reached for a biscuit and spread on some blackberry jelly. Mama crumbled cornbread into her glass of buttermilk and mashed it all up with one of the long spoons. As if that was good manners to turn your food into slop.

"My, that looks good." Miss Gussie looked at Mama's glass. "I think I'll fix me a glass, too."

So that was what the long spoons were for, I thought, watching Miss Gussie root in the refrigerator. She came back to the table and started mixing up cornbread into her glass. She and Mama acted like they were eating ice cream. I wouldn't eat that if you paid me. Their spoons clicked away.

The aunt woman kept busy at the sink, washing out bowls. She seemed a little stiff with my mama. Like she didn't know what to say. I didn't know what to make of any of them, to tell the truth. Now the aunt woman started running water into the sink.

"I know it's terrible to say, but I didn't think we'd *ever* see you again, Clancy Jane," she said. Her broad back faced us, and little waves of fat rolled under her dress. She squirted Ivory Liquid into a stream of water. A chain of tiny bubbles rose into the air and burst.

Mama just nodded and kept eating chunks of soggy cornbread.

"Albert sure will be surprised. Won't he, Mother Dear?" the aunt woman twisted at her waist, looking at us.

"Yes indeed," Miss Gussie said.

The aunt woman smiled at me. "Albert's your uncle, honey. Uncle Albert. He's got the finest dime store. Just full of toys and dolls."

Mama patted her mouth with the napkin. Her eyes met mine. I got the message. You had to be ladylike around here. If you wanted to stay.

"I was sorry to hear about Hart, Sister," the aunt woman said.

"Well." Mama stopped mixing up her cornbread and milk.

They didn't know the half of it. Mama falling down drunk or playing Tony Bennett records and singing "Fly Me to the Moon." Lord.

"But we're all happy that you're home, just tickled pink." She faced the sink, so I couldn't see her face. But her voice sounded strained, like she didn't mean a word of it. Her arms moved up and down as she scrubbed a saucepan. Her blond bouffant jiggled.

I looked down at my plate. I'd picked the pork chop bones clean. I was dying to ask for a piece of that cobbler. But I didn't say anything, lest they think I was a pig. I looked around the kitchen again. It was such a clean place, almost as good as my movie stars' house. Through the windows I saw lightning bugs spark in the trees. I could have sat there forever, it was so nice. Mama picked up her plate and carried it to the sink. She made a motion like she was going to wash it, but the aunt woman scooped it up.

"Nonono, Sister," she said. "I'll do this. You've been driving all day. You're our *guest*. After you leave here, Lord knows when we'll see you again. Or are you planning to move back to Crystal Falls?"

Mama's eyelids flickered. Before she could answer, the back door opened. This pale man walked in. Dorothy's husband. Uncle Albert. Before he noticed us, I stared at him good. He was wearing a blue suit and a navy tie. He had a broad forehead, dark blond hair, and blue eyes. But what struck me most was the *look* in his eyes. I'd seen dogs with this look. When I used to go roller-skating at Jackson Square, to chase the pigeons, I'd see these skinny old dogs. You could tell they'd been kicked and beat a lot.

I couldn't imagine the aunt woman beating a grown-up man, but you never knew. The uncle man's eyes swept around the kitchen and hooked on Mama and me. He glanced back at Dorothy. Then at Miss Gussie. Then back at us.

"Well, goodness gracious," he said. "I just can't believe my eyes. It's Clancy Jane. Miss Gussie said she was bringing you back from New Orleans."

"Hello, Albert." Mama smiled.

"I was real sorry to hear about your husband," he said. "I didn't ever know him, but he sure was brave to go to Vietnam." His voice was sort of watery. Weak. He swallowed hard and gave the aunt woman a nervous glance.

"Your TV show is on, Albert," she said, and stared until he left the room. Before he left, I thought I saw something else in his eyes. I thought maybe he was like a good-natured dog that wouldn't bite until you pulled its ears the wrong way. But I didn't know.

*T*he aunt woman made a big fuss for us to spend the night at her house. She wouldn't take no for an answer, even though Miss Gussie's house was just next door. "Y'all have been driving all day," she said. "You must be dead tired."

Miss Gussie said she wanted to sleep in her own bed.

"Why, you can't sleep at your house, Mother Dear! It's been shut up all week long. It'll be an oven."

"Well, I guess you're right," said Miss Gussie.

"I'm right," said the aunt woman. So we spent the night. The aunt woman made her mama a bed on the fold-out sofa in the den. She gave us her girl's room to sleep in. Through the walls, I heard Bitsy, as big as she was, cry to her mama. "How come *I* have to give up my own bed? How come they didn't go to Miss Gussie's?"

The aunt woman said, "Shhh, little angel. They'll hear you."

"But, Mummie, why'd they come?"

"Shhh, sugar lump. They'll be gone soon."

"When?"

"Soon. Shush, now."

Shush, now? Mother Dear? Sister? Who *were* all those people?

I looked around Bitsy's room. She had herself a four-poster canopy bed. A big dresser with a mirror. Pink swirling curtains on the windows. The walls were pink, the woodwork painted white. I'd never seen so much pink in all my life. Dolls all wrapped in plastic, lined up behind a glass case. A dollhouse decked out with furniture just yea-big. A record player. She even had records in French. I touched everything. I'd never seen anything like it. There was an air conditioner in the window, which the aunt woman turned on, first thing. It blew out mildewy air. But it felt good and cold. Besides, I'd smelled worse.

"The aunt woman thinks we're just visiting, doesn't she?" I asked.

"Well, maybe." Mama smiled. She pulled a gown over her head, then rubbed Jergen's lotion on her hands. "Why do you call her the aunt woman?"

"Because she's all strange."

"Strange? How?"

"A stranger," I said impatiently. "I don't know her. Mama? Are we just visiting?"

"Not really."

"But we've sold all our things."

"I know, I know. It'll work out. You'll see." She eased herself back in the bed, pulled up the covers.

"But I don't see."

"Well, you will. And we're here. So don't worry. Blood is always thicker than water. You remember that."

"Mama?"

"Hmmmm?"

"One more question."

"Just one."

"What's their last name? The aunt woman and them. It's McSomething, I know."

"McDougal. Dorothy and Albert McDougal. And try not to think of her as the aunt woman. You might let it slip. Now go to SLEEP, please."

I rolled over and stared out the window. It was all a-swirl to me. It swirled so hard I couldn't hardly breathe. All those new McDougals. All so strange and quiet. We could have stayed in New Orleans. We had Merry. We had Daddy's things. What if he wasn't really dead? What if somebody else's daddy had gotten blown up? He'd never find us if he came back. What had Mama been thinking?

Miss Gussie was my grandmother, but she was also Mother Dear to the aunt woman and the granny to that girl cousin and that boy with the shaved head. Miss Gussie owned the house next door, which was a good thing. It was real clear that we couldn't live here. I could not stand a room so pink. Earlier, I had noticed the boy cousin's room. He had one all of his own, all decorated with baseballs, flags, and trophies. I reminded myself that I had me a room once, too. With my own bed, which we sold for ten dollars, mattress included.

Clancy Jane

1966

I walked through my mother's house, picking up doodads, trying to remember each figurine and framed photograph. There were tables covered with glass paperweights, stacks of old *TV Guide*s with the crossword puzzles neatly filled in with a ballpoint pen. Ceramic frogs were perched everywhere, as if they'd just hopped up next to the bathtub or beneath a chair. "Just like a real frog might," I whispered to Violet. The truth was, I had no idea my mother had a thing for frogs. I suppose we all have secret things.

The living room was cooler and darker than I remembered, and the air smelled faintly of old wool and mothballs. There were four dark windows, which opened onto the screened porch. The other rooms were brighter, filled with plants. African violets in three colors, white, purple, and pink. Elephant ear plants, with leaves bigger than my hand. Spider plants with baby shoots hanging down like dropped parachutes. Ferns, baby tears, chives, basil, parsley, dill. Mother always did have a green thumb.

What I remembered best of my childhood was Queenie ironing in the kitchen, her waxy smell, a scrubwater scent, the way she shook water on clothes, the steamy *ssssst* of the iron. I remembered the smell of buttermilk biscuits and sweet country ham. Papa sleeping in his maroon chair, his eyeglasses pushed over his forehead. Dorothy locking herself in the bathroom and not coming out until Mother beat on the door and shouted. I remembered helping Mother plant radishes, weeding the lettuce. The only thing she insisted on planting herself was zinnia seeds at the edge of her garden. That was her own special place.

Mother's house had not changed—those wool afghans folded on the back of the sofa, handsewn quilts stacked in the linen press, little crocheted squares she arranged on chairs. There were baskets of fall leaves, books that would surprise you with pressed flowers, the pages slightly stuck together and stained. There were drawers full of keys that seemed to fit no locks. Her linen closet was stacked in neat squares that smelled of lemon sachet. She used to say that busy hands meant a happy life.

*I*t was midevening, and the air was full of blue dusk. I sat on the porch painting my toenails red, China Doll, bloated from Queenie's meal of pot roast with potatoes and carrots. Gravy over noodles. Biscuits. Melons from the garden. Two great big glasses of iced tea. Chocolate pie.

Queenie had long since gone home. I looked up from polishing my toenails. Mother reached into a basket and pulled out her knitting. Her needles clicked. The doctor said it was therapy for her arthritis. She was making an afghan for Violet, her favorite colors, yellow and green. I thought about my secret and felt guilt wash over me.

You can't help this, I told myself. Things like this happen.

The porch was full of pronged shadows. Beneath the streetlight, I watched Bitsy strut up the sidewalk with another girl.

They whispered with their heads drawn together, then they pulled apart and giggled. Our porch was so dark I didn't see how Mother could knit, but her needles switched back and forth, knit-purl, knit-purl. Lights came on next door. Mack's window was open, and phonograph music drifted out. Dorothy came outside, holding a glass of iced tea, and sank down in the hammock. From Mack's room, Simon and Garfunkel were singing "Homeward Bound."

Dorothy lifted her head and hollered, "Mack? Mack, honey? Will you turn it down just a little, sweetie?"

He came to the window and looked down at his mother as if she were a shrilling insect.

"All right, honey?" she said, turning her face upward. Mack slammed down his window, and the music rattled the panes.

Dorothy turned her gaze upon Albert, who stood in the front yard as if he were deaf, trimming the boxwoods in the fading light. His shears made a clean, pinched noise. Behind him, the sky turned pink, then navy, shading to black. Stars popped out between the trees. The moon rose full and hard. Finally he looked toward the street and called out to Bitsy.

"Just one more minute, Father!" she wheedled from the sidewalk. "Please, Father."

"Well, hurry on up," Albert said, and walked toward his garage to put away his hedge clippers. Dorothy got up from the hammock, grunting, and walked over to the porch. She frowned as she cracked open the front door and a blast of music leaked out, Paul Simon singing *Home, where my love lies waiting silently for me.*

"Bitsy? Get in the house *now*," she yelled.

"But, Mo-*ther*," she whined. "It's early."

"Now, Bitsy. I'm late for a bridge game, and you haven't even had your bath."

Bitsy whispered something in her friend's ear.

"Lillian Beatrice!" Dorothy's voice was so shrill it hushed the cicadas.

"Coming, Mother." She waved to her friend and turned up the sidewalk.

"Don't dawdle," said Dorothy.

"I'm *not.*"

"Yes, you are. In the house, right now, young lady." Dorothy jammed her fists against her hips as she watched her daughter walk into the house. At last the door slammed.

I heard the distant noise of cars in town, the shrilling cicadas, the click of Mother's needles, and from the living room the low hum of the air conditioner.

Mother groaned and put down her knitting. "Oh, me," she said, getting up from the rocker. "It's time for Lawrence Welk."

I got up, too, and walked upstairs to wash my hair. When I came out of the bathroom, I noticed the light was burning in Violet's room. She was kneeling on the floor, folding her clothes into a bottom dresser drawer. It made my chest hurt to see how few clothes she owned, how ragged they were. Behind her, on the walls, were old ballerina prints, Dorothy's old pictures.

She looked up and smiled.

"How do you like Mother's house?" I asked.

"Oh, it's real pretty. We've never lived in a place this pretty."

"Don't you love all of her knickknacks?" I smiled. "She's always been a real packrat. Come here, sweetie." I held out my hand and waited for her to take it. "I know things have been real hard for you lately."

Violet looked down at her bare knee, but she didn't let go of my hand.

"And I'm not trying to excuse my behavior," I said. "I acted pretty awful in New Orleans. Daddy's death was a real bad shock."

Violet's eyes met mine and she slowly nodded.

"I'm sorry, honey. I wouldn't have hurt you for the world. But there was more going on than you knew about."

Violet was silent a minute. "Like what?"

"Well, I wasn't in shock just because your daddy died." I paused and squeezed Violet's hand. I wasn't sure if she was ready to hear the truth, but she was my closest kin. For the last twelve years, I had been closer to her than to my own mother.

"There was something else wrong," I said. "At least, I thought it was wrong. And Merry knew about it. It's why she helped us leave New Orleans."

"Why?" said Violet.

"I'm going to have a baby, Violet."

"A *baby*?" Violet said.

"It's from the last time Daddy came home. In May." I pulled Violet's hand over my stomach, which curved just the slightest. "Do you feel it?"

"No." Violet shook her head. "I can't feel anything. Am I supposed to?"

"Well, maybe not now. But later you will." The truth was, I'd loved Hart, but I didn't want another baby. With just Violet, I could manage. With a baby, I was a sitting duck.

"Does Miss Gussie know?" Violet asked.

I shook my head. "And Dorothy doesn't know, either. So it'll be our secret, okay?"

"Okay."

"It's not that I don't want them to know. We just need time to get used to living here. And they need to get used to us."

"But you told Merry."

"She wasn't my mother."

"I don't understand. It looks like Miss Gussie needs to know."

"Oh, she will. I'll tell them all when the time is right." I paused and rubbed my hand over Violet's. "You know, it's not easy to have a new baby in the house. If Mother knew about the baby, she'd only get worked up. And that's not good for her."

"I guess," Violet said. "She is sort of old."

"Anyway, I'll be telling her real soon. Because I'll be showing. My clothes are already tight. They'll be able to see for themselves."

Violet kept her hand on my stomach. "I hope it's a girl," she said.

From the window, the air conditioner purred, swirling the gauzy curtains. I pictured Mother downstairs, all stretched out on the sofa, a *TV Guide* propped on her chest, half-dozing, half-watching bubbles floating above Lawrence Welk's orchestra, high above the Lennon Sisters, who were singing "Moon River."

Violet

1966

*T*he schools in Crystal Falls started the last week of August, the seventh grade for me. Aunt Dorothy took me and Mama shopping on Broad Street. Bitsy went, too, although it was real clear that she wasn't happy about it. Mama had money from our bank in New Orleans and from the rummage sale, but Aunt Dorothy insisted on buying me two dresses.

"No, no, no," she said when Mama tried to stop her. "I want to do it. I wouldn't do it if I didn't want to. Believe me. But the trouble is, Sister, she's going to need scads more dresses than you can afford. All she's got are rags."

Mama blushed.

"And there's Sunday school, too," Aunt Dorothy said.

Sunday school, and we hadn't even been here one week. I could see they tried to mold you real fast, the potter's clay. Thanks to Mama's Bible, I was not ignorant even if I didn't go to church regular.

"But you know what?" Aunt Dorothy was saying. "Bitsy has tons of dresses from last year, and I was going to give them to Queenie to take over to her side of town. But I just know they'll fit Violet. You might have to do an alteration or two. But think of the money you'll save. And Violet will look like a doll. I only dress Bitsy in the finest."

"Really?" Mama said, like she hadn't thought of this.

"Yes, really," said Aunt Dorothy. "Don't you have scads of beautiful dresses, Bitsy?"

Bitsy shrugged. She was almost fourteen. When school started, she would be in the eighth grade. She hadn't spoken three words to me since Miss Gussie had brought me and Mama to Crystal Falls. And when she did talk, she used fancy words I didn't understand. She did that on purpose. I thought maybe I looked or smelled funny. Different. When she thought she could get away with it, she wouldn't have anything to do with me. Her behavior embarrassed Miss Gussie, who made it clear, over and over, that Bitsy was going through a "stage" and would "outgrow it." Like a lizard sheds its skin, I thought.

"I'd just as soon Violet have the clothes as a nigger," said Aunt Dorothy.

While Aunt Dorothy made Bitsy try on an armload of dresses, me and Mama walked down to Uncle Albert's dime store, the Ben Franklin. There were six wide aisles running front to back, all organized into sections. Toys. A whole section of things you could buy for under one dollar. Zippers and thread. Greeting cards, gift wrap, school supplies. Candy and toothbrushes. Baby dresses and diapers. Clothes, underwear, bras, slips, stockings. It was all so neat, just like my new uncle. We bought me socks and cotton step-ins. Uncle Albert gave us a discount and said to me, "Don't you look sweet as sugar? Tell you what, why don't you pick out a baby doll? Pick any one you like."

"Oh, that's so sweet," said Mama. "But I can't let you do that. You've already given us this discount."

"No, no, no. I want Violet to have her a doll," Uncle Albert said.

I looked down the aisle and saw my cousin Mack. He was leaning against the Coca-Cola machine, drinking a 7UP. There was a dust mop propped against the wall, where he'd gotten tired of cleaning the floors.

"Mack?" called out Uncle Albert. "Help your cousin get a doll."

Mack made a face. He was named after his daddy, Albert Dean McDougal, Jr. "I don't know nothing about dolls!" he said.

"I meant for you to *get* it for her, son. They're mostly up high. Can't you see that?"

"Oh." He pushed away from the Coca-Cola machine, set down his 7UP, and glanced at the shelves. He was real tanned from swimming at the club all summer. "I've never noticed."

I didn't want me a doll. There were a million other things I'd pick. But I pointed at a Barbie in a pink plastic carrying case. Mack got a stepladder and reached it for me. The fluorescent light shone through his short hair.

"Is this the one?" he asked.

"Yes. Thanks."

"Welcome." He climbed down the ladder and pushed the Barbie box into my arms.

"Thank you," I said, feeling my cheeks turn hot.

"You already thanked me once," he said and went back to drinking his soda. "But you're welcome anyway."

I walked around a corner and saw Mama standing in the baby aisle. She fingered a lacy blanket and looked up at me. "Oh, you got a Barbie. Wasn't that nice of Uncle Albert?" I nodded.

"Look," she whispered and pointed to a box of Curity diapers. "We'll need plenty of these."

Now I knew how babies got into a woman. First, the woman and the man kissed. Then, if his tongue touched any part of the woman's, that was when it happened. The baby got swallowed and planted. I was only surprised that it took Mama and Daddy so long to get another one. The last time he was home, they kissed right in front of me. I pictured Mama walking, tilted backward like I'd seen pregnant women do. Mama's big belly all pooched out like she'd swallowed one of Miss Gussie's melons. At last I'd get to see, firsthand, what a pregnant belly looked like. All this time, it had been a mystery, how a big stomach looked under one of those baggy smocks.

I glanced up at Mama and said, "Maybe Uncle Albert will give us a discount?"

"Oh, I'm sure he will, honey."

She ran her fingers over a blue blanket laced with white ribbons. I could tell from the way she was rubbing the cloth that she wanted a boy.

From the front of the store, we heard Aunt Dorothy's nasal voice. "Where's Sister?" she asked Uncle Albert. "Sister? Yoo-hoo! Has she been here, Albert?"

I couldn't hear his reply, just a watery mumble. Mama took my hand, and we left the baby things. We turned two corners and walked down the center aisle. Aunt Dorothy was standing in front of the display windows.

"There you are!" She waved at us.

"We've been browsing. This store is wonderful," Mama said. We walked up to the checkout counter. Bitsy was slumped next to her father, holding four huge bags. When she saw the Barbie box I was carrying, she rolled her eyes and muttered something I couldn't hear. She was into cheerleading, boys, and slumber parties, Miss Gussie had told me.

When Aunt Dorothy saw my new doll, she smiled. "Your Mama's really using her discount, I see."

"No," I said. "Uncle Albert gave it to me. Let me pick it out, even."

Something flickered across Aunt Dorothy's face, like she had smelled something bad. Then she smiled again. "Well, wasn't that the sweetest thing? Violet, do you have any Barbie dresses to go with it? A Barbie's not a bit of fun unless you can dress her up. Go pick out an outfit for your doll, honey."

"Thank you," Mama said, "but the doll is more than enough. I already feel terrible. You've bought Violet dresses and given us this discount."

Uncle Albert looked down at his cash register. He licked his finger and polished a spot on the chrome.

"Heavens, one little outfit won't hurt." Aunt Dorothy turned to Bitsy. "Everybody knows that Barbies aren't any fun without outfits. Now just run on and pick out your cousin a Barbie outfit."

Bitsy sighed and dumped her packages on the counter.

"Go on, Bitsy," said Aunt Dorothy. "We haven't got all day. Hurry up."

"Wait, Dorothy," Mama called out. "She doesn't need it. But thanks anyway. You all are too sweet."

"No, Albert needs to finish what he starts," Aunt Dorothy said, watching Bitsy move real slow like down the aisle. She plucked something off the shelf and walked back carrying a pink square box wrapped in cellophane. She held it out to her mother. Beneath the cellophane were a blue dress, tiny blue shoes, a tiny white pocketbook, and a straw hat. Aunt Dorothy took the box, glanced at the price tag, and handed it to me.

"It's just a little love gift from your Aunt Dorothy," she said, smiling, red-faced, holding out her arms, meaning for me to hug her.

School didn't start for another week. I passed time in the kitchen, watching Miss Gussie preserve her vegetables. Miss Gussie had her a maid. Queenie came every single day to polish the silver, change the sheets, iron Miss Gussie's dresses, and push the Electrolux over the roses in the carpet. Sometimes she helped us can the vegetables. Queenie was almost as old as Miss Gussie, and she'd been working here since my mama was a baby. She even remembered my daddy. She said he used to play football for Crystal Falls High and my mama was a cheer-leader. It sounded real romantic to me.

"Dorothy and I used to call you Meanie Queenie," said Mama. "You made us toe the line."

"I sure was strict," Queenie said. "And look where it got us. Noplace is where. You left home and stayed, and it look like Dorothy turn out stricter than me. I want to say to her, 'Doro-thy? It ain't going to do you a bit of good.' It just makes kids want to be wild when you hold in the reins too hard. It just don't do a bit of good."

"I didn't hold in the reins on Clancy Jane," said Miss Gus-sie. "And nothing worse could've happened."

"Well," Queenie grunted, "I know what I know."

I remembered the colored ladies who waited for the street-car on St. Charles. Mama had told me those women were maids, that they worked for the richest families in New Orleans. She said there was no talk any meaner than maid talk. But there was none any more truthful.

Which didn't make a bit of sense to me.

Bitsy

1966

Okay. First, Mummie told Miss Gussie not to go. "New Orleans is no place for a woman your age," she said. "The niggers down there'll cut your throat and won't think twice. Even the niggers up here are getting uppity. Wanting to eat where we eat. Drink out of the same faucets. Go to the same schools." Mummie shivered. "Ooooo, it makes my blood run cold. The next thing you know, they'll be trying to marry white girls. We'll have a whole country full of high yellows before you can say Jack Sprat."

"Are you finished?" said Miss Gussie, lifting one eyebrow.

"Well, it's the truth," said Mummie.

I hated her voice sometimes, the way it screaked up at the edges.

"I just don't see how you can think about driving down there," she went on. "I'll be more than happy to pay for Sister's bus ticket. And her girl's. If you're so determined to get them back here."

"Her husband is dead, Dorothy," said Miss Gussie.

"You've already told me a hundred times, haven't you? And if you ask me, she's just using you to get out of another predicament."

That did it. Miss Gussie's eyebrows slanted down. She gave Mummie a cold look. Her kitchen lights burned all night long, and the next morning her car was gone. I guess she stayed up late to pack.

Mummie said, "That damn sister of mine! After all these years, she just picks up the phone and calls like nothing's happened. She doesn't know how frail Mother Dear is. She doesn't have one damn idea!"

Second, Miss Gussie drove all the way to New Orleans to bring them back here. Mummie gave them my bedroom to sleep in. I had to sleep on a pallet in Mummie and Father's room. Father snored, and Mummie answered in her sleep. I lay there and listened to them oink and snort, back and forth. I kept thinking of my pretty bed and my room full of private things, my bulletin board and my secret drawer. My record player with my stack of French records: How to Speak French in Six Weeks. Mummie had given them to me last Christmas. I was on record two.

I wondered if Violet would snoop, if she would steal one of my glass paperweights, if she would unwrap the plastic on my Madame Alexander dolls, which are going to be collector's items. I wondered if she would thumb through my French phrase book, which was on my bedside table. And all because Miss Gussie's house was too hot and stuffy that first night. Well, it wouldn't have been if she'd stayed put and kept the air conditioner on.

Third. The next morning Aunt Clancy and Violet breezed over to my grandmother's house and staked out bedrooms. Sometimes I had slept over at Miss Gussie's, but I knew those days were over. Where would I sleep? Miss Gussie had a new *petite-fille.* Aunt Clancy had chosen the very room I used to stay in, and Violet took my mother's old room. And that was just

the beginning. Mummie took the both of them shopping and
bought Violet two dresses and promised to give her all of my
old outfits. Mummie smiled the whole time. I thought to
myself, you ought to hear what she says behind your back, Aunt
Clancy. She said that Violet was going to get all of Miss Gussie's
love and attention, and the squeaky wheel got the oil. She had
talked of nothing else.

I didn't mind Violet having my old clothes, but she was a
head shorter than me. Aunt Clancy would be hemming night
and day. Or maybe she'd talk Miss Gussie into it. That's what
Mummie said she'd do.

Then Father let Violet pick out whatever she wanted at his
store. Later, Mummie yelled at him. She said it wasn't right.
What if Violet had picked a fifty-dollar bicycle or the hundred-
dollar dollhouse? This, right on the heels of him giving Aunt
Clancy a discount on Violet's underpants and kneesocks. Mummie screamed that items in our store weren't free. Anything we
took, we had to write down prices in a brown notebook. She
said we had to keep up with these things or else it would inter-
fere with inventory.

"Don't you give them anything else," she yelled at Father.
"Not one blessed thing unless I say so!" Then she turned to
me. "And you'd better watch your step. Keep your distance.
They'll turn Mother Dear against us before this is over. You
mark my words."

Fourth. The first day of school, I was eating breakfast, ham
and biscuits, and who should knock at the back door? Our
maid, Dauphine, let her in. Mummie raised her eyebrows. Violet was wearing my good kelly-green jumper and white blouse
with green piping. She was carrying a red plaid schoolbag, from
Father's store. She even wore a wide green ribbon, also from
Father's store, tied around her braid. She had one long braid, a

thin swatch of mousey brown hanging down between her shoulder blades. Her white kneesocks stopped just below two scarred knees. The scars had turned dark red, almost brown. I asked her how she'd gotten them, and she said, "Roller-skating. I used to chase the pigeons at Jackson Square." The pigeons in Crystal Falls roosted on the roof of the dime store. I had never seen so many scrapes and scars on a girl before, except Mummie, who wouldn't discuss what had happened to her.

Now Mummie looked at Violet. "You want some breakfast, dearie?"

Dearie shook her head, and her braid swished like a snake down her back.

That night Mummie said that Violet had probably run wild in New Orleans. "Like mother, like daughter," she said, and then clammed up when I asked what she meant. But I knew. I hated my cousin's guts. The little *porc*.

"Never you mind," Mummie snapped. "Go do your homework."

"But it's the first day of school," I protested. "We don't even have homework."

"Just find something to do!"

I went upstairs and played my French records. *"Pardonnez-moi,"* I said into the mirror. Unlike my brother, who took little interest in academics, my schoolwork was a source of great pride for me. I was excited about being in the eighth grade. And Mummie said I would be a cheerleader and wear stockings and put my hair up and date football players. She had it planned to a tee how I'd be Miss Popularity. She said the key to everything was beauty and good grades. Not to mention *savoir-faire*. You had to have that.

My homeroom teacher, Miss Sara Moon, was tall and beautiful. Her name puzzled Mummie. "Is she Oriental?" she asked. No, I told her. Absolutely not. You couldn't look any more American than Miss Moon looked. She had white skin, flawless as pearls, and long blond hair she swept up into a French twist. Pretty blue eyes that sparkled. She was real young, fresh out of teacher's college. I longed to be the one she would pick to go outside and bang her erasers against the brick wall.

Which brings me to the next problem.

Fifth. Wouldn't you know, the second week in school, the principal, Mr. Bartlett, who had a wooden leg from World War II and was nicknamed Peg Leg by the students, knocked at Miss Moon's door? The door was all wood, like his leg, except for a rectangle of glass. From my desk, I could see his hooded eyes, his forehead, the bridge of his nose. I sat in the front row, next to Miss Moon's desk.

She got up and opened the door.

Guess who was standing there with Peg Leg, too short to be visible in the door's glass window? My cousin, in my best blue dress with the hand-smocking and a shiny blue ribbon puffed out around her braid. She was wearing white kneesocks. I stared at those scarred knees, little slashes dark as red neons, and I thought to myself, *Mon Dieu!* I knew then I would die if Peg Leg announced that she was my cousin.

"Who have we here?" said Miss Moon, smiling, looking expectantly from Peg Leg to Violet.

"This little lady is Violet Jones," said Peg Leg, putting his arm, which was not wooden, around my cousin. He gave Miss Moon a serious look.

Violet didn't smile. She kept staring at the beige tile floor. The squares were flecked with brown, like a mosaic. Her eyelashes brushed against her cheeks, as if she were shy. I noticed her new black shoes with buckles on the sides. Two pink circles stood out on her cheeks. Why, she was blushing! Something beat joyfully inside my chest. *Joy, joy, joy.* Mummie would have been proud of me. Violet was in trouble, our little lady was. That was why Peg Leg had introduced her to Miss Moon.

"She was in Mrs. Potter's class," said Peg Leg.

Was? I thought, feeling a stab of panic. I'd had Mrs. Linda Potter last year, grade seven. *Was?*

"But we've promoted her to your class, Miss Moon."

"Really?" said Miss Moon, smiling at my cousin with interest.

"She's smart as a whip, Mrs. Potter says." Peg Leg grinned. He leaned toward Miss Moon, and I heard him whisper, "She scored extra high on the tests Linda gave her."

"Oh," said Miss Moon, nodding.

Scored extra high? I thought. What was that supposed to mean, scored extra high?

"You'll make the little lady feel welcome, won't you, girls and boys?" said Peg Leg, facing the class. His eyes skipped from row to row, the way a flat rock skips on water when you throw it just right. Mack could do it. I couldn't. And I couldn't stand my cousin being in Miss Moon's room, either.

"Welcome to the eighth grade, Violet," said my Miss Moon. She gave my cousin an empty desk in my row, the second from the last. *Très bien.* I would be spared having to look at the back of her hair and the ribbon from my father's store every day. But she'd have to look at me. The desk was too big for my cousin. Joy, joy, joy. Her new black shoes didn't quite reach the floor. She was the shortest girl in the eighth grade. And I would be the most popular. The prettiest and the smartest. Mother said it would come true, and I believed her.

Sixth. I was still angry when I thought about it. Mummie said it was best not to think too deeply, to fix my thoughts on something productive or happy, whichever. When it happened, it made Mummie angry too, but she just smiled at Aunt Clancy and Violet and said, "Well, isn't that nice?" She smiled and smiled.

"I could've been a famous actress," Mummie had said over the years. I believed her.

OK. Miss Moon made me, didn't even offer a choice or ask my opinion, she _told_ me to please switch desks with your cousin. I whirled around, looked into my teacher's pretty eyes, and saw that she meant no harm to me personally. I saw in her eyes that Violet was my cousin and rather than force another student out of his desk, she would force me out of mine.

"Your cousin," Miss Moon's voice echoed in my brain. "Change desks after spelling, please."

What could I say? That in eight years of school I had always sat in the first row? I had excellent vision, so I could not squint at the blackboard and feign blindness. I looked at my beautiful Miss Moon and said, "Yes, ma'am."

I fell into a sorry mood. Throughout spelling, I did not raise my hand once, even though I had neatly copied my words and made sentences in _innovative_ (one of the new vocabulary words) ways. All around me, my classmates' arms waved, like stalks of flowers in a field, and I sat there chewing my eraser, my heart broken.

We changed desks, and Violet whispered in my ear, "I sure do thank you for swapping with me. I didn't think I could stand it way back here."

I gave her an icy stare.

Then I discovered why my cousin was so delighted to "swap," as she so crudely phrased it, desks. After I neatly arranged my books and tablets, I slid into the new desk. It fit me perfectly. I sighed, inhaled deeply, and sucked a toxic smell into my lungs. It was a stench like a paper mill. The odor seemed to originate from behind me. I turned and stared at the boy behind me. A tiny *pfftt* sounded, and the boy blushed. His name was Glenn Davis, and he had red hair, red eyes, and so many freckles he appeared slightly *alien* (another vocabulary word). His freckles were not the same size, which gave his skin the appearance of many layers. He was a country boy. He belonged to 4-H and Future Farmers of America. And he had been passing silent gas the whole time. I pinched my nostrils between my thumb and forefinger and breathed erratically through my mouth. I was horrified to think what sort of air-borne germs were drawn into my lungs.

Once, after a particularly audible noise (I couldn't, for the life of me, think of a decent word to describe this boy's condition except "pass wind"), I whirled around to glare at him. He was picking his nose. His index finger was probing his left *nare* (a word from health). I was on the verge of tears. And all because I was Violet's cousin. I was certain Miss Moon would have never made me change desks if this hadn't been a fact.

I made a point to speak to my teacher after school. "I just cannot sit in front of Glenn Davis," I told her.

"Why?" asked Miss Moon. She was sitting at her desk, shuffling papers.

"Because he passes wind and picks his nose," I blurted. "It smells so bad I can't concentrate."

Miss Moon blinked twice. "My goodness, Bitsy," she finally said. "I wasn't aware of that."

I nodded vigorously.

"Hmmm. You have been somewhat quiet today." She stacked the papers in the upper right corner of her desk. "I'll think of something, all right?"

"Miss Moon?" I asked, gathering my courage.

"Yes, Bitsy?" She looked at me. I couldn't read her expression, which intimidated me, in spite of the yellow mums on her desk. I'd given them to her this morning. The mums peeked out of a tall glass vase.

"I just have to sit in the front row," I said. My eyes filled with tears and spilled over. "I've never sat elsewhere."

"I'll change your seat, Bitsy." She reached across her desk and yanked out a Kleenex. She handed it to me.

"*Merci beaucoup,* Miss Moon," I murmured, turning to leave.

"A simple thank you will do, Bitsy," she said.

Seventh. It humiliated me to think about it. And, once again, Mother said not to. It happened right after Miss Moon moved my desk. She moved it—or rather had me push it—to the front row, next door to Violet, who gave me a smile that seemed too eager. Something fell inside me. Now, the whole school year, I would have her at my left elbow. I wondered if she would try to cheat. I hoped she would. A whole image bloomed of Miss Moon snatching Violet's paper. *Ah-ha!*

As I was moving my desk to the front row, I recoiled in horror to see an irregular line of dried mucus glued or otherwise attached to the back of my desk. And all this time I had assumed he was eating them. I marched over to Glenn Davis and said, "You make me sick."

He just stared back with those awful red eyes.

"And you ought to make your mother take you to a doctor," I added, "to see what's making you stink so terribly."

Still, I was utterly relieved to escape Glenn Davis. When we filed out of the room for lunch, Miss Moon had the janitor remove the nastiness from my desk with that awful milky soap that smelled of pine. I rushed down the hall, leaving Violet. I already had my friends who did not want things from me. They

didn't want my desk or my place in the row or my barely outgrown clothes. And I had Claude Edmund Wentworth IV, better known as Meathead, my one true love since the first grade.
The kids called him Meathead because a long time ago, at a
church picnic, he ate fifteen hot dogs. Then he threw up. My
grandfather had worked for his great-grandfather at Citizens'
Bank.

I told Claude and all my friends about Violet's father, that
he had been killed in Vietnam. They didn't know anything
about Vietnam, but most of their fathers had fought in World
War II, like Peg Leg. I stopped talking when Violet emerged
from the cafeteria line. We all watched her look hesitantly down
the length of the table. Good, good, I thought. Sit all by yourself. Claude stood up and waved to her. "There's a seat down
here," he called out. Then he looked at me. "Bitsy, scoot over
and make room for Violet."

"She just the new girl at school," Mummie said later. "This
popularity will soon pass. Just wait and see."

I sat back and waited. And I'd thought the worst was sitting
next to Glenn Davis. I hadn't known anything. I was just preoc-
cupied with other worries. The bottom dropped out of my life
when Miss Moon stood in the front of the room, holding a long
piece of chalk. The blackboard was dark and empty, swept
clean of morning math by yours truly.

"It's time to elect a room chairman," said Miss Moon. She
went on to say that the room chairman would be in charge of
roll call, collecting test papers and homework, and monitoring
the room when she, Miss Moon, was absent for brief periods.

"Any nominations?" asked Miss Moon, raising her eyebrows.

I was astonished when Violet raised her hand.

"Yes, Violet?"

She climbed out of my old desk and shyly looked up at our teacher from under her eyebrows. "I'd like to nominate Bitsy McDougal," she said.

Miss Moon turned and wrote my name on the blackboard, *Bitsy McDougal.*

I realized my mouth was agape. I pressed my lips together. But inside my chest, I felt a flutter, like a trapped bird was beating its wings. *Joy, joy, joy.*

"Any others?" asked Miss Moon.

Glenn Davis raised one filthy hand. He pushed out of his desk and shuffled his dirty shoes. He said, "I'd like to nominate Violet Jones up there in the first row."

Miss Moon wrote *Violet Jones* beneath my name. I sank, just the slightest degree, into my pine-smelling desk. My hip-bones were firm pressure points against the wooden seat.

Unjoy! Unjoy! Unjoy!

"Any other nominations?" asked Miss Wide-Blue-Eyed Moon. The class was silent, hands folded on their desks, eyes rooted to the two names on the blackboard. "Well, then," said Miss Moon, "if Violet and Bitsy will just step into the hall, we'll take a vote."

I got up from my desk, Violet got up from hers. I marched into the hall, feeling my cousin's hot breath behind me. If she thought we were going to have a little *tête-à-tête,* she was wrong. I pulled the door shut and folded my arms over my budding breasts. I wore a bra now.

"You'll win," said Violet. There was a strain to her voice, like each word was a pulled muscle. "I know you'll win."

As I stared at her face, I saw how badly she herself wanted to be room chairman. And she knew she didn't have a chance. She hated me for it, too. I could see that. She hated me for having new dresses and a rich father who owned a whole dime store and a mummie who went to gift teas and played bridge with Claude Wentworth's mother and was socially acceptable. The *noblesse* of Crystal Falls. She probably hated me for having a father. And having my own big pretty house. And a mummie who understood the nature of society, how it worked, how to plan ahead for it. How to make sure I had good manners and was polished to perfection. Mummie said when I grew up I should marry Claude, that he was real cute and money made the world go round. It not only made the world go round, she always said, it could send you around the world.

I saw all of this and then some in my cousin's eyes.

"Well, I'm sure you'll win," I said graciously and smiled one of my mummie's smiles.

Violet bounced on her toes, like a true *enfant terrible.* Her black heels moved up and down on the beige tile. She looked childish and incapable, young and very Jones-like. There were even some at our school. Joneses, that is. It struck me all of a sudden, as hard as a book slapped between my shoulder blades, that Glenn Davis's mother had been a Jones. A distant Jones relative, to be sure. And my stupid little cousin didn't even know it.

I bridled at this new information and made a mental note to tell Mummie. I imagined Miss Gussie having Glenn Davis over to her house to a Kool-Aid party. After he left she would have to fumigate. I knew my mummie would. We seemed to stand forever in the beige hallway, staring at the other closed doors, the white nameplates and rectangles of glass, the tarnished brass knobs, the dusty white light globes on the ceiling. The ceiling had brown water stains, slightly tattered at the edges, the largest of which was shaped like an old man's face, the mouth drawn open, toothless, and screaming.

I knew just how he felt.

Miss Moon opened the door and said, "You may come in, girls."

We filed into the room. Everyone looked blankly at me, then their eyes swept past me. Claude was smiling a strange, slanted smile. I faced the blackboard. There was one name there, and it wasn't mine. My heart dropped to my bowels. Above Violet's name was a smudged, chalky space where my name had been erased. I managed to walk to my desk. I could not bear to see Miss Moon put her arms around Violet's shoulder. "Let's hear some applause for our new room chairman."

Clap, clap, clap. I clapped my hands so hard, my palms flared red. *Clapclapclap.* Violet looked dazed as she stood in front of the board, her name floating in the blackness above her like a crown. Her eyes brimmed with joy that should have been mine. She smiled at me. Then her eyes swept gratefully around the room.

My heart was clapping inside my ribs. It clapped until it shattered into cold red marble. I dreaded going home. Mummie would just die. She would talk this into the ground. She would turn it into my fault—and it probably was. I should have been nicer, prettier, kinder, smarter. I tried to think what she would want me to do. I smiled the prettiest smile I could manage without screaming. In the back of my mind, her voice grew louder and louder: *You'll get her back, you'll get her back, you'll get her back.*

Queenie

1966

*I*t is me who figures it out about Clancy. She is in the kitchen helping Miss Gussie make pepper jelly. I'm ironing. I keep cutting my eyes over at Clancy, like I'm seeing something different each time. She is wearing one of Miss Gussie's aprons, but she hasn't tied the sashes. She's just looped it over her head, letting it dangle.

This morning, I was upstairs changing the sheets, and I caught a glimpse of her as she climbed out of the bathtub. I saw her reflection in the mirror. When she turned sideways, it looked as if she was going to fat. Her belly curved just the slightest bit, like maybe she had gas. Only it had a swolled, solid look to it. The rest of her was pale, thin.

All this time, I've been thinking about it.

"What's that belly on you for?" I ask her now.

She looks at me, then looks away. She keep straining the jelly through cheesecloth.

I say again, "What's that belly on you for?"

Miss Gussie is counting lids to Mason jars. She glances up from the table and straightens her eyeglasses. She gives Clancy the once-over.

"What a thing to say, Queenie," Clancy says. But her

cheeks turn red. "I can't help it if I'm getting fat on your cooking."

Now it's my turn to be quiet.

"And you haven't seen me in years," Clancy says. "I've just gained some weight."

"Then why the rest of you so skinny?" I say back.

"Lord," says Miss Gussie. "Don't tell me you're pregnant."

"Oh, I couldn't be pregnant," Clancy says real innocent like and shoots me a look.

"I bet you are." I thump down the iron, it hisses, and steam rises to the ceiling. "I can always tell when women are carrying. Sometimes I can tell an hour after it happens."

"I'm sure you can, Queenie, but I'll have you know my husband is dead."

"When does a woman need a husband to catch herself a baby?" I say back.

"You shouldn't say such things," she says, and her cheeks turn redder.

"Only a fool don't know she be pregnant," I say and pick up the iron and push it over one of Miss Gussie's blouses.

The whole time I feel Clancy staring hard at me.

"When did you say Hart came home on leave?" asks Miss Gussie.

"May," says Clancy. "The whole month."

"Well, can't you add it up yourself?" Miss Gussie lets out another long sigh. "You used to be a whiz in math. When was your last period?"

"Well, let's see." Clancy sets down the ladle. "I'm not sure. I know I didn't have one last month, but I figured it was from the shock."

"It could be," says Miss Gussie. "But, knowing you, it's not."

"It ain't shock," I say.

"Maybe I should see Dr. Putnam?" Clancy says.

"It wouldn't hurt," says Miss Gussie, staring at her harder. "Let's just hope your emotions are making you late. Because the last thing you need is a baby."

"Five dollars say she carrying," I say, and they all look at me.

The next morning she pees in a jar. Then she gets dressed and takes the jar to the doctor, who tells her what I already know, to expect the baby near the end of February.

"You owe me five dollars," I say, thinking February is a hard time to bring a baby. Winter babies always get the croup and never grow right.

"I knew it," says Miss Gussie. "How in the world are you going to raise two children without a daddy?"

"You did," Clancy says.

"That was different!"

Clancy pressed her lips together. "I'll find a way. And you'll help me, won't you, Mother?"

"Don't you count on me," Miss Gussie says. "I'm old. I don't have that many years left."

"At least I have something left of Hart."

"Oh, for goodness sake, Clancy!" hollers Miss Gussie. "You've already got Violet. You should've been more careful when Hart was on leave, and that's that."

"I wasn't thinking about being careful," says Clancy, her eyes filling with tears. "I was worried sick about my husband."

"You should've told me right off the bat about this baby," Miss Gussie says and shakes her head. In a minute she goes out into the garden to dig.

"You knew you was pregnant before you came here," I tell her later, and she nods.

We're in the garden picking tomatoes. Violet's out here, too. We are getting ready to can tomato juice. Miss Gussie's laying up in the house, a rag on her forehead, says she's got a sick headache, but I know her heart's broke.

"It's like history repeating," she kept telling me.

Clancy looks up at the sky and breathes in air, puffing out her cheeks. Then she blow it out.

"Miss Gussie's mighty upset," I say.

"Oh, she'll get over it," Clancy says. "She just thinks a baby will ruin my life."

"Will it?" Violet says. She hunkers down and snaps off a fat tomato, keeping her eyes on her mama.

I don't say nothing.

"No," says Clancy. "Babies are wonderful. It'll be hard at first. But we'll manage. I'll get a job, and maybe we'll even find us a little house." She pauses and moves deeper into the tomato bush.

After a minute she says, "I'm just dreading what Dorothy'll do."

I hadn't thought of this, but I know it's true.

"That's right," I say. "We'll have to hog-tie Miss Dorothy. She'll have a fit. There's no telling what she'll say."

"What will she say?" asks Violet, turning her face up to me. The fine hairs around her face are backlit by the sun, like fur on an okra.

"Anything bad she can think of," I tell her, looking over at Dorothy's house. "Anything bad at all."

Part Three

Dorothy

1967

Sister went into labor on Valentine's Day, late in the afternoon, and I drove her to the hospital. I was already upset. Last night the colored school burned. Now nigras would go to school, shoulder-to-shoulder, with my sweet children. And there was nothing I could do about it. All of the private schools were in Nashville, and we didn't have enough money for that.

So you could see why it burned me up when Queenie insisted upon going to the hospital with us. She was still wearing her apron, and she filled up the car with the smell of green onions. She'd been right in the middle of stuffing a hen. She sat right next to me, but I kept my mouth shut. Mother Dear and Violet were in the backseat with Sister, who was moaning, "Ohhhh." I pressed my foot against the accelerator. Not because I was in any special rush. I couldn't stand her screaming.

"Can't you hurry?" said Mother Dear, which irritated me just the least, what with my foot smack to the floorboard. As if I had any control over speed limits. We got to the hospital with time to spare. The nurses guided us to the shabby waiting room in obstetrics, which had not changed one iota since I delivered Bitsy in '53. The same old red vinyl chairs. The same plastic plants. The same casement windows with the yellow and brown geometric curtains. The same view of the doctors' parking lot. Dr. Haynes drove a little white sporty thing. Dr. Loring drove the blue Eldorado. Dr. Putnam—Sister's doctor, my doctor, too—drove the long brown Lincoln. I drummed my fingers on the red vinyl and thought of all I needed to be doing elsewhere. Figuring Albert's payroll. Vacuuming under the beds. (My maid, Dauphine, wasn't worth killing. Let me be the first to tell you that she never polished the furniture. Always used a feather duster, scattered lint like so much radiation into the air. These days, if you wanted a clean house, you were better off doing it yourself, believe you me.) Aside from all this work I needed to be doing, it made me edgy to see Mother Dear's blood pressure shoot up as she paced the floor. I could tell it was climbing fast the way her cheeks got so red, like two polished apples. She put me in mind of an expectant father. All she needed was a box of cigars.

We waited and waited. Across the hall, the door to the delivery room was shut. Violet pressed her ear against it. The nurses had said they would bend the rules and let her stay. I thought it was against the law for a minor to do what Violet was doing, but I held my tongue. My own children had stayed home with Dauphine.

I wondered if I should phone Albert. This morning, before breakfast, he had given me a box of dime store chocolates, fresh, not stale. "Happy Valentine's Day," he'd said, planting a clumsy, wet kiss on my cheek.

"Oh, how sweet," I answered automatically. But I longed to say: "Ask me how I'm feeling, Albert. Let me tell you how sick and tired I am." And it was a fact and a half. I was sick and tired of everything. Of Sister's huge stomach, her swollen ankles, and Mother Dear fluttering, a moth drawn to the huge moon of Sister's belly.

The labor room door whooshed open, and Violet jumped back. A nurse rushed out, carrying a wailing baby, Sister's baby. The blanket was white, so I couldn't tell if the child was a boy or a girl. They were all rooting for a boy, but I wasn't. I would have sold my soul for Sister to have another girl. I could just see a baby boy knocking Mack out of first place with Mother Dear. It just irritated me to pieces the way Bitsy sat back and let Violet take over. Bitsy had no fight in her.

"Is it a girl or a boy?" Violet asked.

"A girl," said the nurse. She walked on two erasers, squeaking on the tile, and turned into the nursery. She shut the glass door with her free hand to keep germs from reaching Sister's precious. Mother Dear and Violet stared through the window, watching the nurse weigh and measure the screaming infant, who waved her little fists at all of us, as if she were furious. Her legs wheeled, plump and full, and I was swept away by an urge to have another child of my own. I spread my fingers against the glass and told myself *this too shall pass.* The child was beautiful and not like the Joneses at all. If she was a Jones. We had only Sister's word to go on. The baby had curly blond hair, a surprising amount of it, and translucent fingernails, soft as new shells. Her eyes were squeezed shut, but I could clearly see Sister's features—the round forehead, the small nose, I conjured up an image of Hart Jones—those dark eyes, bowed legs, hair slicked back with salad oil. Violet was her daddy made over.

"She's so tiny, so perfect," said Mother Dear. Her voice reeked of love.

"She sure is," echoed Queenie, who had never, as far as I

knew, disagreed with my mother. Only with me. I was the one
she hated.

"She puts me in mind of Clancy Jane when she was a
baby," said Mother Dear, leaning closer to the glass, no doubt
counting toes and fingers. Mother Dear had always loved new-
borns. She took right over, diapering the child whether it
needed it or not. And she was right there at the first whimper,
springing out of bed and heating up a bottle. She spoiled my
Bitsy and then had the nerve to say I ignored her. It was common knowledge that you had to pull back from a demanding
child. Oh, everything was always my fault! Only Sister was pure
and perfect, as if a near illegitimate birth, Violet's, didn't count.
And now Sister had delivered the child of a dead man. You
couldn't tell me this was normal behavior for a grown woman.

"Does she look like me any?" asked Violet, standing on her
toes, peering into the nursery.

"She sure does," said Mother Dear, who had never seen
Violet as an infant but seemed to have forgotten this fact. The
older she got, the more memories she invented. But it was use-
less to make her admit it. Mother Dear smiled at her new
grandchild, her eyes filled just the slightest bit, and she threw
one arm around Violet, the other around Queenie. "It's just
the *sweetest,* saddest thing I've ever seen," she said.

I just stood there holding my tongue, with no one's arms
around me, telling myself she would snap out of it. A girl was a
girl was a girl. And, thank you, Jesus, I had given birth to
Mother Dear's only grandson. I had no intention of letting her
forget it.

*F*ebruary was a dark month, with the nights falling early, cold
and blank. The stars were hard chips of stellar ice. The lights in

Mother Dear's kitchen burned continuously, although I could not imagine why—Sister was breast-feeding her little precious, which erased the need for formula and sterilized bottles. Sometimes I caught a glimpse of Mother Dear's silver hair as she passed in front of the windows. The vision did not comfort me. Her backyard stretched wide and empty, her garden stalled, feeding itself from deep roots, waiting for spring.

If she had not lost interest in gardening, that was.

I walked over there once a day just to see what was going on, and, without fail, I was sickened at the way she hovered around Sister. *Let me try to burp her,* she said. *Let me rock her a bit longer. Let me try some sugar water.*

Sister played up to her, never raised her voice no matter how much Mother Dear carried on and spoiled the baby. Sister named her daughter Augusta Dee, which told me everything I needed to know. I would never have named a child of mine Augusta Dee. What would you call her—Augie? Usta? Gussie? I sat back and waited. Sister said, "I've decided to call her Dede." If you ask me, Dede is a name for a poodle, not a blond twerp of a girl. Anyway, no one knew where the Dee/Dede had come from. We'd never known a soul named that, except Sandra Dee, and we didn't exactly *know* her. My personal opinion was that Sister was trying to kill two birds with one stone. She got to call her baby what she wanted—Dede and not Augusta, which was an old lady name. She's planned it the whole time. Let me tell you one thing, she might have fooled Mother Dear into thinking she had a genuine namesake, but she hadn't fooled me. It was a plot of Sister's to get all of our mother's love.

But you should have heard Mother Dear. She went around saying Augusta Dee this, Augusta Dee that until I wanted to scream or go stick pins in my eyes. The old fool didn't know she'd been tricked.

Now I honestly thought Violet would get shoved aside, that she would hate the baby, but she mooned over Dede. The truth was, Sister could not handle a newborn baby without Mother Dear and Violet, even though I longed to see her try. She would fail. It was a fact and a half. All Sister did was eat, change clothes, and feed the baby. She moved around the house like she was bone china and could not be touched. Even her skin took on a porcelain sheen.

My own skin was pale, and the circles beneath my eyes were slightly bruised and yellow, as if I had slowly soured, like old fruit. But I was not old. I was thirty-five, not a day older, and if it were not for my tipped womb, I would already be pregnant with a child of my own. A child Mother Dear would pet and make over. A favorite grandchild. She could have loved me if she'd wanted to. I wasn't a difficult person. I wasn't hard to love. I wasn't petty and jealous. I knew it looked that way. I had always spoken my mind, had always told the truth, but I was learning that people hated you for it. Sister told you what you wanted to hear. She told lies. But no one ever called her a liar. That was why I was so honest. Standing in Sister's shadow had marked me, made me turn in the opposite direction, and this was a fact and a half.

Listen to me and listen good: if I'd been Mother Dear's only child, I would have been her least favorite. There were some ugly truths about Mother Dear, and the first truth was she out and out did not like me. If I wanted, I could stand here and name off times, places, and dates she had let me down. Like the time I had that lump in my breast and I was so scared and she would not drive me to the doctor. No, she had to watch *General Hospital* and see if Audrey would get Steve back. Now

I ask you, is this a motherly thing to do? If anyone from her Sunday school class had to get a lump cut out of their breast, Mother Dear would have volunteered to help. At the least she would have made a big pot roast and brought it over. And when I was pregnant, she acted as if I were a cow that would lumber out to the pasture and give birth after a few grunts. I will not even go into how she hardly spent the night with me after my babies were born. You could not dig her out of her house. She couldn't cook me a meal because she was too busy making things for shut-ins and sicklings down at church.

This grated on me: throughout Sister's whole pregnancy, I had walked over to Mother Dear's to check on things. Queenie was always ironing, watching *Search for Tomorrow,* and Mother Dear would be telling Sister one old wives' tales after the other. Her favorite: "Don't raise your arms over your head or you'll wrap the cord around the baby's neck." Sometimes I wished Sister had reached high, just to get Mother Dear's goat, but I think she half believed all those tales. Why else would she have kept her hands folded on her lap?

Queenie and Mother Dear cooked Sister's favorite dishes: spaghetti and meatballs, lasagna, anything with oregano. She grew huge. I thought she might float, her heels rising from the ground, lifting into the cool wintry air, gliding over the town. A breeze would pull her all the way to the Eastern shore, where she would meet a handsome stranger, fall in love, and we would never see her again. Never, ever, ever.

You see how far that notion got me.

Well, at least I had a full, rich life. I had my bridge club, and Sister didn't even know how to play the game. My club was going to Panama City, Florida, in April. I told myself what a lucky woman I was. Getting to take a trip without a husband and kids tagging along. Even so, there was a small, dark part of myself that hated the notion of leaving Mother Dear and Sister alone. They reminded me of best friends, always touching, fixing each other's hair, shopping at the grocery, going to church. I think they were in love.

All through March, I watched Mother Dear watch Sister nurse Dede, her eyes filling with a pure sort of love. I got so depressed over my tipped womb I could barely move. I had this picture of it flopping back and forth like an empty douche bag. Oh, I knew another baby wouldn't change things. Dede would assume the role of queen bee and my third child, girl or boy, would play second fiddle, be shuffled aside, less important than Bitsy even. I was in the kitchen thinking about this, making a pot of tea, when the doorbell rang. I was wearing my bathrobe, so I just cracked open the door, to make sure it was not a peddler. When I saw who was standing on my porch, two little white boys, I opened the door all the way. The boys held a box full of squirming Dalmatian puppies.

"We're selling them for a nickel, Mrs. McDougal," one of them said, reaching into the box and pulling out the fattest one. He turned it upside down, and said, "This one's a girl."

I knew Mack and Bitsy would get a kick out of having a puppy, so I went back into the house for my purse. I found a quarter. "This is all I have," I called out. "Unless you have change for a dollar."

"We'll take the quarter," said the boy, handing me the dog.

But my children were not thrilled. They thought they were too old for a dog. I was the one who had to drag herself out of bed fifteen times a night to let the animal go outside to urinate. It was just like having a new baby in the house. The dog had a million black dots, and I started calling her Domino. She had the pinkest tongue, and I liked the way her toenails snicked into the linoleum.

Having a dog made me think of the first puppy Sister ever owned. She couldn't have been more than four years old. It was a white dog, with long fluffy hair, and Sister called her Smarty Pants. Well, one summer Smarty Pants took sick and died, and Mother Dear buried her in the backyard. That summer, there was a drought, and the ground was so hard Mother Dear could not get the hole very deep. She and Sister just piled a bunch of rocks over the grave. Sister put some flowers, too, I think. One week later, we woke up and found snatches of white fur all over the yard. Sister was going on and on about Smarty Pants coming back to life, but Papa said no, that a 'possum had dug up the body.

"You have to bury them deep," Papa said.

Even though I had the puppy to cheer me up, I started getting real, real blue. It was the sort of blue that made me want to reach up and wring my own neck. I had suffered from blue spells as long as I could remember, but this depression was hard and solid. I felt like a great sow, an ugly troll, and I wondered if I smelled bad, too. I went one whole week without shaving my legs. Albert did not say one word, but he kept his distance. One night I rubbed my thigh against his, and he jerked away.

"Ouch!" he hollered.

"What's wrong?" I asked.

"Your legs feel just like my daddy's used to."

I opened my mouth, but could not speak. My feelings were hurt. I racked my brain trying to remember if Albert's daddy had hairy legs. After a minute I said, "You used to sleep with your daddy?"

"Sometimes," he said. "When he and Mama were fighting."

"Did they fight a lot?"

"Not really."

"Oh," I said. But I began to wonder if I really did have legs like a man's. I got out of bed and went to the bathroom. To tell the truth, I did not have slender, pretty legs. The least I could do was keep them shaved. I rubbed lotion on my legs, then I sheared off the black hairs. (In case you hadn't noticed, I am not a natural blond.) I wiped off all of the stray flecks with a clean towel. On impulse, I sprayed perfume on my throat. When I got back in bed, Albert ignored me. He was stretched out on his back, his hands calmly resting at his sides. After a minute, I brushed my leg against his thigh.

He flinched. "Dorothy, I swear. You're ice cold."

"Cold but smooth," I said. Then I rolled towards him. I wrapped my legs around him and locked my ankles together. Listen, this was not easy. I had short legs, and Albert was a wide man.

"Oof!" said Albert.

I could not tell if he was pleased or displeased. But I'd already gone too far. I held on tight and tried to feel for a reaction. His whole belly was soft and puffed as dough. Risen dough, I thought. Risen yet unrisen. Never mind. I had all the time in the world. I pictured Albert's huge belly as the dial of a clock, his private parts pointing to an incorrect time.

"Ice!" he hissed, trying to push me away. "A block of ice!"

"If you don't want my strawberries," I said into his face, "then don't touch my vine."

"I *didn't* touch it!"

"Did, too," I said, but I felt like a fool. When I rolled off from him and inched over to my side of the bed, he heaved a great sigh. The whole mattress shook. Doomed, I thought. You are doomed. Your mother does not want you and now your husband. Your children don't like you much, either. Poor, poor little Dorothy. My heart sank low in my chest, like a drowned moon.

*M*ost days, I stationed myself beside the living room window, which overlooked Mother Dear's front yard. I watched them come and go with the baby, shuffling to and from the grocery, the baby doctor. Rather than ride to school with Mack and Bitsy—Mack had a used Firebird—Violet caught the bus. Kids leaned out the windows and waved to her. "Violet! Hey, Violet!" they yelled. "I saved you a seat!" All of my worst fears had come true. I wanted to think she was unpopular, a loner, the sort of girl other children pitied, in spite of an initial period of popularity, but I was wrong. She was not a feminine child, to my mind. Her features were too broad to be considered cute or pretty. But she seemed to have a way with people, lots of girlfriends, which shocked me, and once I saw Meathead Wentworth climb off the bus and disappear inside Mother Dear's house. When I mentioned it later to Bitsy, she just scowled.

Mother Dear phoned when she wanted to talk, rather than visiting in person, and me just next door. One day she called, and I was so sad and tired, I could not carry on a conversation. My comments were reduced to throat growls: "Hmmm." "Hmmm?" "Hmm*mmmmm*." "*Hm!*" "Mmmhum."

"Why are you so quiet? Are you sick?" Mother Dear asked.

I cleared my throat. "A little," I said.

"Well, can I do anything?" she asked.

"Now that you mention it," I said, "I've been craving a pot of your chicken soup."

Silence. In the background, I heard Dede fussing. I coughed into the phone.

"Well, Queenie and I are making lasagna. If you want some, just send Mack or Bitsy over for it."

"Lasagna? You know I don't eat Italian!" I almost burst into tears. I knew then I was in real bad trouble. The mental kind, but I couldn't help myself.

"It's all I can offer," said Mother Dear. "It's all I have."

"Sister always loved Italian," I said. Mother Dear *knew* I hated anything with oregano.

"If you need me," she said, "just holler."

I hung up the phone and patted Domino and tried to figure out what to do. I walked into the bathroom, locked the door, and opened Albert's razor. The blade was dotted with dark hairs. Oh, I thought, it's all right for you to have stubble. But not me. Not little Dorothy. I blew hard, the hairs floated into the sink like confetti, and I went to work on myself.

Nobody noticed a damn thing, except Domino, who licked my wounds.

I lost track of time. Whole days went by. By the time Mother Dear phoned, I was running a temperature. I had already been to the doctor. "I'm sick as a dog," I told Mother Dear.

Now. This was the gospel truth. I had a fever of 101, and I knew it was not blood-poisoning like Dr. Hammond said.

"Do you think you can come over for a day, just to help me get on my feet?" I asked.

Silence. "Well, I just bought me a roast, and I have to cook it for a Sunday school party," said my Mother Dear.

I started trembling. I knew I was going to die.

"Could you cook it at my house?" I said. My oven's just as

good as yours. Or let Queenie cook it for you. She isn't sick, is she?"

"Well, that's not the point," said Mother Dear.

"And what is the point?" I twisted the telephone cord around my fingers, watching my skin flush pink, then red.

"It's not her Sunday school party."

"Then let Sister cook it."

"Clancy Jane has enough to do."

I answered her with silence. I had this image of my mouth filling with words. I swallowed hard.

"Dorothy? You still there?"

"I'm here. But I don't know for how long."

"Oh, Dorothy."

"Please help me, Mother Dear. I wouldn't ask if I weren't desperate. I need my Mother Dear."

"Honey, you don't need me."

"I do, too!"

"You never have before. And you don't know what all I've got to do. Put Bitsy on the phone. Let me speak to her."

"She's not your daughter!" I shouted. "She's nothing but a grandchild."

"What?" Mother Dear's voice sounded small. "What did you say?"

"I don't suppose I have a mother," I said, just as mean as I could.

Mother Dear breathed into the phone. "Well," she finally said. Her voice was crisp around the edges. "If that's how you feel."

"Yes. That's how I feel. I feel that you have but one child. And it's not me."

I waited for her to deny it, but she had already hung up. I knew I was mental. I said things I didn't mean, but I couldn't seem to stop or to swallow them fast enough. The words jumped out of my mouth like frogs. I wished I could have taken back what I'd said, but of course it was too late. I gripped the receiver and banged it hard against my forehead. My whole skull flooded with pain. From the floor, Domino looked up at me and whined.

"You're better off without me," I told her and smacked myself again. I saw stars, a burst of white and yellow light, and then nothing but deep black space.

They found me on the floor, bruised and unconscious. Albert and the children. When Bitsy started to get Mother Dear, I screamed, "No! Not her!"

Albert looked puzzled. Then his face flooded with understanding. He knelt beside me and asked if I had been attacked. He whispered it in my ear, and I wanted to slap his face for thinking something like that.

"Dear Lord, no," I said. "I just fainted. I must've hit my head. Now help me up, if you don't mind. Bitsy, go get me an ice pack. A great big one."

"But your forehead," Albert said. "Maybe we should call the doctor. You're all bloody and gashed."

"I must have cracked it on the floor." I reached up to my scalp. I didn't know if it would heal by the time I left for Florida. When women my age turned up with gashes, it caused gossip. It usually meant one of two things: wife beating or alcoholism. I suffered from neither. I liked my daiquiris, but I had never fallen down drunk.

Bitsy brought the ice, and Albert fluttered around me until I stared him down. I was angry at Mother Dear, angry at Sister, angry at myself for being someone they could not love. I carried my ice into the bathroom and shaved my legs. Not that there was a need to. With my face swollen and bloody, Albert wouldn't have touched me with a ten-foot pole. I finished shaving and did not stare at the silver blade. I made up my mind then and there that I was through with the both of them.

*T*en days later, I left for Panama City. The wound had healed to a red line, the shape of a half-moon. It was surrounded by a yellow and purple bruise, which was easily concealed with foundation. I teased my bangs, fluffing them forward. You wouldn't even have noticed it if you saw me on the street.

There were twelve women in my bridge club, most of them wives of successful men. They were not what I would call out-and-out friends, as we did not visit or talk on the phone. We were serious bridge players, dead serious. We even went to tournaments. Master points were awarded to the winners. Then we were rated according to our total points. My goal was to be a Life Master.

We reached Panama City late in the afternoon. We had reservations at a place called the Hawaiian Inn. I had never been to Hawaii, but this hotel seemed authentic. When we entered the lobby, an Oriental boy placed leis around our necks. I thought that was a nice touch. Mine was hot pink. A pretty blond girl served punch into Dixie cups. I took a sip and looked around the lobby. It was full of live plants, island music, grass huts. The hotel was U-shaped, and every room had a gulf view.

I shared a room on the third floor with Cordy Lollar, whose red-necked husband had made a fortune in the wholesale fruit business. Cordy was a sweet, long-legged brunette with huge green eyes. She had two daughters who kept getting into trouble. We tossed a quarter to see who would get the bed next to the balcony, and she won. She acted flustered, but I told her I was just as happy to be near the bathroom. Next door was Betty

Wentworth, Meathead's mother, in her corner suite. It had a living room and wet bar and cost a fortune. Betty was the richest woman in Crystal Falls. Her husband was a big-shot banker, and she'd been to Rio and everywhere. We all followed her lead, which irritated me just the least. That was why we were in Panama City—she was in the market for a beach house. Even if you hated Betty, you had to be sweet or else you'd find yourself blackballed from everything that mattered in Crystal Falls. She was that powerful. That's one reason I was so good to her son. I never called him Meathead. His true name was Claude Edmund Wentworth IV. I called him Claude. He was Betty's only child, but she was so busy flitting here and there, she didn't seem to notice him. When he came to see Bitsy, it was me who baked him cookies. It was me who drove him to the dentist that time he chipped a tooth. It was me who fed him. "Claude, do you want to stay for supper?" I'd say. "Yes, ma'am," he'd say. Let me tell you the truth, I treated him like a son. I tried to be everything his mother wasn't. Even though Claude and Bitsy were young, I was thinking ahead. I had my eye on the IV at the end of his name. I wanted my daughter's future to be secure, and I didn't care if it took both of us to make that happen.

Cordy and I unpacked. Then we dressed in our swimsuits and rode in the elevator to the pool. One by one the ladies drifted down. We played bridge until lunch. Then we went into the restaurant and ordered cute pineapple boats full of chicken salad. After that we divided up into cars and drove to the shopping center, where we bought identical silk bandannas, in twelve different colors. Cordy picked out a powder blue one; Betty's was lemon yellow; I almost got stuck with red before Judy Jules, who was Betty's best friend and roommate, swapped with me. Judy loved red. So I ended up with turquoise, which darkened my eyes and made me feel pretty for once.

We spent the rest of the afternoon lounging around the pool, greased and glistening, smelling of coconut oil, which attracted sweat bees. I lifted my arm to apply the oil. You would barely notice my scars. A suntan was just what I needed. I was white and pale. I lowered the straps on my suit and pushed my sunglasses, a new pair of Foster Grants, over my nose. I settled back, blinking at three gulls wheeling over the pool. The other women lay scattered about. I heard the faint jingle of Betty Wentworth's charm bracelet, the clink of ice in Cordy's gin and tonic. We had all been through the family wars; we had nearly raised our children and were now bone-tired. All we wanted was a week of sun, a few decent games of bridge, a strong piña colada.

That was when I noticed the blond lifeguard in the wrap-around Foster Grants, what we sold at the dime store. He sat on a wooden perch, staring in my direction. His muscles seemed inflated beneath his suntan. His skin was golden brown, like a chicken roasted to perfection. There was a strip of white oxide paste on his nose. I pretended to sleep. There was no hurry. Not with me and my scars, my enormous thighs. It was one thing to show your body at the pool to other women; it was yet another thing to show it to your husband. But I could not imagine unveiling myself to a strange man. I did not even look at myself when I took a bath, it was so awful.

The lifeguard walked toward me, and I shut my eyes. After all these years with Albert, after decades of his soft, doughy body, with his "Yes, honey's" and "No, honey's," I had, in a word, adjusted. Perspiration slid down my backbone. The sun was burning me up, and I thought I would have to buy a can of

Solarcaine. I thought I would tell the young lifeguard that I was flattered but way too old for him.

He walked past my chair, walked past Cordy Lollar's chair, and stopped beside Betty Wentworth. His knee was right next to her nose. She lowered her sunglasses, reached up, as if to adjust her lemon yellow bandanna, and palmed her room key into his hand. He smiled. My mouth fell open. I looked around, but none of the other women had seen. The lifeguard walked away, tossing the key, and climbed back on his wooden perch.

I could have told you what would happen. That afternoon Betty developed a severe migraine. Judy Jules knocked on our door to ask if she could spend the evening with us. "Betty's got one of her sick headaches," she said.

"You can stay with us tonight," Cordy said. "That's all right, isn't it, Dorothy?"

"Why certainly," I said, giving them one of my smiles. But I declined to join them for a seafood supper at the Brass Pelican. I told them I had a headache of my own. After they left, wearing sundresses too young for them, I played solitaire. I spread the cards on the bed, snapping them between my thumb and forefinger. It wasn't long before I heard someone knocking on the door to Betty's suite. Then: footsteps, the door creaked open, silence, a woman's throaty laughter. Betty's laughter. "Well, well," she said. "How nice we look. Do come in."

At last the door slammed, and that made me wonder how long it would be before the headboard began slamming against the wall, my wall, before passionate groans seeped through the Sheetrock. But no. The headboards at the Hawaiian Inn were bolted to the walls. All I could think of was how that boy must smell. I imagined his dark body, the shocking white buttocks, the scent of sweat, Betty's gin, suntan oil. The room next door was so quiet I didn't even hear the scratch of the television.

What were they doing?

I scooped up the cards and shuffled them. The noise startled me, so I set the deck on the nightstand. I walked to the balcony, opened the sliding doors, and let in a gush of salty air. It smelled of blue water, chlorine and sun, coconut oil and sweat. I glanced at the balcony next door, thinking of Betty Wentworth doing whatever she was doing in her silent room and getting away with it. Below, three stories down, the pool glowed like green ice. I gripped the metal rail and stared at the empty lifeguard perch, the POOL CLOSED sign, the umbrella tables, the plastic lounge chairs. The palm trees swayed and shimmered, with coconuts growing from their throats. As I stared at the concrete around the pool, I was reminded of the cheap sort of rock officials paved the roads with in Tennessee. The coconuts reminded me of Mother Dear tending her crops, lettuce and spinach, the crunch of it. Just about now Sister would be rocking her baby girl, and Queenie would be cooking eggplant Parmesan. Albert would be stretched out in front of our television watching *Laugh-In*. Bitsy would be doing her homework, and Mack would be listening to records. *Yeah, yeah, yeah,* those hairy men would sing.

It struck me peculiar that other parts of my life were going on elsewhere. At this very moment they were saying things I could not hear, doing things I could not see.

You couldn't stop it, even if you wanted to.

All these lives going on and on, and still I felt cheated. I leaned forward and squeezed the rail to keep from jumping. I wanted to go home, and I wanted to stay here. The ocean stretched out, a huge quarry, blue ore, the color of the air, and a breeze stirred up again, spicy and foreign, blowing all the way from the Mexican shore, and I told myself, *Your time will come, little Dorothy. Your time will come.*

Miss Gussie

1967

I got up early every morning and drank coffee on my screened porch just to listen to the birds, to watch the pink sun come up behind the mountains. My bones snapped and creaked like old wicker. Clancy Jane and her girls were still asleep, and the house fairly breathed with them. I loved having a baby in the house. Augusta Dee was the most wide-awake child I'd ever seen, and when I held her in my lap, she would stare at me with those blue eyes. Sometimes she put me in mind of Charlie, before the war changed everything. At night, she made noises in her sleep, and I could tell she was happy, that she would have a pretty voice and sing so loud and clear.

From the beginning Dorothy had a throat full of sour notes.

Next door, her house was dark and cold-looking, like the inside of a gas stove. Since she'd gotten back from Florida, she'd had the fidgets. The decorating bug. She hired this new decorator, Mr. Frank everyone called him. He had Dorothy coming and going. She complained behind his back, calling him names which weren't true in the least. Mr. Frank had the patience of a saint.

First, it was wallpaper. Books and books of these leathery pages. Dorothy couldn't make up her mind. She'd pick one, then two minutes later she'd switch. Then he would write down all of her new choices and tote the books back to his car and drive home. He would no sooner leave her driveway than she'd be on the phone, calling Mr. Frank's wife, saying she had changed her mind, that she wanted the blue gingham wallpaper, not the red plaid.

How those people stood her, I'll never know.

It was the same thing all over again when they picked fabric. Mr. Frank believed in re-covering old furniture, which disappointed Dorothy. She had her heart set on French provincial.

Late one afternoon, she called me over to help her pick out paint samples. Dorothy and I peered down at these little bitty squares of color. She tapped one fingernail against colonial blue. Mr. Frank lifted one eyebrow. His eyes were a strange gray, flecked with hazel.

"It's too pastel, don't you think, Dottie?" he said.

He called her Dottie.

Then he went out to his car and came back with a can and a paintbrush. He slapped a long streak of colonial blue right on her living room wall.

"I like it," Dorothy said, stepping back to stare at the blue splotch.

Mr. Frank sighed. "But, Dottie, this shade of blue isn't for a living room. It's, well, it just isn't done. It's a bedroom color."

Dorothy's face fell.

"I know you had your heart set on it, Dottie."

They decided on pale yellow walls and spent the rest of the day choosing carpet. She had to get new carpet on account of that dog. I was already wore out from days and days of listening to them match up colors.

"What about these taupe tones, Dottie?" he asked.

"I don't know," she said. "Don't you think that ecru is just the least off? More of a coffee than a beige?"

"Hmmmmm," Mr. Frank said and held the sample up to the light. "No, it looks fine in this light. Squint your eyes, Dottie. *Then* tell me if it doesn't match."

On and on and on until my ears swelled shut.

I went on home and found Queenie frying bacon. Clancy had read about a hot bacon dressing for spinach in the paper, and she'd ripped it out, asking Queenie if she minded cooking it for supper. Of course she didn't mind.

Clancy Jane was in the living room, tutoring Mack. She had always been smart. There was no telling what she could have done if she hadn't run off to Louisiana. Mack was a big, handsome boy, and he was about to fail until my Clancy Jane got ahold of him.

"Miss Dorothy get her colors picked out?" asked Queenie.

"I reckon," I said and drew up a glass of tap water. From deep within my house, the pipes banged together.

Queenie didn't answer. She kept turning bacon. Her feelings had been hurt ever since Dorothy returned from Florida. She'd brought everyone a present except for Queenie, which was hateful. She'd brought me a plastic spoon rest, filled with seashells and a baby seahorse, its tail curled tightly, like a wound clock spring.

"You could have brought Queenie something," I'd told Dorothy.

"Why?" She lifted her eyebrows. "I didn't even bring my own maid a souvenir. Why should I bring yours something?"

"You didn't bring Dauphine something?" I said, surprised. "After she took care of your family and did who knows what all while you were in Florida?"

"Listen to me, Mother Dear. You can't be too good to nigras."

"Don't you say that word to me!"

"All right, all right. Let me say *colored* then. Is that better? Lord, Mother Dear. You know you can't be too good to them. The moment you do, they'll steal your silver teaspoons. And from there it's anyone's guess."

"Queenie's honest as the day is long," I said. "And I always figured if someone stole something, they probably needed it more than me."

"You'd fire her in a minute."

"I would not! I would never fire her."

"No? You'd fire me if I stole one of your silver spoons."

I shook my head. It was no use to reason with Dorothy. She had gone through maids like you wouldn't have believed.

Years ago, before Dauphine, there was Opal. Dorothy was perfectly able to wash her own clothes, but she'd sit up and watch her stories or play bridge and make Opal dig through the hampers. One time she told Opal to take her coat to the cleaners. It was a fine coat. Albert had given it to her for Christmas (which is another matter altogether—she is so hard to buy for). The coat was pure leather with a blue fox collar. Then Opal came back and said the coat had been stolen out of her car.

"Hell's bells," snorted Dorothy. "I'm calling the police! You just drove to nigra town and hid it in your house!"

"No, I didn't!" cried Opal.

I believed her.

Dorothy fired the woman and hired Dauphine. Don't ask me how she stood it. She kept to herself, and you never knew what she was thinking, which drove Dorothy crazy. Dorothy wanted everyone to like her, even if she didn't like them. If

Dauphine went to Florida and didn't bring Dorothy back a souvenir, the feathers would fly.

Now Queenie lifted each strip of bacon and set it to drain on paper towels. On the counter there was a bowl of boiled eggs. I rolled up my sleeves and started washing the spinach, snapping off the leggy stems. Clancy Jane and Mack walked into the kitchen. He was hugging a stack of books, and his eyes looked vague and blue.

"Can you help me tomorrow afternoon, Aunt Clancy?" asked Mack. "I've got a big test."

"Sure," she said. "And bring more notebook paper."

"You learning anything?" I said, smiling.

"Yes, Miss Gussie! We're all the way to square roots." He smiled, and all of his teeth showed, white.

"You keep at it," I told him.

"See you tomorrow," said Clancy Jane. Upstairs, little Dede started crying. Mack opened the back door, but he just stood there, his hand on the screen, his eyes following Clancy Jane as she went upstairs to her baby. You could tell he thought Clancy Jane hung the moon.

From the open door, a breeze pushed into the room, cool and watery. Then I saw it, a gray titmouse flying straight through the door, over Mack's outstretched arm and into the kitchen. Queenie jumped away from the stove and screamed. I screamed. The titmouse fluttered against the ceiling and squawked at us, fussing. Mack grabbed a broom and started swatting the air, but the terrified bird swooped toward the hallway, up the stairs.

"I ain't going up there," said Queenie, shaking her head. "You know what a bird in the house means, and I ain't going up there."

Mack was already in the hallway, going upstairs to hunt that titmouse. He turned, gripping the broom, and faced Queenie.

"What's it mean?" he asked.

She looked up at the ceiling. "You got to make it fly out the same door it fly in," she said. "Or it mean somebody is going to die."

"Oh, it doesn't!" I said. "But we've got to get it out or we'll have lice all over the place."

"It *does* mean it, too," she said and shot a long, dark glance at the open door.

It was so silent, so hushed upstairs, I wondered if the bird had found a way out.

"Where do you think it went?" I asked Mack. He shrugged and looked toward the window. He walked over and shook the curtains, but nothing flew out.

Clancy Jane stood in the doorway, the baby on her shoulder. "What's going on?" she asked.

"A bird got in the house," I said.

"Oh, my heavens!" she said, hugging Augusta Dee to her chest.

We looked and looked, but we didn't find the titmouse.

The next morning, Queenie and I were changing sheets in Violet's bedroom, and I noticed something gray beneath the bed. I knelt down, my knees popped like crazy, and I saw the titmouse. It was dead as a doornail, lying on its back, its little feet sticking straight up like brown hooks.

Before I had time to think, I screamed. Queenie came running around the bed. Then she let out a scream. I reached under the bed and picked up the bird. It was hard and stiff already, which sickened me just the least.

"Take it out the way it flew in," Queenie said, stepping backward until she smacked against the wall.

I held the bird by his barbed feet and walked downstairs. I went outside, through the kitchen door, and dropped the titmouse in the trash can.

When I came back inside to wash my hands, Queenie was standing in the hallway. Her hands were folded like she was praying.

"Don't you say one word," I warned her. "Not a single blessed word."

*D*orothy's house was a sight to behold. It was yellow and green, right down to the new avocado-colored appliances. Even her mixer was the same dark green. It must have cost a fortune. She took down all the ceramic roosters in her kitchen and put up lemon-and-avocado-striped wallpaper. She bought herself a mug tree, a spice rack, a set of green cut-glass canisters. You could look right through them and see sugar, flour, coffee, tea bags.

"What are you going to do with your old doodads?" I asked her.

"I don't know," she said. "Why? Do you want them?"

We were in Bitsy's room, taking down the pink Priscilla curtains. Bitsy wanted navy blue walls to set off the white French provincial furniture that Dorothy had bought before Mr. Frank got ahold of her. He was a man of taste, and I suspected he was behind the mug trees and the spice racks. But he talked her into painting Bitsy's room a soft celery green, trimmed in darker green, which is just about as far away from navy as you can get. I thought it looked like mashed lettuce, but I swore up and down I loved it. You had to be that way with Dorothy.

"Why don't you have a yard sale?" I suggested to her, thinking of the one Clancy Jane and me had in New Orleans.

"Heavens *no,*" she said. "I don't want the bother. Besides, my yard isn't for sale." She climbed down the ladder, puffing hard, and balled up the pink curtains. I thought to myself that pink curtains would look sweet in Augusta Dee's room. Not that she had one yet. We'd set up the crib in Clancy Jane's room to make things simple, with her breast-feeding and all.

"I'll tell you what. Why don't you and Sister come over here tonight? We'll eat supper. Dauphine's got a pork roast in the oven. Then we can sit down on the floor and go through these doodads. You and Sister can take what you want."

"Well, that's awful sweet." I looked down at Bitsy's Madame Alexander dolls, covered in plastic. They were piled into boxes. Violet was too old, but I thought of Augusta Dee. In a few years she'd love a doll or two.

"What're you going to do with those dolls?" I asked.

Dorothy turned, her eyes narrowed. "I didn't mean the Madame Alexander dolls, Mother Dear. You can't have those! Why, Bitsy would kill me. Just pick something else. Anything else."

I looked at the gauzy curtains, the stuffed bears, the ballerina prints. I didn't want anything from her, not the least thing.

"Well, I'd better scoot," I said, and Dorothy got this long, blue look on her face.

"Aren't you going to eat supper with me?"

I paused. "Maybe some other time."

"Don't tell me I've gone and hurt your feelings," she said, and dropped the pink curtains on Bitsy's bed.

"No, you haven't," I lied. "I was just curious about those dolls is all. Bitsy never played with them a single time. And I just hate to see them sit up in your attic."

Dorothy blinked at the dolls. "They're not the kind of dolls you play with. You collect them. Meg, Jo, Beth, and Amy.

Marmee, too. *Little Women* dolls. And they *are* hers, Mother Dear. *I* certainly can't decide what to do with them. If it were up to me, I'd give them to you right this instant."

I didn't answer because we both knew Bitsy didn't have a say on anything. No more than Mack or Albert. Dorothy was the king and queen, and everyone else had to bow and scrape. She would kill me for thinking such a thought, but there it was. And, Lordy Jesus, I should have been ashamed for thinking it about my own flesh and blood. There had to be something bad wrong with me.

I walked on home, pausing to stare at my garden, the long, grainy rows, the square sections beneath white plastic, held down by slabs of limestone. That boy was buried under the zinnia bed. I thought of his bones all stretched out in the brown dirt. The white sheet had no doubt gone moldy, black as the soil.

Sometimes I thought the Lord had His reasons, and sometimes I thought He didn't know what was going on. I wanted to ask Him, isn't Dorothy enough? Or are You trying to teach me a lesson? He returned Clancy Jane to me, and I was ever thankful, but I just didn't know what He was getting at.

I thought my Clancy Jane would get herself another man. She was so pretty. She had gotten her figure back and wore her hair long, falling in straight panels to her shoulders. I held my tongue when she hemmed all of her dresses too short, like in those fashion magazines she and Violet were always studying at the drugstore.

Sometimes I pretended that Violet and Augusta Dee were my own babies, that Clancy Jane was their older sister. It was kindly like a second chance. I didn't want it to end. Above me the sky was pale gray, full of clouds, and it smelled like rain. I went inside my house and heard Clancy Jane drilling Mack. Violet was stretched out on the rug, reading a *Seventeen*.

Mack pushed back a hunk of his long blond hair. I could see him years from now, working at his daddy's Ben Franklin, wearing a neat blue tie and a white short-sleeved shirt. Dorothy would never let him get too far away. He'd spend his whole life right here in Crystal Falls. As much as it pained Dorothy to admit it, because of Clancy Jane, his grades had shot up. It looked as if Albert would be able to pull strings to get the boy into a little state college next year. Clancy Jane said it would keep him out of Vietnam.

I pushed open my kitchen window. I heard the wind sift through the trees, turning the air green and thick. I heard the low etch of thunder, then the sudden silk of rain. Behind me Clancy's voice went on and on, and the rain washed down hard, overflowing my gutters. I rubbed my aching back and walked upstairs to wake Augusta Dee, who had slept past her feeding. You had to keep babies on a schedule.

Her crib was in Clancy's room. It was Bitsy's old crib, a walnut model with pink and blue balls that the baby could turn when she was older. Dorothy had let us borrow it. Sometimes she could be sweet like that, when she wasn't jealous-hearted. I stood in the doorway, and lightning flashed through the windows. The room seemed separate from the rest of the house, a closed pocket of air. It smelled so light you could tell there was a baby in the house.

I looked down into the crib. Augusta Dee was on her stomach, with her beautiful round head turned away from the window. I saw the curve of her nose, the tiny nostrils, the long eyelashes against her cheek.

Something was wrong. The yellow blanket wasn't moving.

But the room was dark, so I wasn't sure.

I waited for the regular rise and fall of her chest.

Lordy Jesus. *Don't you let this happen.*

I clasped my hand over my mouth.

Her skin was just the least cool, but I knew I could warm her up. Her body was so limp, like one of Bitsy's rag dolls, cold and saggy, but I sank down in the rocker and rubbed her hands. I started singing: *Jesus loves the little children, all the children in the world, red and yellow, black and white—*

I had to wake her up, get her warm. Breathe, child, breathe.

I rocked faster and faster and the storm whirled by and I wished it was me, it should have been me, and the rain beat against the window and the sky was dark as soil and I planted him alive, he was crying for his mama.

Then people came into the room, people old as Jesus.

"What's happening here?" I hollered. "What are you trying to do?"

They were pulling my fingers apart, trying to get to Augusta Dee, wait a minute, stop it, get away, don't you lay a hand on me, you'd better watch it, that boy is rising from the dead, look yonder, he's got a knife, he's coming for you, he'll get you.

My ears filled with the sound of a million birds, they flew around me, beating and beating their wings. I didn't know where my screams ended and Clancy Jane's began.

Queenie

1967

I just pack up my clothes in a sack and move into Miss Gussie's house. When Miss Dorothy tries to make Clancy go to the funeral home, my blood jells. I feel my neck clog up. Clancy just sits in the dark living room, all the lamps turned off, and stares straight ahead, like she's in a trance. She is all wrapped up in a white, gauzy gown and a red plaid robe what belonged to her papa. Her hair falls into her eyes. She don't pay no attention to her sister, who finally gives up and leaves. When Miss Dorothy walks straight to her car, I know what she's up to. All this time she has been champing at the bit to color-coordinate this funeral.

All Miss Gussie's friends come and bring dishes of food, which I lay out on the dining room table, but nobody here has eat in days and days. Miss Dorothy, she comes over twenty times a day, taking a bite of this, a nibble of that. She eat Jell-O salad, sliced country ham, cornbread, doughnuts, fried chicken, chess pies, beans somebody canned last year. She eat until I think she'll burst wide open. But she don't. She just swells up and gets fat like a sow pig. Her panty hose go swish-scratch.

Mr. Albert, he just sits on the love seat and stares at Clancy. He folds his hands and clears his throat. Hours go by, and he don't hardly move a muscle. Mack sits next to his daddy, his hands folded on his knees. They dressed up in suits. Mack owes a lot to Clancy, since he is getting ready to graduate. He tells me he's going to Tennessee Tech and live in what he call a dorm. Now he won't have to go to Vietnam.

Miss Gussie's the one who's in trouble, real trouble. Even though the doctor come and say Dede die of crib death, Miss Gussie don't believe him. She says it's her own fault, she let that baby sleep too late, that she frittered away time over at Dorothy's house.

Miss Dorothy hears this and her eyes fill, but she don't say nothing.

I hear Miss Gussie crying from her room. I crack open the door and go sit beside her and tell her to shore up, that she got to be strong for Clancy, but her eyes shine like blue glass. She's not listening to me.

People fill up the funeral home. They come up to Clancy and put their fleshy arms around her. They smell old and powdery. They Miss Gussie's friends, women who knew Clancy when she was a child. Miss Dorothy sits on the front row. She can't be still. Every few minutes she gets up and rearranges the flowers. The preacher gets up and talks about angels. Then we drive to the cemetery. Then it's over. We go home. We turn on the TV, but we don't watch our stories. We too heartbroke. Poor Violet, she goes to school with her eyes swolled shut, and then she comes home and sits with her mama in the living room. They hold hands.

"I know what's what," Clancy says. "Don't worry, baby. It's not like last time. I know who's dead and who isn't." Then she breaks down and cries.

Clancy is talking out of her head. I try not to listen. I keep busy by making her a bed on the sofa. A whole week goes by.

She won't leave the living room, keeps the door shut and all the lamps turned off. She won't come out except to go to the bathroom. I change the sheets every day. She won't come out and say it but I know she can't sleep in her old room. Not when that baby died there. You can't blame her. First thing after the funeral I took that crib apart with a screwdriver. Carried it up to the attic.

One afternoon I hear Violet talking to Mack. She takes him aside and asks if she can borrow his record player. When he looks at her funny, she says it helped her mama one time before. I can guess what time that was.

"Sure," he says. He goes back home and brings back the record player and a stack of black records. Mr. Albert comes over too, carrying a box of albums. Miss Dorothy's playing bridge, or else he wouldn't be here.

In a little while I hear some music start up. Frank Sinatra's girl, she's singing about how *These boots are made for walkin', and that's just what they'll do, one of these days these boots are gonna walk all over you. Yeah.*

I hope they'll play my girl, Diana Ross, singing one sad song after the other, or Aretha Franklin, *R-E-S-P-E-C-T.*

*M*iss Gussie gets out of bed and spends all day in her garden. She plants and weeds and hoes. I see that she is working around the border, planting orange and yellow marigolds. She plants those every year, and I think that's a good sign.

Things be working out for Violet, too. She stays after school every afternoon, since she's in this thing call a play, something about a wedding. She plays a girl named Frankie. Bitsy plays somebody named Janice. Now I remember. *Member of the Wedding* is what the play is.

The nights Miss Dorothy's not home, when she's out playing bridge, Mr. Albert comes over. He brings a stack of records each time from his and Miss Dorothy's attic. Sometime he bring candy for Miss Gussie and me. It's like everybody love Clancy so much they trying to hold her up and make her get over this grief. Even Miss Dorothy comes over here two, three times a day since the funeral. When she find Mack or Mr. Albert here, she sulls up and says, "Let's don't wear out our welcome. And Sister needs her rest."

One of Clancy's old girlfriends, Martha Sue Moody, she comes to pay her respect. She wear out her welcome fast with me. I don't even recognize her at first, and I almost don't let her in the house. She looks like one of them hippies I see on TV.

"Don't you remember me, Queenie?" she says behind the screen door, and I like to fall down. She got long brown hair parted down the middle. She got round glasses made of gold wire. She got on blue jeans all sewed with patches and a wrinkled blouse that fall to her knees.

"Queenie?" she says again and smiles. "Wow, Queenie."

My lips go numb. I just open the door and nod, like I'm too grieved to talk. When she passes by, I catch a strong whiff of something bad. She used to be so clean and wear ruffles to church, and now she's a hippie and done broke her mama's heart. She and Clancy have been friends since they was babies. They went to vacation Bible school every summer. I look down and see that Martha Sue's wearing sandals, and she's painted blue daisies on her toenails.

I smell trouble, and it smell just like Martha Sue Moody, who now call herself Sunshine Paisley. You call her Martha Sue and she'll ignore you. Every single day this big van stops in front of Miss Gussie's house. The van painted with rainbows, flowers, and stars. Martha Sue hops out in the same old jeans. The man driving look like Jesus. He got a beard down to here and greasy black hair sticking to his back. He got round glasses that make his eyes look too small for his face. He makes my blood turn to ice. All that dirt and hair, like a wild animal. His window be rolled down, and I notice that he's wearing a fringed shirt, like a cowboy's, with something like

painted on the front.

Sunshine Paisley Martha Sue walks into the house. She looks up at me and say, "Peace, Queenie," and spread her fingers into a V. She's brought a bunch more records for Clancy.

"Who's that man?" I ask, peering out the window, watching the van disappear around a corner. Martha Sue's mama just live a few blocks away.

"That's Amos," she says. "He's my old man."

"He don't look so old to me." I keep staring out the window. The van's gone.

She laughs. "He's my *man*, Queenie. You know, like boyfriend? We met at Berkeley."

"Is that a fact?" I'm afraid to ask about this Berkeley. I know about hippies. They're against the war. I've seen it all on the TV. I know about peaceful demonstrations. How they turn the hoses on you and let loose they dogs. I know these hippies don't have nothing to do with me. What does have to do with me, I hold to myself. I don't speak a word. I keep it all inside. I just think about it.

I think about riding to Nashville in 1948. Me and Miss Gussie were taking Mr. Charlie to the VA hospital to get his lungs checked. We couldn't find the hospital and kept driving in circles. Finally we took a bus. The driver made me sit in the back. Miss Gussie followed me. There wasn't no room to sit, so we stood up and held on to plastic hooks. The colored people stared at us but they didn't say nothing. Mr. Charlie was too sick to care. I think about the side door at the picture show here in Crystal Falls, the door that leads one way, straight to the balcony, the colored section.

I think about that pitiful baby's coffin, no bigger than a toy box. I think about Jackie Kennedy losing all those babies, then losing the President. I think about Myrlie Evers and how she's bound to miss Medgar, just like I miss Talley. I think about him bringing bombs to the white soldiers. I think about those four little girls in Birmingham, getting killed by a bomb while they sang at Sunday school.

I think about those three young men killed in Philadel-phia—not Pennsylvania but Mississippi. Two were white boys. It's a war right here, and as much as I love Miss Gussie, she's still a Miss, and I'm plain old Queenie. These things boil on and on in my mind. But I never speak a word.

"Does Gussie pay your social security?" Sunshine Paisley Martha Sue now wants to know.

"My social *what*?" I say.

"Oh, never mind," she says. "I'll say something about it to Clancy. She'll straighten things out." She walks over to the refrigerator and opens it like she lives here. She stands on one

leg and looks inside and lets all the cold air blow out. Then she
grabs an apple and goes into the living room to see Clancy. In
a minute I hear the record player start up. The music runs clear
up my spine and sets my teeth on edge. I don't know where she
found these records, but these people can't sing. They can't
play the guitar, either.

*A*ll I know is I've done some checking. Preacher tends the
yard next door to the Moodys, and he say Martha Sue been
married twice since 1955. She ran off to California with her
second husband, a trailer salesman. She got rid of him and
turned herself into a hippie. Trash is all, just plain trash. Now
she's back home making her poor mama and daddy cry every
night. She brought this woolly friend from San Francisco,
Amos, and they sleep in his van. Preacher says it's been painted
with something called Day-Glo, and they park it in the Moodys'
driveway. Martha Sue's people must be blind. When Amos roll
down the windows, white smoke floats out. Makes Preacher so
dizzy he has to go sit down. He say strange music come out of
that van. And the Amos fellow who look like Jesus, he got dirty
feet.

I just shake my head.

All Miss Gussie says is, "Well, I know it. I know it. But
Martha Sue says she's going back to California real soon."

"How soon?" I ask.

"Soon."

I hint to Clancy that she better look out, that I smell trouble. She puts her arms around me. "I will, Queenie. Don't you
worry. Old Martha Sue is going back to California next week.
She's just cheering me up is all." She draws in a deep breath
and stretches out on the sofa. "Lord," she says. "I don't know

what I'd do without her. And Albert. He and Mack have been the sweetest things, haven't they?"

I let that pass.

"You say they be leaving next week?" I ask.

She nods with her eyes closed.

I go into the kitchen and heat some drippings in the pan. Then I cut white corn off the cob and fry it in the grease. I add sugar, salt, milk, a dab of flour. I've got us a little hen roasting in the oven. I scrape the corn into a dish, then I fix us a toss salad. I toss leaf lettuce, sliced cucumbers, radishes, hard-boiled eggs, red onion rings. I make Clancy's favorite dressing—"Million Dollar Dressing." They say some rich man paid a million dollars to a chef in New York City to get this recipe. Years ago, I got it free from the Wentworths' cook. It's good, too.

MILLION DOLLAR DRESSING

Have ready:

>   4 chopped hard-boiled eggs
>   3 pimentos, chopped
>   ½ pint or more sweet pickle relish
>   1 small can ripe olives, chopped
>   ½ onion, chopped
>   3 eggs
>   1 qt. oil
>   1 bottle chili sauce
>   ½ bottle ketchup
>   Vinegar and salt

Beat 3 eggs until fluffy. Add 1 qt. oil very slowly. Beat again with beater on high speed. Should be smooth. Add mixture to 1 bottle chili sauce, ½ bottle ketchup. Rinse chili bottle with vinegar and salt to taste. Mix by hand until well mixed. Add more vinegar if you want to.

Makes more than 2 qts. Keeps well.

Violet goes off to her play practice, and Miss Gussie goes outside to spray her tomatoes. Through the window, I see Miss Dorothy's car pull out of the driveway. She's gone to play cards or something. After a little while, there's a knock at the back door, and I see Mr. Albert standing there smiling.

I think to myself: maybe Miss Dorothy jealous for a reason. Tonight he's holding a white sack of candy from his store. Chocolate-covered peanuts. He's not a bad-looking man, for all that Miss Dorothy's put him through.

"Here, these are for you," he says to me, holding out the bag. There is some sweat beaded on his forehead. His eyebrows look like two caterpillars.

"Chocolate is good for the soul," he says. "Don't you think so, Queenie?"

"I don't know," I say. "But thank you just the same."

He smiles and pats my shoulder. Miss Dorothy would kill him if she knew he was here every time her back be turned. I watch him go into the living room. Clancy look up from the sofa and smile like she was hoping he'd come. She's got herself on a clean white gown, cut way down to here. I've got the plaid robe in the washing machine. Mr. Albert shuts the door. In a minute I hear some old-fashioned music. I think: uh-oh. And her half dressed.

I sit down at the table and eat me a piece of lemon icebox pie and wait for Miss Gussie to come inside. Now and then I glance at the closed living room door. It's shut tight as a drum. Through the window I see Miss Gussie in her garden, tying up a tomato plant with string. It's still daylight. But it's late. Summer confuses you that way.

Next thing I know, Miss Dorothy be knocking at the back door. She yanks it open. "Oh, it's you," she says. "Where's Mother Dear?"

As if I'm Miss Gussie's keeper. "She's in the garden," I say. I stare at Miss Dorothy's pantsuit, lime green knit stretched over her big thighs. Thighs that could break a man's neck. Her hair's teased, and she's wearing a silver charm bracelet. Dangling from it is a deck of cards, baby shoes, a tiny palm tree. She don't know she's fat.

"You like my new outfit?" she asks, and twirls around. She's got the tiniest feet.

"Yes, Miss Dorothy," I say. "I sure do."

The back door opens, and Miss Gussie walks in. She blinks at Miss Dorothy.

"I thought you were playing cards," she says, pulling off her yellow gloves. She sets them on the washing machine.

"No, I was up at the Piggly-Wiggly. And when I drove downtown, I saw this interesting movie at the theatre. It's another James Bond. I thought I'd buzz over and see if you or Sister would like to go with me."

"Well, that's rightly sweet of you," says Miss Gussie. "I haven't seen a movie in the longest time. Not since *Cleopatra*."

"Then you'll go?" Miss Dorothy acts shocked.

"Yes, I think I just might. Just let me get dressed. Why don't you ask Clancy Jane? She'll get a kick out of you asking."

"Oh, Mother Dear, this is wonderful," says Miss Dorothy. "I hope she'll say yes."

From the living room, I hear an old-fashioned voice singing "Blue Moon." I almost cry out *Don't,* but the word sticks in my throat.

Miss Dorothy waddles across the floor, her green thighs just a-swishing, her charm bracelet a-jingling. I catch a whiff of her. She smells good. Then she opens the door. The music sounds louder. She stand in the doorway, filling it up with her whole self, and sucks in her breath.

She screams, "Aaaaaaaaa!"

Miss Gussie come running. My eyes sweep past Miss Dorothy's big blond head, into the living room. Mr. Albert, he jump off from Clancy Jane, his trousers hooked over his knees, and fall backward to the floor. His arm knock over a table, and all of Miss Gussie's china dogs fall to the floor and shatter. She had one of each breed. They break all to pieces.

Clancy sits up, pulling her gown over her breasts.

"My lord my lord my lord," hollers Miss Dorothy. She falls to the floor in a dead faint.

"Clancy Jane?" says Miss Gussie, standing beside me. Her voice sounds unnatural. *"Albert?"*

My jaw falls open. I slap my hand over my mouth when I see what I see. Mr. Albert scrambles to his feet, pulls up his pants, his face turning redder and redder. It looks like his whole scalp fixing to burst into flame.

Miss Dorothy's on the floor grunting.

"Lordy Jesus," says Miss Gussie. Her eyes fill with water. "What's happening here?"

I don't say anything but I think: Sunshine Paisley Martha Sue. She done brought this thing on.

Clancy's head drops, her shoulders shake. Fat tears fall on her hands.

Miss Dorothy's eyes flutter. I see a slit of blue. After a minute, when she sees that none of us are going to baby her, she sits up, propping herself on her hands. Her legs be splayed apart like scissors.

"YOU!" she screeches at Clancy.

"I'm so sorry, I'm just so sorry," Clancy says. "I can explain, it's not what you—"

"Whore!"

Clancy's eyes fill. Then she gets up from the sofa and the

gown falls down, showing her white titties. She takes off running, pushes past Mr. Albert and me and flies up the stairs. Her door slams. Me and Miss Gussie look at each other. I think it's a good thing I took that crib down.

"Incest!" growls Miss Dorothy. "Adultery!"

Mr. Albert sinks down in a chair and covers his eyes with his hands.

"It's not incest, Dorothy," says Miss Gussie in this weak little voice. "She's just in shock from the baby is all. We all are. Your sister wouldn't hurt you intentionally. And neither would you, Albert. *Albert?*"

Mr. Albert won't look up. Keeps his eyes hid.

"Lord, lord, lord!" cries Miss Dorothy. "I can't stand it!"

I feel so sorry for her. I reach down and help her up. Her arms feel like sacks of feed, Startena, what I used to feed my chickens.

"My god, Albert. I ought to kill you," she says, her eyes bugging out. "I saw what you were getting ready to do. Why, I'll scratch her eyes out and then I'll kill her and then I'll kill you! I'll slap your face! There's laws against this!"

I just stand there, like I'm part of the walls, and wait for Miss Gussie to stop Miss Dorothy from going on a rampage.

"You just calm down," says Mr. Albert.

"What did you say to me?" Miss Dorothy's face floods a deep red. She steps forward like she going to attack.

Miss Gussie grabs her arm. "Calm down, honey. Just calm down. I'm just as shocked as you."

Miss Dorothy stares at the wrinkled sheets all tucked into the sofa. "My own husband!" she cries. "I can't believe this! I just can't!"

"Dorothy, you've got to get ahold of yourself. I'm sure Albert can explain." Miss Gussie reaches out to hug Miss Dorothy, but she jerks away and runs out of the house. Mr. Albert, he don't say nothing. He gets up from the chair, keeping his eyes on the floor, and goes after Miss Dorothy.

I turn to the window and watch Miss Dorothy run across the yard. Her green fanny shake up and down. Then she throw herself at the front door and she's gone. All the way from here, I can hear her shrieking.

Mr. Albert, he cross the yard, real slow like, then he go into the house, too.

"Lordy Jesus," says Miss Gussie, her hand circled on her throat, like she's choking. Her heart look broken. "Fornicating with her own brother-in-law! What could she have been thinking? Her mind's snapped, that's all it can be."

I think: no, they wasn't doing that. Yet. But it looked like they was going to do something. I go into the living room and start folding the sheets. I'm going to wash and bleach them good. I don't want to know or hear any more. I've done took all I can.

*T*he house is real quiet when Violet comes home from practicing her play. She asks where everyone is.

"They've gone to bed," I say. "Your mama's upstairs. So be quiet, hear?"

"Mama's upstairs?" Violet asks, wrinkling her forehead. "Not in *her* room?"

I nod.

"Are you sure?"

I nod again. I can't talk without crying. So I keep busy with my hands. She says she's hungry again, so I fix her a snack. I heat up a plate in the oven. Violet, she's used to sadness in her short life. I've seen that picture of her daddy on her dresser.

That Purple Heart. She sits down at the white table and breaks off a hunk of cornbread and smears it with butter.

"Eat as much as you want child," I tell her. "Just lap it up."

When she finishes, she goes upstairs, and I hear her walk past her mama's door. Then she goes into the bathroom and runs water into the tub. This play has made her happy again. I hear her talking to herself, pretending to be that Frankie girl. Her voice sounds sweet and clear. She don't know nothing is wrong. But she'll find out. Miss Dorothy will see to that. This thing is not over yet.

Now the sky's gone dark blue, and the moon floats high over the mountains. Upstairs, I hear floorboards creak. The house is settling down for the night. I plug up the sink, and while it fills with soapy water, I stack dirty dishes. I wipe the counters. I think to myself that for all of Miss Gussie's goodness, this be a sad house. I think about that dead bird and all the trouble it brought. Then I turn off the faucets. I hear a noise, like the front door be slamming. I dip my hands into the hot water and stare out the window.

Then I see Clancy, she's running around the house, she's running barefoot through the backyard, straight through her mama's garden. Her gown swirls behind her, a flash of gauzy white, lord help me, moving like a rabbit through the trees.

Clancy Jane

1967

*I*ran barefoot through backyards, bruising my feet on sticker bushes and rocks. I stopped at the edge of Martha Sue's driveway, breathing hard. There was Amos's van all painted with daisies, and it seemed to swell with rock-and-roll. Where was Martha Sue? Lights were burning in the house, and I saw her mother pass in front of the square living room window. I couldn't go in there. I might as well go home and face up to the mess I'd made.

I had to get control of myself. I wiped my face with the hem of my gown, pushed back my hair, and sniffed hard. I stared at the van. Martha Sue had told me how her mother wouldn't let her come into the house except to get a drink of water or go to the bathroom. She made Amos drive to the filling station. I hadn't met him yet; I'd only caught glimpses of him when he dropped her off at Mother's house. Martha Sue said he was a genius.

I knocked on the van door. After a moment, Amos rolled down the window. He was a huge, hairy man, with thick wire-framed glasses. Music floated onto the green lawn: *If you're going to San Francisco / Be sure to wear a flower in your hair.*

Amos looked down at my gown, my bloody feet, and said, "Far out. You must be Clancy."

I nodded.

He looked down at my bloody feet. "Hey, are you a Libra?"

"Clancy, is that you?" cried Martha Sue. She was sitting cross-legged in the back of the van, but she scrambled to her feet. "What's the matter? Here, Amos, help me get her into the van."

I opened my mouth, but only strange, numb sounds came out. I kept thinking this was a dream, that I would awaken in my mother's house, or, better yet, I'd wake up in New Orleans, and Violet would still be a baby.

*T*here was never a formal discussion about my traveling with them. After they pulled the truth out of me, Martha Sue said, "Well, that settles it. You can't go back home. Dorothy'll make your life hell. You know she will."

"But I can't leave Violet."

"You're not *leaving* her," Martha Sue said. "Think of it as a little vacation. Just going to summer camp. Things'll blow over in a few weeks, and then you can catch a bus home. You'll get to see the whole country that way."

The next morning, we drove west in a thick cloud of smoke. We breathed each other's air. We were going to "The City," San Francisco, where Martha Sue and Amos lived. He almost had a Ph.D. in chemistry from Berkeley. He had met her in San Francisco. She was working at McDonald's. She and Bobo, the trailer salesman, had left Crystal Falls in 1962 to see the Pacific. After the divorce, she knew she couldn't return to Tennessee. Which meant we were sort of alike. We'd left home early. A birthplace was where everyone else lived and died. Martha Sue said Tennessee was five years behind the times, but I didn't know.

I had every intention of coming back to Crystal Falls. I planned to stay in California a week or two. As soon as we left the mountains, the land changed. From Memphis, we drove north, to Cairo, Illinois, and crossed the Mississippi. We reached St. Louis at dusk. It seemed to grow straight out of the ground like Oz, a metallic city in a dust bowl. On either side of the interstate, the midwestern fields stretched flat and green and endless. There was no curve to the earth.

Oh, Violet, I thought. What have I gone and done?

Martha Sue handed me an ivory pipe. "Don't think," she advised, as if she could read my mind. "Just *be*."

Heat lightning flickered, brightening the land around us. I turned around, remembering a distant lesson from the Bible, Lot's wife. *Don't look back.* Behind us black cumulus clouds formed a shelf over St. Louis, over Kentucky and Tennessee, over my old life.

"No, hold it in, don't exhale," said Martha Sue, taking a drag, showing me how to smoke the pipe.

"Go with the flow, man," said Amos, smiling at me in the rearview mirror. I was struck by the whiteness of his teeth.

Martha Sue's pipe, her awful smoke, seemed stronger than beer. It was a dark green fog that held me by its gravity. It was like standing at the top of a curved staircase and looking down. My pulse changed, I felt it beating in my navel. The air was smooth and slow, filled with a sweet-bitter smell. Where was Tennessee? I had a child? My husband died in Vietnam? Hell no, you won't go. But he did.

When we reached Denver, I knew there was no turning back. I had crossed more than state lines. I felt like an emigrant, my face framed by a calico bonnet, staring at the wagon ruts on the Oregon Trail. Pioneer women had buried their children along the banks of the Platte River—children who had fallen out of wagons, taken sick with the cholera. Any time of the day, you could look off into the distance and see someone digging a grave. I imagined the oxen plodding forward, stirring dust, and, stretching above us, the blue prairie sky, making everything— the wagons and mountains, the rivers and grave markers— shrink.

I wondered if Albert would come after me.

I didn't think he would. He would feel too ashamed. Lord, I don't understand it, but when a person does something wrong, it never feels wrong until later. It's never as evil as you'd imagined. That's how it was with Albert. One minute he was my brother-in-law, and the next minute he was almost naked. At the time it seemed like the most natural thing in the world.

I was just sitting there in Mother's living room, and he was playing old records. "Stormy Weather." "Blue Moon." My head felt disconnected from my body. It was like being drunk. The music pushed me over the edge. And I was already half crazy on account of losing the baby. It was as if I'd been careless with Hart's last gift. I blamed myself. I'd left something undone, I'd caused it. Almost everyone I loved had died.

Johnny Mathis was singing "It's Not for Me to Say."

Albert picked up my hand and said, "Would you dance with me?"

I hesitated. What if Mother came in? But she wouldn't. I looked at his broad forehead, the squint lines around his eyes, and I took his hand.

"I've been looking for an excuse to put my arms around you," Albert said. He pulled me against his chest real tender like. I felt myself go limp. He didn't seem like Dorothy's Albert. I couldn't believe he was doing this. And, I don't know, I was back in New Orleans, Hart was wearing black pants and a white T-shirt. He was smoking a Winston, standing next to the long window in the bedroom, one hand pressed against the wooden sill.

Come to me, Hart.

It felt so good to have his arms around me, I can't tell you how good it was. And the next thing I know, Dorothy was screaming, falling to the floor.

*I*t was a relief to be with Martha Sue and Amos, to have some-one else make decisions. I went along with everything. They spoke a whole different language. They seemed to live in another country. I was so backward they had to explain every-thing to me.

I'd heard about drugs, of course. Back in January the news had covered the Human Be-In. Timothy Leary was there. "Turn on," he said. "Drop out." Mother had gotten up and turned the channel. "Pure dee trash is all," she said.

Martha Sue told me I was getting to California too late. The whole time I was living in New Orleans with Hart and Violet, Martha Sue was careening around the West Coast in a Volkswagen painted to resemble a pink-and-orange flower. She drove from Los Angeles to San Francisco with her hyped-up stereo playing "Eve of Destruction" and "Satisfaction."

"You need a different name," she said. "Clancy's old-fashioned. What about Star? That's a lovely name. It really suits you."

"Sure," I said. But I thought: *Clancy, you're Clancy Jane.* I didn't tell her how much I needed my old name.

As we crossed the Rockies, Amos told me his life story. He had a lab in their Haight Street apartment house, where he made LSD. "It wasn't for money," he said when I looked shocked. He leaned toward the dash, turned up the radio. "Here's my song, man," he said. " 'For What It's Worth.' "

"See, we passed out the microdots at concerts," explained Martha Sue.

"Microdots?" I asked. I didn't understand. I felt stupid, like a country-bumpkin.

"You know, *blotter*," said Amos, looking at me in the rear-view mirror.

"Blotter?" I said and immediately wished I hadn't. I kept thinking of brown paper blotter paper, the kind teachers spread out on their desks.

"It's acid, Star," said Martha Sue. "LSD."

"Acid star?" I said. "What kind of acid is that?"

"Wow, man." Amos shook his head. "The South is, like, permanently dug in."

"She's just gone down a different path, Amos," said Martha Sue.

From the radio, Buffalo Springfield sang, *Paranoia strikes deep / Into your life it will creep / It starts when you're always afraid / Step out of line and the man will come and take you away.*

By the time we reached The City, the "Summer of Love" was in full swing. Martha Sue said, "You've got to stop calling me Martha Sue. That girl doesn't exist anymore. I'm Sunshine Paisley," she said. "But you can call me Sunny."

"All right," I said, but I wasn't sure I would remember.

"And your name is Star."

I didn't answer. I was overwhelmed by the Haight. It was flooded with would-be hippies. Amos kept calling it a bum scene. They explained that the original hippies had a pure inter-est in peace, harmony, and spiritual awakening. With the pil-grimage into the Haight, the streets turned ugly. There had always been Hell's Angels, Sunny told me, but now the rotting hotels, which faced lovely little shops, were full of dirty, stoned kids. The novice flower children drew wolves, drug dealers, pimps. That's when the streets became sinister, dangerous. And the poor children, in their eagerness to be a part of the Haight-Ashbury scene, swallowed anything. They were creating their own versions of flower power.

I would have, too.

It wasn't ugly to me. I understood why they were here.

What I remember best about that whole summer is music: "Sgt. Pepper's Lonely Hearts Club Band," "Light My Fire," "Windy," and "Ode to Billy Joe," which came a little too close to home.

Home was a walk-up apartment in San Francisco, home was a room full of people crashing, home was a momentum, home was relative. All you needed was perspective and love. And The Pill. There I was, twenty-nine years old, disgraced, searching for love, making far too much love, smoking grass, working in a head shop. It had been so long since I'd been with a man. I liked being held. I felt safe. And it made me forget. Sometimes twenty people crashed at our place. Men who were tender, men who smelled like dirty feet, men who had no faces and called me Star. My real name receded, like a piece of wood moving in the slap tide.

And my head was never clear. Maybe I had always been called Star. I had fallen through space and taken root in San Francisco. There was a starved, genuine hippie look about me. My hair was long, parted down the middle like Sunny's, and I smelled faintly of strawberry incense. I wore faded jeans without underwear; I wore a long fringed blouse with a Nehru collar, a beaded headband, sometimes a daisy chain if I could find the flowers in the park.

Most of the time I forced myself not to think about Violet or Mother. There were diversions. I made protest signs. I went on peace marches with Amos and Sunny. I even got arrested and spent a few hours in jail. No one read me my rights. Amos got a bloody nose. Another man was beaten for throwing flowers at a policeman. Before I was released, a hooker with orange hair tried to put her hand up my miniskirt. I started screaming, and the guard came and unlocked the door. "All right, all right. You're free to go," she told me.

My new friends were young. They said they didn't trust anyone over thirty, but they trusted me. I felt sixteen. I told myself I'd go back home in a week, but I kept putting it off. I never bought a bus ticket. It was too hard. I wasn't ready. In the back of my mind was Albert. He hadn't tried to find me. I didn't care. I hoped Dorothy had forgiven him. I learned something from an ex-rabbi, who was now a sort of guru: Absence does not make the heart grow fonder; it creates clear, white spaces. My family didn't know where I was; therefore, I didn't exist for them. I just *was.* It made sense. And there were so many others on the Haight. Runaways. Teenagers from Iowa and Louisville, Atlanta and Houston, New York and Boston. We were all running away, running toward something.

I was fascinated by my friends and their messages: love, peace, freedom. There was a strong bias against the hippies' lifestyle, a feeling that seemed stronger even than the antiwar protest. It didn't make sense to me. Because of someone else's war, I'd lost Hart. Make love, not war. Only hadn't Hart done both, and where was he now?

Mostly I didn't think about my old life. I sucked the pipe and breathed Sunny's air and made signs. We marched from Fillmore to the Panhandle of Golden Gate Park, shouting *LBJ, how many boys didja kill today?*

We held up beautiful signs—

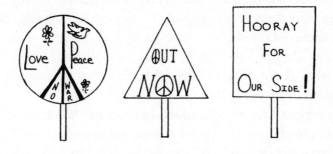

Some people wore coolie hats. The Diggers were there, handing out stew to barefoot teenagers. The Diggers, Amos explained, were anarchists. They wanted you to walk through a twelve-foot wooden frame, and that was supposed to give you a new frame of reference. A guy with bushy dark hair and granny glasses stood up. I'd seen his face in a magazine, or maybe it was on television. He was somebody famous. I looked around. People with short hair and regular clothes had gathered to watch us. Some of them held up signs that said GO HOME, FREAKS.

I turned back to listen to the man with bushy hair. "At this very moment, they're dropping napalm!" he yelled. "Yeah, and somebody's brother is getting zipped up in a body bag! One, two, three, what're we fighting for?"

"Fuck the war!" the crowd shouted.

"Yeah, fuck it," the guy shouted back. "Gimme an *F*. Gimme a *U*, gimme a *C*, gimme a *K*!"

My pulse was beating hard in my neck. Hart, I thought. I was doing this for Hart. Then I was yelling with them.

"Fuck the war, fuck the war!"

* * *

I found myself longing for a past I never had. I lived through Sunny's memories, her recollections of the Haight's early days. How could California—with all of its mystics, swirling lights, and psychedelic festivals—have existed in the same time and space as Crystal Falls? That, to me, was the biggest mystery. And what about New Orleans? I hadn't thought any city was stranger.

Sunny and Amos advised me not to write home, but it was the middle of summer. I'd been gone weeks and weeks. I knew they were worried sick. All except for Dorothy, who probably wished I was dead. I pictured my sister leaving for Sunday school, her sad blond face, her puffed sleeves and bouffant hair. I pictured Mother and Queenie, stringing beans on the porch. And Violet. Lord, Violet had lived through worse on account of me.

I couldn't bring myself to call home. I would have felt their voices as small hooks through the telephone wires. I couldn't have stood it. Instead I mailed a postcard featuring the Golden Gate—it was a solid, American structure, something Hart would have appreciated. He would have understood that I had successfully jumped off into another oblivion.

> *Dear Mother & Violet & Queenie,*
> *Hi! I'm here for the summer. I'm fine. I love you all.*
> *Please forgive me for leaving without saying good bye. I'll be*
> *back soon and then I'll explain everything*
>
> > *Love,*
> > *Clancy Jane*

On the other side of the world, boys were getting blown apart, but the war was *here,* right outside our windows:

> *Ho, Ho, Ho Chi Minh—*
> *The NLF is gonna win!*

The Haight grew dark. You could feel it coming. Drug dealers had moved into the flophouses, capitalism had arrived. People were dying, killing each other. You didn't know who to trust. Panhandlers cruised the streets, wearing signs that said WILL WORK FOR FOOD. Then they would take their money, buy a loveburger for a quarter, and get high on a nickel bag.

Sunny got it into her head to drive to New Mexico. Some of her friends had dropped out and were living on a pig farm down in Abiquiu. The three of us climbed into the van and drove south. I closed my eyes and listened to the radio. The Rolling Stones were singing "Mother's Little Helper."

At dusk, the van broke down in Ventura. Amos opened the hood, and steam poured out. Cars whistled by like so many rockets. Amos had friends in L.A., so we decided to hitch. It amazes me now to think how brave and reckless we were, standing on the freeway, our thumbs pointed up, fifty dollars between us, two long-haired women and woolly Amos. A beat-up red Chevy, full of construction workers, picked us up. I took one look at the crowded car, four men holding metal lunch-boxes and hardhats, drinking Pabst, and I was flooded with black paranoia. I wanted to run. The men stared.

"Well, get in if you're getting in," said the driver. Sunny and Amos crawled into the backseat, wedging themselves between two men with crew cuts. I slid into the front seat, between the driver and a young man with bad breath and pimples.

"I'm Luddie," said the driver, grinning. He had yellow teeth. The air inside the car was full of tobacco, beer, perspiration. There was an American flag decal on his windshield. The guy next to me looked young, maybe seventeen. His name was embroidered on his pocket, Stanley.

"Where you people from?" said one of the crew-cuts.

"San Francisco," said Amos. I was grateful for his deep voice, for his whole masculine presence.

"You aren't one of those hippies, are you?" asked the driver.

"Oh, no," said Amos. "We're on our way to a retreat."

"Catholics, eh?" said Luddie. Something changed in his face. I caught Sunny's eye, and she smiled. Amos was staring out the window. I tried to relax. It's going to be all right, I told myself. It's going to be all right.

The car turned off Ventura Highway, speeding down a series of streets where the houses were clumped together, squat and shabby.

"Where're we going?" I said, and Sunny gave me a look that clearly said *Hush, be cool.*

"Just going to let Don and Buddy off," the driver said and stopped in front of a peeling white wooden house, which was surrounded by a chain-link fence. A brown dog stood on its hind legs and yipped when the crew-cuts climbed out of the backseat and walked up to the gate.

Luddie revved the motor and angled into the street. "Find something on the radio, why doncha, Stanley?" he said.

Stanley leaned forward and twirled the dial until he found a baseball game. It scratched over the static. Luddie kept driving. The landscape changed from city to wilderness within the space of a few miles. Still, he kept driving. I wanted to turn and look at Amos and Sunny, but I was firmly pressed between Luddie and Stanley. I stared through the water-speckled windshield, taking in the tall oaks, the yellow bushes. It was almost dusk. Way up in the sky, seagulls wheeled. We were close to the beach. The clouds were a deep, dusky blue and dropped down low. We kept driving. Stars popped out, no one said anything, I smelled the ocean. San Francisco seemed like a long way away.

I tried not to panic as the red car angled up a scrubby hill, through a spindly oak forest. I glanced out of Stanley's window and saw the ocean. The gulls squawked, flew white against the dark blue sky. Luddie veered off the road, throwing me into Stanley, and drove up a pinkish dirt path. He parked the car in a clump of tall yellow bushes. I looked straight ahead, too frightened to breathe. Further up the road, the bushes were black from a recent fire. Here, everyone talked about spontaneous combustion. You couldn't trust summers in Southern California.

You couldn't trust anyone.

Luddie pulled on the emergency brake and turned up the radio. Jimmy Gilmer and the Fireballs were singing "Sugar Shack."

"Stanley? Take that rope and tie up the man hippie," Luddie said, and his teeth appeared, like yellow corn. "We'll get to him directly."

My heart beat wildly, as if ripping from my chest.

Sunny screamed and reached for the door handle. Amos's arms flapped forward. "Wait a minute. You can't do this!"

"Can't do what?" Stanley said. He turned, as if smiling, and socked Amos's jaw. It made a solid noise, and Amos slumped forward, moaning.

Luddie grabbed my arm. He reached in the backseat and grabbed Sunny's hair. She was still screaming. Stanley jumped out of the car, pulling Amos into the dirt. There were muffled groans. Then Amos was wrapped up like a rodeo calf. His glasses were bent, the lenses crushed. A thin line of blood trickled out of his mouth. His eyes were open.

"I'll take her," Stanley said, pointing at me.

Luddie gripped Sunny by the hair. She clawed at his hands, and he slapped her. "Well, all right," he said. "But hurry it up." He pushed me forward. Then he slapped Sunny again. She screamed, and he clapped his hand over her mouth.

Stanley came toward me, unbuckling his belt, jerking down his zipper. Behind me was a cliff, a shelf of rock above the lights of Ventura. They looked tiny, distant. I sucked in air and ran in the other direction, toward the ocean.

"Get that hippie bitch!" cried Luddie.

Stanley cursed. He lunged forward, locked his arms around my knees, and I fell hard against the ground. My lungs went flat. I couldn't breathe.

"It's time to pay me and Luddie back for the ride," he said, flipping me over. I kicked him in the chest and tried to scramble to my feet. He pinned down my arms with one hand, digging into me with the other.

"Stop it!" I yelled. "Listen! My husband fought in Vietnam!"

"You must think I give a shit." Stanley's breath was hot and nasty.

"You don't understand. He's dead!" I hollered. "They killed him!"

"So? I'd fuck him, too, if I could."

I opened my mouth and vomited on his neck.

"Commie hippie cunt," he said and slapped me. He ripped off my blouse. Way off in the distance, I heard Sunny's screams. I couldn't breathe. He would suffocate me if I couldn't get my breath. No, no, no. Please stop, don't, you mustn't, *fortheloveof godstop.*

And this isn't happening this is nothing i'm not here mother is showing me how to weed the beans first you have to figure out what's a weed and what's not that's a girl you've got it and you're part of the air you're a tree a piece of bark a blade of grass this is california where the freaks are fuck the war fuck the war can't you smell the ocean open your eyes beyond the trees there are a million stars.

Bitsy

1967–1968

First, I left play practice early and I was in the kitchen, making a chicken sandwich, when Mummie came charging through the front door. She ran upstairs, screaming, "That bitch, that low-down bitch!" Domino paced the floor, whining. She worshiped the ground Mummie walked on and vice versa. From upstairs, I could hear Mummie's wails. I immediately went *en garde*. I set down the bread and followed her. She was in her bedroom throwing Father's things in a suitcase, muttering something I couldn't understand.

"Mummie? What's wrong?" I asked.

She didn't answer. She sobbed so hard water dripped out of her nose.

Mack came out of his room and stood in the doorway. "Mama?" he asked. "What's wrong?"

"Your father is a whoremonger," she said, snapping the suitcase shut. She wiped her eyes with Father's T-shirt.

"He is not," I said.

She whirled around, her eyes narrowed. "Was I talking to you? Just get out of here!"

I held back the tears. She'd never talked to me that way before. Then I ran downstairs, two steps at a time.

Second, Father came running through the front door and sat down on the sofa and burst into tears. Never before had I seen him cry, not even when his own mother died. His sobs were a deep bass, frilled around the edges like a choirboy.

"Not you, too," I said, but he didn't hear.

Mummie never did come downstairs. That evening Mack saw a police car over at Miss Gussie's. "Now, that sure is strange," he said, and he picked up the phone. When my grandmother answered, he said, "Miss Gussie, you wouldn't know what's going on with my mama and daddy, would you?"

As he listened, his face changed.

"Uh-huh. Yeah." He nodded like she could see him. "Do you know where she went?"

He hung up the phone and dug in his pockets for his car keys. Then he ran out the front door, leaving it wide open, letting out all of the air-conditioning.

"*Attendez!*" I hollered. "Mack! Where're you going?"

"I don't have time to say," he called out. "I've got to go find Aunt Clancy. She's done run off."

"Aunt Clancy?" I hollered back, but he had already gone. None of this made a bit of sense.

Then Mummie thundered down the stairs, her face all screwed up and blotched with red marks. "Where did your brother go?" she asked, rushing to the door, looking into the yard. "I heard him drive off."

"Why don't you calm down and tell me what's going on?" I said.

She slapped me so hard my neck snapped backward. Before I could catch my breath, Father got to his feet and stared at Mummie.

"You're one mean woman," he said. His voice was cold. "Don't you slap her if it's me you're wanting to hit."

"I'm not mean! I'm not! Anyway, how can you say that after what you just did?" Mummie dropped to the floor, a heap of lime green fabric. She looked up at me. "I'm sorry, Bitsy. Listen. I didn't mean to hit you. Oh, my *God*. I don't even know what I'm doing!"

She reached up and grabbed a hunk of her hair, pulling with all of her strength. I could see white scalp lift from her skull. Her eyeballs were huge and white, like two eggs, the yolks flat and blue.

I just stood there, holding my face. "Somebody tell me what's going on!" I cried.

She answered by snarling, rocking back and forth on her heels. Domino whined and scooted under a table and started growling.

"Mummie, don't!" I cried. I used to think she knew everything. That she was a *grande dame.*

Father sighed and shook his head. She was still hunched on the floor, whipping her body back and forth. He hunkered beside her.

"Dorothy?" His voice was gentle. "Sugar? Try and get ahold of yourself."

"Arrrrr," said Mummie.

"Dorothy?"

"Arrrrrrr!"

That did it. He stood up and rubbed his hands on his slacks. Something fell behind his eyes, a pale shutter. Then he went upstairs.

Third. This was the worst: Aunt Clancy. I could not believe she did what she did. As soon as Father went upstairs, Mummie turned to me. "I opened the door, there they were. Wrapped around each other like stripes on a candy cane."

"I don't understand," I said. I wanted her to hush. I wished Father would come downstairs and make her hush.

"What's to understand? Your father's pants were down. Tied up in knots around his ankles. He was kissing and climbing all over Sister. Oh, it was awful!"

My eyes filmed over. Not my father. She was lying. I couldn't feature him acting romantic with any woman. He wasn't that sort of man. I knew all about how babies were made, but I was certain my parents had outgrown the need for such things. When I tried to imagine how I was made, my mind turned white and blank, like a sheet of paper, and that was the end of it. I couldn't for the life of me imagine my father and another woman—any woman.

"I'd like to cut her titties off." Mummie said.

I was waiting on the front porch when Mack drove up. I ran down the driveway. "Let's go over to Miss Gussie's," I said. I wanted to find out the other side of the story.

"This ain't like Aunt Clancy," Mack whispered as we crossed the yard. Miss Gussie had the police in an uproar. She was begging them to search the town with flashlights and dogs. They wouldn't do it. They said Aunt Clancy hadn't been missing long enough.

"But she was wearing only a nightgown," my grandmother was telling a policeman.

The policeman nodded and wrote something down in a tiny notebook. Violet was sobbing, holding on to Queenie. The whole front of Queenie's dress was wet. Aunt Clancy hadn't bothered to leave a note, which I thought was cruel. Or real desperate.

From our house, the porch light flashed on, and Father came out of the house. He was carrying a suitcase. Mummie came running after him, screaming as she zigzagged across the front yard.

"Just get out of my life," she yelled, trying to kick him. "Go on, get! You're nothing but a dog shitting in other people's yards."

I reached for Mack's hand.

"Daddy? What's wrong, Daddy?" Mack hollered.

Father didn't answer. He climbed into his Buick, the taillights blinked red, then the car lurched out of the driveway.

"You can't leave me, you turd!" screamed Mummie. She chased his car down the street, beating on the trunk. "Is it because I didn't shave my legs? Is that it? You tell me! You tell me right now!"

The policeman looked up from his notebook. Miss Gussie's hand went to her mouth. Violet blinked. Queenie shook her head.

"Mama!" yelled Mack. He took off after her.

"Come back here, you ugly bastard!" she screamed. "Nobody'll have you but me!"

She ran down the street, her arms thrust in front of her, screaming my father's name over and over.

*M*ummie tried to turn my grandmother against Aunt Clancy. Miss Gussie wasn't having any of it.

"Yes, Clancy Jane was wrong to do what she did," said my grandmother, "but she deserves our forgiveness!"

"She does not," Mummie snapped.

"The Bible says forgive and forget," said Miss Gussie.

"It also says Jesus wept," snapped Mummie. "But that didn't keep him from getting nailed, did it?"

Father moved into the ladies' lounge at the Ben Franklin.

It was a drab brown room with a sloped ceiling. There was a yellow vinyl sofa, two kitchen chairs covered in the same padded vinyl, and a white enamel table. The room smelled of dust, cheap perfume, and dirty stockings. On the shortest wall, there was a door leading to the roof. Next to the door was a picture, *The Last Supper.* When me and Mack were little, we used to go up to the roof and throw pebbles onto the sidewalk. We'd laugh when we smacked the pedestrians.

Mack helped Father move his things to the store, but when Mummie found out, she tried to make him feel guilty.

"Mack, sweetie, don't you know anything?" she said. Her voice was so reasonable it was hard to believe she had chased Father's car down the road. "You can't make things too easy for your father or he won't come back home," she said, lifting one side of her forehead.

"Are you sure you're telling the truth?" Mack asked.

"About what, sweetie?"

"You know what. Aunt Clancy and Daddy."

"It's the truth. Believe it." Mummie grimaced, pulling her lips into a tight line.

"I just can't believe Daddy and Aunt Clancy would do something like that. I don't understand why."

"That's easy," Mummie said. "She's a woman, and he's a man. She didn't have a husband, so she figured she'd take mine. She didn't even have to stretch to do that. We were right next door. She took what was handy."

"I don't know, Mother." Mack shook his head. "It doesn't add up. That's not how Aunt Clancy is."

"You don't know how she is. You just *think* you do." Mummie gave him a chilling glance, the first one I'd ever seen her give him. "You're either for me or against me. There's no in-between. If you're on her side, then move out."

Mack moved out that afternoon and got a job frying burgers at the Rocky Top Cafe. He rented a filthy *chambre meublée* for three dollars a night down by the railroad, where hobos lived. He refused to come home, even when Mummie begged. We hunted him down. She was terrified of being alone, terrified that he would lose his deferment. Terrified that he'd turned against her.

"We'll just forget this whole thing happened," she pleaded. We were standing in his apartment. It smelled musty. He had a metal cot, cardboard boxes full of his clothes. A cheap portable radio sat on the floor. Spanky and Our Gang were singing "Sunday Will Never Be the Same."

"I don't care whose side you're on," Mummie said. "Just come back home, and we'll make a fresh start."

Mack sat down on the cot. The springs went *yink!*

"I wouldn't have gotten so upset if you hadn't taken her side," she said.

"I didn't take anybody's side," Mack said. "I'm just trying to see things clearly."

"This wouldn't have happened if Albert hadn't brought those records over. Music makes people think of things they ought not to."

Mack rolled his eyes.

"Don't look at me that way. You know it's true. I'm not deaf. I hear those songs. 'Light My Fire' and all that. Don't think for one minute that I don't know what that means."

Mummie couldn't see my face, so I grinned at Mack. He grinned back.

Mummie looked at him and blinked. "Well, sweetie, go ahead and laugh if you want. This is serious. What if Sister's pregnant? Did that ever cross your mind? I can just see her having a baby with its little brain stuck on the outside of its head. A retard."

"Her and Daddy aren't related," he said.

"I don't care." She walked over to a cardboard box and looked inside it. She started folding Mack's shirts. "You don't go around stealing your own sister's husband."

"She didn't steal Father," I said.

"What?" She twisted her whole body to look at me. "Is he here now? No, I don't see him. Do you?"

When I screwed up my mouth to keep from crying, she looked satisfied. Then she turned to Mack. "I don't blame you, sweetie. Sister just took advantage of her situation. It was Mother Dear's fault for coddling her. Queenie's, too. And it's Bitsy's fault, too."

My mouth dropped open. *"Moi?"* I said.

"Bitsy?" Mack said, looking at me. "She hasn't done anything."

"Well, she's just so silly. All she's got is a pretty face, just like Sister, and that won't last forever."

I swallowed hard. The back of my throat hurt.

The corners of Mack's mouth tucked down. His eyes went flat and blue.

"Don't look at me like that," she said.

"You ran him off," said Mack.

"I did not." She smoothed her hands over a blue flannel shirt. "But go ahead. Hurt me. I'm strong, I can take it."

Mack's eyes filled.

"You pick up these boxes and come home with me right now. You're just a baby. You don't know how mean the world is. You need me."

"I'll go to Vietnam before I live in the same house with you," he said.

Fourth. Which is just where he went. He joined the Marines, and by the end of November he was in Vietnam. After he left, Mummie took on the role of War Mother. And he wouldn't even write her. She watched the news every night. She took out the *V World Book* and kept it open to Vietnam.

"I knew it," she said, shivering. "They look just like Japs."

"What do the Japs have to do with this?" I asked.

"They almost killed my papa," she said. She meant Miss Gussie's husband, Charlie, who had died before I was born. I didn't know much about him.

"He didn't get killed in the war, did he?" I asked.

"Almost," she said, rubbing her arms like she was cold. "Nearly. I don't want to think about it. That's why I hate the Japs."

"But they're not Japs, Mummie. They're Vietnamese."

"It doesn't matter. They're all the same to me."

Mostly I kept Mack's letters to myself, clipped in my diary. Mummie mailed him long letters written on Big Chief tablets, which he swore he burned. He asked me to make her stop sending money. American dollars were worthless over there.

His letters made me want to cry, because I knew he was suffering and scared to death. I hated Mummie and Aunt Clancy. I even hated Father.

December 9, 1967

Dear Bitsy,

The guys here used to tease me about being from Tennessee. They said What's this? You wearing shoes, man? I told them I was from Tennessee & I was proud of it. None of the guys here believed I had me a sister named Bitsy. Don't you mean Betty? they asked. I said No & showed them your picture & they saw for themselves how cute you are. They all whistled. I told them you could speak French. That's what the gooks talk. Now everybody in my squad wants a date with you. Hahaha. I told them you wouldn't date no horny bastards.

It's not so bad here, honest. It's real hot & the mosquitoes eat us alive & we have to shit in the weeds but we don't see nothing—we don't see Charlie. The guys tease and say there's nothing out there but mud & rice. I like to believe that. Except when it gets dark. Here, the nights will make anybody believe in ghosts. Whole trees seem to move & you can't tell what's whispering, the leaves the mosquitoes or the VC. See, you don't know who's the enemy & who's not. You've got your NVR, the North Vietnamese Regulars, who are the out & out commies. Then you've got your sneaky bastard VCs—the Vietcongs, rebels who smile at you by day & cut your throat at night. They're all over South Vietnam.

At night we have these three-man listening posts. We go out & hunt for Victor/Charlie. You can call them either one, take your pick. Other times, since Charlie won't come out, we do S & D, which is short for Search & Destroy missions. At first I thought, gee whiz, I'm gonna get to cut me off some ears like I seen some guys do. And one guy found a dink skull, and he burns a candle in it. It's not that you want to cut up bodies, but when you see a dead U.S. soldier, somebody you've known and talked to, you get mean. But mainly we just search. I haven't even fired my gun, although one of the guys shot a pig. I can hear artillery popping all night long like fire works. It don't seem real. It's like a part of me is numb. It's like coming home from the dentist & one whole side of your face is numb & your lips don't feel like your own lips.

The next place they're sending me is Phu Bai. We're going to support operations on the DMZ, but don't tell anybody—this is classified information. I'm looking forward to drilling holes in dink asses. Phu Bai is about ten km from Hue, which my commander calls the "imperial" city, whatever that means. You know me. I'm still dumb as mud. But they say Hue is a pretty neat place. You pronounce it like Way or Whey. There's a river called the Perfume, so I don't think it's a bad place.

Tell Daddy & Miss Gussie that I'm A-OK. Give them & Dauphine & Queenie a hug for me. I guess Daddy is still living down at the store? I know you miss him as much as I do. He writes me good letters. Before I left I asked him what happened, and he said he didn't understand it himself. I couldn't get anything out of him. Could you? Nobody gave Aunt Clancy a chance to explain her side. So we don't know for sure. Don't hate her, Bitsy. She was so lonely and broke up. I just hate this thing has torn up our family. But you just can't talk to Mama like she's a regular person. You know this is true. I hope Aunt Clancy's home by now. If not, I'd sure appreciate her address. I've been writing everybody I know almost. I still can't write Mama, and I sure wish she'd stop sending me all those letters. Being here has taught me that losing things marks you. I've been thinking a lot about Hart, even though I never knew him personally. And I feel this powerful need to write Aunt Clancy. You ought to tell Violet her daddy was a brave man to have volunteered. We humped near An Khe, and I thought about him getting blowed up. I don't know why he came back here a second time. He must've had balls. Or been a crazy one. And he was old, 29. Most of the guys are my age. But they seem real old. The C rations taste like shit, although the peaches aren't too bad. I sure

*miss Dauphine's and Queenie's cooking, all those biscuits &
fried squash fritters. I'd better stop thinking about it, or I'll
make my stomach growl. The water tastes rotten, like drinking piss. That's because the streams are full of shit—human
and cattle. They treat the water with iodine pills, and that's
what makes the water taste so bad. The guys here told me to
write home for Kool-Aid. Can you send me some? Well, we
gotta go dig some foxholes, so I'd better sign off. Hope y'all
have a happy New Year. They call it Tet over here, & I think
there's going to be a cease fire. The dinks celebrate it in a big
way. Don't Worry!!!!!*

Love,
Mack

Christmas was awful. It started out normal enough. Mummie called Mr. Frank and had him decorate the whole house
with magnolia leaves, white pine, and holly. He draped an artificial garland over the banister. He put green and gold ornaments into a huge brandy snifter. He put up a tree and sprayed
it with this stuff that looked like shaving cream. He made a
partridge and a pear tree out of *papier-mâché* pears, a ceramic
bird, and tree branches. She told Mr. Frank to send the bill to
Father.

She played carols on Mack's old stereo. The house was full
of men's voices—Bing Crosby, Nat King Cole, Andy Williams.
She went outside and tied a big red bow on our mailbox. She
hired a man to outline our house with blue lights. I didn't
understand why we were celebrating *Noël*. Mack was in Vietnam, Father was living at his store, and she was stuck with me.
She talked me into helping her sew a popcorn-and-cranberry
garland for the tree. It was fifteen feet long and took five whole
days to make.

When the house was finished, Mummie said, "What do you think?"

"*C'est magnifique,*" I said.

"*Deck the halls with boughs of holly,*" she sang, throwing tinsel icicles on the tree. "*Fa-la-la-la-la-la-la-la-la.*"

It rained Christmas Eve. We sat in the living room, staring at the tree, listening to the Mormon Tabernacle Choir, waiting for Father to come over. He arrived after supper, bringing with him the scent of fresh air and dampness. He carried a huge poinsettia beneath an umbrella. "Merry Christmas, Dorothy," he said, setting down the plant, then the umbrella.

"Have you been busy down at the store?" she asked him.

"Oh, yes! Very busy."

"I'm so glad." Mummie smiled. She was wearing a red velvet dress that flattered her. She looked real *bon vivant.* "Won't you join us in a glass of eggnog?"

"All right," he said, looking uncomfortable. He sat down on the sofa and smiled at me. He didn't take off his hat or coat. He didn't take off his gloves. I noticed he was wearing a brown and beige knitted scarf. Hand-knitted.

Mummie brought him a crystal cup of eggnog. I could smell the bourbon in it. She put on a Nat King Cole record. That song had always made me feel cozy. Now it made me see how my life fell short of blowing snow, roasting chestnuts, and reindeer who knew how to fly. Father sipped eggnog and watched us open our gifts. He gave Mummie a box of chocolate-covered cherries and a blue sweater. He gave me a pearl necklace. We gave him a silver money clip. After he'd finished the eggnog, he said he had to be going.

"But you just got here," said Mummie.

"I'd stay if I could, Dorothy. But I'm due at the Jaycees?

We're having a Christmas party for the little crippled children? We do it every year, remember?"

"Oh, yes. I do remember." Mummie stared down into her eggnog.

He stood, and I walked him to the door. Mummie trailed behind. He kissed me on the cheek. Then he bent to pick up his umbrella. As he straightened up, he almost bumped into Mummie.

"Well, good night," he said, patting her arm. Then he stepped outside into the rain. He ran to his car without opening his umbrella. I stood in the doorway, wishing for snow, wishing this day would end. I watched the blue lights around our house reflect in the damp street.

Mummie stood next to me. "I spend god knows how long getting this house perfect," she said, "and he stays five minutes."

*F*ifth. On New Year's Eve, I caught Mummie plucking out all of her eyebrows. She sat cross-legged on the bathroom vanity, staring into the mirror, the tweezers snapping like a small dog.

"Get out of here!" she yelled into the mirror.

"What're you doing?" I asked. I didn't realize until that moment how much I wanted her to lie. To say she had a medical reason for removing facial hair.

"I'm plucking my eyebrows. What do you *think* I'm doing?" She lifted what was left of one eyebrow and stared me down. Later, she took Father's razor and shaved off the stubble. Without eyebrows her face seemed huge, startled, alien. I knew then that Father would never come back home.

I went into Mack's room and stared through the plaid curtains. I could still smell his scent, that boyish, spicy smell.

Through the window, Miss Gussie's house looked dark. She and Violet went to bed with the chickens. They didn't know what to do when it got dark. I did. The day I turned fourteen, I was allowed to date. I had a ten o'clock curfew. Mostly I went out with Claude Wentworth, who played football and was my one true *amour*. I'd loved him since the first grade. It drove him crazy when I whispered his name in French, *Boulette*—it meant meatball, but it was as close as I could get to the real thing. My dates with him pleased Mummie to no end, and hardly anything made her happy these days. Sometimes guys with bad reputations called, but I was afraid to say yes. There was too much gossip buzzing around town about my family. Father had converted his office into an apartment. He went to the furniture store and bought a king-sized bed and a dresser and a big color TV. He even had a hot plate, but mostly he ate out. Over the TV, he had a map of Vietnam, and he used a red Magic Marker to chart places Mack had been.

Mummie said he was just trying to make her look bad. She could barely hold her head up. I didn't want to add to the trouble. She believed Queenie and Dauphine talked about us behind our backs. Mummie's suspicions grew worse after Dauphine quit.

"It's a deliberate plot of the nigras to overthrow white people," Mummie said.

To tell the truth, I didn't see how Dauphine took it as long as she did. Since Father left, Mummie had gotten dirty. She wouldn't pick up after herself. Time and again I saw her stick Milky Way wrappers underneath the sofa. She'd let trash pile up, then yell at Dauphine to vacuum it up. She wouldn't wash herself, and she wore her bra until the straps were filthy. Then she'd go yell at Dauphine for being a no-good, lazy nigra.

"All you people are good for nothing," she yelled.

I was so ashamed of Mummie. She'd changed so much. She was all forehead. She could play a role on *Lost in Space*. I hated it when she stood in front of the mirror and sketched two arched, feathered lines over her eyes just to look normal. We saw Miss Gussie and Violet in the yard, and they just looked at Mummie and pretended not to notice. They were polite that way. But Mummie was developing a reputation all on her own. She was getting more and more eccentric. When Dauphine quit, there was more to do around the house. I kept thinking how lucky the Wentworths were, and I was more and more determined to marry into that family.

The Wentworths' house was cool and dark and smelled of cinnamon apples. Everything was so clean. I loved going over there to watch TV with Claude. Miss Betty wasn't real friendly. She made comments like, "Are you joining us for dinner again, dear?" All my life I'd thought of the noon meal as dinner; supper was what you ate at night. I just didn't fit. My father wasn't rich enough, and my mother was too strange. Father had a business, of course, but it couldn't compare to what the Wentworths owned. They had maids who wore black uniforms and set the dining room table with silver and the sprigged china, even for breakfast. How could I fit into that family, with a name like Bitsy? Little Bitsy McDougal. That was the first strike against me. I wanted to scream from the top of my lungs, *My name is Lillian Beatrice!* But I never did. My real name sounded even more stupid than Bitsy. Besides, you couldn't yell in public and keep a reputation.

Mummie tried to play on my grandmother's sympathies. She groveled. She talked like a little girl, she asked for advice about my father, whether she should divorce him or ask him to move back home. I knew for a fact that she was waiting for him to make his first move.

Miss Gussie acted cool and polite. She refused to give advice about my father. She stayed next door. She never came over to visit us, so she didn't know what was going on at our house. It was just me and Mummie. I wished for something different. I wished I was old enough to marry Claude. I wished Mummie would run off so I could go live with Miss Gussie. All my grandmother seemed concerned with was Violet. She was growing. They were always down at Father's store, buying things for my cousin, getting their discount.

"I don't see her buying you anything," said Mummie, wrinkling her forehead. She was in the bathroom drawing on eyebrows, like war paint. I didn't see why she bothered when she didn't even wash her hair. It was a dirty, dull blond, almost brown. It was so oily it looked wet. She didn't shave her legs, either.

"I don't need anything," I said. But I was lying. I needed to get away from her.

"Well, excuse me for breathing," she said. She put down the eyebrow pencil and glanced at me. "Don't you have anything to do? Go clean up your room."

"It's clean."

"Your closet isn't. It's full of things you've outgrown. And you've got winter dresses all mixed in with your summer skirts. Plus, you've got a world of filth under your bed."

I walked upstairs and flopped down on my bed, happy to be alone. I hated my celery green walls. I never knew if Mr. Frank had picked out the color or if Mummie had. It was a secretive hue. I'd tacked up posters from floor to ceiling. Last Christmas I'd asked for a black light and a guitar, but Mummie had given me a white, fake-fur hat-and-muff set that made me look infantile. I'd given her a yellow cardigan. She said it was

too big and returned it. She never said what she'd exchanged it
for, and I forgot to ask.

I pushed away from the bed, turned on my record player,
and put on a French record. Then I walked over to my closet. I
piled all the old dresses on a chair, my good ones on the bed.
When I was finished with the clothes, I sat down on the floor
and began sorting my shoes. I heard a noise behind me, and I
looked over my shoulder. Mummie stood in the doorway.

"Que voulez-vous?" I asked.

"Stop talking that stupid pig Latin!" she shouted. She
crossed the room and snapped off the stereo. The voice on the
record receded in slow motion, *"Est-ce qu'il va faire beau?"*

"It's not pig Latin," I said coldly. "It's French."

"Ha! You hope it is," she sneered. Then she pointed to the
piles of clothes and shoes. "What in god's name do you think
you're doing?"

"Cleaning my closet," I said.

"Cleaning! You make me want to laugh. You've done nothing but make a mess! What do you plan to do with these?" She
gestured to the stack of dresses on the chair.

"I don't know." I reached into the closet for another shoe.
"Maybe I'll give them to Violet."

"Violet?"

I looked up, and when I saw my mother's face, I knew I
should have kept my mouth shut. Before I could say anything,
she walked across the room and jerked the shoe out of my
hands.

"Okay! I was only kidding!" I held my hands over my head.
I was afraid she would hit me with the shoe. "I didn't mean it!"

"You'd better not mean it. I'm not giving anything to that
little bastard. I never saw Sister's marriage certificate. And I
don't want her twerp wearing your hand-me-downs. Why,

people might confuse the two of you. They'll see a girl in a blue velveteen dress and she'll be picking her nose and they'll think it's you."

"They won't."

"They will, and they'll think it's you." She shook the shoe in the air. "Violet has a mother. Let her mother provide, just as I provided for you."

I looked down at the floor to keep from smirking. What a laugh. We both knew who paid the bills around here: Father. It came to me that no one paid Violet's bills except Miss Gussie. At least my father was alive, even if he didn't live with me.

"Anyway, who put this notion in your head, Miss Generosity?"

"You did. You told me to clean my closet." I stared at her. I was getting mad. "I was just following orders."

"Why, you no-good, ungrateful smart mouth! I'll show you!" She threw down the shoe, grabbed my arm, and pulled me over to Miss Gussie's house. I didn't fight back. She opened the screen door and shoved me inside the kitchen. Miss Gussie and Violet were standing at the counter, canning tomato juice. As Miss Gussie looked at us, her eyebrows drew together.

"Dorothy? What's wrong?"

"Let's get one thing straight," Mummie said, breathing fast. "There will be no more hand-me-downs from my house. I'm sick and tired of you using my child to get things for your precious matchgirl!"

"What are you talking about?" Miss Gussie said.

"You know good and well! You've been filling Bitsy's ears about how pitiful Violet is, haven't you? You'd do anything to get our old things."

"What?" Miss Gussie's face sagged. She looked over at Violet. I glanced at her, too. I couldn't see her face. It was hidden by a panel of dark hair. Her fingers were stained red from the tomatoes. She was wearing thin cotton shorts. Miss Gussie had made them, and they were pressed so neat and nice. I looked down at my matched shorts and blouse and felt ashamed. I was still jealous, I couldn't stop it, but I knew it wasn't her fault that she lived with Miss Gussie. We didn't have whole families. I never thought it would happen to me. I didn't know a single person at my school whose parents were divorced.

Mummie opened the screen door, letting in a rush of heat. Then she turned to glare at me. "You come home where you belong," she said in the same tone she used on Domino. As she walked down the porch steps, the door clapped shut behind her.

Miss Gussie sighed. "Why your mother gets on these tangents I'll never know."

"I'm sorry," I said.

"Oh, honey." She put her arms around me. "It's not your fault."

Later, Violet and I walked to town. We went to Father's store once or twice a week. That was the only way I got to see him. He'd give us a few dollars and treat us to cherry Cokes at the drugstore. We found him upstairs in his office, sitting at his desk, tapping keys on an adding machine. There was a half-eaten doughnut at his elbow. Next to the doughnut were pictures of me and Mack. There was even a picture of Mummie. Father leaned back and looked at us. His tie was off, and his shirt was open at the neck.

"Bitsy, I didn't know you were coming today," he said. He didn't seem happy to see me, which was the last thing I needed. I already felt like I didn't have a mother, not a normal one. I wanted to make her pay for driving my father away. Some nights, for lack of something to do, she ranted and raved. She blamed Aunt Clancy for everything. She said history repeated, that her sister had a habit of running off and disappearing. Whole years could pass without a single word.

"I'm the steady one," said Mummie. "No, indeed. You won't catch me abandoning my family."

No, I thought, you'll just shave off your eyebrows.

Sometimes I thought my cousin was luckier than she realized. She never mentioned Aunt Clancy. In the beginning I wondered if she were dead. Hit by a car, starved to death, buried in some shallow grave, sold into white slavery. Things like that happened all the time. Then Miss Gussie told us that Aunt Clancy was living on a pig farm somewhere out west. Violet even flew out there to visit. All by herself. Miss Gussie let her. I didn't have the nerve to ask, but I wondered what a pig farm was, exactly. Did they raise them for pets or to slaughter? An image rose in my mind, of a roasted suckling pig, an entree on a menu, *cochon de lait.*

Just then, a woman in a pink uniform stepped out of the lounge. She was straightening her skirt. When she saw me, her eyes almost popped out of her head. I recognized her as the waitress from the doughnut shop around the corner. I didn't understand what she was doing upstairs in my father's store. His face turned red as he gestured to the greasy paper sack on his desk and the doughnut. Beside the sack was a full bottle of 7UP.

"Dory was just bringing me some lunch," he said. "You know Dory, don't you?"

"Hi, girls," she said.

"Hi," said Violet.

"Nice to meet you," said Dory.

I didn't say anything. It wasn't nice to meet her. She had no business here. I wanted Father to come back to us.

"Aren't you going to say anything, Bitsy?" said Father.

I shook my head.

Dory blushed all the way to her scalp. She was almost pretty, in spite of her hair being too dark, teased a mile high, and she was wearing too much mascara. Her eyebrows were arched, like brushed mink, and her irises were dark brown. She was the sort of woman my mother would dismiss as low-class, a gold digger. Somebody a man could catch a nasty disease from, a *demimondaine*.

"Oh, me," Father said as he reached into his back pocket and opened up his wallet. He handed me two hundred-dollar bills. "Here, honey," he said, fitting the bills into my hand. "Why don't you and Violet go buy yourselves some pretty things?"

Dory stared at the floor. Her breasts rose and fell under the pink blouse. I smelled her cheap perfume. There was something comforting and motherly about her breasts. I thought about Mummie jerking the old shoe from my hands. I thought of her smooth forehead, the shelf of bone over her burning eyes, the sketched brows. She was horrible. I didn't want to grow up and turn into her. Father hadn't turned to Aunt Clancy on accident. He would have turned to any woman who gave him half a chance. There wasn't anything I could do about it.

"*Merci,* Father." I leaned over and kissed him on the cheek. Then Violet and I ran down the stairs, through the store, and into the street.

*S*ometimes you think you've seen the worst, and you haven't. The end of February, we got a telegram from the Marines.

Mack had been wounded in action at Hue. And all this time we'd been relieved that he hadn't been sent to the Khe Sanh. Mack said it could have been worse, but not by much. A rocket-propelled grenade exploded near him, and Mack caught shrapnel in his right leg. He wrote me a letter from a hospital in Japan.

March 10, 1968

Dear Bitsy,

The medics keep teasing me, saying the RPG was coated in pure VC shit. Now I got me a bad case of gangrene, I kid you not. I told them maybe it was NVR shit. Victor/Charlie does this on purpose with booby traps and mines, to cause infections and blood poisoning. I don't know & I don't care. The medic in the field hospital said my leg was pretty bad. When he was cleaning the wound, he picked out everything from rocks to wood slivers. Do you know how big an RPG is? It's about the size of a grapefruit, but I've seen them bring down helicopters. When they got the bleeding stopped, they sent me straight to Japan. They've tried like hell to save my leg, but it's green & black and smelly. It oozes pus & stinks like a dead cat. They're still giving me medicine to keep my blood from getting poisoned, but it looks like I'm gonna lose my leg. Right below the knee. I don't like to think about that. They say I was lucky, real lucky, that I got me a million dollar wound. But that just makes me feel bad. I've seen so much worse. Do you remember the colored guy I wrote you about? Lenny Boy King, from Valdosta, Georgia? He told the best jokes I've ever heard. I even wrote you some, remember? He got hit with an RPG round, and it blew off his arm at the shoulder. I have written his mother. When the medics were carrying us out, the VC opened fire. I never saw the bastards,

I just heard their guns, tat-tat-tat-tat. They have those good AK-47s from the Chinese. Anyway, this medic was carrying my stretcher & all of a sudden he fell to his knees. Blood was pouring out of him. He got shot twice in the gut, one bullet went in above his dick & came out his asshole. It blew it clear off. The other medic & my sergeant threw the guy on top of me & they picked up the stretcher & ran like hell to the helicopter. The whole time, the VC were firing. Tat-tat-tat. The choppers were going whap-whap-whap. I saw the medic in the hospital & it looks like he's going to be OK. They've reworked his plumbing & now he shits into a bag on his side. I'm not sure when I'll get out of here. I don't want to come home but I don't have no place else to go.

Love,

Mack

When Mummie heard the news about Mack, she vomited two whole days. It was terrible. She gripped the toilet and heaved until blood vessels ruptured in her right eye. Miss Gussie finally had to call her doctor. He was a Yankee, but he looked like a regular Dr. Kildare. Dr. Byron Falk was stitched on the pocket of his *blanc* coat. He gave Mummie a shot, and she slept for twelve hours. I hated to leave her alone, so Violet came over to keep me company. She understood about Vietnam. She talked about her daddy, and I knew she had to miss him. My father lived across town, and I missed him. I imagined losing him. I imagined Mack's infection getting worse. I worried that he'd die and get sent home in a casket. Like a crate of fruit, a side of meat. Just the other evening the news showed flag-draped boxes. I knew they were full of dead boys. The reporter said some of the boxes were empty—some were practically empty. The rows went on and on like reflections in a three-way mirror.

The evening news was full of death. When Martin Luther King got murdered, I was sleeping. The news showed cities going wild—people breaking windows, getting clubbed by the police. Nothing bad was happening in Crystal Falls, but Mummie locked all our doors. We slept with the lights on. We weren't taking any chances. Mummie took to her bed for days on end. Domino whined and sulked around the house. I thought to myself, *c'est la guerre*. I was worried sick about Mack. Even though he was in Japan, his letters failed to calm me. I was afraid something would go wrong, that I'd never see him again.

April 26, 1968

Dear Bitsy,

I heard about Martin Luther King getting murdered in Memphis. I don't understand it. Why did James Earl Ray have to go and do that? If he wanted to shoot somebody so goddamn much, why didn't he come to Vietnam? Something like this makes me want to puke. I'm ashamed to say I'm from Tennessee. I hate this fucking war. Tell Queenie how sorry I am, but don't tell her I cursed. I would like someday to take her to Washington, D.C., to see where King marched. I'm glad that fat fucker from Texas isn't running again. Daddy says he's voting for Bobby Kennedy. I hope Miss Gussie does likewise. I'll write her too. I just pray that the U.S. pulls out soon, but I don't see how. We're dug in. It would take us a year to ship out all the Jeeps & chinooks & tanks & stuff. I guess you heard what Westmoreland said, that he had to destroy Hue to save it? Did you ever see me on the news? Kennedy's the one who'll stop sending kids over here. They look younger & younger all the time. I can't get over it. Some of them here in the hospital are helpless as babies. They've got to be turned, they piss on themselves, they don't have no arms or legs. So you can see I got out of this lucky. What's 1½ legs? There's a guy with one arm, and he told me that having one arm isn't much better than having none. The guy from the next bed said at least you can wipe your own ass. He's paralyzed from his neck down & smokes cigarettes through a hole in his neck. Sometimes, when I hold his cigs, I want to cut loose & cry. But I don't. I hold it in. I can't cry here. Nobody does. It wouldn't do any good. It won't until we're out of here.

Your brother,
Mack

I came home from a date with Claude, who had been trying to get into my bra all night, and found Domino scratching at the bathroom door.

"What's wrong girl?" I said. She looked up at me and whined. I opened the door and gasped when I saw the blood. It was all over the pink tile, all over Mummie. I knelt beside her, thinking she'd been murdered, and stared at her arms. The blood was coming from her wrists. There was a razor blade on the sink. Her eyes were open. Domino lowered her head and sniffed the blood. All I could think about was calling an ambulance.

"I'll get some help," I said. When I stood up, her hand closed on my dress. I looked down at her bloody hands, surprised at her strength.

"Don't call anyone but your father!" she hissed. "Promise!"

"But you'll bleed to death!" I cried.

"No." She shook her head and pulled down hard on my dress, smearing the fabric with red fingerprints. "Call him."

Father came over and said she hadn't cut an artery, that her wounds were superficial. He stopped the bleeding by wrapping each wrist in heavy gauze bandages.

"Look. White cuffs," she said, holding up one arm. "I always wanted some."

Then she looked at my father. "This is silly, Albert. Why don't you come on home? I can't tell you how empty this house has been without Mack."

"We'll talk about it later," he said, cutting his eyes away from her.

"No." Her jaw turned square and hard. "Let's talk about it now."

"Dorothy, you're not well. Besides, there's nothing to discuss."

"Oh yes there is." She turned to me. "Bitsy, ask your father if he wants to come back home."

I shut my eyes.

"For god's sake, Dorothy," Father said quietly. "Leave her alone."

"Go on, Bitsy. Ask him."

I looked at my father, but before I could speak he came over and put his arms around me. "No, sugar. I'm staying put for now." I'd never heard such sadness in his voice. It was as if he were telling me that someone had died.

"What do you mean, you're staying put?" Mummie's forehead wrinkled. One eyebrow was smeared into her hairline. She blinked, pushing tears out of her eyes. "You're not trying to tell me you want a divorce, are you? Because if you are, I won't give you one. Not in a million years."

He looked over at me, and in his eyes I saw Dory and her pink uniform, her whole decorated self. Why, he thought she was pretty, just beautiful! That's what counted. I was filled with longing for a mother like that, with eyebrows and soft breasts, with the soothing aroma of fried doughnuts and chocolate icing in her hair. Someone with cool hands who would push my bangs from my forehead. Someone who would look down at me and ask, *"Qu'est-ce qu'il y a?"*

I would answer, *"Je suis perdue."*

"Ça ne fait rien, ma chère," she'd say. *"Ici on parle français."*

Part Four

Violet

1971

Mr. and Mrs. Albert McDougal
request the honor of your presence
at the marriage of their daughter
Lillian Beatrice
to
Claude Edmund Wentworth IV
on June thirtieth nineteen hundred seventy-one
at seven o'clock
First Baptist Church
Crystal Falls, Tennessee

R.S.V.P.

Reception immediately following
at Crystal Falls Golf and Country Club

*R*ight after we graduated, Meathead gave Bitsy a marquise diamond—one carat. It was one of his mother's rings. Bitsy's daddy gave her a blue Mustang convertible. It had blue leather bucket seats and an eight-track tape deck. Meathead's parents gave him a red Corvette. With a nickname like that you'd think he had a face like a pot roast. He didn't. Even if he was a bit of a mama's boy, he was real handsome, like a blond Warren Beatty: two great big dimples framed his mouth; dark blue eyes that were so clear and polished you wondered if he used Windex; one red mole above his lip, which made him look sexy. When he and Bitsy stood side-by-side, they looked like a picture from *Modern Bride.* They'd been voted Mr. and Miss Senior Class and cutest couple. He was college-bound, Tennessee Tech, which made his mama ill. She wanted him to go to a famous college, like Harvard or Yale, but he was marrying Bitsy instead. My cousin planned to work at a bank in Cookeville, Tennessee, while Meathead went to Tech. They were going to live in the married students' apartments.

Me, I was going to college, and I didn't care if I ever got married. The boys I dated were not pretty like Meathead. Some were downright ugly, but they were smart, straight-A students. That made up for a lot in my opinion. Miss Gussie said, "You just date those boys on purpose, so you won't fall in love and ruin your plans for college."

I just laughed. I had me a full scholarship to the University of Tennessee. I was going to be a marine biologist. Or maybe an ornithologist. I couldn't decide.

"Love's the furthest thing from my mind," I said. It was the truth. Love was a waste of time. "And just look at me," I added. "I'm not the prettiest thing to walk the earth."

Queenie was listening from the other room. She hollered out, "And you ain't the ugliest, neither."

"Some people might argue you down," I hollered back, but she just grunted. I was sort of plain, and that was the naked truth. I didn't care. I wanted to get a Ph.D. I wanted something solid. Love was pure air. I wasn't ignorant. I knew about attraction, how it could make you do foolish things. When I was younger, Meathead used to flirt with me to make Bitsy mad. It worked, too. Push a button, and watch Bitsy jump. She wasn't stupid, and she wasn't plain. Even when we were young, she was beautiful. She had long blond hair that she rolled on empty lemonade cans. We didn't even look related. We didn't act related. She loved Dionne Warwick and would dance around the room singing "I Say a Little Prayer" until my eyes crossed. She'd cry every time Glen Campbell sang "Wichita Lineman" on the radio. Her favorite movies were *Chitty Chitty Bang Bang, Dr. Zhivago,* and *The Sound of Music.* She walked out of *2001* when the monkeys began crawling over the monolith. She'd never heard of *I Am Curious (Yellow)*. She thought *Easy Rider* didn't have a plot. She hated "The 59th St. Bridge Song," "Ohio," and everything by Canned Heat. She said "Going Up the Country" made her think of Mack getting wounded at Hue. When the National Guard killed those students last year, she said, "Those students shouldn't have egged them on."

When she announced that she was getting married June 30, Aunt Dorothy was fit to be tied. She got all agitated and said June 30 was wrong, wrong, wrong. That the moon would be in Scorpio, or some such nonsense. She begged Bitsy to get married between July 6 and August 14, when the moon and planets were in harmonious alignment. She was real into astrology and wouldn't get out of bed until after she'd looked at her chart. She even read her dog's horoscope. She didn't know Domino's exact birth date, so she estimated that the animal was a Pisces. Just to make sure, she'd even phoned the little boy who sold her the dog, but the boy couldn't remember. She made Domino a chart, then she made one for each of us. Queenie said it was witchy and stuck it in a drawer and laid a Bible over it.

"You've just got to change the date," Aunt Dorothy begged.

"I can't," Bitsy said. "I'm going to be a June bride, and that's that."

"Well, be my guest," Aunt Dorothy said, folding her arms. "But you'll be getting married under a taint."

"So?" Bitsy narrowed her eyes. "I've lived under one my whole life."

Aunt Dorothy's mouth puckered. Then her smooth forehead drew up and wrinkled. She looked so weird. Some people weren't happy unless they were stirring up trouble, going from one crisis to the next. I don't like to name names, but my aunt was one who was always in a state. "Miss Dorothy be like the sunshine," Queenie once said. "Some days she shines strong, and other days she don't come out at all."

Now Bitsy's voice changed to sugar. "Oh, Mummie, forget about those silly charts for once! Are you going to be sweet and help me plan things or not?"

"I wouldn't touch this wedding with a ten-foot pole," she said.

*B*itsy spoke in French when she asked me to be in her wedding. She called it *dame d'honneur,* which was her fancy way of asking me to be her maid of honor. I didn't speak French, but I figured it out. I could almost speak it after listening to her the last five years. Me, I'd taken Spanish in high school. What I'd really needed was Latin, but Crystal Falls was too backward for that.

Bitsy's wedding was going to be huge. More than 350 invitations were mailed. I know. I helped address them. I licked stamps until I wanted to scream. But something good came out of all that work. My mama was coming to the wedding. She hadn't been home in years. She lived on a hog farm in New

Mexico, what she called The Garden. When she left us, it took her a whole summer to write. She sent a postcard. Then she sent beads made out of polished stones just yea-big and a poster that said "Flower Power." She sent paper jewelry. Real hippie stuff. I couldn't believe it. I kept all of her letters and postcards in a shoebox. At night I listened to music and wondered if Mama was listening to the same songs. I propped the portable radio next to my ear, and it was almost like the songs were being whispered. The lyrics spoke of California and wild hippie nights. Mama had started out being a simple song, like "Doo Wah Diddy Diddy." I didn't know for sure, but I suspected she'd gotten real complex, like that song "Light My Fire." Then it came to me that our lives didn't resemble music; it was more like math, an algebra equation:

$$Y \text{ (Hart)} + X \text{ (Clancy)} = Z \text{ (me)}.$$

Z could have been anyone.

I cried for two solid weeks when she disappeared. No letter, no phone call, no explanation. I heard three different versions of that mess with Uncle Albert—Miss Gussie's, Queenie's, and Aunt Dorothy's. The most important version—Mama's—hadn't been heard. I just knew she'd come back and clear everything up. I thought maybe she had been getting something out of Uncle Albert's eye. A piece of lint, maybe. Or they could have been in love. I didn't think so, but I wasn't sure. I hadn't seen what Aunt Dorothy claimed she'd seen. I tried to remember if I'd done something to cause it. It didn't matter. Mama was gone, and I missed her. No one, not even Miss Gussie, could take her place.

In those days I still didn't think of my grandmother's house as home. It was such a new memory. I couldn't reach back into my childhood the way Bitsy or Mack could and know that the roses in the bedroom wallpaper had always been the same. I was just now getting used to nighttime creaks, the house expanding and contracting. I thought I might grow up and move away before I got accustomed to every little thing.

In Crystal Falls you didn't see mothers running off. But there was nothing you could do to stop one who'd gotten it in her mind to run. The same went for men. Uncle Albert was living in a new brick house. Now that he wasn't dating Dory, he dated widows. He and Dorothy were still married, only they hadn't lived together since 1967. She just went right ahead and acted like nothing was wrong. Bitsy's wedding invitations were proof. Mr. and Mrs. McDougal, my foot. Uncle Albert gave her money right and left. And Miss Gussie said that his dime store wasn't doing any good at all, what with the new K mart down the street and its super-duper low prices.

But I didn't know.

I never talked about Mama. I held everything in a clear glass box within my chest. That whole summer I moved slowly, afraid of shattering my insides. It wasn't until after she moved to the hog farm that she phoned us. It was early September, the first time I'd heard her voice in three months. She said she'd been through some rough times, but everything was fine now.

"Are you ever coming back?" I asked, first thing. I missed her, but I was confused. I didn't know if she still wanted to be my mother. I was just a kid. I didn't know anything.

There was a long pause. I heard static on the line, like a needle scratching against fabric. She finally said, "Sure, I'm coming back."

"When?" I gripped the receiver. I wanted to see her face. I had to know that I hadn't invented her voice.

"Soon, baby. Real soon."

I started crying. I didn't believe her. Miss Gussie got on the phone and talked to Mama. They made plans for me to fly out to New Mexico all by myself.

When Mama picked me up at the airport in Albuquerque, I saw that she was a real live hippie. It embarrassed me to death. And she looked younger. She had on a baggy dress, all fringed like an Indian's, and sandals a man would wear. Her toenails were not painted. Her hair hung past her shoulders and was parted down the middle. She hugged me so hard I thought I would stop breathing.

"Oh, baby!" she cried, squeezing my neck. "Oh, Violet!"

She was driving a beat-up van which was painted orange and pink and red, like a huge tattoo. It was like sitting inside of a carnival ride. We drove a long time. I'd never seen such dry, dead land. It looked like pictures of the Holy Land with that sharp blue sky and mountains carved up like bones.

Mama lived all by herself in a real little adobe house surrounded by other little houses. There were even some tepees, and actual people lived in them. I couldn't figure out why they called it a hog farm. I didn't see so many hogs. And I didn't see why they called it The Garden, either. There wasn't much agriculture. It was real dry there. You couldn't get blood out of a turnip.

She had a little easel set up in front of a window, which overlooked dust swirling over some mountains. The mountains there were strange—they didn't have any trees or grass. They were huge, bare rocks, grained with different colors. Her paints were neatly laid out on her desk, watercolors and oils. Her desk wasn't anything more than an old door suspended over two filing cabinets. Next to the easel was a wineglass full of bird feathers, what she called her totems. Above her bed was a poster, MAKE LOVE, NOT WAR. Another poster showed a yellow submarine. That came from a Beatles' song. Mama and I had always listened to the same bands. She taught me to hear the layers in music. I remembered what Miss Gussie had said about rock-and-roll singers. She called them Yippies, Hippies, and out-and-out sinners. "I don't know what the world's coming to," she always told me and Queenie. My heart sank when I saw an astrology book on the shelf. I wondered how much of Aunt Dorothy she had in her. They were, after all, blood kin.

Mama said she'd sold some paintings, and she showed me her canvases. I was amazed that she knew how to paint, but she said she'd learned a long time ago. I flipped through them, thinking they were good even if the colors were too strong. There were pictures of red-brown rocks, mountains of clay, beneath a hard blue sky. There were pictures of enormous flowers with insects crawling on the petals. There were dozens of pictures of Indian babies. Mama said she couldn't paint them fast enough. She told me she sold them in a gallery.

When she wasn't painting, she and Sunny made Indian jewelry and sold it at craft fairs. The jewelry was real pretty. She gave me a silver necklace studded with turquoise and a ring all wound up like a snake with turquoise eyes. Sunny lived in another adobe house with a great big loom, and she raised sheep. She called my mama Star. Sunny said she would weave me a blanket for five dollars, and I could pick the colors. She dyed the wool with herbs. Amos was her boyfriend, but he was getting ready to move to Boulder, Colorado, to be a monk or something. He seemed to be a dope fiend. He wore a black patch over his right eye, but I didn't have the nerve to ask what had happened.

Mama's new life was built around natural things—solar power and organic gardening. I didn't know what to think. Women breast-fed their babies right in the open. Men walked around with their hair tied into ponytails, like a girl's. A lot of them had college degrees, even Ph.D.s. "Wow," they said when the least thing happened. They didn't seem as awful as I'd seen on TV. They were just regular people. In a way they were neat. They didn't believe in the war that had taken my daddy, but at least they were trying to do something about it.

That night Mama slept on a cot and gave me her bed. It had a heavy blanket—red, yellow, and black on dark cream wool, woven with Indian patterns. I had trouble relaxing. From one of the other houses, I heard tambourines, guitar music, and low scratchy voices. They were singing "Monday, Monday." There was a window over Mama's cot, and I watched the moon skate over the rocks. I didn't have a memory of falling asleep. Twice I heard something howl, and I closed my eyes. Then it was morning.

We went outside to the iron pump and filled our buckets. Mama handled the pump like she'd been doing it her whole life. Her gestures were full of new knowledge, and somehow they made me feel older. My hands ached as we carried the buckets back to the kitchen. She seemed used to hard work. I wasn't. Miss Gussie and Queenie did everything for me. I had no idea that living could be so complicated—water, warmth, food. She reached down and fed piñon into the stove. Red sparks drifted out of the grate. She told me that piñon was a kind of scrubby pine. It reminded me of cedars back home. We were getting ready to make bread, whole wheat. The hippies divided chores—baking and sewing, gardening and baby-sitting, laundry and hog-tending. I was glad someone else was doing the laundry. Mama said it took all day. The hippies had to haul bucket after bucket of water to a kitchen. The temperature in the kitchen would already be high due to summer heat, but the hippies had to stoke up a fire anyway. They fed kindling into the grate while water heated in huge, steaming pans. Then they poured the boiling water into larger pails and hauled them back outside to metal troughs, like horses drink from. They spent all morning stirring, adding soap powder, hauling rinse water, wringing out clothes.

We hadn't seen each other all summer, and it soothed me to watch Mama sift brown flour into a bowl. It was a chipped glass bowl, the kind my grandmother had in her kitchen. Mama's kitchen counters were clean and bare except for a basket of pears. The yellow Formica buckled in places next to the sink. It had been scrubbed until the pattern had faded. There was a narrow kitchen window over the makeshift sink, which was nothing more than a stainless-steel sink fit into the Formica. It drained into a bucket. We had to empty it several times a day. I'd never before thought about plumbing. It had always seemed meant to be, like water draining into the ponds and lakes after a heavy rain.

I loved the way her house smelled, like air had been drawn from the iron pump. There was a cold, metallic bite to the water, a steely edge that seemed to settle everywhere like gray dust. I tried to set everything into my memory as I greased the pans. They were heavy cast iron. Mama kneaded the dough, thumping it with the heel of her hand. Behind her the narrow window was all sky, blue and cloudless. Way off in the distance a blackbird circled. Specks of flour wafted in the light. I ached to live here. I didn't see why I couldn't. There wasn't much space, but we could find me a used bed at a junk shop. And if Mama needed privacy we could divide the room with a quilt. Or we could get a bigger house and send for Miss Gussie and Queenie. We could do that. But if she wanted me to live with her, why hadn't she mentioned it? I hadn't brought enough clothes, just one of the old green suitcases.

Thump, thump went Mama's hands like a slow pulse. She was wearing a long purple dress. Beneath her eyes were matching circles, carved half-moons of color. She looked thinner, as if the bright southwestern air had whittled her down. She didn't look like someone from Tennessee. I knew then I had lost her.

"Are you staying here forever?" I blurted, surprising myself.

"Here?" The thumping stopped. She glanced up from the dough. "Oh, no. Not forever. I don't think so. Why?"

"Because." I swallowed hard. I was afraid I might cry. From outside, I heard someone singing "Sunshine Superman" as they chopped wood. Nothing here seemed real. Not this kitchen or the red fire in the stove. It was a dream, and I'd wake up. Mama would say, "Upsy-daisy, Violet. You'll miss the bus. Hurry, hurry."

"Because what?" she said. Her hand was frozen against the dough.

I felt something drip down my face. Tears. I wiped my chin on my sleeve. "Because I can't see you leaving. Can you?"

"Oh, baby, don't cry."

"I'm not. So, are you going to leave or what? It doesn't matter." I didn't mean it. I was testing her. I wanted her to say *Sure I'm leaving. I hate this place. I'm going back home with you.*

She lifted one hand from the dough, as if to touch me, then she looked down at her sticky palm. "Oh, dear. I don't want to get you all messy."

"I don't care. I like messes." I wiped my chin again.

"Baby." She put her arms around me.

"Why'd you have to leave?" I said, pressing my face into her shoulder. I already knew the answer, but I wanted to hear her say it.

"I don't know. Something just snapped." Her voice was tiny.

"But why?" I opened one eye and saw purple fabric. I'd gotten her whole shoulder damp.

"Oh, that awful stuff with, you know, Albert."

"But that didn't matter." I pulled back to look at her. We were almost the same height.

"No. I guess it didn't. I realize that now. I don't think Albert meant any harm. When he touched me, Violet, it was like a daddy's touch. You know what I mean?"

I wasn't sure, but I nodded. She looked out the window. I looked, too. The blackbird was still circling.

"Then you'll come home?" I said.

"No." The word was so faint, almost whispered, I wondered if she had really said yes. She touched my face, and I smelled dough and yeast, her whole floury scent.

"You lied. Just a minute ago you said you weren't staying here forever." I pulled away and leaned against the counter. "So you lied."

"Oh, Violet. I just meant not *now*."

"You lied!" I was hollering. I wanted to run away. If I'd been in Crystal Falls, I would have disappeared. I wouldn't have written, either. "You don't want me. You just don't want to be a mother anymore. You want to be a stupid hippie. You want to be sixteen again. That's all you want."

"That's not true." Her eyes filled. The irises looked like wreaths of algae. "Don't say that."

"Why? You never called. You just sent those crummy postcards. Those stupid, ugly beads." I knew I sounded like a brat, but I couldn't stop. I was so mad. "You don't even have room for me if I wanted to live here."

She wiped her eyes. Her whole face looked pale. "There's always room, baby. Always. You know that."

"I don't know it. And you didn't have to move here. A

stupid hog farm. It stinks. This stupid bread stinks. I hate it all."

"You don't know what happened."

"I do, too!"

"No." Something in her voice was different, harder. "In the beginning I *was* running away from home. I was so ashamed. My life kept getting these kinks, and I couldn't work them out."

"So what? Mine did, too. But I stuck it out." An image of Daddy came to me, and I started crying. "You should've, too."

"No. You're strong, Violet. You really are. You're like my mother. She can stand anything. Even when Papa was so sick, she kept going to Sunday school. She baked pies for old people. She planted her lettuce and corn—"

"I don't care about that!"

"Well, maybe not. But you will someday."

"I won't."

"Oh, listen, honey. The reason I came here isn't important. What really matters is why I've stayed."

"What's that?" I wiped my cheek.

"Something real bad happened." She looked back at the dough. Her bottom lip jerked. She reached behind her, blindly searching for a kitchen chair. She sat down and rested one grainy palm on the oilcloth. I walked around the table and sat down, too.

"It happened to the three of us. Me, Amos, and Sunny. San Francisco had turned ugly. We heard about this place in New Mexico. It was full of good people who'd gotten sick of it all. Good people who had done nothing but carry signs."

I just stared at her hands, all crusted with the wheat flour. She was talking about things I didn't care about.

"The whole world had gone crazy, at least in California. You wouldn't believe how many peace marches turned into beatings. People getting clubbed over the head. Thrown in jail. Innocent people. If you had long hair, you were a troublemaker. God, I'll bet the FBI has a file on me. Anyway, we packed the van and drove south." She looked up at me and smiled with one side of her mouth. "You know, real hippies aren't bad. They're gentle people. With a pure way of seeing things. They cut through the layers. That attracted me, Violet."

"Really." My voice was pure ice.

"I never planned on staying in Abiquiu. Just a week, maybe less. Then I was going to ride the bus back home. I missed you so much, baby. Anyway, on our way here, Amos's van broke down. We were in Ventura, California. Ever heard of it?"

I shook my head and looked out the window. The blackbird was gone.

"Well, it's next to the Pacific. Some men gave us a ride." She folded her hands, locking her fingers. "We didn't know they were bad."

"Bad?" I looked up, my attention caught.

She shut her eyes. Tears gathered in the corners. Outside a hacking sound started up again as someone else began chopping piñon.

"It's hard," she said and then paused, blinking. "It's still hard to talk about it."

"What?" I sat up straight.

"It's like, you've heard about, I mean . . ." She broke off and wiped her cheek. A piece of hard dough fell away. She looked at me. "You know what rape is?"

I nodded, starting to understand. Earlier in the summer, the police caught a man who'd raped an old woman. We were scared to death. Miss Gussie loaded a shotgun and kept it hidden in the bedroom. So I knew what it meant, but with all my strength, I wished I didn't.

"Well those men, those bad men, they raped us."

I was silent for a beat. "Us?"

"Amos and Sunny." She paused. "Me."

My hands clapped against my mouth. I felt sick.

"They left us for dead. They blinded Amos in one eye. That's why he wears the patch. But that wasn't the end of it. When the police came to the hospital, they told us we'd brought it on ourselves. There Amos was, one whole side of his face mashed in, and it was our fault."

I got up so fast I knocked over my chair. I pressed my face into her cool, purple lap. Her legs felt solid. She smoothed my hair down my back. "Why?" I said, my voice muffled by her dress.

"Because of what we were, what we stood for." Her voice cracked in the center of each word. "We were stupid to hitchhike."

"No. I meant why do men have to do that?"

She was silent a moment. "I don't know, baby. But most men aren't like that."

"Those men could've killed you."

"Well, they did. A little. A chunk of me, anyway." She lifted my chin. "But, hey, it's over. I'm here. And I need to stay here a bit longer. Until I get my nerve worked up. Until I'm whole again. Or nearly whole. This place has broken away from the rest of the world. It's a place to heal. Does that make sense, baby?"

No, it didn't, but I just hugged her tighter. I knew then that she'd let me stay, only I didn't need to. It wasn't necessary. Not in the way it was for her. We just held each other. Outside the chopping had stopped. Now the wood made a hollow, knocking sound as the man stacked his kindling. From far away I heard a piglet squeal. I looked up at Mama and wiped my face. "Your dough is getting hard."

"What? Oh." She reached down and laid her hands back on my face. "It can wait. There's no hurry."

*I*n spite of her forecast, Aunt Dorothy planted herself right in the middle of Bitsy's wedding plans. She studied *Bride.* She concocted color schemes. She called caterers. She came to our house and borrowed things. Nothing was ever brought back. Bitsy was bad about borrowing, too. They might as well have robbed us. They didn't seem to know that they were stealing. But I'd go next door, and there would be Miss Gussie's meat-loaf pan sitting on the counter with a pound cake in it. Or I'd see my new fingernail polish, which Bitsy borrowed before I ever got to use it, and the bottle would be half-empty. I didn't have the heart to ask for things back. But it was getting to the point where I told little lies when they asked to borrow something. I wasn't the only one.

"I know good and well you all have got scissors," Aunt Dorothy said when Queenie acted like she couldn't recall where she'd put them.

"Why do you need scissors?" I asked her. "I thought the whole thing was being catered."

"If *you* ever get married," Aunt Dorothy said with forced patience, "then you'll learn a thing or two about caterers. They don't make rice bags, for instance. And that's why I need scissors. I have all of this blue and white netting and nothing to cut it with."

I wanted to say, Why not use your teeth? But I didn't. I went and got the scissors.

Sometimes I thought Aunt Dorothy used borrowing as an

excuse to talk to us. She'd talk to anybody. Queenie said she did it to hear the sound of her own voice. If she thought we weren't listening, she'd talk louder and LOUDER. Sometimes she'd say, "If you all aren't interested, then I'll go home." But she never went home. She'd just change the subject. Most of the time she was upset with Bitsy. My aunt said she hadn't given her a proper amount of time to plan the wedding. She said it was customary for the bride's family to foot the bill for everything except flowers and the rehearsal dinner, which was the groom's responsibility. My aunt let out a weird giggle and said that Albert had a big surprise coming to him. She said the Wentworths did, too. She couldn't wait for them to see the flowers.

From the beginning, Miss Betty said she didn't want to be involved in the planning. She seemed bored by the whole thing, except when she didn't get her way. Sometimes I went to the Wentworths' house with Bitsy. It was a mansion. Tall ceilings. Mirrors with gold frames. Maids polishing the furniture. The whole house smelled of wax. Miss Betty was always on her way somewhere else. She'd have her pocketbook over her arm, her keys in her hands. She wore diamond rings and gold bracelets and drove a brown Mercedes. Bitsy called her Mrs. Wentworth. She called Bitsy Sugar Pie. If you asked her a question, she'd answer like she was doing you a big favor. She did not seem crazy about Sugar Pie. She was polite and gave us these thin-lipped smiles. Sometimes she'd walk out of the room while Bitsy was still talking. The next day I'd see her picture in the paper, a luncheon or fashion show. She was real big into society.

The only time she got upset about the wedding was when Bitsy let it slip that her mother was against serving alcohol at the reception. Miss Betty's eyes narrowed. "If that's the case, Sugar Pie, then you're crazy for having the reception at the club. You might as well have it at the church, even though I've always loathed churchy affairs. They smell so *chalky*."

"But the invitations have already been mailed," Bitsy said.

"Do what you want, Sugar Pie." Miss Betty threw up her hands. "Just keep me out of it."

Bitsy's eyes got big, but she didn't say one word. The next thing I knew, Aunt Dorothy had backed down. Bitsy said that in addition to champagne, two kinds of punch would be served. My aunt used to play bridge with Miss Betty years ago. After Uncle Albert moved to his store, Aunt Dorothy dropped out of her clubs. She got out of the social whirl, so to speak. Now all she seemed to care about was that dog of hers and watching soap operas. And trying to find a Mother-of-the-Bride dress. She and Bitsy drove to Nashville, like they were a regular mother and daughter, but they came back empty-handed. Aunt Dorothy swore she was going on a diet, that she wouldn't eat anything but cottage cheese and peaches for a month.

"The problem is, I can't find me a dress because of my waist," she told me and Queenie. "It's just so teeny-tiny."

Later Queenie said, "She can't be fit because her thighs be big as country hams."

There was also a problem with Mack. Miss Betty was worried about him being an usher on account of his leg. And that was the least of it. When Mack was discharged from the hospital in Japan, he went straight back to Saigon. He said he'd forgotten something. He returned to the States with a Vietnamese wife. Nobody could say her real name, but she could speak good English. French, too. Mack said to call her Sloopy. He said it was from that song "Hang on, Sloopy."

Aunt Dorothy liked to have died when Mack limped off the plane. Sloopy was out-to-here pregnant. My aunt bit her lip so hard she had to dab the blood off with a handkerchief. Her lip swelled, and when she talked, her words had a blunt, muffled sound. Uncle Albert got Mack started in the remodeling business. Mack could look at an old house and see things most people couldn't. He saw skylights, lofts, gingerbread porches. He hired a small crew, mostly other veterans, and they were right busy. He bought five acres in the country and built a ranch house for his new family. He said he built it for practice.

Miss Betty was opposed to Mack being an usher. She asked how he was supposed to seat the guests. "I don't want to hurt your feelings, Sugar Pie, but I don't see how he can participate. I know it's sad and everything about his leg, but I'm just thinking of the overall effect."

"He lost his leg in Vietnam, Mrs. Wentworth," said Bitsy. It took a lot for her to say that. She was scared of the Wentworths.

"Mmmhum. Well, do what you think is right."

"He can use his wooden leg," said Bitsy.

"As I was saying"—Miss Betty paused, studying her bracelet for loose diamonds—"do what you think is right."

When Aunt Dorothy found out, her face turned red, and she grabbed Bitsy's shoulders. "Betty Wentworth can go straight to hell. She's a fine one to talk about what's right! And she's not paying for this wedding, not one red cent!"

"What about the flowers?" asked Bitsy.

"They're a drop in the bucket! Why, I could travel around the world three times for what this wedding's costing. And you listen here, your brother *will* be an usher, and I don't care what she says!"

For once, I agreed with Aunt Dorothy.

But when Bitsy asked him, Mack shook his head. "Hell no, I don't want to be in no wedding," he said. "I was barely in my own."

A seamstress made the bridesmaids' dresses. The design

was straight from _Romeo and Juliet_. They were blue, with capped sleeves. The whole affair was going to be color-coordinated, which Aunt Dorothy insisted upon once she'd gotten over her astrological prediction. Everything from the rice bags to the mints would be blue and white.

The bride herself had chosen a Juliet gown with a Juliet cap with a long, luxurious veil. Her engagement picture, which sat on Miss Gussie's TV, showed her long blond hair, falling way past her shoulders. Her eyes were a lovely gray-blue. Me, I just let my hair grow long and it hung down my back. I parted it down the middle and tucked a panel behind each ear.

We spent whole afternoons in Bitsy's room, listening to records, looking at bride magazines, stretched out on Bitsy's bed, the air conditioner blowing across our legs, rippling our long hair. On her white dresser was a framed photograph of Meathead, his senior picture.

Above her dresser was a poster I'd given her last Christmas: WAR IS NOT HEALTHY FOR CHILDREN AND OTHER LIVING THINGS. We turned the pages slowly, looking at pictures of Waterford and Royal Doulton and Lenox. From the record player, the Beatles were singing "I Am the Walrus." I'd brought _Magical Mystery Tour, Abbey Road,_ and _The White Album_ from my house. I spread them on the bed and stared at the covers.

"Do you remember when everyone thought Paul was dead?" I asked Bitsy.

"Paul who?" She looked up from the magazine.

"Paul McCartney."

"Oh, right. The Paul-is-dead rumor. That happened ages ago. You remember the silliest things." She shrugged and picked up _The White Album_. "It was stupid. Like this album. It's all white. What did they do, run out of ink?"

It was my turn to shrug. I was thinking about "Revolution 9." When played backward the phrase "number nine . . . number nine" was supposed to sound like "turn me on, dead man." I scooted across the bed and reached for *Abbey Road.* On the cover, Paul was the only one who was barefoot. That was supposed to be a sign of death. And his armband on the inside cover of *Sgt. Pepper's* said OPD. That was supposed to mean "officially pronounced dead."

Bitsy got up and put on a stack of new records. She flopped back on the bed. Gordon Lightfoot started singing "If You Could Read My Mind," a typical Bitsy song. She picked up the magazine and parted her pretty lips and released a long sigh. She said, "I think I should've picked out Sculptured Grape for my pottery. It would've been cuter than the Sculptured Daisy. Don't you think so, too?"

She'd done this once already, changed every one of her patterns. That was embarrassing. You should have seen the way the jewelry store lady rolled her eyes and drew lines through the old choices on Bitsy's bridal card. Aunt Dorothy's dining room table was covered with wedding gifts—Wedgwood china, Waterford crystal, Reed and Barton sterling. To tell the truth, I didn't care about china patterns. I didn't care about gift teas or honeymoons in Florida. I was so full of this wedding I figured I wouldn't need a separate one for myself.

"No," I said to Bitsy, "I like what you've picked out."

"You really think so?" she asked around a wintergreen Life Saver. "You don't think that baby food might stick between the daisies?"

"Baby food? Why would you care about that?"

"Because I just do." She looked down at the magazine. Her eyelashes were long and dark. Little purple veins were stitched on her lids.

"Well, that's stupid." I rolled over on my back and stared at her sideways. "You don't feed babies off of dishes. You feed them out of plastic bowls with little animal decals stuck all over them. Your daddy sells them. Anyway, you won't be having a baby for years and years. Not until Meathead finishes college."

"I wish you wouldn't call him Meathead. His name is Claude. And we might have one before then."

"You'd better not!"

"You sound just like Miss Gussie. Old and fussy."

"It's the truth. Besides, Meathead would kill you if you turned up pregnant."

"No, he wouldn't. I mean, he hasn't yet."

I just stared.

"You might as well know the truth, Violet." She drew in another sigh. Her eyes got watery.

"You promise not to tell?" I nodded.

"I'm pregnant."

I looked down at her stomach. It looked flat to me. The word kept ringing in my ears: pregnantpregnantpregnant. I pictured her all swelled up. My mind skipped back to Mama, when she'd been carrying Dede. I couldn't imagine a baby coming out of Bitsy. I couldn't imagine her being a mama. It had to be a mistake.

"How do you know?" I asked.

"The doctor told me. He said I'm three months. It's due in December. A Christmas baby. Won't that be nice?"

I couldn't answer. I was horrified.

"Don't look at me that way," she said, and her eyes went flat. "We were going to get married anyway. We just got carried away. Anyway, we just did it once or twice. I swear it. That's why I didn't get on the Pill."

"I don't care about that." I sat up and crossed my legs Indian-style. "What did Meathead say?"

"*Claude* said nothing." Bitsy shrugged and looked at his photograph. "I don't think it's really hit him yet."

"What're you going to do when it does?"

"I don't know. He likes doing it. Maybe I can keep him distracted."

"Bitsy, this is awful!"

"No, it's not. It's nothing. I don't even feel pregnant. I swear it's nothing at all."

"Have you told Miss Gussie? And what about your mother?"

"No." She shook her head. "Nobody knows. Well, except for Miss Betty. We had to tell her, of course. She wouldn't have agreed to the wedding otherwise." Her eyes narrowed. "You know what she did? She tried to talk me into having an abortion. Can you believe it? She said she'd pay for everything."

"What did you say?"

"I told her to forget it, that I was having my baby. When I reminded her that she was talking about her very own grandchild, she backed down. She said I'd have to starve to keep the baby little. Then after it's born, she's going to tell everyone it's premature."

"Who'll believe her?"

"I can't worry about that now." Bitsy looked down at the magazine. Her forehead wrinkled as she stared at a Metlox pottery advertisement. It showed a newlywed couple sitting in a kitchen full of sunlight and bay windows. They were eating breakfast on plates with red and black roosters. From the record player, Mick Jagger started singing "Nineteenth Nervous Breakdown."

"I don't want to talk about it anymore," said Bitsy. "Claude loves me, and that's all that matters. Let's just look at these china patterns." She squinted at the page. "What do you think? Should I change patterns or what?"

I just looked at her pretty face and wondered if she could read my mind. I was thinking how stupid this whole marriage thing was. Love was like summer, I wanted to tell my cousin. Love was like the painted daisies on your china. Love was your daddy hanging out at the doughnut shop, it was your mother picking white meat off of chicken breasts for Domino, it was my mama living on a hog farm painting pictures of other people's children. It was you giving Meathead what he wanted so you could get what you wanted.

"I love the daisies," I finally said, and she heaved a big sigh and crunched down on the Life Saver.

"I do, too," she said. "I really do. It's cheerful. I'd hate eating off of roosters every day. Wouldn't you?"

"Yes."

We stared down at the Metlox picture, which showed the rooster strutting—one pointed claw stuck forward. Then I licked my finger and turned the page.

Miss Gussie

1971

Two days before the wedding, Violet drove me and Queenie to the Nashville airport to fetch Clancy Jane. She listened to loud music the whole way. The only one I liked was something about a McArthur's Park and a cake getting ruined by the rain. At the terminal, we sat in front of picture windows, watching the airplanes. Some people stared at Queenie. The man next to her got up and moved. When Clancy Jane came off the airplane, she looked fairly normal, not like you'd expect a hippie to look. She wore old-timey glasses with wire frames. Her hair was braided over one shoulder. She wore shoes and a yellow dress with a shawl. There was not a speck of make up on her face, which made her look peaked. She hugged me so hard I noticed bruises on my ribs the next day.

When we got home, I looked across the yard and saw Dorothy sitting on her porch. She was tying up rice bags—white netting with blue bows. I waved, and she waved back. When Clancy Jane waved, Dorothy got up and went into her house and slammed the door. She left the rice bags just sitting there.

"She's still mad at me," Clancy Jane said, staring at Dorothy's house.

"Yes, she's mad all right," I said, surprising myself, but

Clancy Jane didn't get it. She had brought a tiny oil painting for Bitsy's wedding gift. It was a morning glory.

"Did you paint this?" I asked.

"Lord, no. I wish I had. It's by Georgia O'Keeffe." Clancy squinted down at the picture. "I know her. Well, I don't actually *know* her, but I know some people who do. Don't tell Bitsy, but I got this painting for practically nothing. O'Keeffe was going to throw it away. But it'll be worth a lot someday."

I didn't say anything. But I could tell that Bitsy wouldn't like it. She was into early American, and she'd already decorated Meathead's old bedroom with gold eagles, braided rugs, and afghans. They were living with the Wentworths until Meathead started college in August.

After supper Violet went upstairs to help her mother unpack. I just sat awhile on the screened porch. It was quiet. The lightning bugs floated over the grass, blinking yellow, like slivers of topaz streaking the air. I wondered what the early settlers thought of fireflies. Tonight they looked like hundreds of fairy lights. The cicadas echoed, like voices in a well. The moon skated through the trees, spreading cool light over my garden, over the old graveyard. The land here had gone sky high, it cost a fortune, but I had no plans to sell until I was good and ready. Dorothy wished I would, so we could all live high on the hog. But I'd hate to look out and see houses, other people taking out the garbage or watering their lawns. The city had crept toward us, and we had neighbors up and down the road. But if you saw the view from my back porch, the old fields sloping into the trees, you'd think this was still the country.

Next door, the lights burned in Dorothy's kitchen. Things weren't right over there. Bitsy said as much. And I didn't think she was stretching the truth. All you had to do was look at

Dorothy's forehead, that scratchy place where her eyebrows used to be, and you'd know things were wrong.

Dorothy had gotten into horoscopes real big. She called herself a Capricorn. Even kept up with that dog's horoscope. She was losing her grip. Her house got dirtier and dirtier. When I'd walk inside, the smell would rush up my nose. It was more than a doggie stench. It was as if the house itself had an odor deep down. She lost interest in life. I think she was grieving for Albert, but she'd never come out and say it. Instead she stopped playing bridge. I wondered if she was ashamed to have those ladies come over and see all that filth. Piles of unopened mail on the kitchen counter. It was a wonder the electric department didn't cut off her lights. I didn't open my mouth. After Mack lost his leg, she let Bitsy run wild. Let her wear those boots and short skirts that showed all of her private parts. And she seemed relieved when the girl up and announced her wedding plans.

The year Albert left, she spent a fortune on Christmas decorations. Then she went and left them up. Year after year. I'd go over there on Labor Day, and there would sit her tree, the tinsel blowing in the cool, air-conditioned breeze. She said it cheered her up. I wondered if she did it to spite Albert, to make him feel sorry for her. I heard he'd broken up with that Dory. Now he dated widow ladies. They brought him pies and cookies. Nobody fussed at him to change the fuses or to repair the screen door. I had an idea he was happier than he'd been in years.

*T*he Wentworths hosted the rehearsal dinner at the country club. It is a one-story cinderblock building, painted beige, all covered with English ivy. There are old, crank-type windows on one wall. Beyond the windows is a great big blue swimming pool. On one side of the room was a bar where the young people gathered. And two kinds of punch, Christian and spiked. In silver bowls. That was Miss Betty's doings. In fact, the whole rehearsal dinner was her doings. Everything was white, which seemed a trifle pale to me, but I wasn't real up on decorating.

A violin player strolled around the little tables. Each table was set for six, with starched white cloths. Centerpieces full of lilies, daisies, Queen Anne's lace, and snapdragons. Candles flickering from silver and crystal holders. Napkins folded into tulips. Sterling silver stretched on either side of the plate. Three kinds of crystal. Waiters in tuxedos carrying champagne on silver trays. There was a strawberry in each glass.

Lord, I'd never seen such fanciness. It was out-and-out elegant, like something you'd see on TV. It reminded me of that tour Jackie Kennedy gave of the White House. And all this for the two families and the wedding party. The room was fairly full. I spotted Mack over by the spiked punch. He was wearing himself a new suit with a blue carnation. He gripped a cane. One leg of his suit was neatly pinned below the knee. Sloopy was standing next to him, just a-smiling. They had themselves a baby boy, Christopher, my great-grandchild, but he wasn't at the dinner, of course. He was with the baby-sitter, Mrs. Jolene Tucker, who used to be in my Sunday school class. Mack and Sloopy lived in the country, the sticks nearly, in a two-bedroom brick house. It was just as neat as a pin. You could eat off the floor. They had chickens, a horse, and two golden retrievers. Mack could hunt like anybody with two legs. The VA had fitted him with an artificial limb, but he said it bit into his stump. He wouldn't use it. And he wouldn't talk to Dorothy unless he had to. Not after the way she'd carried on the night Christopher was born. She went on and on about how that baby looked

Oriental and that her papa would die and don't anyone expect
her to baby-sit it. Lordy Jesus, Mack's face turned red. It was
like all the love he had for his mother had gotten thrown away
in his cut-off leg.

Now Albert walked up to his son and slapped him on the
shoulder. Albert looked mighty fine in his dark gray suit. His
hair had turned silver around the temples. Handsome. He
kissed Sloopy's cheek. When I looked at my grandson and his
chopped-off leg, I couldn't help but think of Hart. Sometimes
I wondered if he was still alive, wading through the jungle, a
victim of amnesia. But they'd sent back his dog tags. A piece of
them, anyway. He was dead as a doornail. Mack wouldn't talk
much about Vietnam. He said people ignored veterans. It
hadn't been that way after World War II. Come to think of it,
my Charlie wouldn't talk about the Pacific, either. Dorothy
would beg to see his scars, and he'd say, "Oh, me." Once in a
while, he'd pull up his shirt to make her hush. I always thought
all wars were the same, but they really aren't.

A waiter walked by, and Albert reached for two glasses of
champagne. He handed one to his son. Albert said something,
and Mack laughed. Dorothy fluttered on the other side of the
room. She acted like Clancy Jane wasn't there. She walked over
to me and hugged me so hard my punch swayed in the cup. I
caught a whiff of hairspray mingled with perfume. She looked
awful. Someone should have told her she shouldn't wear that
shade of pink. With all her blond hair, pink made her look
washed out.

"Betty Wentworth went all out, didn't she?" Dorothy whispered.

"She sure did." I took a sip of punch.

"Well, wait until she sees the reception tomorrow night,"
Dorothy hissed. "It'll knock her eyes out."

Meathead's great-aunt Sylvia walked up to us. "Hello, Gussie," she said, ignoring Dorothy. "I just heard that your Clancy Jane is an up-and-coming artist out in New Mexico?"

I nodded.

"I'm quite interested in art with a southwestern flair," said Sylvia, working her back to Dorothy.

Dorothy tapped her on the shoulder. "Excuse me? I'm an artist, too."

Sylvia didn't acknowledge her. "Would you be so kind as to introduce me to her after dinner?"

"Why, certainly."

Dorothy narrowed her eyes. Then she walked away. She went straight over to Miss Betty. Dorothy had this strange smile on her face. I knew that smile. It meant she wouldn't let up, wouldn't stop until she'd created a scene. Miss Betty saw her coming and inched backward until she was up against the windows. Behind her the pool sparkled. Dorothy stood smack in front of her, her mouth moving a mile a minute. Miss Betty's eyes darted around the room. She inched away from the window. I saw her lips move, *Excuse me excuse me excuse me.*

I wondered if she thought Bitsy came from a strange family. But I could have told her a thing or two about her husband's people. It would have shocked her drawers off. My people, the Johnsons, had been country folks. The Hamiltons were good stock, too. They went way back, all the way to the Revolutionary War. That was how they'd gotten the land in Tennessee—it had been a grant. This wedding had brought everything into focus for me. I thought how funny it was that my granddaughter was marrying a Wentworth. It chilled me just the least.

Miss Betty, having escaped from Dorothy, went around the room whispering that it was time to be seated. I sat next to two bridesmaids who kept giggling. The waiters carried trays of food. They brought shrimp cocktail. Then they cleared that away and brought a cold soup. Cucumber. They brought tomato aspic. They kept the wineglasses filled. They brought stuffed Cornish hens, rice, asparagus, and hard rolls. They brought pecan pie with a dollop of whipped cream. They brought coffee that smelled of orange peels and spices. It burned the back of my throat.

Throughout the meal, the Wentworths smiled. They made toasts to everyone but the bride. Albert, bless him, stood up and toasted his daughter. "I'd like to make a toast to my lovely daughter," he said. "And I'd like to wish her the best of everything in life and her marriage."

Dorothy, not wanting to be outshined, stood up. She raised her glass, weaving slightly. It was real clear that she'd been dipping into the wine. She said, "I'd like to make a toast to Meatball. I mean, Meathead."

She raised her glass, drained it, and sat down. Her pink dress made a ripping noise. No one said anything. Bitsy gave her mother a long, dangerous look. The Wentworths kept smiling. I thought Miss Betty's face might crack down the middle she was smiling so hard. Meathead smiled, too, but he was looking at the bridesmaids at my table. One of the girls stared right back at him, and it seemed to me that her eyes were eating him alive. You didn't see that, I told myself. You didn't see anything at all.

But it preyed on me. After the meal, I tried to get Bitsy alone. Those bridesmaids were all over her, like mosquitoes. Sylvia grabbed my elbow and begged me to introduce her to Clancy Jane. The violinist went home, and the young people went into the bar and unplugged the jukebox. They rolled it into the ballroom, plugged it in there, and started dancing barefoot. The Wentworths stood back and smiled some more and tried to act like they were happy. My legs felt weak. I found an empty table and sat down. My bones ached. The room whirled around me; it whirled hard and fast like my whole life. At last Violet drove us home. I fixed a glass of hot milk and laced it with honey and brandy, but I still couldn't sleep.

The First Baptist was an old church, with four white columns, stained glass windows, and polished mahogany pews. The Wentworths and Hamiltons had been coming here to worship since before the Civil War. It had served as the backdrop for many a wedding in Crystal Falls—fancy weddings, simple weddings. On account of Dorothy's bragging and planning, I was more or less expecting a fancy one. Since Violet was in the wedding, Clancy Jane drove us to the church. We had us each a corsage—white and blue daisies, blue carnations, baby's breath, a blue-and-white satin bow. I wore a blue dress that Violet had helped me pick out. I wore gloves to hide my age spots. Outside the vestibule was a guest book. The pen had a fat white feather. I signed my name, *Gussie Hamilton.* Then an usher held out his arm. We stepped into the vestibule. Right off the bat I noticed that the right-hand side, the groom's side, was overflowing.

I saw doctors. I saw dentists. Lawyers. Merchants. Real-estate agents. Bankers. They were spilling over to our side of the church. The young man escorted me to the second row. Each row was decorated with blue and white flowers and blue candles. The altar was hidden by white gladioli, daisies, and snapdragons. Creamy roses, blue hydrangeas, maidenhead ferns. A cool florist's smell hit me all the way to where I was sitting. Dorothy had told me that it was traditional for the groom to pay for the flowers, and I thought it was a good thing that the Wentworths had so much money. Still, I'd raised Dorothy better than to take advantage of people. She'd let this wedding go straight to her head.

Clancy Jane was escorted to the pew behind me, and Queenie sat next to her. Miss Betty walked down the aisle wearing a blue chiffon dress that swirled just below her knees. The candlelight caught her diamonds. She slid gracefully into a pew and fixed her eyes on the altar. Music started up from the piano. Bitsy had picked out love songs for her wedding. Just the other day she'd said the pianist was playing "Cherish" and "Never My Love." I couldn't remember the others. Behind her back, Violet called it music to vomit by.

At last Dorothy herself came swaying down the aisle, giving off a big wind of Chanel No. 5. Her diamonds caught the candlelight, too, but they looked like cut glass. Her hair had been teased and sprayed into a square, which made her whole body look peculiar. She was wearing a floor-length aqua dress, which turned her skin a sour color. She sat in the pew all by herself, and I felt terrible for picking out her flaws. She turned back to me. She didn't glance once at her sister. "Well? What do you think, Mother Dear?" she whispered.

"Beautiful." I'd always felt real conspicuous talking in church, especially at weddings, what with the ushers coming and going. It didn't seem like the music was loud enough to cover our voices.

"Yes, yes," hissed Dorothy. "I ended up using two separate florists to get enough flowers. They tried to stick me with mums, but I wouldn't hear of it. Mums are so common. Those florists were mad as wet hens. Wringing their hands, calling each other names. But it all worked out, didn't it?"

I nodded.

"Shhhh." Dorothy twisted her head, staring toward the rear of the church. "It's starting."

A side door opened, and the preacher popped out like a Jack-in-the-box. Meathead and his daddy came out, too. Tiny sprays of white roses and blue daisies were pinned to their lapels. They weren't smiling. If it hadn't been for their tuxedos, you would have thought they were pallbearers. The wedding march started up, *DA-NA-NA-NA,* and everyone shifted in the pews. You could hear their whole bodies turning. The ushers walked down the aisle, followed by the bridesmaids. They looked so sweet in their blue dresses and broad-rimmed hats. You'd never guess that one of them had been making eyes at the groom just the night before. They held tiny flower baskets, too. Violet was last of all. She was the maid of honor. Her dress was baby blue, trimmed in white ribbons, and she carried a basket of flowers. She had on a huge white straw hat, which set off her dark hair. She looked like an angel. She had on lipstick, and her cheeks were pinker than usual. Even her eyes seemed larger, the lashes fringed. I guessed that Bitsy had talked her into wearing makeup. I just hoped she would leave it on a spell and not rush home and scrub it off. This new plainness was Clancy Jane's doings. Like mother, like daughter. I just sat back and looked at Violet to my heart's content, proud that she was mine.

Then I saw Bitsy, all dressed in white, with the least touch of blue. One hand was tucked in the crook of Albert's arm. The other hand held a huge bouquet crammed full of special order flowers—lily of the valley, bone white irises and daisies, roses and baby's breath. It was half as tall as Bitsy. Her face looked gauzy behind the veil. I couldn't make out her features. She didn't look real. The music paused for a few moments, and the train of her gown made a slick, scraping noise as she walked forward.

Honey, stop, I wanted to say. It's too hard. You'll run

through that love in no time flat. You'll be bored stiff in four years. All the young people get divorces now. Just look at them on TV. And that groom of yours has a wandering eye.

"Who giveth this woman?" asked the preacher.

"I do," said Albert. He released Bitsy's hand and stepped backward. He sat down next to Dorothy. She reached forward and squeezed his arm. He kept his eyes on his daughter.

It went fast. It was one of those new double-ring ceremonies you read about in the paper. Then it was over. Everyone filed out of the church, murmuring softly to each other. Then they drove off to the reception at the country club. I waited with the rest of the family while the photographer made the newlyweds pose. Bitsy Wentworth, I thought. I never would have believed it. Never in a million years. The photographer lined the two families up for a group picture.

"Smile," he said.

Miss Betty drew her lips together as if she had a penny between them. Dorothy, standing between Albert and Mack, showed all of her teeth.

I went with Mack and Sloopy to the reception. They didn't act like husband and wife, didn't hardly say one word to each other. She stared out the window while we drove across town. He talked to me about my garden. I told him I'd been feeling too lazy to plant my usual crops. Just some tomatoes, corn, cucumbers, squash. Not a single flower. This was the first year I hadn't planted zinnia and sunflower seeds.

"God almighty, look at this shit," said Mack, peering through the windshield. Cars were sprawled all over that country club. We had to park way down at the tennis courts and walk nearly a mile, with Mack just a-hopping. He leaned hard on Sloopy's arm.

When I walked into the ballroom, I saw at once that

Dorothy had gone too far. Spent too much money, which is just as bad as being cheap. She'd gone and hired a band. They were playing something old-fashioned and sweet. The young people weren't dancing. I wasn't surprised. I'd learned from Violet what they liked, that jerky, screaming music. They were crowded around the buffet. The table was something else. It seemed to sag under the weight of all that food. I saw boiled shrimp. I saw caviar on toast points. I saw sugared pecans. Crab puffs. Oysters wrapped in bacon. Country ham in beaten biscuits. Smoked turkey in muffins. Tenderloin of beef in home-made rolls. Cheese straws. Cheese balls. Cheese fondue. Chocolate fondue. Strawberries dipped in white chocolate. Snails stuffed with something smelly. Chopped-up liver on crackers. Marinated artichoke hearts. A hollowed-out water-melon filled with fruit balls and berries. Cocktail wieners in currant sauce. Stuffed Gouda cheese. Frosted grapes. Fudge. Lemon squares. Pecan tassies. Two bowls of punch, vodka and strawberry, and champagne. There was also an enormous blue-and-white wedding cake, six layers, with a plastic bride and groom on top.

It was almost ridiculous. Just looking at it took my appetite away. The other people were digging in, pushing through the line, filling up their plates, taking a sample of this, a sample of that, laughing and dropping things on the floor, eating like there was no tomorrow. I knew what caterers charged—per person, per menu item. And Dorothy had invited more than 350 people.

All right, I told myself, looking down at the buffet and the people's hands just a-digging. It's none of your business. Bitsy is Dorothy and Albert's only daughter. Of course they wanted her wedding to be special. But I didn't understand why the caterer hadn't said, "HOLD it, Dorothy! You're going overboard! You can get by with half this food! Nobody will even remember what you served a year from now!" I knew where the bill would be sent—Albert—and my heart broke for him. That poor man. He didn't make that kind of money. Someone should have told her she had way too much food. They should have told her that one main meat, like the tenderloin, would have been plenty. And she didn't need cheese straws, stuffed Gouda, *and* cheese fondue. She needed one cheese, one sea-food, one fruit. Wedding cake was plenty for dessert. She didn't need that champagne, either. It was as if she thought if one thing was good, four would be the best of all.

Miss Betty walked up to the buffet and stared down the length of the table. Dorothy sidled up to her.

"Well?" Dorothy asked. She was grinning hard.

"Pardon?" said Miss Betty.

"What do you think?"

Miss Betty gave her a cool look. "About what?" she said.

"Why, the reception," said Dorothy. Her smile slipped a notch. "What else?"

Miss Betty turned her attention back to the table. She didn't say a word.

"It's gorgeous, don't you think?" said Dorothy. "It's—"

"If it's anything," snapped Miss Betty, "it's overdone."

"It's not!" said Dorothy. Her whole face caved in.

"Why, it's a waste of money, considering everything."

"Considering *what*?" Dorothy's temple began pulsing.

"Well, you *know*."

"Know what? Stop beating around the bush, Betty." Her forehead jerked up. Her painted brows moved like two worms.

"You don't know, do you?" Betty said.

"Oh, for heaven's sake!"

"Never mind," said Miss Betty, waving one hand. Her

smile was frozen. "Forget I said a word. Everything's lovely, just perfect. It's a four-star reception. You have my compliments."

"Wait a minute, wait a minute," said Dorothy. "What don't I know?"

"Well. I just meant . . ." Miss Betty's eyes moved in circles. "I just wondered if you knew how much food you'd have left over. That's all."

"Oh. Well, I sure do. We'll fix you up a doggie bag, and you can take some home."

Miss Betty's eye twitched.

"It *is* delicious food." Dorothy smiled. "You get what you pay for, don't you? Would you say it's lavish?"

"Would *I* say it?" Miss Betty paused and gave a tinkling laugh. She lifted one real eyebrow. She seemed to be thinking *This is my only son's new mother-in-law?*

Dorothy looked so confused I ached for her. I walked up to her and touched her arm. Her skin felt cool and mushy, like thawed turkey.

"It's a fine reception, honey," I said, but I stared straight at Miss High-and-Mighty Betty. I wasn't scared of her. I remembered when she was a little girl and her daddy sold shoes on the square. "You should be proud of yourself, Dorothy."

Miss Betty returned my gaze. One eye flickered. Then she turned and worked her way into the crowd like a fish swimming toward deeper water.

Bitsy and Meathead drove off in a blizzard of rice to Daytona Beach, Florida, for their honeymoon. Violet, who did not catch the bouquet, flew back to New Mexico with her mother for two weeks. Just me and Queenie were left. The green yard stretched between us and Dorothy. At night she cut off her air conditioner and opened the windows. I could see her standing in front of a wooden easel, dabbing paint onto a canvas. Every

now and then, she would stand back and stare at it. I was dying
to see it. When I asked her what she was painting, she said,
"Me. I'm doing a self-portrait of me."

I didn't say anything. I tried not to think of anything. When
I finally saw it, I was surprised. She'd painted herself as a thin,
beautiful Dorothy, wearing a straw hat, her arm looped around
Domino's neck. It was a good likeness of that dog, but she
herself looked fairly frightening. It was something in the eyes.
She would not look right thin.

Sometimes Queenie helped me in the garden. She bent slowly.
Her spine curved. She looked old. I worried that she would die,
and I would grieve myself sick. But it turned out that I was the
one who was dying.

"What's these bruises on your arms from?" asked Queenie.

I held up my arm. There were four bluish marks. I hadn't
even noticed.

"And look at your legs," she said. "What's caused them
purple spots? All speckled like."

"It's just from varicose veins," I said, looking at my legs
this way and that.

"You ought to let Dr. Falk look at you," she said.

Dr. Falk was my new doctor. He was a Yankee. When he
talked, each word sounded as if it had been pinched, hard. But
you didn't have to wait all day to see him.

"I'm not letting him look at nothing," I said. "He'd just
want to stick me in the hospital and run tests. You know how
those new doctors are. They don't know beans about sickness."

"I don't care," said Queenie. "When Violet gets back from
New Mexico, she'll make you go see Dr. Falk."

First thing, he put me in the hospital and stuck a great big needle into my breastbone and the pain liked to have killed me. He called it a bone marrow.

"You didn't have to dig to China, did you?" I said sharply.

He just hung his head. He was as cute as could be, married with three little blond-headed girls. I heard his wife liked to play tennis and spend money. She was a Yankee, too. Amelia was her name. I heard they were having trouble, but you never knew the truth about doctors. People liked to talk and create trouble where none was.

They put me in a semiprivate room, next to the window, and I had me a view of a cedar grove. The woman in the next bed, Sarah Sue Walker, had lung cancer, like what my Charlie had. Her son drove up from Nashville every other evening. He was an archaeologist, and he brought chocolates and flowers. He talked on and on about his job. I was not one to eavesdrop, but I glanced up sharply when I heard him telling her about some skeletons that had been unearthed when the new state highway had been built.

My head almost swiveled off its hinges.

"Skeletons?" I blurted out before I had a chance to think. If I'd had time to think, I would have kept my mouth shut, but I didn't. I guess that's where Dorothy got it.

"Yes, ma'am," the archaeologist said. Then he went on to say that he'd determined the bodies were from a family cemetery, from the mid-1800s.

"You mean you can tell what year a person died from just the skeleton?" I asked.

"Oh yes, ma'am," he said.

"That's real interesting," I said, but my heart flip-flopped. I cleared my throat and smoothed my hand along the sheet.

"Does this happen often?" I asked. "Skeletons being found?"

"All the time," he said. "Just all the time. Especially when people build houses or install swimming pools. They don't always report it when they're supposed to."

"They're supposed to?" I said.

"It's a misdemeanor if they don't," he said. "It's all in the law books."

"Well, you learn something new every day," I said. My legs were fairly shaking beneath the covers. I had no idea the world was so modern and could look into your past and dig up all your secrets.

Queenie walked in mumbling, "Lord have mercy, I could have walked here faster than Preacher drive me. Thought I'd never be here." She was holding a shopping bag by its string handles. I knew it was full of food she'd packed to fatten me up. I was relieved to see her, even though I knew I couldn't eat a bite.

"Lord have mercy," she said, taking one look at me. "What's gotten into you? All pale and shaky. You look like a goose walked over your grave."

"Not a goose. A bloodhound," I said. Sarah Sue Walker and her son watched us thoughtfully from across the room.

"Say what?" Queenie set down the bag, walked over to my bed, and felt my forehead. "Why, you're burning up! Don't they keep thermometers at this hospital? Where's that nurse?" She shook her head and strode out of the room.

The nurses came with more pills, and I forgot about graves and grave-digging. I forgot about the soil holding secrets. The whole thing slipped further and further in my mind, the way pickle jars get pushed back in a refrigerator. Pretty soon, you forget you have pickles at all.

* * *

*N*ow. I had to get ahold of myself and shore up. I had me a blood disease. Cancer. Leukemia. My veins were clogged up with white cells that didn't know what to do with themselves. They were blind, deaf, and dumb. They crowded out the smart cells. Dr. Falk held up his hand and ticked off medicines he planned to give me. He said my face might bloat up and I might get a hump on my back. Lordy Jesus, I thought. Wasn't the disease enough?

"Lymphocytic leukemia is very serious," Dr. Falk said. "There's two types, acute and chronic, and you've got an acute case."

He explained what acute meant.

I didn't say anything. I would have to get that kind. I just sat back against the white pillow and let his words sink in real slow like. We were all alone in my hospital room. Sarah Sue Walker had gotten moved to intensive care the day before yesterday, and it was as if she'd dropped off the face of the earth. Normally Queenie would have been sitting with me, but she'd gone home to check the mail. I knew I had to tell her. She was the only one.

"I'm not sure how long you've had it," he said.

"Well, you ought to be. You're my doctor."

He breathed in and opened my chart. "Yes, but you haven't been to my office since, let's see, 1967."

"I wasn't sick."

He looked up from the chart and blinked.

"How long will I live?" I said.

"It's mostly an asymptomatic disease until the end."

He explained what asymptomatic was.

"Am I near the end?" I asked.

"It's impossible to tell, Miss Gussie."

"Well, how long would you guess?"

"I don't like to make guesses." He paused. His eyes were dark blue. He was a right nice-looking man for a doctor. "Guesses sound so much like promises. And I don't like to break promises."

"Well, of course not. Just make a guess anyway. I won't hold you to it. I need to know."

"You might live another year. Or you might live six months. It depends on several things. Right now your platelets are real low."

"Platelets?"

"They're blood cells. When you cut yourself, they make your blood clot."

"And mine are low?"

"Very." He nodded. "You'll want to be careful and not bump yourself hard."

"You mean, if I fall down the bleeding might not stop?"

He nodded.

I stared out the window and tried to think. I hadn't expected this. Twelve months, six months. It hit me that I didn't have something you could cure, exactly. I felt like a roast that someone had stuck into the oven and set a timer and I'd stop browning in twenty-four weeks.

I wanted to think it wasn't fair, but I was an old woman. It was fair, after all. All you had to do was look at all of the little children with this leukemia. I thought of Hart, struck down in his prime, him and that baby blown to pieces. I thought of Dede going to sleep and never waking up. I didn't know what was worse—sudden death or the lingering kind, what got my Charlie. To tell the truth, both kinds were bad.

I was clear on one thing. I looked up at Dr. Falk, who was still standing next to my bed.

"Let's just keep this between us," I said. "At least for now."

"I don't understand, Miss Gussie," he said. He put his hand on his head.

"Let me put it this way," I said. "I don't want you telling my family about this leukemia thing."

He just stared, his hand stuck to the top of his head. Then he said, "Well, okay. If that's what you want."

"That's what I want," I said.

"You'll tell your family, then?" he said.

"I'll tell them nothing."

"Nothing?"

I shook my head. "Not until I'm good and ready."

"Just don't wait too long," he said, and his voice went straight to my bones.

I hated the idea of telling them. I didn't understand it myself. It was just a notion, a strong feeling. I did not want to be coddled. And I knew they'd try. I wanted things to go on the way they always had. To happen like they were meant to happen.

I wanted to work in my garden and drive my car and mow my own yard. I wanted to shell butter beans on the back porch with Queenie.

I didn't want people feeling guilty.

I could see Clancy Jane moving back home. I could see Dorothy coming over fifty times a day and making me wish I had a quicker disease. And Violet might not go to college. She might get her a job at the A&P or the bank. And Bitsy, why she'd probably have a baby or two, just to give me another great-grandchild before I died.

I didn't want to speed up anyone's life.

Me and Queenie would do what we could, for as long as we were able. I didn't know how long that would be. And then

I'd have to tell Clancy Jane and the others. But I wasn't keen on telling Dorothy ever.

That afternoon she knocked on my door, holding a pink African violet.

"Yoo-hoo," she said, peeking into the room, her forehead up to here. She'd forgotten to paint on brows.

"Come on in, Dorothy," I said and pushed back against the pillows. "What pretty flowers."

"Did the doctor find anything?" she asked, sidling up to my bed, arranging the violet on the bedside table that already held my telephone, roses Queenie had picked in the side yard, a jug of ice water, a blue basin, and my Jergen's lotion.

"Not a thing," I said.

Dorothy sighed hard and said, "Well, that's good. I knew he wouldn't. You just push yourself too hard is all. You just push too hard."

After a while she got up and went home. But it was a real long time before I fell asleep.

Dorothy

1971

Near the end of July, during a heat wave, Sister moved back to Crystal Falls. I was suspicious, but I kept my doubts penned up, like dogs in a manger. "Get! Hush! Go lie down!" I would yell, and the dogs crouched down, staring at me with yellow eyes. It was the most awful thing you could imagine, almost like being paranoid.

Sister moved into Mother Dear's house lock, stock, and barrel. I could not believe it. "What's going on?" I asked. I thought something had gone wrong for my sister out in hippie-land. I thought she had come home to lick her wounds. I was just dying to find out. Mother Dear didn't say one word. I knew she was glad to get her favorite girl back. But something nagged at me—finally I realized it was Mother Dear herself, the way she looked. Her face had widened, round as a harvest moon, and she was weak. You should have seen her arms give out when she was stringing Kentucky wonders. She had to rest her wrists on the sides of the bowl. Purple bruises popped up on her arms, and I stared at them enviously.

"How did you get those bruises?" I asked.

"Thin skin," she answered.

I didn't believe it. She had always claimed that her skin was thick as buffalo hide. Mine was, too, and just as scarred.

Since Sister had moved back home, something had been set off in all of us. I took up the slack time by visiting Mack and Sloopy and little Christopher, who was almost out of the Terrible Twos. Mack was glued to Walter Cronkite, watching the news—boys being carried off on stretchers, in helicopters beating the air like giant Mixmasters. I thought it was a shame the way the TV showed those boys bleeding every night. Then Walter Cronkite switched to a college campus where the students were throwing eggs at the National Guard. Mack slapped his good leg and cursed.

"Calm down," I said. "It's just the TV." I had natural disasters on my brain. I was worried about earthquakes and such. It was all laid out in Revelation. You can read it for yourself. I did not know, in all honesty, how much longer I could stand it.

"This isn't no goddamn movie, Mama," Mack said.

I didn't like his tone, but I had to go easy on him. When it happened, when he lost his leg, I went around asking the Lord why it could not have been me. Even though no one believes me, his horoscope for that day had said DO NOT TAKE RISKS.

"It's real. It's the goddamn gooks killing Americans and nobody cares!" he yelled.

"Walter Cronkite cares," I said.

"I can't take this fucking shit no more."

I didn't say a word. Sometimes he talked so trashy, you would never know he was my son. You would never know he had a successful business, even if it was all due to Albert. Mack had never cursed before he went to Vietnam, and that was the gospel truth, so the war had done something to his personality. Warped it.

He leaned back in his La-Z-Boy and reached for the Pabst can on the little table. His amputated leg looked like the limb of a dead tree. I could not stand to see it sticking out of his bluejean shorts—that pink nub, the little *x*'s of skin puckered and stitched together.

Instead, I looked around the room. I was sitting on a tan Naugahyde sofa. Hanging over it was a sailboat painted on black velvet. Tacky, tacky, tacky. But it was spotless. Sloopy was in the kitchen now, mopping the floor. Baby Christopher watched her from the playpen with his cute little slanted eyes. I never dreamed he would turn out as cute as he had, but I could see all of us mixed up in his little round face.

Sloopy lifted the mop from the pail, watching the water stream down into the bucket. She was forever cleaning something. I had always heard Orientals were neat as pins, even if they placed little value on human life. Like leaving babies up on mountaintops. She never talked about her relatives who were left behind in Vietnam.

"They're taking over the damn country," he went on, flipping his hand at the television. "Just look. Those ones with the hair. Look at them marching. I lost my leg for those fuckers, and they don't even give a shit. Don't that beat all?"

I tried to keep my family together, in spite of the deck being stacked against me. Albert should never have left, but he was hot-to-trot for other women. Oh, I saw it now, even though I hadn't seen it coming with him and Sister. At least he didn't marry that trashy Dory, who was just after his money. Let me tell you one thing, that would have been a laugh and a half.

After he got rid of her, I thought he would come back to me. I was ready and waiting. It just made good sense, but he never did. He lived all by himself in a new subdivision by the shopping mall, what used to be a cow pasture. There were not any trees. Plain as all get-out. I did not see how he stood it after I'd taken pains to bring color and harmony to our home. He might as well have been living in Nebraska. His yard was flat as a flitter.

I heard that he dated well-off widow ladies.

Just the idea of it burned me up. Me sitting home, him painting the town. Buying women steak dinners when he had expected me to cook every night. I worked my fingers to the bone to keep him happy, but, no, that was not good enough, was not sexy enough. All I had was Domino, so at least I was not entirely alone. Plus she could understand human language. She knew whole phrases: Food To Eat, Water To Drink, Poopoo, Pee-pee, Go Outside, Shake Hands, and Sic 'Em.

I decided to make the best of things and throw a party. I drove to the Hallmark store and bought these cute invitations. I wrote out PLEASE JOIN ME FOR AN AFTERNOON COOK-OUT. I invited Mother Dear, Sister, Mack and Sloopy, Queenie, Bitsy and Claude, and Violet. The truth was, I had not forgiven Sister for trying to seduce my husband, but I couldn't very well have a party without her. Or Queenie. I had to pretend everything was water under the bridge.

I had a knack for decorating, just like I had once had a knack for painting pictures. Even though it was an afternoon party, I hoped my guests would stay until the evening. I'd bought plenty of beer for Mack. I didn't care if he got so drunk he couldn't stand on his leg. He loved me and knew I hated being alone. I strung up colored lights in the trees, and they looked so pretty I thought I'd leave them for Christmas. I set out matching paper plates, napkins, and cups (pink and orange flowers). You should have seen the spread on my redwood picnic table. I fixed Domino a plate before my guests arrived. Grilled corn (cut off the cob, since her teeth were bad). French fries with ketchup. Potato salad. Kentucky wonders. Deviled eggs. Watermelon. Brownies with two inches of icing. Domino licked her paper plate. No one could ever beat me cooking, even though Queenie liked to think she could.

An hour before my guests were to arrive, Bitsy called and gave her regrets. I was stunned. I almost burst into tears. We lived in the same town, and she treated me like I was a distant relative. I had barely seen her since the wedding, and that was two months ago. Although she would not come right out and say it, she had her own crowd. A life without me.

"My neighbors are starting to ask questions," I told her, squeezing the receiver. "They wonder why they never see your car in my driveway."

"I have to spend time with the Wentworths, too," she explained. But I knew she was lying through her teeth. "And I'm helping Claude buy his college clothes."

"When are you moving to Cookeville?" I asked.

"Well, Claude's going the end of August, but I'm thinking about staying with the Wentworths."

"Don't you want to be with your new husband?" I said. I could just hear the gossip now.

"It's kind of hard to explain over the phone."

"Then come to my party."

"Oh, I don't know."

I was silent.

"I'll try," she said.

No one showed up except Mack, Sloopy, and Christopher. Sister called at the last minute and said they were all sick. I knew she was lying because I'd seen her pulling weeds earlier. I just ignored the slight and tried to gloss it over with small talk. Sloopy smiled and nodded to everything I said. I told her how I'd tried to make things run smoothly. I knew how, I told her. I had style. I was just dealing with rude people.

Toward the end of the afternoon, a red car angled into my driveway. We all stared. It was Claude's Corvette. Heat lightning flickered over the trees. He and Bitsy got out of the car and walked around the hedge. I just stared her down. She was wearing a white cotton smock. Her stomach pooched out.

"Hey, Sissy," said Mack. He hopped over to her. Then he reached down and patted her belly. "Put on a little weight, ain't you?"

"A little," she said. She twisted her rings.

Claude shoved his hands into his pockets and stared at the cloudy sky. He looked furious.

Bitsy sat down and reached for an ear of corn. It was real clear that she was not going to explain her condition. "You're not *pregnant,* are you?" I blurted out.

She giggled, took a bite of corn, and nodded.

I braced my hands on the table and slowly got to my feet. I stared hard. "This isn't funny! How'd you get this big? You haven't had time!"

"The usual way, Mama." Mack snorted and had to wipe his nose on his sleeve.

I ignored him. "How far along are you?"

"Not real far."

"She's five months," said Claude. He did not sound proud. I had a terrible feeling about this. I looked down at my fingers and counted. Five months.

"That means . . ." I broke off. My eyes swept to her stomach.

"That's right, Mama," said Mack. "Count them fingers. She must've been three months gone when she wore white."

"Mack!" said Bitsy.

I wanted to slap her face. The little liar. The little sneak. I sat down so hard the redwood bench went *thunk*. No one spoke a word, no one breathed.

I turned to Mack. "Did you know she was pregnant?"

"No. But I can count."

"Most people can." I faced Bitsy. "And they will."

It thundered hard and started raining. We picked up the food and ran into the house. Sloopy made two or three trips. Those people were used to water. When I got dried off, I found everyone in the living room. They were watching the evening news—gunfire and body bags.

Claude shook his head and said, "What a waste of lives. What a waste." He thought he was special with all of the Wentworth money and his high draft number, what his daddy got with political pull. "We shouldn't be in Vietnam," he said. "It isn't a winnable war."

Well, that did it. You couldn't say something like that to a veteran of any war, least of all a veteran with a cut-off leg. I could see Mack's eyeballs turn red and glow. His lips turned blue, and he crushed a beer can in one hand.

"You don't know *anything*," Mack said, his lip curled back. "We can win that war, easy."

"How?" said Claude, real cocky like.

"By establishing front lines," said Mack, ramming his fists together.

"That's ridiculous," said Claude. "There's no way we can do that without using a million men."

"We can, too!" cried Mack. He got up, hopping on one leg

to the bookcase. He pulled out the V *World Book.* "I was there! Were *you*? Hell no, you weren't. Rich boy!"

"Now, let's don't get into name-calling," said Bitsy. She rubbed one hand over her belly. I felt no connection to the child growing inside of her. I hated her for making me into a fool. Mother of the bride, indeed. I must have been a laughing-stock. I could have told her a thing or two about having babies. How they make a man ashamed of your body.

"I didn't *have* to be there," said Claude. "Everyone knows it will take countless lives to establish front lines. The U.S. will have to deploy a million men. And they will have to occupy every single village and hamlet. It just isn't feasible."

"You don't know shit!" yelled Mack. He flipped through the *World Book,* found the section he was seeking, and thrust it into Claude's face. "The war is strictly economics. Johnson didn't want to win it because it's good for the economy. Nixon's the same way."

"That's not true," Claude said. "Nixon wants to win the war. He can't!"

"He can, too!"

"Look, are you saying you're smarter than Westmoreland and Kissinger?" Claude's eyes nearly bugged out of his blond head.

"I never said that. But I might be." Mack narrowed his eyes, and in his face I saw a different arrangement of myself and Albert. It shocked me.

"Listen, Mack," said Bitsy. "The U.S. can't win the war."

"We can, too!"

"Stay out of this, Bitsy." I reached for her arm, but she shrugged me off.

"No," she said. "We can't win unless we drop an atomic bomb."

Mack jerked up the *World Book.* "You're right! We should drop a fucking A-bomb!"

Sloopy looked into her lap, tears dripping out of her eyes.

"It isn't morally feasible," said Claude. "Look at the criticism we got for bombing Hiroshima."

I leaned back in my easy chair. I could not take another minute of this or my mind would snap clean in two. I had lived through a world war, not a skirmish. I knew a thing or two. I knew about ration stamps. I knew about men coming home changed and scarred on the inside. I stared at my daughter's rich husband. I hated him for making her pregnant and ruining her life. I decided then and there I was through calling him Claude.

"Meathead, you are an educated idiot," I said coldly.

"Yes! That's right, Mama," said Mack. "That's what he is!"

"Why, Mrs. McDougal," said Claude, looking so much like Betty I could have slapped him. "That's an oxymoron."

I ignored him. But I had an idea he was trying to say I was a cross between an ox and a moron. Maybe a bull steer and an idiot. "We would've won the war with Japan even if we HADN'T dropped the bomb," I said firmly. "We established front lines on Okinawa."

"Okinawa was two to sixteen miles wide, Mrs. McDougal," said Claude.

I just hated his guts.

"It was wider than that," yelled Mack. "You don't know shit!"

"Aren't you ashamed?" Claude said.

"Of what?" Mack narrowed his eyes.

"Of being a Vietnam veteran."

"Hell, I'm not ashamed." He blinked hard. "I'm not, I'm

not! I just did what I was told. I did what I thought my country wanted."

"What about My Lai? The U.S. didn't want that, did they?"

"You stupid ass. My Lai was a fucking bomb factory. So are most of the villages from Qui Nhon to Da Nang."

"You've got an answer for everything, don't you?"

"It wasn't my fault!" cried Mack. "You don't know shit!"

I had always heard that bad luck came in threes. Or was that death? I could never remember. Around the end of August, Bitsy decided to move to Cookeville with Claude (so he could get a college education, and what was my daughter getting?). On Labor Day, Mack up and left Sloopy. He wanted a divorce. When I pressed him for an explanation, he said Sloopy didn't approve of his drinking. He was sitting at my kitchen table in his old chair. He was drinking beer. I didn't open my mouth.

"And things weren't too good in the bedroom, either," he said.

I closed my eyes. I didn't know what to say. While I'd never been one to discuss the marital act, I had never turned Albert away. It had always struck me funny that he'd never seemed to require it. I didn't even think he'd ever had relations with that Dory. I believed men should use their private parts and not talk about them so much. Anyway, it had been much too long. I'd forgotten.

"She nags all the time. I just don't need this shit, y'know?" Mack drained the rest of his beer.

"Hush, just hush," I said, shutting my eyes. "Don't say that word!"

"It's the truth. It *is* shit."

I sighed and stared at my baby son, who had been turned

into a fiend by war. Then my head cleared, and I saw Christopher's smiling face.

"But what about your child?" I said. "Don't you just hate to see him grow up in a broken home?"

"Christopher will be fine, Mama. You wait and see. Just because my marriage is over don't mean I've stopped being a daddy."

But it did.

I begged him to move back home with me, to save money if nothing else, and he said he would consider it. I believed him. I cleaned the house, top to bottom, and I filled the freezer with his favorite foods, even ice cream sandwiches. I bought a case of beer.

Well, he never moved in. I was just heartbroken. Now both of my children were gone for good, and I wouldn't get another chance to do things right. To baby them and wait on them and really be a mother. (Now that I had the time to do it.) I had lived alone for a long time, and I was getting mighty tired of it.

Bitsy came home one weekend—staying with the Wentworths, of course—and I told her how disappointed I was. She just laughed.

"Mummie, I hate to be the one to tell you this, but Mack's not moving in with you," she said.

She was so pregnant she looked ready to bust. All stomach, which meant it would be a girl. It burned Bitsy up when I told her that. She got so mad. Sometimes I just didn't know about her. There Violet was, getting herself a college degree in Knoxville and talking about graduate school, and there was my own Bitsy, wasting her life picking out color schemes for a nursery in some rat-hole apartment in Cookeville, Tennessee. And she had been so smart in school, smart as a whip. She could speak French like nobody's business. Our church offered a course in

interior decorating, and she flat refused to take it. No, she was
making a career out of spending Meathead's money and having
babies. I had already planned for all of my grandchildren to call
me Grandmother Dear, even though I hadn't been sure if little
Christopher's first words would be English. When he was a
baby, I had nightmares about him calling me Soon Lin or Mama
Chow. But he spoke English like a regular child. He called me
G'an Maw.

"I don't know what you're talking about," I now said to
Bitsy, blinking hard. "Mack told me he would think about moving here, and I think he will."

"Don't hold your breath, Mummie."

I just stared. With Bitsy you could never tell when you were
being baited and tricked. Sometimes I would see her car in
Mother Dear's driveway, when she was supposed to be in
Cookeville taking care of Meathead. I just knew all of them
were sitting around the kitchen table laughing at me.

"He's got a girlfriend, Mother," said Bitsy. She giggled and
snorted. "That's why he left Sloopy. And wait until you see her.
Lord. Her name's Earlene. She drives a school bus. A great big
yellow one."

I didn't believe it. I narrowed my eyes.

"I don't have the faintest idea how they met," she said.
"Unless it was at the Thirsty Turtle."

"The what?"

"Thirsty Turtle. It's a fancy beer joint on the Nashville
Highway."

I chewed my lip, hard, and tasted blood. I'd lived my whole
life in Crystal Falls, but now I realized that the town had
changed right under my nose. It had things I knew nothing
about. The Thirsty Turtle, indeed.

"You are lying through your teeth," I said. I could have just smacked her across the room. "Mack wouldn't go to a place like that."

"It's the truth," she said. "He goes there all the time. You just think Mack can do no wrong. You would support anything he did."

I didn't say anything. I couldn't feature him going with a woman bus driver.

"You wouldn't care if he'd left Sloopy and Christopher for a hooker," said Bitsy. "You wouldn't blink an eye."

"Mack wouldn't go with a hooker!" I screamed. I felt my face turn hot. "You always have to criticize your brother's taste just to elevate your own."

"I do not."

"Well, he wouldn't go with a hooker."

"Not when he gets it free from that Earlene," said Bitsy. "She's got a reputation as long as Interstate 40. And I'll tell you something else."

"Don't you tell me anything!" I cried.

"You can't see reality. You never could: You just distort the truth until you end up with a version you can live with."

"I do NOT!"

"You'd approve of any old thing he dug up."

"I would not. I wouldn't tolerate him marrying a nigra. I draw the line at that."

"Well, it's a shame he hasn't married a black woman. Because I think you love Mack so much, you'd overlook it. I think it would be the only way you'd overcome your prejudice."

"Prejudice!" I spat out the word. "How dare you talk to me about prejudice! I don't have a prejudiced bone in my body. I've always been good to the coloreds!"

"You make me sick!" Bitsy made a face and stormed out of the house. Her car squealed out of my driveway. Well, let her drive like a bat out of hell. A pregnant bat. If she lost her leg in a car wreck, then I would have a matched set of children. And I already had enough to worry about. Sister sucked up to my Mother Dear night and day. And every time I turned around, Dr. Falk's car was in the driveway. He was a married man, too. With three little children.

Anybody with eyes could see Mother Dear was sick. She could barely get up and down the porch steps. Sister was always helping her up. Then Mother Dear would have bruises where she had been gripped.

Sister and Queenie guarded her night and day. They swore up and down that nothing was wrong. But when I visited, I took note of the bedside commode, the metal walker. Those were not the normal things you would find in a sickroom. Not to mention the amber bottles of pills lined up in the kitchen window.

"What're these pills for?" I asked.

"This and that," said Sister. She and Queenie treated me like I was pure dirt. An outsider, not blood kin. It made me so mad I wanted to slam my head into a wall. I wanted to stick pins into my lip. I even thought about being a vital organ donor. I imagined myself stretching out on a metal table. The surface would be cold and firm, and my skin would break out in goose-bumps. The surgeon would raise one gloved hand, gripping a scalpel. He would slice into my body, as if I were a shaved lamb, and remove a lung, eyeball, or kidney. He would hold my organ in his hand and run to the next operating room and stick it inside of a sick person. Someone eat up with cancer. People would say, "Oh, wasn't she kind and Christian like?" But I did not want praise and glory. I did not want to be made famous on the six o'clock news. I wanted the hole, the loss of my vitals. My son would never know how much I envied his stump.

"There is something wrong with Mother Dear," I told Sister. "And don't you try and say it's her arthritis."

"It *is* her arthritis," snapped Queenie. She lowered her eyebrows, and I could have slapped her until her teeth rattled. Would she never retire? She had probably been stealing Mother Dear blind all these years.

"Well, I'm going to call up Dr. Falk," I said. "I'll just ask him."

"Why don't you do that?" said Sister.

But when I called Dr. Falk, he was real evasive. I could hear his voice curving away from me, just like it probably curved away from his wife. I could not pin him down.

"Is it the pip or what?" I demanded. "And you'd better tell me straight out."

"Uh, pip?" said Dr. Falk.

"Haven't you ever heard of the pip?"

"No."

"I swear, you Yankees ought to think twice about moving south. The pip is what kills baby chickens."

"Mrs. McDougal, I'm not a veterinarian," said Dr. Falk. "And I cannot discuss your mother's condition with you."

I felt my blood turn to ice. I hung up the phone and marched straight back to Mother Dear's and demanded to know the truth.

"I'm just down in my back is all," she said. She was sitting in the porch swing, which faced the backyard. It was early October. Her garden had not been plowed under, and I could see brown stalks of last summer's corn. There, at the edge of the garden, was the bald place where she had always planted flowers. I remembered her pulling up my dress and slapping my bottom. *Get out of my sunflowers, Dorothy!*

"Where has summer gone?" I said. The swing screaked back and forth.

"It's still here," Mother Dear said.

"What?" I gave her one of my looks.

"I said it's still here."

"Where?"

"It's hiding."

"I wish you'd make sense. Are you having a garden next year?" I watched her face.

She breathed in and out, but she didn't answer.

"Let me ask you one question," I said. "Why is Dr. Falk over here night and day if you're not sick?"

She smiled and looked at me sideways. "He comes to see Clancy Jane, I reckon."

I drew back and stared. "What do you mean?"

"He's got a crush on her," Mother Dear said. "Big as the world."

Well! The cat was out of the bag. You could've knocked me over with a feather. I sat down in the swing and set it to swaying. I hated imagining Sister with a man when I didn't have one. I didn't like it at all, the things that were swirling in my mind.

"Is this serious?" I asked as soon as I found my voice.

Mother Dear nodded. "Real serious," she said.

"But he's married." My mind skipped back to Albert, back to him and Sister on the sofa.

"I think it's a real unhappy marriage," said Mother Dear. "They've been separated for some time."

"I don't care. He's still married, isn't he? That ought to tell you something. And I sure wouldn't want someone doctoring on me who'd cheated on his wife."

"I can't believe that Clancy Jane would have actual relations with a married man," she said.

"No?" I wanted to laugh.

"No, indeed not."

"Well, have you forgotten my Albert?" I paused to let his name sink in. "This makes two married men for Sister. That we know of."

Mother Dear gave me a long look, but she didn't say anything. She knew I was right, but she would die before admitting it.

*I*t was the worst autumn I could remember. The unseasonable warmth was ruined by continuous rain. In spite of it being November my grass shot up overnight, wet and glistening, too damp to mow. Mother Dear's garden was a shaggy square of weeds. It rained ten straight days and nights, as if the sky had a great big tear and was slowly leaking blue water. My basement flooded. And it was full of doodads. Domino and I stood on the top step and looked down at the water. It was not especially deep, only two inches or so, but it was enough to ruin everything. There was Mack's old salt map of Tennessee. Bitsy's rocking horse she had worn the springs off of. I wanted to wade into the sludge and pluck that map from the water.

But I didn't want to get my feet wet, so I shut the door and went back into the kitchen. Domino's toenails clicked on the linoleum behind me. I poured a fresh cup of coffee, then sat down and propped my elbows on the table. My shoulder blades felt like two chicken bones. I tried not to think of all the work waiting for me in the basement, once the water receded. If it receded. The radio had issued flood warnings across the county. And floodwater was not clean. It seeped from the ground and left behind a brown sediment. Plus, after the flood of '45, Mother Dear had been scared to death we would all contract typhus.

I tried not to think of mildew taking hold on my dirty laundry, popping out like a black rash. I would have to mop up that water and haul each full bucket up the basement steps. All by my lonesome self. Not a living soul cared if I up and died. What I needed was a change of scenery. It would have been easier for me to kill myself than take a trip somewhere. To San Francisco or New York. I would be scared to death in a great big city.

Domino walked over to her basket. It was a big wicker bed with a plaid mattress. It creaked as she jumped in and circled twice before finding a comfortable position. I looked at my telephone. It hung on the wall, black and dead. No one ever called me. I called people, but it did little good. I always felt like I was interrupting them. Take the ladies down at church. They were always meeting for Bible study or ceramics. After Albert left, I spent a whole lot of time down at church, and let me tell you one thing, I have never seen such bossy women. And gossips, my Lord. They all wanted to know what had happened to my eyebrows. I told them that I had a skin disease, and that shut them up.

I thought about calling Mack. There was no telling what that boy was doing. Bitsy had told me the truth. He was living in sin. Living in a trailer park, with him building houses right and left, and him with only one leg. Living with that Earlene. (Bitsy had been right—Earlene did drive a school bus.) You would have thought that Mack might have learned something from his father's doings. I worried about him building those houses. I didn't see how he could with just one leg, but you couldn't tell him a thing.

I knew it would do no good to call Bitsy—she was never

home. She was off spending Meathead's money on a nursery. I
hoped she spent it all. She never worked at the bank a single
day, and I was glad. I thought of her driving around Cookeville,
Tennessee. It was raining cats and dogs there, too. She was big
and pregnant, and she wouldn't come to my house for Thanksgiving dinner.

I hadn't been invited next door, either. I was not about to
call them and invite myself. Let them sit in the parlor, where
Sister had tried to take my Albert in sin. Let them watch *All
My Children* and worry all day about Tara and Phillip. I knew
Queenie watched it. She watched *As the World Turns,* too. She
talked about Lisa as if she were a friend. Lisa did this, Lisa said
that. I wondered if Queenie hated to see weekends come.

I know I did.

Rain scratched at the kitchen window. The sky held a
strange blue darkness. The house felt huge. Beneath my feet, a
floorboard creaked as the house contracted in the dampness.
For a moment, the years dropped away, and the children were
still home and nothing had changed. Dauphine would be
stuffing the turkey, and Albert would be fitting a bow tie at his
throat. I never meant for it to end this way, me all alone, sitting
in the kitchen, drinking a cold cup of coffee, waiting for the
rain to stop. I prayed that I would sleep through Thanksgiving.
I couldn't even remember which Thursday it was supposed to
be. Already I was dreading Christmas, even though my house
was fully decorated.

*I*t rained the day before Thanksgiving. The ground seemed to
shrink beneath the dampness. There was no way I could dry
out my basement. Everything I had down there was ruined. I
went into the kitchen to put on a pot of coffee, and I just hap-

pened to look over at Domino. She was stretched out on the linoleum, and I thought for a minute she was dead.

"Domino?" I cried.

She lifted her head and looked at me with her muddy eyes. Her spotted tail moved in just the slightest wag. But she didn't sit up and thump her tail against the floor, the way she always did first thing in the morning. I felt tears rush into my eyes. Oh, Lord. Let my Domino be all right.

"Domino?" I said, trying to rack my brain for something to cheer her up. I picked up a can of Mighty Dog. "Food to eat!"

Domino just lowered her head and let out a long sigh. I ran upstairs and got dressed and brought down a blanket. I coaxed Domino into the car, covered her with the blanket, and drove to the vet's office. Dr. Harmon took one look at my precious and said, "Domino is one sick doggie, Mrs. McDougal."

As if I did not know! And I just hated for him to call her a doggie.

"I need to keep her a day or two," said Dr. Harmon.

"You mean *hospitalize* her?" I had not expected this. "But what's wrong?"

"Well, Mrs. McDougal, it appears to be heart failure." He scratched his head, as if he were not certain. "I'm going to start her on some medicine. Can I reach you at home?"

I had not counted on going home. I just stared at Domino, who was stretched out on the steel table, breathing hard. She was so weak she couldn't sit up. And normally she hated coming to the vet's. Her toenails would screak against the metal table.

"Mrs. McDougal?"

"I would rather stay, if you don't mind," I said.

"Well, all right. Suit yourself." He reached down and

picked up Domino in his arms, grunting with the effort. Then he disappeared into the hallway.

In a minute his receptionist poked her head into the exam room. "Mrs. McDougal? Wouldn't you be more comfortable in the waiting room?"

She was not being polite. I could tell. She merely needed the exam room for another animal. I picked up my purse and Domino's blanket and listened to the empty sound of my heels on the linoleum as I walked toward the lobby.

I did not know how much time passed. I held a magazine in my lap, *Dog World,* and stared out the picture window. The rain fell sideways against a dark gray sky.

"Mrs. McDougal?"

"Yes?" I looked up. Dr. Harmon stood in the doorway. I did not like the way he was staring at me.

"I think you'd better come back."

I swallowed hard. "Back" was the room reserved for serious cases. In all the years Domino and I had been coming to this clinic, I had heard him mention the back room. This is the place they took car accident victims. Dogs that had been run over. Once a whole family brought in a collie. They had her wrapped in a bloody sheet, and Dr. Harmon said, "We'd better take her on back."

Domino had trembled all over like maybe she was going to be next.

Now, I got up and followed Dr. Harmon. Before we reached the back room, I heard Domino grunting. Her eyes were closed, and she was stretched out on a metal table. Her chest sawed up and down. I knew then she was breathing her last, and that, when she died, I would have no one.

"Domino?" I whispered. "Oh, Domino."

She opened her eyes, and when she saw me, she lifted her head and grinned. She was trembling all over.

"I just don't think it's any use," Dr. Harmon said. "I hate to see her suffer like this."

"Can't you do something?" I cried.

"Ma'am, it's out of my hands."

I felt my eyes bulge. Domino went back to grunting and wheezing. I burst into tears. It wasn't long before the wheezing stopped. Dr. Harmon did not look at me as he placed the worn blue collar in my hands. I told him I wanted to bury her myself. He wrapped her in the blanket and carried her to my car.

"Are you sure you're all right?" he asked me.

I just stared at him, the murderer. I did not know, I was not sure, but I wondered if Domino would still be alive if I had not taken her to his office. Maybe I should have treated her myself. And if he planned to send me a bill, he could send it until the cows came home. All I could think of was Domino. She had looked so pitiful lying on that cold metal table. They had not even thought to put her blanket over her. She always had shivered, even when I turned the heat up.

I walked out into the parking lot, feeling the rain strike my body, and yanked open my car door. Lightning flashed over Dr. Harmon's office. A moment later, a huge boom shook my car. I gripped the steering wheel. I couldn't look in the backseat to save my life. Instead, I concentrated on the blurry windshield. The rain came down hard, like a flurry of gray moths, and I wondered if the sky was crying for my Domino.

I knew I was in shock, but I looked up at the sky and said, "Weep! For I cannot!"

"Hurry, little Dorothy," I told myself. I stabbed my key in the ignition and pulled out into the street. I started singing "Old Rugged Cross."

I didn't think I could stand it. "Suffer the little dogs to come unto me," I shouted.

I just kept thinking of her lying on her side, grinning at me.

When I angled into my driveway, I got out of the car and strode to the garage and found me a shovel. Rain slashed down. I sloshed all over the yard, trying to find the best spot for Domino's burying place.

Then I looked across the yard, and my eyes rested on Mother Dear's garden. That clear space where she always planted the zinnias. During my childhood, it had seemed like a magic edge. Mother Dear tried her best to keep me away, but I'd hide in the tall sunflowers. Domino had liked the shade there, too. I thought about asking Mother Dear if I could bury my dog there, but I was afraid she'd say no. I'd just have to sneak and do it. With the ground all torn up this time of year, who would know it was my Domino's resting place? Later on I could have a fountain installed. Or a sundial. Mother Dear would never guess it was a grave marker.

It took all my strength to carry Domino to the edge of the garden. I set her down, and the rain fell against the blanket. I didn't feel real good myself. Then I started digging. I was almost blinded by tears and rain. I glanced up at my mother's house. Dr. Falk's white sports car was in the driveway. No telling what he and Sister were doing. Queenie and Violet were probably cooking giblets. Mashing sweet potatoes for a soufflé. Getting ready for a family dinner without me. Well, let them. I squinted at Mother Dear's kitchen window. I saw curtains, a light burning over the stove. It would be just like Sister or Queenie to spy on me. I hoped they were. I thought I could make out their thin faces from behind the screen. I didn't care. I wanted them to walk out here and stop me. I'd tell them about Domino. That would hush them. They knew she'd meant the world to me.

Then I got sad again. Oh, Domino, I thought. You are the only one who ever loved me. What am I going to do without you? Then I remembered Sister's first dog—what was her name? Oh, yes. Smarty Pants. I remembered the day Mother Dear buried that dog, how the ground crumbled like something hard and stale. I remembered white fur blowing across the yard like dandelions. *You have to bury them deep,* Papa had said. You have to bury them deep.

I thrust the shovel into the dirt and pushed it deeper with my foot. The soil came up easily, heavy and black, from all of the water. I kept digging, but I made little progress. The rain kept falling. Now and then my shovel made a sucking noise in the mud.

My Domino needed a casket. Mahogany would do, but there wasn't time. Sister could come running out of the house any minute. I paused, breathing hard, and stared into the hole. It was not a pretty hole, but it was deep. I leaned over and scooped out more dirt.

The tip of my shovel struck something hard.

Good, I thought. I have struck limestone. A picture formed in my mind, of me laying Domino against a nice shelf of rock. Why, I could not have planned it better. Then I saw that my shovel had not hit limestone. It had struck a bunch of ribs. I dropped to my knees and peered into the hole. Attached to the ribs was a piece of decayed white cloth. The ribs were attached to a breastbone, a long backbone full of notches and spikes. There was a whole skeleton buried down there, and no telling whose it was. Lord, Lord, Lord, Lord. I crouched on my heels. Thoughts were buzzing inside my head like bottle flies.

I supposed the next step, before I called the police, was to ask Mother Dear herself. Maybe there was a family story that went with this skeleton. My whole body pulsed with suspicion. Suddenly it made sense, after all these years, why she had carved an island at the edge of her garden. Mother Dear knew who was buried here. She and Queenie had killed somebody. Or maybe just Queenie had, and Mother Dear was protecting her. Maybe Queenie had killed a Fuller Brush man or a Bible salesman. A Kirby vacuum cleaner man. And it was just my luck that Queenie was watching me right now, figuring out a way to hush me forever. She could put rat poison in my tea. She could push me down the stairs. She could bury me right here, on top of these bones, and no one would ever know. They would believe anything she told them. "Miss Dorothy got mad at me and said she was leaving town and never coming back," she would tell the family. And they would believe her. It was that simple.

I knew my days were numbered. I had already made it easy for her. She didn't even have to dig a hole. All she had to do was cover me with dirt. I glanced down at my hands. They were black and grainy. My dress was so wet I could see through it. I looked down into the hole. There was no way I could bury my dog with a stranger. And I did not want to confuse the police. I knew one thing: I was going to catch my death of cold if I stayed out here in the rain, and wouldn't that make it easy for her? She and Sister could get Dr. Falk to prescribe me some poison pills. I needed to go inside where I could think.

I left everything the way it was and slogged back to my house. I stood in the kitchen, dripping water all over the floor, and tried to figure out what to do. The first thing I laid eyes on was Domino's basket. The plaid cushion was dented. If Domino were alive, she would have growled and scared off Queenie. My eyes filled. Well, I would just have to bury her later. In another spot. With a regular tombstone. I went over to the sink and drew up a glass of tap water. It tasted rusty and was probably full of typhus. I spat it out.

Behind me the kitchen was quiet. My life would never be the same. I felt dizzy, like maybe I was dying, only I was too heartsick to call an ambulance. I stretched out on the linoleum. I closed my eyes and prepared to meet my maker.

Miss Gussie

1971

I didn't believe my eyes. A fat woman was standing in my garden, just a-digging. She held a shovel, her elbows moving up and down. Mud was flying everywhere. I shook my head and blinked hard. The woman was still shoveling damp soil. If I hadn't gotten up to take my pill, I would have missed it. I just happened to look out the window. Beyond the glass panes, rain grated in the blue silence. It was almost evening.

"What in the world," I said, moving closer to the window. My legs creaked. They were bruised and skinny. I stared hard at the fat lady. She was wearing a scarf and a black coat. A blue blanket, with something stuffed inside, lay at her feet. Her calves were broad and fleshy. I knew one person in the world with legs shaped like that.

"Dorothy?" I said, leaning closer to the panes. I couldn't feature what she was doing, what with the rain coming down so hard. And she was digging right where she shouldn't. In my old flower bed. Where Charlie and I had hid that boy. I had been feeling too poorly to plant zinnias last summer and that whole section had gone weedy. I gripped the windowsill until my knuckles turned white. That was just like Dorothy, always digging up trouble, didn't know when to stop. I strained to see what was inside that blue blanket. Dorothy kept shoveling dirt. I'd never seen her work that hard before.

She dropped to her knees and stared down into the hole. Lordy Jesus, I thought to myself. I should have planted my tomatoes. I'd been stupid to hoard that part of the garden for flowers. Maybe I'd just set it off, drawing emphasis to the very thing I wanted to hide.

Now she was walking back to her house. She yanked open the door and disappeared inside. The kitchen lights turned on. I saw her standing in front of the sink. I looked back at the garden. The soil around it was piled high. I sighed hard, and my breath fogged the glass. I didn't have much of a choice. I would have to take care of things before Dorothy called the police. That would be her next move. It would have been mine if I hadn't been guilty.

I was wearing nothing but a gown, but I didn't have time to change. I pulled on my flannel robe and the knitted slippers. Then I walked down the hall like an old, old woman. When I passed by the living room, I heard Clancy Jane's voice.

"Gin," she said, laying down her cards. She, Violet, and Queenie were playing rummy with Dr. Byron Falk. Now that his divorce had come through, he spent most of his time over here. When he started shuffling the cards, I crept in the kitchen. On the counter was a coconut cream pie with one wedge missing. A twenty-five-pound turkey was defrosting in the sink, floating in clear water. Clancy Jane had invited Dr. Falk to eat Thanksgiving dinner with us. I inched open the back door. Rain sprayed onto my robe. I heard laughter from the living room. Queenie's laughter was strongest.

"Hush your mouth," she said, laughing. "I ain't playing no more cards with you."

"Oh, come on," said Violet, shuffling the cards.

I stepped outside and leaned into the wind, bending my

head toward my chest. The rain fell in solid sections like blowing wheat fields. My slippers skidded in the damp grass, and I fell down hard, knocking my head. I reached up and felt a goose egg on my scalp. It hurt like the dickens. I slowly got to my feet. My bones ached, and I was soaked through and through. By the time I reached the hole, I was out of breath. I looked down at the blue blanket. Wrapped inside it was that poor old dog. Domino's spotted fur was drenched, as if she'd drowned. Dorothy had worshipped that dog. I shielded my eyes with one hand and looked toward her house. Her kitchen lights were still burning. I bent down to see if the dog had been hit by a car, but I couldn't tell. I wondered what had happened. Her hind legs were starting to get stiff. I squatted and peered into the hole. Dorothy had dug it right deep. It was starting to hold water. That wasn't all. My heart pumped faster. The bones were there, all right. Bones like old shells. Bones that had held up the boy's body. We'd buried him in his clothes, covered him with soil, and the whole time his heart was ticking beneath the curved arch of ribs.

"Mother!" he'd cried. He had meant Willadean Wentworth, of course, long dead, drowned without ever knowing the truth. When Dorothy was little, I tried to keep her away from this part of the garden. I didn't want her running and skipping over tainted soil. Contrary as ever, she was drawn to the spot. I was forever hollering at her. It didn't do a bit of good. She was so stubborn. She didn't understand. She just wanted to help me plant zinnia seeds. She wanted to make the pretty flowers grow. She didn't know what was down there. In my mind's eye he was still alive. He would always be alive, inhaling dark soil into his lungs.

All these years later, it had come back to haunt me. Aside from me, Dorothy was the only living witness. Even though she couldn't have a memory of it, I was convinced that night had marked her. The least I could do was bury her dog. I'd just have to talk to her later and smooth it over. I pulled hard on the blanket and pushed Domino into the hole, grunting with the effort. My head was throbbing something awful. I picked up the shovel and began slowly filling the hole. My arms wouldn't lift more than a scoop of mud at a time. I felt a chill coming on, as if my own bones were slowly working their way through my skin.

I remembered the spring of 1932—it came late and cold. Charlie and I planted rows of corn, and we did not speak. He wouldn't go near that end of the garden. If it was tended at all, it was tended by me. It was at the east end of the yard, next to the oak tree, and I worked in the shade. I blocked off the bad part with a rock border and planted zinnias, marigolds, four-o'clocks, and peonies. I planted sunflowers in the back. Charlie watched from a distance. His face seemed pale and angular, hard-boned. When he came down with a case of summer flu, he asked me to make him up a bed in the guest room. I said all right. He said he was afraid of infecting me and Dorothy. Fine, I said.

Every afternoon, while Dorothy slept in her buggy beneath the oak, I worked in the garden. Every now and then I'd glance up at the old Hamilton land. The field stretched out green and wavy beneath the wind. The honeysuckle didn't bloom until the middle of June, but when it did, it was thicker than ever. The barbwire fence sagged beneath its weight. The smell pulled at me, almost like a longing. I filled the house with sprigs of it, breathing the deep smell as if it could purify me. By July the vine had stopped blooming, and the scent was gone. I sat on the porch, the baby in my arms, and listened to the whippoor-wills calling back and forth. The corn was so tall, I could barely see the land behind it. Charlie was inside listening to the radio.

Jack Benny's voice drifted onto the porch. All summer Charlie's
flu came and went. His shirt gaped open at the neck, making
his bow tie sag. He was letting this thing eat him alive, it was
shrinking him, and there wasn't a thing I could do.

It took all my strength to fill the grave. Come April, I would
have to remind Clancy Jane to plant zinnias. I leaned against
the shovel, thinking I'd rest a minute. The rain fell harder. My
windows were yellow squares, blurred slightly around the edges,
making the whole house seem like one light. I looked down at
my robe. I was a sight. The fabric was plastered to my legs like
a dirty eggshell. You couldn't even tell the flannel was pink.

My head was aching, and I was half-dizzy. I wondered if I
had the strength to get back inside the house where it was warm
and always summer. The yellow light from the windows seemed
closer. I felt the heat of it on my face. I had to get inside and
tell them that it was all right, that I had buried Dorothy's dog
for her. If only I weren't so tired. If only my head didn't hurt
so bad. If only it weren't so soothing to lie here and listen to
the rain. If only Clancy Jane hadn't worn that poodle skirt. I
told her not to hem it so short. "Oh, my god," she cried out.
"It's Mother. Byron, come quickly." I felt confused for a second. Then I remembered. Mama was calling me. Her kitchen
had a wood stove. It was early of a morning, and rain was beating on the tin roof. The windows were steamed up. I rubbed
my hand on the glass and looked outside. A gray sky stretched
low over the trees. Mama and I cut out biscuits and set them in
a greased pan. I licked my finger and wrote my name on
another pane, GUSSIE. I fed kindling into the grate. The wood
was damp, and it sizzled. The heat from the stove fogged the
windows up again, and all you could see of my name was
G   SIE. Mama looked out the window and rubbed her hands
together. "Just listen to it pour!" she said. I hugged my knees
and waited for the biscuits to rise.

Dorothy

1971

*T*he phone rang, and I opened my eyes. I hadn't died. I was in the kitchen, lying on the floor. Outside the storm raged, clawing at the windows. But it couldn't reach me. I was safe. My house was secure as a vault. The phone kept ringing. I scrambled to my feet and answered it.

"Dorothy, I've got bad news." It was Sister. I thought to myself: *you and me both.*

"You need to come to the hospital as soon as possible," she said. "We're all here. And don't bother getting all dressed up, either. Get here as fast as you can."

"The hospital?" I said, irritated. What now? I thought. Then it came to me: Bitsy! Bitsy has gone into labor!

Before I could say another word, Sister said, "You need to hurry. It's Mother. She's real, real sick. She's dying, Dorothy, and I don't have time to explain."

"Dying!"

"Bitsy's here. Violet's on her way. We're in room 107."

"But I don't understand!" I cried. "Why is Mother Dear dying?"

"Just hurry, Dorothy." Sister's voice broke. "I'll explain it all when you get here. I can't talk anymore. I've got to go." She hung up without so much as a by-your-leave. Well! You could have knocked me over with a feather. First Domino, then the skeleton, and now Mother Dear. It was more than I could stand. But at least Queenie had not seen me. I looked down at my muddy clothes. My hands were solid black from digging the grave. I didn't have time to change or bathe. I wiped off my arms with a tea towel and grabbed my pocketbook and charged out the door.

Halfway to my car, something made me stop and turn around. I looked back at Mother Dear's garden. Something was different. I couldn't see Domino's poor old body. I ran toward the grave, slipping twice in the mud. When I reached the garden, sure enough, Domino's body was gone. The hole had been refilled. The shovel was on the ground. Then it came to me: the murderer had done this! The murderer had covered up the bones and stolen Domino's body. That same murderer was probably watching me right now. Lord God, help me. I ran screaming to my car. I got inside and locked the doors. Then I drove straight to the hospital. I had it all planned. I was going to tell them that a murderer was among us. When I reached Mother Dear's room, they were all gathered around the bed. Sister eyed my wet clothes, but she didn't comment. There, in the center of the white sheets, all shrunken and grunting, was Mother Dear. Her head was muddy. I looked down at her hands. They were as dirty as mine. I didn't understand it. Her eyes were closed, but her mouth sagged open. She drew in a jagged breath and held it. When she didn't exhale, I looked up at Sister and Queenie. At last the room filled with a long, whistling breath.

Sister stood in front of the window, backlit by the gray sky. She was crying. Queenie kept wiping her own eyes with a balled-up Kleenex. Bitsy sat in a chair, her stomach huge and resting on her knees. Tears streaked down her fat cheeks. She had gained far too much weight during her pregnancy. Claude put his hand on her shoulder, and she reached up and grabbed it. Mack was hunched over in the corner, and standing next to him was a scrawny girl in blue jeans who kept rubbing his arm. It was Earlene, that school bus driver. She was snapping a piece of chewing gum. She was no improvement over Sloopy, let me tell you.

Mother Dear started breathing hard, and we all turned to watch.

Lord, Lord, Lord.

All I could think of was Domino and her missing body. I wondered who the murderer was. My brain couldn't soak up anything else. Sister walked over and put her arms around me. "How'd you get so wet, Dorothy?"

"Well, it's a long story. I've been at the vet's." My eyes blurred over. "Domino died."

"Oh, no." Sister squeezed my shoulders. "I'm so sorry, Dorothy. It couldn't have come at a worse time, could it?"

I wiped my eyes and sniffed hard. "Would you please tell me what's happened to Mother Dear?"

"It's the saddest thing," said Sister.

"We found her in the garden," said Queenie. "She was digging to beat the band."

"What?" I froze.

"She was delirious. She must have thought it was planting time," said Sister, her voice breaking.

"In all this rain, too." Queenie wiped her eyes. They looked muddy and deep.

"What did she say?" I grabbed Sister's blouse. "Why was she digging!"

"I don't know." Sister peeled my hands away. "She

couldn't talk. She must have fallen and hit her head. See that bruise? She was unconscious when we found her. Byron says she probably got confused and wandered outside. She must have thought she was planting. Then she collapsed. When she hit her head, it caused a hemorrhage of the brain."

"Hit her head? You mean, someone bashed her skull in." My eyes swerved around the room, searching for the guilty party. I was twitching all over.

"No one hit her."

"You don't know that!"

"She fell, Dorothy."

Sister looked down at Mother Dear's dirty arms and went to the sink for a washcloth. She wrung it out, came back to the bed, and started wiping down our mother's arms.

Dr. Falk cleared his throat and looked at me from under his eyebrows. "Miss Gussie had low platelets, Dorothy. And when she hit her head, her blood couldn't clot fast enough. She hemorrhaged."

"Platelets, my foot!" I cried. "Something's not right here!"

"Excuse me?" said Dr. Falk.

I opened my mouth, but I forgot what I'd started to say. All I could think of was murder. We were all doomed.

"Oh, Dorothy," said Sister. "Mother didn't want you to know she had leukemia. She thought you would go to pieces."

"Leukemia?" I looked away from Sister and stared at Dr. Falk, who averted his eyes to the floor.

"It's the truth, Mummie," whined Bitsy. "Miss Gussie didn't want you to know."

"Say *what*?" I cried. I could not believe my ears.

Bitsy nodded and started weeping. She reached up for Claude's hand.

Lord, Lord, Lord. It was beginning to make sense. Sister

leaving her hippie colony and coming home. Mother Dear's face puffed up like a blue moon. The bruises, the weakness. And I could just hear Mother Dear saying she did not want me to know. My eyes filled as I stared at Judas-Bitsy, my own flesh and blood.

"Do you mean to tell me that my own mother had leukemia and no one had the decency to tell me?" I stared them all down.

Silence. The only sound was Mother Dear's snagged breath. "Mack?" I said. "Did you know?"

He looked down at the floor. Then he nodded. Earlene rubbed his arm, and I saw that she had known, too.

Sister squeezed my shoulders. I jerked away. "How long has she been sick?" I asked, keeping my voice low. I wanted to show all of them how civilized I was. I knew they were expecting me to curse or slap someone's face.

"Since July," said Judas's husband. "She's been sick since Bitsy and I came back from our honeymoon."

My nostrils flared. I didn't even look at him. He wasn't blood kin. And he had stolen my daughter and turned her into a rich Judas with too many notions. From the bed, Mother Dear was sucking in air like a broken pump. This was the final insult. First, she had robbed me of her love. Then she had robbed me of her death. What had she imagined I might do? Cry? Throw myself on her? *Bother* her? No, I would have tried to make her final days happy. That was all.

I was too mad to cry. She might as well have slapped my face. Something blinked on and off, like neon, inside my skull. Once again, Mother Dear and Sister had left me out. Not to mention Queenie. I vowed it would be the last time.

"Since I'm obviously not part of the in crowd around here," I said, "would somebody like to explain why Domino's body was stolen and what that skeleton is doing in Mother Dear's garden?"

"What?" said Sister.

"That dad-blamed skeleton. Don't tell me you don't know about it."

"What are you talking about, Mummie?" said Judas-Bitsy, drawing away from me like she had caught a whiff of a bad smell.

Queenie gave me one of her if-looks-could-kill voodoo stares.

They were all in this together. I had to call the police before one of them moved the bones. If I had to make a bet, I'd pick Queenie as the murderer. I glanced down at my dress. I looked white trashy, like maybe I didn't practice principles of good hygiene. I knew what they were thinking: *Dorothy has flipped her lid. Her brain has cracked into a million pieces.* But it was a lie, a bald-faced lie, and I hated them all. I started to tell them, but I didn't. I held my tongue. I had to be careful or I'd find myself in the garden. I felt Queenie's gaze. My mother exhaled loudly, as if she were exasperated. I just knew she'd be all right. She'd open her eyes and tell us what she'd been doing in the garden. I waited and waited, but she never took another breath.

"Good-bye, Miss Gussie," Queenie said, kissing my mother's hand. Sister's eyes watered.

"What're we going to do now?" sobbed Judas-Bitsy.

No one said anything.

"We'll call the funeral home, that's what we'll do," I said. Everyone stared at me like I had said something wrong.

Judas-Bitsy pressed her face into Claude's chest, and her shoulders moved up and down. Sister and Queenie were hugging each other and boohooing. Dr. Falk put his arms around them. I just stood there watching. My eyes were dry. I could not stand it. Let them manage on their own. Let them pick out the casket and deal with the undertaker. I knew about these things, and they didn't. I strode out of the room, walked straight to my car, and drove home. I locked all the doors so Queenie couldn't get to me.

The kitchen phone rang all evening. I ignored it. If my family thought I was going to sit at the funeral home when half the town knew my mother was dying and I did not, they had another thought coming. I had no intention of being a laughing-stock. Later, someone rang the doorbell. I opened a kitchen drawer. I didn't have a gun in the house. I'd have to beat them off with my rolling pin. Then they walked around to the back door, jiggled the knob, and beat on the glass. I heard voices rising into the rain. It sounded like Sister and Mack, but I could have been mistaken. After a few minutes, they went away.

*N*ow this is what happened, you can take it or leave it: I got madder and madder. It rained and rained. The weathermen predicted flash floods and winds up to thirty miles per hour. I could not sleep a wink. I sat in Mack's old room and stared down at my mother's house, trying to figure out what to do. I couldn't see much because of the weather.

I tried not to think about my whole, ugly life, but it was hard. I thought if Mother Dear had been a Chinese woman, she would have set me on a mountain to die. If she had been a hippie, she would have gone to an abortion clinic and had me scraped out. I thought of my church, the way it was color-coordinated, decorated in dark maroons. The walls were pale mauve, the carpet burgundy, and the pews were upholstered in mini-print mauve and blue. You would not think Christians cared if things matched or not, but they seemed to mind in this

town. One of our members owned a sewing shop, and she sold
the church the fabric at a discount. I heard she made a profit. I
never liked the maroon. I thought of the matching burgundy
flower arrangement on the altar, the carved letters beneath it:
DO THIS IN REMEMBRANCE OF ME.

"Do it, Little Dorothy," I whispered. "Do it to them before
they do it to you, sugarbabe."

"Do what?" I said aloud.

"Just do it," I said back. "Do anything. Do it, doit, doit-
doitdoitdoit."

The rain shot hard and fast out of the sky. There was no
telling how many bodies were buried in Mother Dear's garden.
I imagined a long string of farmers and Fuller Brush men, their
lives snuffed out for reasons I would never know. It hit me, all
of a sudden, what I must do, and I could have just killed myself
for not doing it earlier. I picked up the phone and called the
police. "I'd like to report a missing body and a murderer," I
said, breathing hard into the receiver.

"Your name, please?" said the dispatcher.

"Dorothy McDougal. And I'm pretty sure my mother's
maid just dug up a whole skeleton in our backyard. I think she's
trying to hide the evidence. She might have killed my mother,
too. And she stole Domino. Her body, I mean."

"One thing at a time, ma'am," said the dispatcher. I gave
him my name again, Queenie's name, and our address.

I was disappointed when only one black-and-white car
pulled into Mother Dear's driveway. There were no sirens, no
wheeling blue lights. Just a pear-shaped policeman, wearing a
dark gray raincoat, who took his own sweet time getting out of
his car.

I hurried like I didn't have a whole lot of time. I ran downstairs, through the rain, to Mother Dear's house. I felt death everywhere, like a dark smell. *Come to me,* it said. *Come to me.*

They were all in the kitchen. The policeman was drinking a cup of coffee, and he and Sister were laughing at something Queenie had just said. Then they saw me. They stopped laughing. You could see the smiles drain from their faces. Here my mother was, not even buried, and they were having a party.

"We were just going to call you again," said Sister, picking up her coffee cup, getting up from the table. She walked over to the counter and poured a fresh cup.

"Ma'am?" said the policeman. "We've got it all straightened out now."

I just stared. I knew that he had believed their lies.

"Have you checked the grave yet?" I said.

"Ma'am, there wasn't no need." He cut his eyes at Sister.

Sister set down her coffee cup and walked over to me. She put her hand on my arm. "Dorothy, it's not what you think."

"One of you stole Domino's body. Then you filled in the grave. Hid that skeleton. Covered it up."

Queenie just sat there, giving me the Evil Eye.

"Then you cracked Mother Dear's head in with the shovel."

"Oh, honey." Sister squeezed my arm and looked to Queenie for help. "I'll just call Byron. He can give you a pill, something to calm you down."

"No!" I screamed.

The policeman stared at me like I had a disease.

I stared right back. "Go ahead," I said. "Lift your eyebrows at me. You could've at least *checked* the garden. Go check it now."

The policeman shifted his glance toward Sister, and I knew then who was running this show. No telling what lies she had told him. Queenie picked up her coffee cup and stared at me over the rim. She wouldn't let me get away with this. I knew too much. My days were numbered. I had to find a safe place to hide.

"You can't fool me," I said, feeling my face draw into a hideous snarl. "You're all in it together."

Behind me, Sister started sniffing. The policeman stared into his coffee cup.

"So you're not going to check out that grave?" I said, giving him a hard look. I wasn't afraid of him.

"No, ma'am. I don't see a need to."

"Then I'll go dig it up myself!" I headed toward the door, but Sister caught my arm.

"Calm down, Dorothy," she said. Her face was inches away from mine. Then she looked at the policeman. "She's in shock."

"The hell I am," I said and jerked away from her grasp. I saw no love in her eyes. They were blue and cold. Now that Mother Dear was gone I was just one more person to share the inheritance with. I knew what she was doing. I stepped backward, keeping my eyes on my sister the whole time. When I reached the hall, I started running. I ran across the yard, into the safety of my house, and locked all the doors.

I was so scared, I lost track of time. Before I knew it, the farm report came on the radio. The announcer said flash floods and thunderstorms were on the way, for people to evacuate to high ground. I imagined Town Creek swelling against its banks. Now a good flash flood was just what I needed. Slowly, it came to me what I must do. I put on mascara, blue eyeshadow, lipstick, and blush. I drew two, curved eyebrows and feathered the edges to make them look real. I sat down at the kitchen table and wrote out instructions for my funeral in case they killed me before I could hide. Then I rummaged in Albert's old dresser for a set of keys to the dime store. It was the safest place I knew—they would not think to find me there. If he had changed the locks, which I sincerely doubted, I would simply smash out the back window. I knew for a fact and a half that he did not have a burglar alarm. He couldn't afford it like the Big K's and Dollar Generals could.

It was a little after dawn. I got an umbrella, sneaked out to my car, and drove to the square. It was raining to beat the band. The creek had topped the bank, spilling across the road, like a tide. The water was not deep, but the creek continued to rise. An emergency crew was already at work, stacking sandbags in front of the buildings. I did not see Albert's car.

I angled my car down the narrow alley. It sank into the water. I parked in back of the new travel agency, which was on the other end of the street from the dime store. I knew all about covering tracks. I got out of the car. Dirty water gushed all over me. I opened my umbrella, stepped into the deep water, and waded up the back steps to the dime store. I fit the key in the lock, the tumblers moved, and I pushed the door open. The old floor creaked beneath me as I felt my way through the darkened storeroom. It smelled dusty, faintly sweet. I remembered all of the times I wrote out his payroll checks and made the bank deposit and he did not appreciate it. I looked toward the front of the store. Someone had stacked sandbags in front of the glass doors. Even so, water had seeped in, buckling the green tile.

I went upstairs to Albert's office. I was surprised to see that nothing had changed. The walls were the same dull green; his desk was cluttered with old pictures of the children. There were no photographs of his women, no feminine touches. But there wasn't time to linger. I had to make sure they weren't coming after me.

I went into the ladies' lounge and opened the door, which led to the roof. I stood there a moment, listening to the storm coming down. If this wasn't a flash flood, I don't know what was. I made sure I had my umbrella and walked up the rickety stairs to the roof. Rain swarmed out of the sky, each drop stinging like an insect. All around me, the air hummed. I stood on the edge of the building that faced the direction of Mother Dear's house. I glanced down the full two-and-one-half stories and got dizzy. It was much taller than I imagined. The creek water had covered the sandbags around the courthouse. I looked down again. The water had a coppery sheen. It was not real deep, perhaps four feet, but it was steadily rising.

I opened the umbrella, remembering the day Papa and Mr. Wentworth stood on the roof of Citizens' Bank, and oh, Lord, what would they think of the town now? The whole square had changed so much. Crystal Falls seemed like a great big city. I looked at everything, every single detail: posters of Jamaica and Australia in the Dreams Do Come True Travel Agency; beveled glass in the windows of the Tulip Deli and Catering; rows of eyeglasses in Elmer's Vision Center ("New Glasses In One Hour"). I saw lawyers' offices decorated to look like boutiques, with striped awnings and stained glass doors. I saw metal filing cabinets in the Century 21 office; the little tubs of toppings in Salads 'n' More. The round tubs of ice cream and the frosted windows of Baskin-Robbins. The pink walls of Velma's House of Hair where they fried my hair the last time I had a permanent. I did not see how Albert's Ben Franklin had lasted all these years, how he scratched out a living.

The rain fell like little pellets, hurting my skin. I stood tall, holding in my belly, pushing back my shoulders. Across the road, at the Burger King, an emergency crew, outfitted in yellow raincoats, piled sandbags in front of the doors. The visibility was so poor they did not realize I was on the roof of the five-and-dime in the middle of a flash flood.

I wished Albert could see what Sister had driven me to. I could stand up here and tell the whole town what Queenie did, and that I, no doubt, was her next victim. I pictured Albert rushing over to Mother Dear's house, digging out Papa's old silver canoe, and making Mack and Bitsy paddle with him to the square. I imagined reporters, emergency crews, ladders and trampolines, the mayor himself. They would dig up the bones in the backyard, and everyone would realize how mean they had been to me.

I was hit, all of a sudden, by the coincidence of it all. It was real, real strange that both my mother and Domino were dead. It could not be anything other than a plot. Someone wanted my share of the inheritance so they would not have to go back to living in a hut. Selling cheap jewelry on the street like a hotdog vendor. I pictured all of those pill bottles, the purple bruises on Mother Dear's arms. Clancy Jane coming back to town the way she did. Leukemia, my foot. Dr. Falk was probably in on it. That was why they had kept it a secret. They had been poisoning my mother, and I would have figured it out, and now I was next.

I did not have a soul to turn to. My own husband had left me. My children thought I was a fool. I had dug up an actual skeleton and no one believed me. It hurt too much to think I had been reduced to this.

A person could not recover from a slight of this nature. I thought about everything. From the scars on my arms to the scars on my heart. My whole life did not make sense. My mother was laid out at the funeral home, dead at the hands of the people she loved best. She had probably discovered that skeleton in her garden.

I knelt down, clutching the umbrella, and the tar surface of the roof dug into my knees. I looked toward the open door. Beyond it, I heard a noise. It was a firm noise, like someone had stumbled on the staircase. They had come to get me. They had watched me drive away, and they took a back road to get here so I wouldn't know it. I got up, staggered to the edge of the roof, and, Lord help me, I heard footsteps on the stairs, a dry, scraping noise.

There was nowhere for me to hide. Without thinking, I stepped backward. My foot came down hard on air. The whole time I was falling, I heard Albert's voice calling my name *Dorothy, Dorothy, Dorothy!*

$\mathcal{B}$itsy

1971–1972

$\mathcal{T}$he phone's been ringing off the damn wall," Claude shouted when I walked into the kitchen.

"Don't you yell at me, Claude Wentworth. Didn't your mother teach you not to yell at pregnant women?"

I shook my umbrella, and water sprayed everywhere. He stepped backward. I wasn't up to this. Here it was, the day before Thanksgiving, and Miss Gussie was being laid out at the funeral home. I'd been there with Aunt Clancy and Violet, helping them choose the casket, a nice cherry model.

"I'm not yelling." His eyes dropped to my stomach, then came back to my face. "Where have you been?"

"At the funeral home, where do you think?" I pushed wet hair out of my eyes.

"You don't know what's happened, do you?" he said, more gently.

"No, what?"

"People have been calling right and left about your mother."

"Mummie?"

He nodded. "I don't know how to tell you this. She fell off

the roof of your father's store. Nobody seems to know how it happened."

I stumbled backward and sat down hard in a kitchen chair. The baby rolled and kicked inside me, as if it were shocked, too.

"But she's alive," Claude said. "They've got her at the hospital. She's broken her hip. And one of her legs. I think she jumped."

"Je ne me sens pas bien," I said, shutting my eyes. All the breath left my body, but I could just see her jumping off the Ben Franklin's roof. I really could.

"Oh, come off it, Bitsy! Talk normal, would you?"

"You used to like it when I talked French."

He wouldn't look at me.

"I can't believe she'd jump," I said.

"Why not?"

He lifted one blond eyebrow. The older he got, the more pug his nose seemed to get. And that red mole got bigger. I wondered what he'd look like when he was old.

"You don't have to be so mean about it," I said, rubbing my *estomac* to remind him of what I was growing.

He stared as if I were the biggest mistake he'd ever made. I wondered if he'd been talking to his mother. Mrs. Wentworth thought her baby son should have married a college girl. Somebody whose mother had eyebrows. She never came right out and said this, but she didn't have to. She was ice cold to me, in a polite way, of course. Claude and I left Tennessee Tech every weekend and drove back to Crystal Falls. We stayed in his old bedroom. It had football pennants—Harvard, Yale, Stanford, Princeton. He'd never planned on going to a state college. It wasn't my fault that his grades in high school had been terrible. I'd made straight A's and B's.

I didn't feel at ease around his family. Mr. Wentworth was never home, and he was almost never at the bank. He was chairman of the board. He played endless rounds of golf at the club. He wore bright slacks—lime, magenta, canary—and matching knit shirts with alligators. He drove a gold cart with a sun canopy. His golf bag was burgundy leather. Each wood was sheathed with a matching cover. When he wasn't golfing, he was in the clubhouse drinking Scotch and water. Sometimes the colored bartender had to carry him out.

Mrs. Wentworth called her husband Claude. She also called her son Claude. It could get confusing with both men answering to everything she said. She had her bridge games, teas, fashion shows, and clubs. She had agendas and schedules. Sometimes she would join Mr. Wentworth in the cherry-paneled den for a drink. It was just like in a movie. The bar was long and polished, and behind it was a mirrored wall. The wall was lined with cocktail glasses. There was a silver ice bucket with silver tongs. The Wentworths sat on opposite ends of the room, tinkling ice in their drinks.

Did you have a nice day? he asked.

A fine day, and you? she answered.

Splendid.

Then silence, except for tinkling and measured breathing. Sometimes a maid passed a silver tray full of things with tooth-picks. As much as I hated being at the Wentworths, I hated our apartment in Cookeville more. I didn't know anyone. I was so lonely. The apartment was full of wedding presents, but I disliked cooking because of the roaches. Sometimes I'd walk to the campus to wait for Claude. I'd sit on a green bench and watch girls with long, swinging hair. Girls with tight blue jeans and short skirts. My feet were so swollen I had to wear tennis shoes. Sometimes Claude would forget to meet me, and I'd sit on that bench for hours. Finally I'd get up and waddle back to the apartment.

I'd known him my whole life. We were different. He hated peanut butter cookies, and I loved them. He'd get so mad when I'd bake them on our shiny new cookie sheets. Also, he liked his shirts ironed, and I didn't own an iron. We'd gotten one as a wedding gift, but I'd exchanged it for a knife sharpener. It was funny how we fought over little things, and before we knew it, we'd be screaming at each other. And all because I'd done something silly, like put bell peppers in the meat loaf. Mrs. Wentworth had spoiled him, but I knew he'd change when the baby arrived.

Now Claude gave me a funny look. The baby kept rolling inside of me. "I hate to say this, Bitsy." He paused. "But this is just typical of your family."

I knew it was true, but I didn't say anything. She was, after all, my mother.

*S*he's going to be all right," Aunt Clancy said after Mummie came out of surgery. Aunt Clancy's hair was pulled back into a ponytail which almost reached her waist. She didn't have on one of her hippie outfits. She was wearing heels and a navy blue dress. It looked like one of Violet's outfits. My aunt had been a hippie so long, she didn't look right in regular clothes. There were circles under her eyes. I knew she was grieving for Miss Gussie. We all were.

Dr. Byron Falk was with her, and he kept rubbing her neck. They were in love. He had a wife and everything. I'd just seen him the day before when he'd pronounced my grandmother dead. I wondered if he remembered coming to our house and giving Mummie a shot. Aunt Clancy met him last summer when she returned to Crystal Falls. She drove up in a beat-up van. A man with one eye brought her. He looked like a weirdo from California, like someone from Charles Manson's family. He unloaded boxes of clothes and her paintings. I was relieved when he left. There wasn't much of a market in Crystal Falls for art, but there were some semi-hippies who lived downtown. They were an older couple, in their late thirties, and they gave my aunt a job at their craft shop. They made macramé, pottery, and woven blankets, and they even let Aunt Clancy sell some of her paintings.

Right before Claude and I moved to Cookeville, Aunt Clancy told me about my grandmother's leukemia. She made me promise not to tell Mummie. I kept my promise. It grieved me to think Miss Gussie wouldn't live to see her second great-grandchild. Because of Mack's divorce, she hardly ever got to see Christopher. I loved her house because it had a good smell. When Claude and I came home from Tennessee Tech on weekends, I visited her. She would be sitting on her screened porch, a quilt wrapped around her knees, and my aunt would make us a cup of green hippie tea. I didn't ask what was in it. Besides, it tasted good. Aunt Clancy didn't eat red meat. She made fresh bread every morning. Since my grandmother hadn't planted a big garden, Aunt Clancy went to the Farmer's Market to buy vegetables. She threw out all the white sugar and flour. Queenie said, "Just how am I supposed to cook?"

"I'll do the cooking," said my aunt.

"That's what I was afraid of," Queenie said back.

"There's no brain damage," Dr. Falk now said. He was from up north. He had one arm around Aunt Clancy.

"Thank goodness," said Father. When he'd heard about Miss Gussie, he'd gone straight to Mummie's house. He found a note she'd left on the kitchen table. The note had frightened him. It all but said she was planning to hide in the Ben Franklin. He drove through the flooded streets to the square. He went inside the store, calling out her name, and she began screaming from the roof. Now he pulled the note out of his pocket and handed it to me. "I think you should read this, Bitsy. Give it to Mack when he gets here. Where is Mack, by the way?"

"We can't find him," said Aunt Clancy. "I think he's gone off in the school bus with Earlene."

Claude raised one eyebrow. I knew that look, what he was trying to say. That we were weird. And there I was, about to give birth to our child. I was worried sick that my nerves would bring on the baby. I unfolded the note.

To Whom It May Concern

By

Dorothy McDougal

In the event of my death, which will likely be first-degree murder, my will is at Cecil J. Sweeney's office. Certain people are out to get me because I know what's in that hole. They know who they are. That's why I'm going to lock myself in a certain dime store. I don't want certain people to find this note and tear it up. I want my children to get it. I have definite ideas about how I want MY own FUNERAL to be. I want everything perfect to the last detail.

1. I want an all-white color scheme. This includes a top-of-the-line white casket. I want a white satin lining with a ruffled white pillow.
2. I want to be holding a bouquet of white roses.
3. Dress me in the white dress I've got laid out on the bed. Use the matching shoes and white panty hose.
4. Be sure to have Velma Dean fix my hair and face. My make up is on the bed, too. (Look for a little plastic zipper bag.) Also, tell her I want white nail polish.
5. I want to wear my diamond earrings and my pearl necklace. All my rings, too.

6. Arrange silver candelabras around my casket. Use white beeswax candles.
7. Notify all florists that I have requested WHITE FLOWERS ONLY!!!!!!! (This is important for the overall effect!)
8. Serve refreshments. I always thought funerals should have decent food, not those stale doughnuts. Call my caterer. Albert has always paid my bills. Serve milk punch in a silver bowl. Try to follow the all-white color scheme. (Some suggestions: finger sandwiches, divinity, coconut layer cake.)

I crumpled the note and threw it to the floor. Claude reached down and picked it up. His eyes switched back and forth. "Holy cow," he said. "She's really flipped her lid."

Aunt Clancy and Dr. Falk exchanged glances. Father gave a polite cough. I stared at the wall. We still had Thanksgiving and Miss Gussie's funeral to get through.

*B*yron Falk took Aunt Clancy, Queenie, and Violet to the Hermitage Hotel for Thanksgiving dinner. Claude and I ate with his family. I didn't know what Mack and Earlene were doing. Mr. Wentworth talked about his stocks and golf scores. Mrs. Wentworth asked Claude about his grades. No one mentioned my family. No one commented about the baby. My stomach was huge, full of life, but they didn't seem interested. I wanted to say, *"Je suis enceinte!"* Only they wouldn't have understood. They didn't speak French.

We buried my grandmother the following day. There was a big turnout. People wanted to learn firsthand about Mummie, if she'd jumped or fallen. The gossip was something awful. There Mummie was, laid up in intensive care, in no condition to receive visitors, so people came to the funeral home to feed on our grief. I could spot the curious ones right off the bat.

They came in pairs, dressed in black, perching like vultures in front of my grandmother's coffin. If they hadn't had the decency to send flowers, I didn't give them the time of day. Miss Gussie's Sunday school class sent a huge wreath, and so did the Senior Citizens Club. The undertaker, Mr. Howland, kept track of the flowers, who'd sent what, and wrote everything down in a little book. Death was a strange way to make a living, but Mr. Howland seemed good at it. He smelled of Old Spice. I didn't care for the way he kept referring to Miss Gussie as "Mother."

"We want Mother to have a good coffin liner, don't we?" he'd told Aunt Clancy in the display room, when we'd gone to pick out a casket.

It rained the whole time Miss Gussie was laid up in the viewing parlor, but it stopped the day she was buried. It was as if someone had switched off a current. I stood there in the cemetery, listening to the dripping trees. I almost screamed when Violet touched my hand.

"Look," she whispered, pointing to the sky.

"Look at what?" I didn't see anything. I thought maybe she'd seen a bird or something.

"The sun. It's shining." She squeezed my arm, like I should find profound meaning in what she'd said, but I couldn't. She still had her mother, even if she was a hippie, and I didn't have anyone.

Although it was Thanksgiving weekend, Claude had driven back to Tech to study for exams. I packed my suitcase and told Mrs. Wentworth that I was going to stay with Aunt Clancy and Violet for a few days.

"I think that's a good idea," she said. She was sitting in the dining room surrounded by piles of cookbooks. She was planning the menu for her annual Christmas party. She did not mention my mother.

"It won't seem the same without Miss Gussie," I said.

"I guess not. How long will you stay with your aunt?" She didn't look up from her cookbook.

"I was planning to leave Monday. Then I'm driving to Cookeville."

Mrs. Wentworth set down her cookbook. "You're welcome to come back here, Sugar Pie. I mean, don't you think Claude needs to concentrate on his exams?"

"But I miss him, Mrs. Wentworth."

She looked at me for a long moment, her eyes dropping down to my stomach. She sighed. Then she picked up her cookbook. "I'm going to scream if I don't decide on the menu."

*R*ight before Mummie was discharged from the hospital, Father signed papers on her. He didn't want to send her to the state mental hospital, but the private ones were too expensive. So that was how she ended up in Central State.

Fall semester ended the second week in December, and Claude and I returned to Crystal Falls. Father and I drove to Nashville, that's where Central State is, to visit Mummie. Winter was in the air the morning we left. I could still see evidence of the flood—scummy waterlines on telephone poles and houses, sandbags stacked near the entrance to businesses. On the bridge were little snails that resembled seashells.

During the drive up, Father explained about the side effects of Mummie's medication. He had already visited her twice, and he tried to prepare me. I wasn't interested. I was so pregnant I felt like a seed pod, ready to burst. My fingers were swollen. I couldn't wear my diamond ring or my wedding band. I wondered if people thought I was an unwed mother. My back ached, as if my bones were slowly spreading. I hated being pregnant.

"The doctors are giving her Thorazine, which makes her wink all the time," Father said. "So just pretend like you don't notice."

"Okay," I said.

"She doesn't look like herself. She looks . . . I don't know, real *witchy*." He glanced at me. "And that's not all. She thinks the FBI has her under surveillance."

"She *what?*"

"She thinks they've got her room bugged. She thinks they're out to get her."

"But why?" I stared out the windshield.

"The doctors say she's paranoid," Father said.

Central State was the most depressing place I'd ever visited. We drove past redbrick buildings with dark windows. The idea of Mummie being there made me sad. An orderly took us into the dayroom. It was full of green and yellow vinyl chairs. The stuffing had burst out of a sofa, but someone had taped it up. A television was screwed into the wall. Music came out of ceiling speakers, the kind of music you hear in elevators. Right off the bat, I smelled pine disinfectant. The nurse unlocked a steel mesh door, and Mummie came out. The first thing I noticed was her rolling limp. The heel of her hand mashed against a slick wooden cane. Most shocking of all was her hair—it had turned completely white and fell in strings around her ears. There were deep circles under her eyes, cutting purple grooves into her flesh.

"Did anybody follow you here?" She limped over to Father and gripped his sleeve with her free hand.

"No, Dorothy," he said. His voice was low and smooth.

"Are you sure? Because the FBI uses unmarked cars. So does the TBI."

"No one followed us, Dorothy." He patted her hand. "Aren't you going to say anything to Bitsy?"

"Why, that's not Bitsy. That's a fat frog you've brought to confuse me." Her eyes twitched as she glanced down at my stomach. Then she turned back to Father. "Albert, please. Get me out of this hog pen. They're watching me night and day. It's awful!"

"I will, Dorothy. I will," he said, licking his lips. "When you're better, sugar."

"I am better!" She grabbed Father's lapels and pulled him forward. "I want out of here this instant! Today, not tomorrow. You don't know what I'm going through. They're watching me through hidden cameras, and I can't even go to the bathroom in private."

"I know, sugar, I know."

"You don't know, either! These women go around farting and picking their noses. It's their hobby. I *hate* it here!"

I glanced around the room. A thin, silver-haired lady was sitting in one of the yellow chairs. She looked like someone's grandmother. She caught my eye, and I smiled. She recoiled, as if terrified, and dropped to the floor. She started barking, throwing her head back. She scuttled towards me on her hands and knees, showing her teeth and growling. Mummie released Father's lapels and stepped between me and the dog lady.

"Stop that," Mummie scolded, shaking her finger at the old woman. "You get over there and lie down. Go on, get."

The woman cocked her head, whimpered, and scooted backward on her knees. Then she scrambled to her feet and walked over to the yellow chair.

"You just get over there and lie down like a good puppy,

that's a girl." Mummie limped across the room. She reached down and stroked the woman's head. "Her is a good, sweet girl."

*I*t was good that Mummie was not herself because Miss Gussie's will was not fair. She left her house to Aunt Clancy and Queenie. She left Violet one of the buildings downtown, rented by the ice cream place. It had not flooded much. And they had a five-year lease. Mack got the land behind my grandmother's house. Twenty whole acres of trees and broken monuments. He said he was going to develop it. Mummie and me got the Salads 'n' More, but they'd been flooded out. We had to pay for repairs before they could reopen. Miss Gussie also left Violet her collection of ceramic frogs, ten glass paperweights, and her Citizens' Bank stock certificate. Claude said I'd gotten screwed. He said I could take it to court, but I shook my head. I didn't want anything. On Christmas Eve, Aunt Clancy flew to Las Vegas with Dr. Falk. They got married and came back the same day.

Since Claude was doing last-minute shopping with his father, I drove by myself to Queenie's. Violet had decorated a cedar tree with all of Miss Gussie's ornaments. I recognized some old ones Mack and I had made out of tuna cans. Queenie brought out a platter of cheese and crackers. Violet sat on the sofa drinking from a carton of eggnog. She was wearing jeans with one ragged knee. She watched thoughtfully as Dr. Falk played with Aunt Clancy's hair. They planned to live at his old house on Tulip Road. Violet told me she was going to stay with Queenie. She thought Dr. Falk was square, but I liked him.

"I'd like you with short hair," he said to my aunt.

"I wouldn't," said Violet.

"Oh, I have my own style," said Aunt Clancy, smiling. Her eyes crinkled in the corners. She ran her fingers through her hair, and it fluffed around her shoulders. She held up her left hand, admiring the gold band. Dr. Falk kissed her fingers.

"I'll bet Santa's bringing you a surprise tonight," he said. Aunt Clancy gave a girlish laugh.

Violet rolled her eyes and took a long swig of eggnog.

He swept her hair into a French twist. "You ought to see yourself, honey. You're dazzling."

"You missed your calling, Byron," said Violet. "You should have been a beautician."

Queenie laughed, covering her mouth with one hand.

"Well, maybe," said Dr. Falk. "But you have to admit she looks beautiful like this." He kissed Aunt Clancy's neck. Then he released her hair. It swooshed to her waist.

On the last day of December, New Year's Eve, I had my baby, a little girl, seven pounds on the dot. The doctor gave me gas. I didn't remember anything. When I gave the baby a normal name, Jennifer Leigh Wentworth, Claude's mother acted offended. I think she wanted me to name the baby after her, Betty Junior. No one said a word about the baby being "early." Claude seemed disappointed that I'd had a girl. He didn't give out cigars. His mother didn't help matters. She stood at the nursery window and studied the baby. She kept telling everyone how much Jennifer Leigh didn't look like Claude. Her eyes dared me to say different.

I dreaded going to her house, even though she had set up a crib and all kinds of baby things in Claude's old room. Everyone seemed to think I belonged with the Wentworths. No one bothered to ask what I wanted. I longed to go to Miss Gussie's house, but it wouldn't have been right.

After New Year's, Claude went back to Cookeville, leaving me and Jennifer Leigh with his mother in her deep house that smelled of silver polish and whiskey. I didn't put up a fight.

"It's really so much easier for you to stay at Mother's," said Claude.

"Yes," I said. I was scared to be alone with the baby. As soon as I was able, I put her in the car seat and drove over to see Queenie.

Mack was living in Mummie's house with Earlene. She parked her school bus in the side yard. Even though it was January, she took down all the storm windows and screens and scrubbed them with a toothbrush. Queenie said, "That girl works like a man." We watched her haul out everything from the basement. Then she asked me and Mack what we wanted to keep. I'd always known Mummie was a packrat. As I stared at the rusted tools, mildewed clothes, and boxes of old Christmas cards, it seemed real clear that her mental state was spread out in the sunshine. No normal person hoarded trash. Of course Mack and I said we wanted nothing.

"Good," Earlene said. She dumped the boxes into the back of Mack's truck and drove to the dump. I almost liked her. She had a settling influence on my brother. Around the end of January, they started remodeling Mummie's house. Mack unfolded blueprints and told his men where to set up little wooden stakes. The stakes were connected with string and jutted out into the backyard. They waited for the weather to warm up so the concrete men could pour the footing. Mack was building a Florida room, three walls of pure glass, off the kitchen. He also waterproofed the basement. Upstairs, he knocked down walls and made a huge master bedroom. He and Earlene drove to Dalton, Georgia, and bought wholesale carpet. Down came Mummie's green and yellow wallpaper, and up went purple and maroon stripes. Earlene had the most god-awful taste, what I called the "double-wide decor"—curtains with dingleballs, a waterbed that always seemed to have the same tiger-striped sheets on it, a bookcase filled with romance novels, the thick type with hot pink covers and titles done up in blue ink.

I thought I might borrow a book until Violet saw them and punched me in the ribs. She was home for a long weekend. Claude was still at Tech.

"Oh, god," she said, laughing. "Romance novels. Why am I not surprised?"

"Well," I said. "At least she reads."

"No," said my cousin. "That's not reading. That's a coma of love."

I didn't see what was wrong with that, but I didn't say anything.

By the end of February, Mack and his men had cleared off most of the old Hamilton land. The air was full of bulldozers, knocking down trees. The city made them hire the funeral home to move the family graveyard. Queenie and I watched from the glider. Some of the graves were so old, the caskets had disintegrated.

I got tired of watching, but it was better than sitting alone at the Wentworths' house.

"You got any pie, Queenie?" I asked. Now that Aunt Clancy was married, Queenie had started cooking real food again.

"Fresh-baked apple," she said, and nodded toward the kitchen. "Help yourself, baby doll."

*V*iolet drove a tan Volkswagen that she'd bought for three hundred dollars. Sometimes I'd drive down Tulip Road and her car would be parked in Aunt Clancy's new driveway. I imagined my cousin driving down Interstate 40, moving between Knoxville and Crystal Falls. I never envied her, not the first time, because I always saw my life as natural and normal. I didn't need an education. I had an Mrs. degree, and she was working on her BS in biology. She said she was studying to be an ornithologist. I pretended like I knew what that was, but later I looked it up in the dictionary. I couldn't help but think of her as the Bird Woman of Tennessee.

I was just dying to ask if she was still a virgin. She was bone thin, with long dark hair that she pulled back into a ponytail. Her fingernails were chewed off to the roots. And while she had contact lenses, she mostly wore these huge tortoiseshell glasses. She even looked like a woman biologist, just like I looked like a happily married woman. You'd never know I was stuck in Claude's boyhood bedroom. I'd almost gotten out of the habit of being married. I didn't have to cook or keep up with his clothes. Mrs. Wentworth's maids did all of that. Claude would come home nearly every weekend, bringing his dirty laundry. He'd hold the baby a few minutes. Bernice would fix him pancakes, grilled shrimp, chef salads, biscuits, and meat loaf *sans* bell peppers. He made love to me quickly, without passion. He kept his eyes open when he came, but he never looked at me. I felt used, like an inflatable doll. Afterward I'd listen to him breathe. By Sunday afternoon he was ready to drive back to Tennessee Tech with a basket of folded laundry in the trunk.

I suspected I was losing him to those college girls. I desperately copied everything Mrs. Wentworth did. I grew long fingernails, and I wore my hair long and curly. I bought makeup at Cain-Sloan's and learned how to shadow my eyes. First thing every morning, I weighed myself, and if I went one pound over

110, I went on a starvation diet. I even stopped speaking French. I dreamed of having a little house, of inviting other couples over to dinner. We would eat on the wedding china and silver. Claude would open a bottle of French wine, and I'd pretend that it tasted good. I dreamed of fixing up our house. Jennifer Leigh's room would be wallpapered in pink hearts, and she would have a white crib with a pink, ruffled canopy. Claude would work at the bank, and everyone would say I took such good care of him, the way I ironed creases into his shirts and trousers. I'd get Queenie to show me how to make jellies and biscuits—things I had not learned from Mummie. I figured I could make it last forever. The cute life with cute baby and the cute, blond husband with the pug dog nose.

I found myself driving around Crystal Falls to kill time. The baby was asleep, so I asked Bernice to watch her. I said I wouldn't be gone long. Claude was due home from Tech—spring break—and I wanted to take a bath and roll my hair before he arrived. I drove into the country, right by Mack's old house, Sloopy's house now, and I got a chill. I saw Christopher running across the yard, chasing the chickens, and I was overcome by an urge to stop and say hello. Not that I felt right about it. After all, I was Mack's sister. But I found myself turning down the long driveway. I noticed that Sloopy needed more gravel. It had washed away, and grass had sprung up in the center, scraping the underside of my car. That sound gave me a real bad feeling. I couldn't help but think of the work Mack had done on Mummie's house.

The kitchen door opened, and Sloopy stepped onto the carport. She was wearing a cotton dress, the type a country woman would wear, and her hair was pulled back into one long braid like Aunt Clancy's. Her face split into a smile when I got out of the car; she ran down the gravel drive. I swallowed hard and buttoned my sweater. It was late March, and wild buttercups bloomed in the fields. They weren't really wild. Miss Gussie had once said you could always tell where old houses had stood because of the buttercups. I looked back at Sloopy. When I shut my eyes, I could see myself coming out of her house, running down the same grassy driveway.

"Bitsy!" she cried.

"I can only stay a minute," I said because I knew I was going to cry, and I didn't want her to know it. "Christopher sure is having fun chasing those chickens."

"Oh, yes. You will come inside?" She was already opening the door, walking into her house. "I just make ice tea, you want some?"

"No, thank you," I said. "I really can't stay. I just wanted to say hello and see how you were doing."

"Oh, so-so. We get by. How's your little baby? You have a girl, yes?" She smiled and folded her arms. Behind her, the kitchen counters were wiped clean, and a dishrag was folded by the sink. Christopher's drawings were taped to the refrigerator. Through the window, I saw trees, cows, and blue mountains. In the living room, I looked at the plaid sofa and Mack's old La-Z-Boy with the little beer table standing beside it, polished and waiting. At the other end of the room, a walnut television played the theme song to *Gunsmoke.* For some reason, her TV was the saddest thing I had ever seen. I hated my brother for leaving her. I could see Claude going off, too. I could see myself waiting in his old room, waiting for him to come back. I didn't understand what men wanted.

I pictured Sloopy watching Matt Dillon and Chester and Miss Kitty. She might have glanced now and then out the window, then risen from the plaid sofa as my car turned into her driveway, saying to herself in English rather than French, because that's how much my brother had changed her life, "Now, who can that be? Who can that be?"

When I returned to the Wentworths' house, Claude was sitting with his mother in the cherry-paneled den. When Mrs. Wentworth saw me, she glanced at her son. I wondered if I'd done anything wrong.

"Is Jennifer Leigh all right?" I asked.

"Funny you should ask." Claude glared at me. "She's fine."

"Bitsy," Mrs. Wentworth said quietly, "the next time you go off and leave the baby, would you kindly let me know?"

"I told Bernice," I said. I didn't understand what the fuss was all about. I usually took Jennifer Leigh everywhere I went.

"Bernice doesn't run this house. She's hired help. So in the future, I'd appreciate it if you'd let me know."

"You've never complained before," I said.

Mrs. Wentworth threw up her hands and looked at Claude. "I can't reason with her. You try." She got up and left the room.

"Go ahead, Claude," I said. "Reason with me."

"Don't talk to Mother that way," he said.

"I thought I was talking to you." I sat down and stared at him. He was wearing brown corduroy trousers and a navy V-necked sweater *sans* shirt. His neck looked smooth and vulnerable, with a tuft of blond hairs at his throat. A long time ago I had counted those hairs. He resembled a little pug-nosed boy, someone who was pretending to be a grown-up.

"This isn't easy." He shifted on the sofa and glanced up at me. He rested his arms on his knees. His hands dangled like two dead flowers.

"You haven't flunked out, have you?" I asked.

"No. In fact, my grades are better than ever." He paused

and looked down at the floor. His cheeks flamed red. "I think we've had it."

"Had what?" I wrinkled my forehead.

"The marriage has had it." He scratched his jaw. Finally he looked at me. "Actually, I don't think I want to be married."

"That's too bad. Because you *are* married. To me." Tears rushed into my eyes and spilled over.

"I'm not trying to hurt you, Bitsy. But Mother says you trapped me."

"You trapped yourself."

"I didn't. And it's not fair." He lifted both hands and spread them wide. They were steady. His eyes held an amused expression. I realized he was enjoying himself, the high drama of it all. I imagined him in four years: he would be sitting at his father's desk, turning down some farmer for a loan.

"I can't join a fraternity," he said. "You can't join a sorority."

"We can, too!"

"No. It wouldn't be the same."

"What are you saying?"

"Well, we're already not living together."

"No? Then why do you come home and fuck me every weekend?"

"Don't talk like that." His eyes narrowed. "You sound so trashy. Like that thing your brother lives with."

"Maybe I am trashy."

"You said it, I didn't." He folded his hands and stared at his mother's polished glass and chrome coffee table. It was arranged with brass boxes, candles, magazines, glass paperweights.

"What about the baby?"

"Don't worry about the money. I'll pay for everything."

"Okay, Okay. Are you saying you want a divorce?"

"No, I didn't say that. I just think we ought to live apart for a while. It's the best thing. Mother says we got married too young."

I couldn't answer. My lips were jerking. I had no place to go. I'd have to get a job, a baby-sitter. Oh, god. It was awful. I'd have to make a whole new life from scratch.

"Who knows? Maybe we'll get back together." He lifted his hands again.

"Don't count on it. You always hated waiting in line."

"What?"

"I'll find somebody else."

"Good luck."

"Rat fink!" I stood up.

"Bitsy—"

"You go to hell!" I ran out of the room and crashed into Mrs. Wentworth. She had been listening at the door.

"What on earth. . . ." She frowned.

I ran up the stairs to Claude's old room. The baby was sleeping, her little rump pooched high in the air. I started packing. In the back of my mind were our wedding gifts in that awful apartment. I wondered if I'd get them back. Claude was rich, he could buy more, but I needed those gifts. I closed the suitcase, carried it to the hallway, and set it beside the door. From downstairs, I heard Claude and his mother talking.

Well, I told you. You wouldn't listen.

I know, I know.

Something made me walk down the hall and turn into Mrs. Wentworth's bedroom. I strode past the king-sized bed, past the windowseat, and entered her dressing room. It smelled so rich and floral, I felt dizzy. I stared down at the marble counter. It was arranged with jars of perfumed soaps, crystal cologne bottles, and silver brushes. In the center was an enormous fabric-covered jewelry box. The fabric matched the draperies in her bedroom. I opened it and looked inside. Pearls, diamond earrings, emerald rings, sapphire bracelets. She loved her jewelry more than she had ever loved Jennifer Leigh. I grabbed a handful of little things, turned sideways, and stared down into the toilet. The porcelain bowl was clean, full of sparkling water. I dropped earbobs and rings, pearls and brooches. They splashed and sank to the bottom. Then I reached for the handle, flushed, and watched everything disappear. The bowl filled with clear, fresh water.

I'd watched enough of *Perry Mason* to know what to do. I picked up a washcloth and rubbed away my fingerprints. My head started spinning. I leaned over the toilet and spit into the bowl. I thought I might be sick. If flushing her jewelry was the best I could do, then I was in big trouble. It was too late to stick my hand down the toilet. I pictured the rings floating to the bottom of the septic tank. I wiped my mouth and stood up. The room swayed. I stumbled into the hallway, and I could still hear his mother's voice droning like a bumblebee.

It's for the best. Oh, my poor baby. Don't worry. You'll get your life back.

I packed my car, carefully strapping Jennifer Leigh into her seat. She cooed and waved her arms. I reversed out of the driveway and stared up at the house. Claude was somewhere inside with his mother. It had always been his mother's house. Minutes later I pulled into Queenie's driveway. Next door, I saw bulldozers carving a hole for Mack and Earlene's new swimming pool. The whole field was full of roads and framed houses. One house had a black roof, with little holes for skylights.

I got out of the car and reached for the baby. Queenie was

in the garden. Way up in the sky two birds chased each other. The sun felt strong and new. The sky stretched over us, making the framed houses look like matchsticks. I was so scared. I'd be divorced and living in Crystal Falls. With a baby. Men would think I was an easy lay. Maybe they'd be right, maybe they'd be wrong. Maybe it depended on the man. I held on to the baby, as if for balance, and walked toward the garden, toward Queenie, my new life.

Clancy Jane

1972

I'd been dreading the party for weeks. It was on Memorial Day—a black-tie cocktail buffet given by Byron's partner. The invitation was propped on the kitchen desk. Every now and then I blinked at it—black paper lettered in silver, as if to underline the formality of the evening. I stared longingly at the tiny inscription, *Regrets Only*.

"I just don't know about this," I said at breakfast, shaking my head. We were sitting at the round table. I stared out the bay window. A male cardinal fluttered down to the bird feeder.

"Don't know about what?" Byron tapped his spoon against his cereal bowl. He ate Corn Flakes every morning, but he embellished them with berries, nuts, raisins, or banana slices. Once I even caught him adding a mixture of Concord grapes, raspberries, and brown sugar. We had gotten married in Las Vegas, and the justice of the peace had worn red cowboy boots. If Dorothy had been around, I might have asked her to figure out my astrological chart. But I'd never asked anyone's advice about love. Neither did my daughter. She was in love with a graduate student, Lawrence Prescott III. "You'd better watch guys with Roman numerals at the end of their names," said

Bitsy, who ought to know. I always forgot how many numerals Meathead had.

"I don't know about this party," I said, looking into my own cereal bowl, plain granola from the health food store in Nashville. "I'm not the party type."

"Aw, Clancy. Don't get shy on me."

"I'm not shy." I briefly closed my eyes and imagined the rhythms at the hog farm—feeding kindling into the stove, kneading bread. I ached for those chilly nights under the stars, passing a pipe, humming something from *Sgt. Pepper's Lonely Hearts Club Band.* Now, of course, I lived in a sprawling brick house on Tulip Road. It had bay windows, polished wood floors, carved mantels. I liked it, but Byron wasn't satisfied. He said it looked dated and called Mr. Frank, who suggested a different color scheme—jade and sapphire.

Byron reached across the table and tugged my braid. "God. All that hair. You'd look so pretty with shorter hair. So up-to-date and fashionable."

I looked out the window, watching the cardinal crack open a sunflower seed. "You used to wrap my braid around your arm."

"I still do." He reached for my hair again and began looping it around his wrist. "You wouldn't have to cut it all off. Just to your shoulders."

"I like my hair." It fell to my waist, long and straight, parted down the middle. I remembered wearing a beaded headband, a crown of daisies. I remembered making love to men whose hair was longer and straighter than mine.

"Okay, so don't cut it." He twirled the braid like a jump rope. "Hey, what are you going to wear?"

"Wear?"

"To the party, *baby*. You haven't forgotten that it's formal?"

I shook my head. "Isn't that a fancy way of saying it's a prom for grown-ups?"

Byron just smiled.

The afternoon of the party, I bought an ivory taffeta dress. It reminded me of a dead magnolia, but it was the only thing I could find without sequins. Still, there was nothing worse than a pile of ruffles on a woman who was used to bell-bottoms. Then I dithered back and forth over shoes, disgusting myself. Didn't I have anything better to do? I tried not to think how much I had changed. I finally settled on a pair of bone pumps, which matched the dress so closely they looked dyed. While I waited for the clerk to put my shoes in a box, I picked up an evening bag. Maybe I needed one of those, too. Anything black-tie made me nervous. My idea of a party was sitting on rush mats, listening to Iron Butterfly, feeling my pulse rise out of my body and scatter like a million fireflies.

After I left the shoe store, I walked around the square. I slowed down in front of the Ben Franklin. A woman with glasses and a sagging chin stood in front of the cash register. I could see all the way to the back of the store, and I remembered buying things for Violet and Dede. I abruptly turned and walked down the sidewalk, past Rich's Drugs and the Western Auto. I stopped in front of Velma's House of Hair. I stared at the posters of glamorous women. Beyond the poster was a row of mirrors and pink swivel chairs. On the back of each chair was a name spelled out in gold glitter: Velma, Angie, Lucinda, Kathy. I shifted my package, opened the door, and took a deep breath. The air was scented with hair spray and permanent solution. I thought of Byron twirling my hair. I thought of the party—all those sharp-boned women with long eyelashes. I wondered if they'd compare me to Amelia, Byron's ex-wife, if they'd make fun of my long hair.

Five minutes later I was sitting in one of the pink chairs, watching Angie shake out a pink apron. The plastic crinkled as she slipped it around my shoulders. "What did you have in mind, hon?" she asked, looking at my reflection in the mirror. Her eyes were dark blue, outlined in black pencil.

"Maybe just a trim?"

"Hon, you need the works, and I don't mean Summer Blond." Angie picked up my hair with both hands and looked at it skeptically. "And, law, these split ends. When was the last time you had your hair done?"

"I don't know. A long time ago."

"You really need it colored, hon." She chewed her gum fiercely as she stared at my hair. "We could frost it."

"Not today. Just a cut will do."

"Okay, hon. It's your hair. You tell me to cut an inch, and I'll cut an inch. Not one speck more." She blew a bubble and it popped against her upper lip.

"Maybe you should just cut an inch?"

She sighed and rolled her eyes. "Hon, you've got a foot of split ends. I mean, we're talking major damage here."

I squinted in the mirror. The ends were slightly fuzzy. Had Byron noticed? "Well, all right." I shut my eyes and leaned back against the pink vinyl. Angie's gum popped as she held out a section of hair. The scissors made a crunching sound, and I pictured green apples, the tart kind that draw up your mouth. She twirled the chair around, and I watched a little boy scoot across the floor on his stomach. His nose was running. "You bad boy! Stop doing that, Raymond!" warned a woman who was sitting in Lucinda's chair. "Stop it right now, or I'm going to get up and spank you!"

Raymond ignored her and kept scooting. He looked up at me and grinned. "Me is a dad doy," he chirped and scooted toward the Coke machine. The woman sighed and leaned back in the chair. "I swear, I can't do a thing with him," she said.

When Angie was finished, I looked in the mirror. It was shorter than I had expected, just above my shoulders. With wide bangs. I hadn't counted on bangs. I looked like Prince Valiant.

"Pretty snazzy, huh?" Angie grinned.

"Yeah. Real snazzy." I climbed out of the chair. My whole head felt lighter. I stopped dead when I saw the piles of hair on the floor. They looked like murdered animals.

Byron was unzipping the tuxedo bag when I walked into the bedroom. "Hey, hey, *hey*," he said, grinning. "Now if we can get rid of the sprouts and yogurt!"

"I hate it." I swallowed down a sob.

"You're not used to it, that's all." He put down his tuxedo and crossed the room. He smoothed his hands down my hair. "So slick and shiny. And it swings when you walk."

"Who cares?" I shrugged off my bell-bottoms and walked naked to the closet.

"I care." He reached for my wrist and pulled me to the bed. "I was just teasing about the sprouts, I really was. And I can eat red meat at the hospital." He brushed his lips against my throat. "But I draw the line at yogurt."

"Yogurt's good for you," I said.

"Is it?" He moved on top of me.

"We're going to be late for the party."

"Hmmmmm?"

"Late," I said. I was having trouble thinking clearly. I closed my eyes and saw myself standing in my mother's kitchen. All last summer, Byron made house calls. Sometimes he'd sit with me in the kitchen. He'd eat a piece of zucchini bread and drink herb tea. He seemed fascinated with my life. He couldn't believe I didn't eat red meat. While I talked, his knee pressed harder and harder into my thigh. One afternoon, while Mother was sleeping, he asked me to come into the kitchen. "What?" I said. "I can't stand it any longer," he said, backing me up against the refrigerator. He lifted my hair away from my neck. He kissed my throat. I didn't know what to do. I was always helpless around a passionate man. He was a Yankee, and his accent cut through me like those miracle knives on TV. They'll cut through boards and tin cans. They'll cut through anything.

*Du*sk was falling when we turned down the long driveway, which was illuminated by dozens of hurricane lanterns. The house had six white columns and long French windows. It belonged to Byron's partner, Dr. Eugene P. Clayborne IV. And Mrs. Clayborne.

"Where're you taking me, Byron? Tara?" I grabbed the sleeve of his tuxedo, wrinkling the fabric.

"Relax, Clancy," Byron said, laughing. "You look beautiful."

I shook my head, and my hair swung forward. I swallowed hard as a young man rushed forward to open my door.

"Everyone's in the garden, sir," he said to Byron.

As we walked up a series of pea-gravel steps, Byron admired the landscaping. Two weeks ago, he had spent seven hundred dollars on new shrubs for the house. "It needs something else," he kept saying, staring at the boxwoods and holly, dark green against fresh mulch. He bought twenty-four rose-bushes, and when we were finished, the whole yard looked overdone. "I really like it," he said, stepping back to admire it.

People were gathering beneath a white, gauzy tent, which was suspended over the brick patio. I didn't know any of them. In the center was a long buffet table. The food was arranged on silver trays: cheese straws, raw vegetables, tiny quiches, caviar, fried mushrooms, boiled shrimp on crushed ice. Outside the tent was the bar, and several men waved at Byron. While he fetched our drinks, I wandered through the garden. A violinist was playing old songs, like "Days of Wine and Roses"— square music, the type Richard Nixon liked. There was a pool at the farthest end of the patio; candles floated on plastic lily pads, swirling in the blue currents. A curved path, lined with pink flowers, led to a gazebo. I smelled money everywhere.

Bitsy might have known some of these wealthy people. I seemed to recall that her ex-mother-in-law ran around with several doctors' wives. When Byron came back with the wine, I drank it quickly, for lack of something better to do. I looked slowly around the patio. All of the women seemed to have shoulder-length, bobbed hair. With bangs. They all seemed to be wearing taffeta dresses. I held out my empty glass.

"Oh, already?" Byron looked surprised. As we made our way to the bar for a refill, he introduced me to a surgeon and his wife, who barely said hello. She said something like, "Hmmm." Then she looked up at Byron and smiled. "I noticed your daughters were taking tennis lessons at the club," she said. "They're just the cutest things."

"Thanks." Byron smiled politely and touched my elbow, guiding me toward the bar.

"Was she one of your wife's friends?" I whispered.

"Sort of."

"Sort of?" I lifted one eyebrow.

"They played tennis together. Don't worry about it."

A waiter passed with a tray of wine, and I reached for

another glass. No one talked to us even though Byron received plenty of nods from afar. We walked around the pool, then sat down in the gazebo. He nudged me. "We can do this."

"Do what?" I took a swallow of wine.

"Have a party. I know the caterer. You wouldn't have to lift a finger."

I looked into the wineglass. There was probably some peculiar logic at work here. I'd cut my hair, so of course the next step was a party. "Hey, are you hungry?" Byron didn't wait for an answer. He set his wineglass on the wooden rail and got up. He headed toward the buffet. While he was gone, two women—a pale, raw-boned blonde and a chubby brunette—walked over to me. They were wearing pastel taffeta dresses. Both had beaded evening bags tucked under their arms. After a minute or two of chitchat, it became clear to me that they, too, were second wives. Leave it to the outcasts to sniff out a soul mate. The brunette smiled at me with her whole painted face. Her name was Sally. She had bangs, too. Her eyelashes were as long as my little finger.

"Where do you and Byron go to church?" Sally pushed the hair from her face. Dark strands were caught in her earrings. She unraveled them with her fingernail.

"Church?" I said, then felt ridiculous. "We don't go to church, exactly."

The women exchanged glances. The blonde, Ellen, recovered first. "Well, that's okay. It's just fine if you don't go to church."

"Not everyone has to go," said Sally. She sounded oddly apologetic. "I don't get much out of the sermons anyway. I get everything I need from the music. Hymns say it all, don't you think? And charity work. I get a lot out of that. Would you like to have lunch next week? Wait a minute. Next week is out. What about week after next?"

"Gee, I don't know. I'll have to check my calendar," I said.

"I know just what you mean." Sally gave me a serious look and nodded. She opened her evening bag, pulled out a green leather book, and flipped through the pages. I looked down and saw a tiny calendar. Each day had its own box.

"Let's see, the twenty-sixth is free. In fact, I don't have a thing planned." Sally looked up. "Are you free?"

Before I could answer, Ellen tapped her friend's appointment book. "You're also free on the twenty-ninth and thirtieth."

"What? I've got two whole days open? Let me see." Sally squinted down at the book. "How did this happen? I can't believe it." She looked up at Ellen. "What are you and Peter doing that weekend? We could go have dinner, go to a movie."

"Um, we have plans."

"You do?" Sally kept staring.

"We're going to that luau."

Sally looked horrified. "What luau?"

"Excuse me," I said, standing up. I walked straight to the bar. Behind me I heard Sally saying, "What luau?" I glanced at the buffet table. I knew I should eat *something,* but I was too depressed to think about food. Especially this food, the deadly puff pastry made with white flour. If I was going to die, I'd rather do it with alcohol.

"White wine, please," I told the bartender. He handed me a fresh glass. It was beaded with moisture. I turned and faced the patio. I didn't see Byron. I was depressed. My new life seemed hopeless. I couldn't see myself campaigning for phone numbers and tennis dates. Working hard to keep all the little boxes on my social calendar filled. I wondered if small town people became smaller in order to fit. Perhaps they had to. Their brains contracted, *they* contracted. It was a pulling inward, of notions and expectations. I turned back to the bartender and got a fresh glass of wine. I drank it in four swallows and held out my glass again. Five glasses of chablis, on an empty stomach, does strange things to the human brain. Mine was no exception. The party made me edgy, and alcohol blunted the corners. I didn't like the pretense, the stuffiness and exaggerated manners. I didn't like being all dressed up. I thought about climbing on the table, staring down at everyone, and saying, "I'm going to tell you all a little bedtime story, set in Ventura, California."

Byron came up behind me and squeezed my arm. "You're having an awful time, aren't you?"

"God, *no,*" I said gaily. "I'm having a ball."

"No, you're not. Let's go home."

"Not yet." I veered back to the bar.

He caught my arm. "You don't need another glass."

I lifted one eyebrow, then looked down at his hand.

"Let's go home, baby," he said in my ear. "I'll bring you a whole bottle of wine. In bed."

"In bed?" I said loudly. A woman behind Byron turned and blinked.

At the end of the garden the violinist was playing "Moon River." I couldn't believe I was here. Hadn't these people ever heard of real music?

"Clancy." It was Byron's voice, very patient.

"I don't know," I said, feeling obscurely bullied. He gripped my arm and I lurched forward. My left knee buckled; I threw my free arm out for balance and shouted, "WHOOPS!"

Byron caught me. His arm was like a piece of metal. I didn't miss the sudden hush in conversation, the swiveled heads. I navigated down the pea-gravel steps without stumbling once, but when we reached the driveway, the valet parker was nowhere in sight. Byron studied the assortment of keys on the wooden board and picked out his chain.

The cars were parked across the street in an empty pasture. We walked in silence. The night air felt good against my face. There was no moon, and I couldn't see where I was going. Halfway to the car, my shoe sank into a cow flop. I yanked hard, learning forward, and my foot slipped out of the shoe. I screamed and fell into the grass.

"Clancy?" Byron whirled around, his eyebrows stitched together.

"I fell down." I giggled. "I lost my shoe."

"It's not funny," he said. His tuxedo blended into the darkness as he searched for my shoe.

I waved my hand. "Oh, just forget it," I said airily. "I don't need that old shoe. I'm not Cinderella. And I've already left the ball."

"Cinderella, hell," Byron said. He hunkered down and plucked my shoe from the cow flop. "Here," he said, dropping the shoe into my lap. I pulled off my other shoe, gripped them tightly, and walked barefoot to the car.

"God, what if someone saw you?" he said, holding open my door.

"It doesn't matter." My taffeta dress made a crinkling noise as I slid across the seat. I dropped my shoes on the floorboard.

"It *does* matter, too." He slammed the door.

"Why?" I asked, but he couldn't hear. He was walking around the car. He was a very proper man in a proper profession. I was a very improper woman, a different sort of woman. Perhaps it was a lack of morals or good sense, but I didn't care what people thought of me.

When he got into the car, I said, "I can't live this kind of life, Byron."

"What, you can't take falling down drunk at parties?" He jammed the key in the ignition. The radio came on. The Who was singing "Won't Get Fooled Again."

"I don't have anything in common with these people."

"You haven't tried." Byron drove out of the pasture, leaving a trail in the fescue.

"They don't even care that Nixon's bombing Cambodia."

"So get them involved. Make them care."

"Oh, sure. Maybe I ought to organize a demonstration? Carry a sign? In case you haven't noticed, no one carries signs in Crystal Falls."

"No."

He turned onto the highway. If the shoe fits, I thought, wear it. All I'd tried to do was get through the night. All I'd wanted to do was have fun. I wasn't worried. Drinking was something you could stop. You couldn't stop being crazy. I reached down for my shoes. Then I rolled down the window and breathed deeply. The air smelled dark and herbal, of freshly mown grass and wild onions. I leaned out the window, gulping warm air.

"Clancy? What are you doing?"

I answered him by leaning further out the window. I threw the shoes as hard as I could. They skipped down the pavement and rolled in the ditch.

I awakened to rain and looked across the bed. I rubbed my forehead—it was threaded with pain. Byron was sleeping, his mouth open, one hand propped on his chest. He was still wearing his tuxedo. A wasp droned into the room, struck the ceiling, and emitted a long, dull sound, like a tractor. It smacked against the windowpane, buzzing forward with all its might. Then its wings drooped, as if it were puzzled by entrapment. Dejected, it crawled toward another pane. Its wings fluttered. The buzzing started up again as it tried to fly through the glass, toward the trees, which seemed to be waving and clapping.

Queenie's voice rose up and blew around me, a sweetened breeze: *You not trapped, girl. Not unless you nailed to the floor.*

I got up and swallowed three aspirin. Then I tumbled back into bed and I closed my eyes. *Sleep it off, that's right, just sleep it off.*

I woke up that afternoon. Byron's half of the bed was empty. There was a cryptic note beside the telephone: GONE TO HOSPITAL.

I packed a suitcase and drove south, navigating down rough-paved roads in Alabama. I found a radio station that played old songs—"American Pie," "Ohio," "Incense and Peppermints." Each song brought back a specific memory. ·

I reached Destin, Florida, that evening and checked into a cinder-block motel. The room smelled of sulfur. On the dresser were a clock radio and a hot plate. I opened the glass doors, but it was too dark to see the beach. I pulled back the cold linen, curled up in the bed, and dreamed of nothing.

The next morning it was still raining. I brushed my hand across the bed. Empty. It took me a moment to remember I was at the beach, and the rain must have followed me. I must have slept through the night. I sat up, hugging my knees, and stared out the glass doors. The tide slapped forward, green and foamy. The Gulf of Mexico stretched out beneath a gray sky. The horizon was blurred. My mouth tasted grainy, but my breath was clean. Dry as a bone, dry as a stone, cold sober. Not for long, not if I started thinking. You could count on it.

I reached for the phone and dialed Byron's number. He answered on the first ring. "Jesus, Clancy!" he hollered. "Where the hell are you?"

"In Florida," I said.

"*Florida?* What the hell are you doing there?"

"You know why."

"No, I don't." He sighed. "Are you always going to solve your problems by running away?"

My eyes filled. I hated him for saying that. "I think you're a shallow person, Byron."

"I am not."

"You're never satisfied. First, you fell in love with me because I was different. Then you couldn't wait to change me."

"I wasn't exactly trying to change you."

"You didn't like my hair, you didn't like my clothes. You think I'm out of style, you think—"

"Wait a minute. You don't know what I think."

"Then tell me."

He sighed. "I just want you to come home."

"What about the party? I embarrassed you."

"It doesn't matter." He paused. "Come home, and we'll straighten everything out."

"I don't like straight things," I said and hung up.

Home wasn't on Tulip Road. It never was. Home was the same place it had always been. I got out of bed, opened the suitcase, and found the whiskey bottle. Wild Turkey. I carried the bottle back to bed. I leaned against the headboard, remembering the New Orleans days. Whatever had happened to my old record player? All those old songs Hart must have listened to in Vietnam. I took a long swallow of whiskey and pictured myself falling to the floor in New Orleans, a heap of liquor breath—all these years later I was still falling. My mouth burned as I took another drink of Wild Turkey. The clock radio on the dresser clicked on, playing an old song, "These Boots Are Made for Walkin'." I remember when Nancy Sinatra recorded that song, right after she divorced Tommy Sands. She asked for one dollar in alimony. The next summer, I ran away with Sunny and Amos to California. I distinctly remembered the smell of patchouli oil. There was a poster that said FAR OUT. Sunny said it meant we'd traveled a long way from our old lives. She was still weaving blankets in Abiquiu; Amos was in divinity school at Yale. Neither of them could believe I'd married a doctor, but they wished me the best.

Sometimes I imagined an alternate self, what I would have become if I'd stayed in New Mexico: long, gray hair, an aged hippie growing organic vegetables, fertilizing the soil with hog shit, painting portraits of Indians. My hands would be grained with dirt. The air would be drugged and heavy, like sweet tobacco. Someone would be strumming a guitar, singing that old song by Country Joe McDonald—"I-Feel-Like-I'm-Fixin'-to-Die Rag":

> *And it's one, two, three,*
> *What are we fighting for?*
> *Don't ask me, I don't give a damn,*
> *Next stop is Vietnam . . .*
> *Come on, mothers, throughout the land,*
> *Pack your boys off to Vietnam;*
> *Come on, fathers, don't hesitate,*
> *Send your sons off before it's too late;*
> *You can be the first one on your block*
> *To have your boy come home in a box.*

I pictured my old kitchen. The linoleum floor, swept clean. You could eat on it and not get sick. The checked tablecloth, a jar full of zinnias, sunlight pouring through the windows, the smell of wheat bread wafting.

I thought about Byron's house on Tulip Road. The day I had left there was an arrangement of old English roses in the entry hall. The arched windows in the sunroom were flooded with light. An artist from Nashville had been commissioned to paint a bouquet on the floor.

What I remembered most clearly about his house was the view from the sunroom, the neighbor's white clapboard. The blond mother and children, the tire swing in the largest oak, the blond cocker spaniels sleeping on the porch. After they moved to Atlanta, I realized how much I had depended on them. The yellow lights from their windows. Children bouncing a basketball. The wife walking the dogs. I grieved. Their house didn't sell for months. It was empty, dark, silent. I kept thinking how I used to sit on the wicker sofa, a glass of wine at my elbow, watching someone else's life. I remembered letting the room grow dark, wishing with all my strength that I lived any-where but Tulip Road.

I thought about love, how sick I was of it. I hated the idea of falling in love. I'd never known any sort of fall to be pleasur-able. "Oh, I fell down the stairs, and it felt so *good*!" Whenever I thought of falling, I thought of Dorothy dropping past the dime store's windows, thudding against the pavement, her mouth filling with floodwater. I thought of myself hanging from the bridge and changing my mind. Once you let go, the pull of gravity was irrevocable. Nevertheless, I fell in love with Byron Falk. Under normal conditions we wouldn't have met. He'd been my mother's doctor. He left his wife, Amelia, and she went around town bad-mouthing me, saying I was part of his change-of-life crazies. They had three blond daughters, ages fourteen, twelve, and eight. I imagined Amelia's narrow face, her burning eyes, her arms spread like wings around her babies.

Just for the record, Amelia, he pursued me.

The whiskey was working. I closed my eyes and tilted my head against the wall. I remembered last summer, the heat of it, Byron backing me up against the refrigerator, making love to me, no, he wouldn't wait, I wouldn't wait. It wasn't long before he moved to Tulip Road and spent all of his time showing me how good Yankees were in bed. That whole season burned blue, like a pilot light.

I fall backward into summertime dusk. We're at Mother's house. While she sleeps, pieces of her life break away. Dorothy's house is dark, but her car is in the driveway. It is early September, and the air is heavy, full of piano music drifting from the open windows of the living room. Byron's three daughters, on loan from Amelia for the weekend, are playing "Chopsticks." Because he never seems to know what to do with them, he brings them to my mother's house.

From the hammock, I watch heat lightning flare over the hills, then fade into the blue light. I glance toward the house as Byron crosses the porch, holding two glasses of wine, and walks barefoot down the steps. When he reaches the hammock, he hands me one glass and sets the other beneath the hammock. He puts his hands on either side of my neck and begins to rub my shoulders.

"Your hands are cold," I say, and reach back to touch his cheek.

"Are the girls making too much noise?" He has a nasal accent. He grew up in Michigan, near Lake Huron. "Should I make them stop?"

"Oh, no. They're fine."

"You think?" he says, and picks up his wine. Earlier, the girls

had swarmed across the grass, catching lightning bugs, but they had soon grown bored and had wandered into the house for something to drink. Minutes later, I heard them arguing over sheet music they'd found in the bench. Then the piano started up.

"Thank God," Byron had said then, but he kept glancing up at the house. I sensed that his relief was edged in guilt and a tarnished image of weekend parenting. He didn't seem to know what to do with so many females.

Now he sits down in the hammock, making it swing. Grass is stuck to the soles of his feet. He dips two fingers into the wineglass, fishing out a melted ice cube. I look up at the house, ablaze with light, the windows bright rectangles. One window is dark, the curtains drawn, and behind it my mother sleeps. Her house slopes into a vast yard, the rear surrounded by a honeysuckle vine. Beyond the vine is the old Hamilton land. A long time ago, when I was a girl, I thought it was haunted. At night bobwhites would call out back and forth over the gray tombstones, and Dorothy would whisper, "Hear the ghosts, Sister? They're coming for you. Shhh! Listen!"

Now Byron's girls are singing "Bye, Bye, Blackbird." Since his divorce, the children spend alternate weekends with him. I think of his girls as three blond birds, une, deux, trois. Three babies, three gestations, twenty-seven months of their mother's life. The girls resemble Amelia—blue-eyed blonds, with long, difficult curls, like pencil shavings.

"Scoot over, hammock hog," he says. I shift my weight, and wine sloshes on my wrist. I rest my head against the pillow and fan my skirt across my legs. From the trees, cicadas shrill like voices chanting in a church. I rub my bare foot against his chest, imagining his heartbeat swelling beneath my toes. It is almost time for him to leave. As if reading my mind, he says, "Why don't you come home with me tonight? I'll smuggle you into my room."

"I wouldn't dare," I say, looking sideways at the house. The

girls are singing, violently banging the piano. Make my bed and light the light. *"Not after what Amelia told you,"* I add. *Two weeks ago, Byron pronounced Mother stable enough for me to drive with him and his daughters to Gatlinburg. It was just for the weekend. He rented a chalet, which overlooked the town, but we ended up sleeping in separate rooms. The girls, excited by the novelty of another woman in their father's life, crawled into my bed and begged to hear fairy tales. Byron slept in one of the bunks intended for the girls. We ate steaks at The Brass Lantern and let the girls pick out souvenirs, little black bears with red leashes. It seemed to me that traveling with children had a way of transforming lust into something banal or smoldering. I hadn't realized how much his daughters resented me until after we returned to Crystal Falls. I was having lunch with Byron in the hospital cafeteria when a striking blond walked up and glared down at me.*

"Amelia," said Byron, *setting down his iced tea so hard it sloshed onto his tray. Two nurses from the next table kept looking over their shoulders.*

"I have a bone to pick with you," she said. *She was tall and leggy, with blue eyes. Right away I saw the resemblance to her daughters. She lifted one arm, and gold bracelets rattled. Byron had described her as the "queen of the doctors' wives," which struck me as most unflattering. I imagined her playing tennis, drinking piña coladas, planning whole months at a time on her calendar, desperately filling up the blank spaces.*

She did not acknowledge my presence, which suited me just fine, but she narrowed her eyes at Byron. "The girls said you took a person with you to Gatlinburg," she said.

"So?" Byron said. *His eyebrows came together.*

Amelia's lips parted as she gathered a long sigh. She rolled her eyes. Her chest moved up and down beneath her tennis sweater. "I can't believe you said that."

"Said what?" Byron threw down his napkin and looked at her from under his eyebrows. "Look. I'm in the middle of lunch. What is it that you want?"

She narrowed her eyes, and I noticed her nose was rather beaked. The line of her jaw was firm. She rested both hands on the table and stared down at Byron. "I won't, I absolutely won't have the children exposed to strange women. Our divorce isn't even final yet. I can take you to court. You'll lose visitation rights. I swear it, Byron. And you know how accommodating I've been. Do you hear me, Byron? Do you hear me?"

Now I sit up in the hammock, set the wineglass on the grass, and look up at the house. The girls are still playing the piano, singing "Humpty Dumpty," their treble voices rising, falling. I imagine their fingers pecking hard against the ivory keys, I imagine Amelia falling from a stone wall, arranging pieces of her life. Above the hills, heat lightning bleaches the sky the color of bone. Byron rubs his hand along my bare leg. "Come here," he says, and reaches for my hand.

"But the girls," I say. "It's too risky."

"It's dark. They won't see us. Nobody will."

I glance one last time over my shoulder. The back porch is empty, illuminated by light from the windows. The glider moves back and forth in a humid breeze. Through the window panes, I see his daughters' blond heads bent over the piano, their lips moving.

I pull up my long skirt, revealing a flash of white thigh, and lean back in the curved ditch of fabric. The hammock sways as he shucks down his jeans, moving toward me. I hook my arms around his neck, breathing in the honeysuckle. The girls sing and sing, hitting clef notes, falsetto giggles. I feel the timbre of it entering my skull. The cicadas shrill from the privet hedge, and high above the yard lightning flickers like raised eyebrows. The air is full of strange light, like a photograph negative. From the house, the singing *abruptly stops. The piano bangs shut. The screen door yawns open on its hinges, footsteps ricochet across the porch. Then his girls are running down the hill, running toward the hammock, flying across the grass, blond hair fluttering in the air like feathers.*

$\mathcal{J}$anis Joplin was singing "Me and Bobby McGee." I opened my eyes. For a moment I couldn't remember where I was. The air was full of whiskey. While I had slept, the bottle had over- turned, staining the sheet brown. Thank god, it wasn't all gone. I pulled up on my elbows and stared out the window. It was still raining. The beach was empty, full of dangerous waters. A current pulled the seaweed east. It would be so easy to slip down, weightless, easy as falling asleep on cool linen. What did my mother always say? *Good night, sleep tight, don't let the bed- bugs bite. You made your bed, now lie in it.*

Back home it was almost spring. The trees were still bare, a network of thin branches twisting upward. Blackbirds would etch across the sky, flying over my mother's old house, over the house on Tulip Road. His tuxedo would be hanging like a skele- ton in his closet.

When my head cleared, I phoned Violet's dorm room. It rang and rang. Finally she answered.

"Mama?" She sounded sleepy. "Is that you?"

"Hey, how are you?"

"Fine. Mama? Um, I can't really talk. See, I've sort of got someone here?"

I sat up in bed. "You mean, like, a *guy*?"

"Mmmhum."

"In your dorm room?"

"Mmmhum."

"Oh, my god."

She laughed, and I heard linen crinkling.

"This is so weird." I smiled into the phone. "Shouldn't I be yelling at you or something? God, I feel so *old*."

She laughed. "See you soon, Mama."

"See you," I said, but she'd already hung up. I held the receiver against my cheek. Somehow, I couldn't imagine her making love. Not my baby girl. Not when I'd diapered her. I remembered that old trailer in Louisiana, the sharp smell of the alcohol stove. It seemed as if I'd been a mother my whole life. I kept thinking I'd have time to make things right, but each time I failed her, I failed myself. When I failed myself, I failed her.

I poured the rest of the liquor into the sink. Then I packed my suitcase. It was dusk when I drove into Crystal Falls. I drove past Byron's medical clinic, past the turn off to Tulip Road, past shopping centers and manicured subdivisions, until I reached my mother's house. I parked the car next to Bitsy's Mustang and looked up at the screened porch. Queenie was sitting in a wicker rocker, and Jennifer Leigh was bouncing in a walker. Bitsy was stretched out in the swing reading *Glamour*. I remembered the old days, with Mother, Papa, and Dorothy. Queenie would bring out a pitcher of sweet tea, the ice clinking. The porch was long, with a gray washed floor. Mother wore a floral cotton dress. Her starched white collar was folded like two napkins. At the edge of the yard, her garden was a green blur. It was hard to believe that I couldn't pick up the phone and call her, that I would never again hear her voice. A piece of my gravity was gone, and to keep from floating, I had to fill my pockets with rocks.

Queenie got up from the chair, walked across the porch, and opened the screened door. Behind her, Bitsy laid down the magazine and got up from the swing. She scooped up the baby and stared at me.

"Girl, I declare," said Queenie, drawing her eyebrows together until her forehead wrinkled. "Dr. Byron's been calling here night and day. He's worried sick."

I walked up the porch steps and put my arms around her, smelling her scrubwater scent, which seemed to have burned itself into the fabric of her apron. A sob tore loose from my throat, and I felt her hand on the back of my head.

"Lord, girl," she said. "You're home now. Don't you cry. Queenie's here, Queenie's here."

Queenie

1972

*I*t's high summer, and they all home now. Clancy, Violet, Bitsy, and Bitsy's child. When I call the baby Little Bit, Bitsy act like I done lost my mind. "Her name is JENNIFER LEIGH," Bitsy says real loud, like I'll remember it better if she shout. But that baby look just like a little Bitsy to me, and she act like Miss Gussie. When her mama not around, I call her what I want. At least her name not Little Dorothy. Who knows what would happen then?

Last spring, Bitsy come over here with bad news. It's the middle of the afternoon. I am in the garden planting lettuce. Bitsy is crying, and so is Little Bit.

"What's wrong with you?" I ask.

"Claude wants a divorce," says Bitsy, her face screwing up.

I just keep sifting soil over the seeds.

"Didn't you hear me?" says Bitsy, juggling Little Bit up and down.

"Of course, I heard you." I stab my spade in the ground. As I stand up, my knees pop. I'm getting too old to do this, but there is something soothing about working in the yard. Planting seeds and seeing them poke green out of the dirt. And it gets you out of the house without going too far.

"What am I going to do?" wails Bitsy, looking like her mama, what they done locked up and throwed away the key. Dorothy jumped like she was a bird that forgot it know how to fly.

Then I focus my eyes good and look strong at Bitsy. I see Mr. Albert's cool blue eyes and his dimple chin. Her blond hair is all tangle, and her makeup drips black streaks down her cheeks. Sometimes I think Dorothy would have played bridge the rest of her life if Albert hadn't been caught loving on Clancy Jane. But it comes to me that two wrongs don't make another wrong. Bitsy's her own self. None of it's her fault, just like Little Bit can't help that her own daddy, that old Meathead, done forgot she was born. She don't even know he's gone.

"Come on in the house, child," I tell her. "It's too cool out here for that baby."

She follows me into the kitchen and sits down at the table. Little Bit puckers up her mouth and her chin quivers. I reach for that child and she clings to me like she can smell the milk on me.

"Can we stay here for a few days?" asks Bitsy. "I would stay with Father, but those widow ladies will get on my nerves. And Mack's not exactly living alone."

I tell Bitsy, I say to her, "You come right on and stay as long as you like." It's true that she has no place to go. Her mama's house been took over by Mack and that Earlene. They live together like all the young peoples do now. They have tore down walls in Dorothy's house. They have cut holes in the roof and put in windows. They have put in a swimming pool. They have put in a little separate pool that swirls hot water. They tried to get me in it, and I said over my dead body. Those blue pools glow all night long. Dorothy's house once had three bedrooms upstairs, but now it's not got but one. Mack calls it a loft. It's got a whirlpool bath that you have to climb up marble steps to get to. Plants growing all over the place. All of this in front of a stained glass window that shows two naked womens.

Mack's making something out of himself by building houses. He's got the whole backyard filled up. It used to be Miss Gussie's land. Now he calls it Hamilton Place. He's made him so much money, he driving a brand-new truck, and Earlene's got her a Cadillac with a sunroof. She still drives that school bus, says she needs to do her own thing. I look up at Bitsy and think I might like the company. There's nothing like a baby in the house to make you young.

She moves in and set a crib up in the guest room. Then, next thing I know, here come Clancy Jane herself, wanting to move in, too. Like it be catching. She's left Dr. Byron and won't hardly take his calls or talk to him. She tells him that she won't live in that pretty house of his. And when I go for my checkup, he cries and begs me to tell her how much he loves her. That he don't know what he did wrong, but if she'd tell him, he'll make it right.

*T*hen it be June, and the air conditioner break down, and we get distracted by the heat. Violet comes home from college. She brings a young man with her. Somebody like her that studies birds. His name is Lawrence Prescott III. He fixes the air conditioner. They sleep in her old bedroom, and there's just one bed, but only Bitsy complains. She's jealous but she don't know it. Me, I think it's terrible, under Miss Gussie's own roof, but I don't open my mouth.

One day it pours down rain, and they stay holed up in they room. The rest of us are downstairs, waiting for the storm to pass, but we're real tense. We're drinking green tea. Bitsy gets up from the table and walks to the kitchen door. She looks out the curtains. "They ought to get married if they're so in love," she says.

"Why?" says Clancy Jane, turning to look at her. "So they can have a baby and get a divorce?"

"I didn't say that." Bitsy's face turns red.

But I know what she mean. It be a real long time before Violet and Lawrence come downstairs. And when they do, they're barefoot.

Then Lawrence, he finally goes back to the college in Knoxville, and the rest of us breathes a sigh of relief. There's nothing worse than one man in a house full of womens. After he leaves, us all sits on the porch and take turns rocking Little Bit, who's cutting a tooth.

Violet says she's in love but she doesn't want to get married. She says she wants her career, that she's not different from a man.

"I hope you're different," says Bitsy. "And if you ask me, you're getting the short end of the stick."

"I'm not getting the short end of anything," says Violet.

I roll my eyes and wonder how long us womens can live together without us killing each other. I don't see how, I sure don't.

*I*t's deep summer, and I go back to Dr. Byron's office for these dizzy spells. He listens to my heart and tells me I have to slow down.

"I can't do that," I say.

"You don't have a choice, Queenie." He reaches in his pocket for his prescription pad.

"You sound like Clancy Jane," I tell him.

His face falls. "Is she all right, Queenie?"

I nod, wishing I hadn't opened my big mouth.

"Queenie?" He stared down at the pad. "Would you mind if I moved in with all of you?"

"Say what?" I'm shocked. I couldn't live with no grown man. Violet's boyfriend was bad enough.

"Do you think she'd let me?" says Dr. Byron, his eyes watering up.

"Lord have mercy, I don't know. What you going to do with that big house of yours?"

"Sell it." He wipes his eyes with the flat side of his palms. "Will you tell her that we'll never have to go to another party as long as we live? I don't care if she grows her hair to her ankles. Will you please tell her all that, Queenie?"

I just sit there in his office like a bump on a log, listening to him rattle on, and I nod my head. He blows his nose and hollers for his nurse to come take my blood pressure. Then he writes out a fresh prescription for my heart pills.

"I don't know," says Clancy Jane when I get back home. She's giving Little Bit a bottle of apple juice. "I can't see him living here, can you?" She wrinkles her nose. "He'll never do it. He can't give up that house."

From Clancy Jane's lap, Little Bit stares at me. Her lips curve around the nipple, and juice leaks out of her mouth.

That afternoon, Mack and Earlene walk over. She's got on short shorts cut up to here, and the rest of her hanging out. You can see her parts what belongs in a bathroom. Mack's got his wooden leg on beneath his jeans, and he's gripping a cane. The cane got diamond snake eyes.

Clancy Jane makes a pitcher of tea and we all get to talking. Bitsy starts begging Mack to put us in a gazebo.

"Oh, I know *just* where to put it," she says, standing up,

walking to the screen door. She bends her knee against the mesh. "Right where the birdbath is."

"Can't do that," Mack says. "Too much limestone."

"So dig it up," she says.

"It's too much rock. We'd have to dynamite." He picks up his cane and points at the garden. "If it was me, I'd put it right there."

"Where?" says Clancy Jane. She walks over to the screen door. She's just a tad taller than Bitsy, but she seems smaller.

"At the east end," says Mack. "Near that oak tree."

"But that's where Miss Gussie's flower garden is," I say.

They all turn to look at me.

"Well, I know," he says, "but that tree'll shade you in the summer. Plus you'll have more privacy."

We all stare at the new houses in the field.

"And there ain't much rock there," he says.

"How much would it cost?" asks Clancy Jane.

"Well, I don't really know." Mack scratches his head. "It depends on how fancy you want to get. If we make it big enough, we can put a hot tub in the middle."

"And let's put a great big ceiling fan, too," says Bitsy.

A slow smile spreads across Clancy Jane's face. "It does sound nice. We can hang ferns and wind chimes. And we can put in a curved walkway and landscape it with spider grass and rocks. Maybe we could even put in a rock garden. Can't you just see it?"

"No," says Violet. She's all sulled and grieved over Lawrence Prescott III being in Knoxville.

"I can see it," says Bitsy, handing the baby to me. The baby look at her mama like she lost her mind.

"Well, come on, then," says Mack. "Show me where you want it, and I'll put stakes in the ground for you."

"Let's do it, Aunt Clancy." Bitsy giggles and pulls Clancy Jane's arm. Violet shakes her head, but she gets up and follows them. I hold up Little Bit and say, "What we going to look like in a gazebo? What we going to look like in a hot tub? We going to look like two carrots floating in a bowl of soup?"

A few days later, Mack and Earlene drive up in a backhoe. They start digging at the edge of Miss Gussie's garden. The motor be so loud I can't hear myself think. We stand at the window and watch.

Little Bit crawls up to her mama and beat on her legs. Bitsy picks her up and says, "She'll never take a nap."

Next thing I know, a pile of bones go flying in a chunk of dirt. Mack hops up on his one leg and stares down at the bones. Earlene switches off the motor and stands up. She jumps off the backhoe and runs over to the skeleton. We all go outside to look at the bones. It's a whole skeleton.

"Lord have mercy," I say, rubbing my chest. It gets heavier as I stare at the skeleton. I can't believe my eyes. There's dog bones, then there's bigger bones, with white cloth stuck to the chest bones. And I even think I see a metal button shining.

We just crowd around the bones and stare.

Earlene whistles, touching the skull with her boot.

"Good grief," says Bitsy, hugging the baby.

"How old is it, you reckon?" says Mack. "Maybe it's an Indian?"

"It looks real old to me," says Clancy Jane, wrinkling her nose.

"Look yonder at them scraps of white rags," says Earlene. "Lord. It's corroded."

"I'll bet Lawrence would know if it's old," says Bitsy.

"He wouldn't, either," says Violet. "He's not an archaeologist."

My blood pressure keeps beating in my ears. It's bad luck to find bones. They're squatting around the bones. Earlene picks one up, holding it this way and that.

"That's gross, Earlene," says Bitsy.

I think I've got to sit down where it's cool. "Lord, it's hot out here," I mostly say to myself. Then I go back into the house. I start taking out ingredients for a nice pecan pie. I'm all dizzy from the heat and commotion. The girls come inside directly, and they don't even scrape they feet on the rug.

"Scrape your feet," I tell them. They take off they shoes and go in the living room.

"Isn't that the strangest thing?" Clancy Jane says. We're all alone.

"It's bad luck," I say.

"Oh, Queenie." She smiles.

"Don't you 'Oh, Queenie' me. Hand me that Crisco, baby."

I'm already measuring out flour for the crust. I'm thinking that this skeleton has something to do with Miss Dorothy. Maybe she was in love, and she killed the man. I don't know, I just don't know. Clancy Jane takes the flour sack from my hands. Her eyes are so blue I think I can jump off in them. It's always a weary load, and the thing about white people is it's always their load you're carrying.

"Oh, Lord." Clancy Jane covers her mouth with her hand. "I just remembered something. Do you remember when Mother died? Dorothy said she'd found some bones out there? She said her dog's body had disappeared?"

I nod. The hairs lift on my neck. "She called the police on us. She was talking out of her head."

"Maybe she wasn't. She kept telling us there was a skeleton in the garden." Clancy Jane combs her fingers through her hair.

She don't look like herself with short hair. "Remember how we found Mother in the garden? She'd been digging something. I never understood what she was doing out there."

"Maybe she buried Miss Dorothy's dog?" I say.

"Reckon she did? But she was so sick."

"Well, somebody buried it."

"Maybe Dorothy did it and forgot?" Clancy Jane's forehead wrinkles. "But that doesn't explain the other skeleton."

"Don't ask me," I say.

"We certainly can't ask Dorothy," she says.

This is true. The longer she stays at the mental place, the worse she gets. It upsets Bitsy too much to visit, but Mr. Albert still keep up with her. He must feel sorry for her. Responsible. He is a fine man, and Dorothy never knew it.

Mack and Earlene come into the house. Mack gets out the phone book and starts looking in the Yellow Pages. "I've got it figured out," says Mack. "You know out back, where the old graveyard is?"

Me and Clancy Jane nod.

"Miss Gussie and I used to walk through that old graveyard," he says. "Maybe some of the Hamilton kin got buried further back?"

The kitchen is so quiet you can hear a pin drop.

Clancy Jane's eyebrows draw together, like she's puzzled, but she doesn't say anything.

"No telling how old that grave was," Earlene says.

"There's people who'll know," says Mack. "I've heard other builders talking, and you can get into real trouble if you don't report something like this."

Bitsy comes into the room, holding Little Bit on her hip. She opens the refrigerator and grabs a bottle. "Oh, what's the fuss? Just dig him a fresh grave at the edge of the yard and forget it."

"I don't think that's legal," says Mack. "I ought to call the police, or somebody."

"I'll bet people dig bones up all the time and never tell a soul," says Bitsy.

"Maybe so," says Mack, scratching his head, "but I think it's a misdemeanor to dig up a grave and not tell anybody. Maybe it's even a felony."

"What does it matter?" asks Earlene. "I mean, who's going to tell?"

The kitchen is full of everyone breathing in and out.

I've said all I'm going to say. They can call who they want. I sift flour for the piecrust, keeping my back to the girls, who are too quiet. I fill a bowl with brown sugar, vanilla, butter.

The baby spits out her bottle and says, "Kee!"

It takes all my strength not to turn around and pick her up.

Some man comes to look at the bones. He pulls into the driveway in a white truck with the State of Tennessee written on it. He is a real nice young fellow with a sandy beard, and you wouldn't have believed how Bitsy sidled up to him, purring like a mama cat. He look through her like she's not there. He asks if he can sift through the dirt for clues. Go ahead, we say.

A week later, he comes back. The sheriff comes with him. We all gather in the backyard. The expert says the skeleton was a white man, and he died in the early 1930s. He thinks it might have been 1932.

We all say we can't feature how it got there.

The state man tells us the body was buried pretty deep, which makes him think it was a genuine grave. If it had been a murder, he explained, then it would have been shallow.

"Why don't you check dental records?" asks Bitsy. She's been reading up on this in the *World Book.*

"I wish I could," says the state man, not looking at her. "But X rays weren't invented in 1932."

Bitsy blushes, but she acts like she's hot and goes into the house for a glass of water.

"Maybe it's from the old family graveyard?" asks Mack, pointing at the edge of the yard. The new houses are outlined in the afternoon light. He's already sold I don't know how many, and they not finished yet. Pretty soon, we're going to have us neighbors. They'll stare out they windows at us and we'll stare back.

The state man looks toward Mack's subdivision. "There's still graves out there?" He sounds alarmed.

"Nah. We got the funeral home to move all the graves and headstones," Mack says.

"Was your family still using the cemetery in '32?" the state man asks.

"I don't know." Mack lifts his shoulders.

"There'll be burial records at the courthouse," the state man says.

"No, sir, they ain't complete," the sheriff says. "A flood ruint the records in, let me think, it was in the forties. Anyway, this garden ain't nowhere near that old cemetery." He's got a great big gun hanging from his waist, like it a body part. He's got little half-moon stains of sweat under his arms. His shirt is stretched tight over his stomach. He purses his lips and looks at Mack. "Wonder if your people buried any slaves out there? In the old graveyards, they used to bury the colored separate."

Mack shrugs.

I think: *Move on to the back of the bus, Queenie, just move on back.*

"There weren't any slaves in 1932," says the state man. "And besides, he was a white man." He goes back to sifting dirt.

The sheriff turns to me. "You're the only one who was around then," he says to me, taking off his hat. His hair is damp and matted. He wipes his head with a handkerchief. "Everybody else has passed away, I reckon," he adds.

I shake my head. "Yes, sir, but I didn't come to work here until 1938."

The sun is falling hard and solid. I walk across the yard and go sit on the screened porch.

In the next day or two, reporters come and take pictures. There's an article in the paper: MYSTERY SKELETON FOUND IN BACKYARD. And it is a real mystery, one that happened right here in Miss Gussie's backyard. No one ever figures it out. The city of Crystal Falls has to get themselves a court order to move the bones to the cemetery, even though most everything was took by the state man. Finally the city puts up a tiny gray marker, carved with nothing but 1932.

Clancy Jane's just a-working on her rose garden at the edge of the yard. Beyond the roses, I see the honeysuckle tangled on the old bob-wire fence, and through the fence I see the sun shining on the old Hamilton land. Way off in the distance, I see the houses, which have been bought by Yankee engineers and doctors. Sometimes, when the nights are still, I can hear traffic from the highways. Things have changed so much I can't make sense of it.

Clancy Jane spreads out pine bark over the mulch. Then she stands up and waves to me. She walks toward the house, stripping off her gloves, and pauses by the new gazebo. It's white. She's got ferns hanging. The hot tub water swirls, the color of the sky, pale blue, and reflects off the ceiling. The girls have got it fixed up so cute with wicker chairs and a white ceiling fan. Flowers planted all along the curved walkway. Clancy Jane's just like Miss Gussie for the world. Got her a green thumb, too.

"Afternoon, Miss Queenie," Clancy Jane says when she sees me staring at the water. "I wish I could get you into this hot tub. You'd just love it."

"I wouldn't," I say under my breath. But I smile.

"Oh, you would. It would help your arthritis."

"Maybe. What you been planting?"

"A Queen Elizabeth," she says and rubs the back of her hand over her forehead, leaving a trail of dirt.

"You know what I've been thinking?" she says. "I've been thinking that we need to take a little trip. We could fly to Washington and see the monuments. What do you think?"

I say, "I don't know."

"We can fly up there," she says. "We'll go in style. First-class. I've already talked to Violet and Bitsy. They said they'll go if you'll go."

"Me?" I wave my hand. "Lord have mercy, you don't need me tagging along on no trip."

"Yes, we do. We'll see the Lincoln Memorial and tour the White House. Or we can go somewhere else. We can go to New York or California or anywhere you want."

I try to get it straight in my mind. I can't feature me in Nashville, Tennessee, much less Washington, D.C. I can't feature me flying on no jet plane. The screen door bangs, and the girls walk out barefoot into the grass. Violet's got on Lawrence's plaid shirt, with the elbows rubbed out, and I don't think she has much else on. Bitsy looks like she's ready for a date. She's got on makeup. Her hair is curled, and she's wearing white slacks and a pink blouse that needs to be ironed.

"Where you going?" I ask her, and she says nowhere. She's holding Little Bit, who is chewing on a piece of cookie. Her whole chin is speckled brown. She reaches for me and says, "Kee*eee.*" Her eyebrows wiggle just the least when she tries to talk. Clancy Jane takes the baby from Bitsy and swings her around. Little Bit gives a belly laugh. Clancy Jane sets the baby in the grass. Little Bit, she scramble off and beat on the screen door.

"She's one smart baby," Violet says. "She knows where the air conditioner is, doesn't she? She wants inside where it's cool."

"She's smarter than us," says Bitsy, fanning herself. "It's hot as a firecracker out here."

"You going with us to Washington?" says Violet, looking at me. "Please say you will."

"I reckon I might," I say.

The girls cheer together and kiss me on the cheek. Then they take off running into the house, skipping over the baby.

"Those girls," says Clancy Jane, smiling. She opens the door for Little Bit. The baby crawls inside, her hands slapping on the kitchen floor. I hear a noise in the driveway, and I turn to see who it is.

It's Dr. Byron's white sports car. He gets out and stands in the driveway. He and Clancy Jane just stare at each other. Then he reaches into the front seat of his car and pulls out a sign. He holds it up. He's made it out of construction paper and a yardstick. I read slowly, moving my lips.

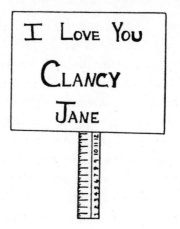

I hold my breath, waiting to see what she's going to do. She don't do nothing except stand there like she's gone blind.

"Don't make him crawl," I say. "Go to him now, girl."

She walks to his car, and he hands her the sign. After a minute he picks her up, swings her around, and they fall backward into the grass. They start laughing. He pushes her hair out of her eyes, and I think to myself that we'd better clean out an extra closet for his things. I turn back to the house, climb up the porch steps, and sit down on the swing to rest a minute. I push off with my feet and close my eyes, swaying back and forth. I imagine the jet airplane—a long silver bus, only I won't have a ride in the back. I'll hand the stewardess my ticket, and she'll take me to the first-class seats. She'll bring me magazines and a pillow and a glass of something with bubbles in it. And we'll fly over Miss Gussie's house, over the gazebo, over the subdivision, and disappear into the clouds, with the sunset behind us. The sky would be all pink and gauzy, the way heaven must be, with the moon and the stars and planets above us. And way below, the lights of Washington would shine, and I would take Little Bit's finger and stick it against the window and say that's Washington, D.C.

I open my eyes and gaze into the green yard, and I see Miss Gussie standing in front of her garden, the way it used to be. She's young, her belly is swelled out to here, she's carrying Clancy Jane. I blink hard, and when I open my eyes, she is still there, just as plain as day. She moves through the rows, a beautiful young woman all backlit by the sun. I feel young, too. I look down at my lap, and I see somebody else's long brown legs poking out of a calico dress. Why, I haven't worn a dress like this since . . . oh, I was a young thing. Young as can be.

The smell of summer rises. Heat shimmers over the honeysuckle, over the bob-wire fence, over the fields of Queen Anne's lace. The katydids roar. Light shines everywhere like it's something you can touch. All around me birds are singing. Miss Gussie's waiting. Then she holds out her hand and I get up from the swing and together we step into the corn.

Author's Note

I would like to thank Nick Fielder, state archaeologist of Tennessee, who provided information on the disposition of skeletons and pointed me in the right direction for further research; Paul Miller for providing background information about sixties' and seventies' music; Alex Humphrey, who served in Vietnam from 1965 to 1966, for answering my many questions; my father, Ralph Helton, for his stories about the Marines in World War II; my mother, Ary Jean, for listening to many long-distance readings and for her suggestions, such as the instructions for Dorothy's funeral; Robert VanHooser, chairman of the board, Lebanon Bank, for his memories of the Great Depression; Will D. Campbell, Randall Elisha Greene, Shirley Hailstock, Dr. Diana Gabaldon, and Wanda Rader for early readings, encouragement, and friendship; Allison Adams for her cheerful voice on the telephone and for helping with permissions to lyrics, among other things. I'd like to express deepest appreciation to Lisa DiMona; to my husband, Mahlon, for his tales of the sixties; to my sons, Trey and Tyler, for being good sports.

Most of all, love and thanks to Jane Hill, who made this book happen in the best way.

About the Author

Michael Lee West's fiction has appeared in *First for Women, Wind, Southern,* and other magazines. A registered nurse, she lives with her husband and two sons in Lebanon, Tennessee.